SABER DOWN

HARRISON KONE

THM

Ten Hut Media
tenhutmedia.com

This is a work of fiction. Names, characters, businesses, places, events and incidents are either the products of the author's imagination or used in a fictitious manner. Any resemblance to actual persons, living or dead, or actual events is purely coincidental.

ISBN: 978-1-964007-25-0 (Paperback)

ALSO BY THE AUTHOR

David Shaw

Into the Valley of Death

Saber Down

The Defection Protocol

Invictus

Never miss a new release!

To find out more about Harrison Kone and his books, visit

severnriverbooks.com

To Harry, my namesake and grandfather – philosopher, teacher, playwright, Marine – thank you.

"These are the times that try men's souls." – Thomas Paine

PROLOGUE

Near Kandahar,
Afghanistan

The Marine Corps Special Operations Officer bounced in the passenger seat as the Humvee sped toward the target village. The Afghan Commando that drove bobbed his head to the music that played from the miniature Bluetooth speaker resting next to the gearshift. The Marine officer, although semi-fluent in several languages, including Pashto and Dari, had difficulty deciphering the message of the fast-paced lyrics, but he smiled and bobbed his head alongside his new friend.

Captain David Shaw had met Lieutenant Masood al-Sabir six months prior at the start of his deployment, and, save for a few instances, the two men and their teams had raided together nearly the entire duration. The Marine captain glanced into the back seat where Corporal Kyle Reyes and Sergeant Taqi al-Attar conversed. Reyes was explaining to al-Attar the pronunciation of the English word *queue*.

"I don't understand," al-Attar said in his thick accent. "Why do you not pronounce the *u-e-u-e*?" Reyes laughed, and Shaw grinned.

"*Breedmal*," al-Sabir started, referring to al-Attar's rank in their native tongue, "do not try to understand. These English-speakers are strange." A hearty laugh echoed from his lips as a playful hand shot out toward Shaw's upper arm. The Humvee veered, and al-Sabir's hand quickly snapped back to the wheel to straighten the vehicle.

"You alright there?" Shaw jested. Only slightly embarrassed, al-Sabir laughed but kept both hands on the wheel.

"Hey Boss, everything good?" came Staff Sergeant John Wyatt's voice through Shaw's communication headset. Shaw pressed the push-to-talk device (PTT) fixed to the upper left on his plate carrier to initiate his response.

"Yeah, the good lieutenant might be drunk," he joked. Al-Sabir's eyes, filled with concern, snapped toward Shaw. A declaration like that over the radio could prove fatal to his career, but Shaw simply smiled and winked. The Afghani, despite all the missions alongside American military personnel, had yet to understand their humor, but he laughed when he realized the captain's intentions. He shook his head back and forth and cracked a smile.

"You are going to have to look after my children when I am gone," he said. Shaw's eyebrows perked up.

"Why's that?"

"Because, how do you Americans say?" he paused, searching for the right phrase, "you are going to be the death of me." Shaw laughed and patted al-Sabir on the shoulder. Al-Sabir wore a satisfied smile as he turned his attention back to the road. He could not put into words the happiness he felt connecting with the Americans. He looked at the endeavor as a critical part of his mission in building a trusting relationship between their forces, not simply on their joint-unit level, but every positive interaction was a stone placed on the foundation of US-Afghan friendship. Al-Sabir intended to do his part in building an Afghanistan where his young children could prosper, and that relied on a healthy relationship with the United States.

"We're coming up on the village," said one of the commandos in the lead Humvee. Al-Sabir cut off the music and hardened his expression as they roared through the village perimeter.

The unexpected wave rolled over their vehicle pressing each man deep into their padded seats. The concussive blast radiated down the column, disorienting the warriors, if only briefly. A pillar of black smoke spiraled into the air as the lead Humvee smoldered from the IED blast. Bullets thudded into the row of idle vehicles rumbling in the middle of the street. Against the armored vehicles, the rounds popped like the crackle of popcorn, but the Marine Special Operations Team attached to the company of Afghan Commandos kept their cool amid the ambush.

Nearly twenty years into the Global War on Terror and despite his numerous engagements involving ambushes, the thrill still triggered an adrenaline dump with which Shaw was all too familiar.

"Where's it coming from?" Reyes shouted. Al-Attar searched frantically up and down the mountainside to his left in the direction of the incoming rounds. Flat, simple buildings dotted the slope in tight formation.

"Contact left!" came Master Sergeant Beasley's report through the comms.

"Good copy, B," Shaw replied, keeping his voice calm yet commanding. "Can we get through?"

"Negative, the lead Humvee is blocking the path. We'll need to secure the area," Beasley replied.

"Alright, Sergeant Wu, I want our guardian angels to light up that slope," Shaw ordered.

"Yes, sir," Sergeant Wu responded. As a United States Air Force Tactical Air Control Party Specialist (TACP), Sergeant Peter Wu, trained and authorized to call in all manner of danger-close aerial support, did as instructed.

"Alright, boys, you know the drill," Shaw stated into the radio as he threw open his passenger door. He helped al-Sabir out his side of the vehicle and remained low behind the Humvee's protection. "Reyes, on me!" he shouted. Reyes, the newest member of their team, quickly slid to his side. Shaw peeked around the front of the vehicle and engaged the muzzle flash from a second-story window just over one-hundred meters away. Reyes, laying his carbine flat against the hood of the Humvee and presenting as little of himself as possible to the enemy, opened fire as well.

"Grenade!" came the shout to his left. Shaw's eyes snapped that way and targeted the Soviet-era explosive. How? The enemy wasn't close enough, were they? The average distance a man could throw a grenade was around twenty to thirty meters. The situation had to be more dire than he anticipated.

Shaw watched as al-Sabir scooped up the explosive and arched his arm to throw it back. Shaw, immediately recognizing the threat, grabbed Reyes and drove him to the ground.

The explosive shockwave lifted the dust off the vehicles and rattled the two Marines as they fell. Disoriented, Shaw remained motionless while his insides recalibrated from the blast. The unnerving sensation demanded a moment's rest, but he did not have the luxury to wait for his organs to settle. He rose to one knee and checked on his teammate.

Reyes lay unresponsive, but alive. Shaw tapped into his communication headset, "Adams, I need you at delta!" the Marine captain urged. He glanced upward toward the two commandos who now were nothing more than a heap of blood, guts, and flayed flesh. Al-Sabir's severed head, his expression contorted in horror, met Shaw's gaze. He quickly looked away.

"Copy that, Boss," came Adams' response.

"Hang in there, buddy," Shaw said to the unconscious Reyes. The chorus of gunfire around him drowned out the shouts of the commandos and Marines who fought against the assault. Shaw glanced around quickly, taking note of their surroundings. Before he could assess further, the deep bellowing of a heavy machine gun cut through the chatter of the small arms fire.

Shaw recognized the sound immediately. The Soviet-made DShK 1938 fired the 12.7x108mm anti-material cartridge similar to the US .50 Browning Machine Gun round. If hit, the round would cut him in half, and his body armor wouldn't protect him in the least.

"I can't get to you!" came Adams' reply through Shaw's headset. Adams was the bravest corpsman Shaw knew, if he couldn't make it to them, things had to be worse than he originally thought.

"Wyatt, can you take out that gunner?" Shaw asked his team sniper.

"On it, Boss," came the sniper's reply. Shaw stole a peek over the hood of the Humvee and picked up the bright muzzle flash of the barking machine gun. He ducked quickly as bullets skirted up the side of the vehicle.

"We've got technicals inbound!" came Beasley's voice through the radio, referencing improvised fighting vehicles outfitted with heavy machine guns, a favorite of al-Qaeda insurgents.

"York, put that AT4 to use!" Shaw ordered referring to the anti-tank weapon at the Marine's disposal. Shaw checked on Reyes again, and satisfied his condition was stable, rejoined the fight. Shaw braced his M4A1 carbine against the front corner of the vehicle, took aim, and opened fire. He squeezed off single shots, and, through his EO Tech holographic sight, he quickly engaged the enemy combatants.

The unmistakable, hollow report of an RPG-7 reached Shaw's ears, but before he could react, the old Humvee he used as cover ripped apart. The concussive force launched him diagonally away from the vehicle, and he bounced against the hard dirt before rolling to a stop. His insides felt like soup, and his entire body tingled, but he mustered the strength to rise.

Shaw clumsily raced back toward Reyes, who through his prone position had miraculously escaped death. Staying low, Shaw gripped Reyes' drag handle fixed to the rear of his plate carrier and pulled him toward the next vehicle. His shoulder erupted in pain as a round shredded through the flesh. Shaw spiraled downward and instinctively grabbed his bloody shoulder. He tried to ignore it for Reyes' sake.

Shaw grabbed a handful of sand as he pulled himself forward. His body shrieked with every movement, commanding him to stop, but the warrior fought onward. His long, dark hair, wet with sweat, clung to his face and beard, mixing with the dust, dirt, and blood splattered on his face. The man's blue eyes, fixed on the next Humvee, beamed in bright contrast to his dusty, bloodied complexion. The vehicle only sat twenty feet away, but the distance appeared as miles.

Glancing back to the unconscious man he dragged, his mind predicted the coming event. If he didn't increase his speed, they would most certainly die. There were simply too many hostiles to remain exposed. The rest of his team provided cover fire, but he feared it wouldn't be enough.

He gritted his teeth and fought the pain as his lifeblood escaped through the gaping hole in his shoulder. He felt each thump of his heart as the pain pulsed through him. He rose to his feet and took three steps before searing heat ripped upward through his legs and back. He staggered and gaped at the fresh spray of blood on the sand before him. He shouted, not in distress or fear, but in anger and determination. The shout of a man bearing a weight he refused to relinquish; the shout of a man striking fear into death itself, denying the darkness its prize.

Two more steps.

One more step.

A high whine echoed through his ears, and various explosions shook him to the ground as a barrage of missiles detonated around him. The Marine felt hands grip him, pulling him behind the Humvee as the Marine Corps AH-1Z Super Cobras swirled overhead pounding the enemy with an array of cannon fire and rockets. Dirt leapt into the Afghan sky like great, brown geysers as the attack helicopters, like wasps, buzzed around the village.

"I got them!" a Marine shouted as he and an Afghan commando dragged the two wounded men further behind the Humvee.

"Shaw!" another shouted as he slid to the wounded Marine's side. He immediately ripped into his individual first aid kit (IFAK) and began patching the man's stomach.

"Wyatt," Shaw groaned. He coughed and blood spewed from his lips and splattered his face.

"You're going to be alright," Wyatt insisted as he packed the stomach wound with the clotting agent. Shaw's eyes popped open as the pain from Wyatt's work crashed over him.

"Reyes?" he weakly managed to say between coughs. Wyatt glanced up at another teammate working on the wounded Reyes. He received a thumbs-up.

"In better shape than you," he joked, but Shaw felt the gravity in his tone. "He'll be alright," Wyatt added. Shaw smiled lazily, and his eyes closed slowly. "Stay with me!" Wyatt shouted. Another Marine, York, hurried to Wyatt's side to tourniquet Shaw's legs.

"How is he?" he asked anxiously as he wrapped a tourniquet high on Shaw's thigh. Wyatt offered him a grave look before turning his attention back to his wounded compatriot. York cursed as he ripped another tourniquet from his own kit just before Shaw fell into darkness.

PART I

THE TERRORIST

1

Shaw awoke and snapped upright, covered in sweat. He groaned as his injuries protested his movements. He panted, and his chest heaved. The Marine felt every tingle of pain from a myriad of wounds on his body. He must be on pain meds, because the pain was subtle and his mind hazy. His bright eyes, weak and tired, scanned the room. He was in a hospital. The television in the corner sat dark and silent, and a variety of monitors occasionally flashed and hummed in guttural tones. He exhaled as he slowly settled himself back into the bed. The last thing he remembered...

The Marine touched his stomach as the dread set in. He tore the sheets off his body and ignored the pain in his shoulder. He almost cried when he wiggled his toes.

"Thank God," he said as he fought against the rimming of fresh tears. He inhaled slowly and shuttered as a wave of chills passed over his body. He did his best to cover himself again with the sheet, but he missed his left foot. He pressed his lips tightly together to suppress his emotions. He should be paralyzed. He covered his face with a hand and then dragged it down his dark beard before gazing out the window to behold the green trees and brilliant sky.

He wasn't in Afghanistan.

A knock at the door drew his attention. A nurse, barely in her twenties, entered offering a warm smile. He returned her smile with a half-hearted grin. He needed to know where he was.

"How are you?" she asked sweetly. She wore her brown hair pulled tightly into a neat bun, and her eyes glowed with kindness.

"Where am I?" he asked.

"The Naval Hospital Camp Lejeune," she responded as she made her way to gaze at the monitors. Shaw relaxed when he heard her answer. How long had he been out? He rested his head back on the pillow. "I'm May," she said, "and I've been your nurse." Shaw offered her a better smile than before.

"David Shaw," he greeted. She activated the bed controls and raised him to a reclining position before she assessed him.

"I know, Captain," she answered. She noted his long dark hair and grizzled beard. He wasn't an ordinary Marine, if there was such a thing as an ordinary Marine.

MARSOC Raiders weren't held to the same grooming standards as other Marines. As an element of United States Special Operations Command (SOCOM), the Marine Forces Special Operations Command (MARSOC) served as the special operations component of the Marine Corps, and those serving within the elite organization were some of the best the Marines had to offer.

Shaw's brow was sharp and permanent creases lined his forehead. He was quite attractive, and he reminded May of a frontiersman, rugged and capable. He spoke with a slight southern accent but only barely noticeable, and he held an aura of respect and intelligence she found delightful, even though a bit intimidating. "You were pretty banged up. Shot six times," she said. Shaw almost laughed. "You spent a few weeks at Landstuhl for surgery and post op, and now you're here for recovery. Everything looks good though," she added. "We'll need to change your bandages soon."

"Hello, Captain," greeted a man from the opening door. Shaw glanced up at the older man as he entered. He was tall, at least six inches taller than

Shaw's sturdy six-foot frame, and thin with hands worn from combat and a face no different. His short silver hair, neatly combed, seemed to shimmer in the florescent light.

"General Weber," Shaw greeted. He tried to make himself more presentable by sitting up, but the general waved his hand in disregard. The officer fiddled with his cover as he moved to Shaw's side. Most might consider it unusual for the commander of MARSOC, a major general, to visit one of his team commanders, a captain, but Shaw held a special place in Weber's heart. Not only had he wished for the man to become his son-in-law, a dream he and his wife still held onto despite the failed relationship between their daughter, Caroline, and Shaw that ended the year prior, but Weber had personally recruited Shaw into Detachment One, MARSOC's predecessor, in the early 2000's. He had never regretted it.

"How are you holding up, Son?" the officer asked.

"Ready to get back to it," Shaw was quick to reply. Weber grinned and nodded as he walked around the bed.

"You always are," he said affectionately. "I brought you some things. I know the guys wanted to video chat with you." Weber held up the laptop bag. "Honestly though, I didn't know you would be awake. You weren't when I called in this morning," Weber finished.

As a captain in the 2nd Marine Raider Battalion, Shaw served as the Team Commander of a fourteen-man Marine Special Operations Team (MSOT). A master sergeant served as Team Chief and assisted him with team operations. The team was split into two identical squads, called Tactical Elements, each led by a Staff Sergeant as the Element Leader. As commander of his MSOT, intelligence gathering, mission planning, preparation and training, logistics, and mission execution demanded his full attention.

He could receive a name from up the chain of command, obtain the intel from local sources needed to locate the target, recon the area, prepare a plan of attack, coordinate support forces, and accomplish the mission with the utmost diligence and expertise. There was nothing he would rather be doing. Every choice held real time consequences, whether good or bad, and produced life-altering results. You couldn't get that with a desk job, not in the military, and not anywhere else. The operation tempo was fast, and Shaw liked it that way. It meant less time twiddling his thumbs and more time dirt napping those who sought to destroy the United States and her allies.

"Your boys have been pushing me to put you up for a commendation for what you did for Corporal Reyes," Weber said. Shaw's eyes widened.

"Did he make it? Is he okay?" Shaw hurriedly asked as he recalled the Marine. The general's smile widened as he took in Shaw's concern.

"Yes, Captain. He's fine. He's still in Afghanistan with the rest of the team." Shaw issued a sigh of relief. Reyes' injuries must not have been nearly as severe as his own if he was recuperating in a field hospital. "About this commendation," Weber continued.

"It's just a piece of metal," Shaw interjected. The major general smirked.

"I told them you'd say that," he said. Shaw grinned as his mentor gazed out the window. The Marine captain looked down at his hands, rough, cut, and peeling, as he felt a wave of sorrow enter the room. May must have felt it too. She offered Shaw a sympathetic half-smile before leaving.

"What is it, sir?" Shaw asked. The older officer sighed and turned to face him. His hard eyes grew soft, and he found it difficult to break the news to his captain.

"You're a good Marine," he started, "always have been." Shaw had a hunch where this was going and broke eye contact. "I remember the first time we met all those years ago." Shaw would make it easy for him. "You were fresh out of training and on your first deployment..."

"Sir," Shaw said before a big sigh, "I understand." He wouldn't dare show Weber the emotions that assaulted his spirit. Deep down he knew he was more than a Marine, but he couldn't fight the pain and anger swirling inside. On September 11, 2001, he had enlisted, third in line at the recruitment office. He was nearly halfway through his first semester at Duke University when he watched the towers fall. His parents had protested heavily, claiming he was throwing away his full-tuition scholarship, but he didn't listen. Duty drove him forward.

His grandfather had served as a Marine machine gunner in World War II, so Shaw hadn't struggled with which branch to join. He had obtained a Force Recon contract with the Marine Corps, meaning he would head right to the heart of the action after receiving the highest quality combat training the Marine Corps could provide.

"I pushed to get you an instructor position, but even the commandant said nineteen years were enough. I'm sorry, Son," Major General Weber said. Shaw nodded his acceptance and stared at his feet, feet he could move. He was grateful for that, but he remained silent. "You'll have the Navy Cross. I promise."

"Sir, I don't..." But Weber cut him off.

"Not for you, Captain, but for my sake," he said. He snapped to attention and rigidly saluted the man in the bed. It wasn't a salute to return, and Shaw knew he couldn't ask for a greater sign of respect than that. Shaw had never seen him in that state, so full of remorse and sadness.

"I'll see you around, sir," Shaw said.

"Aye, Son," he responded, "you will, and I'll tell Caroline you're back stateside." Shaw smirked; she was the last person he wanted to see after the way they had left things, and he doubted she would even bother to make the trip. Weber returned a knowing grin, tucked his cover under his arm, and left the room.

As the door closed, Shaw directed his gaze back out the window as he tried to decipher the mix of emotions whirling inside him.

2

Camp Leatherneck,
Helmand Province, Afghanistan

Staff Sergeant John Wyatt brushed his fingers along the wall as he walked down the bland corridor. He held a ruggedness about him, but with his short, tousled blonde hair, tan complexion, and lively blue eyes, he looked like he belonged on the beaches of California instead of in the mountains of Afghanistan. He wore a light gray jacket and woodland camo-patterned, combat pants. The famous Raider skull, embroidered on a red diamond against a blue background surrounded by the five white stars of the Southern Cross, adorned his sleeve. The patch alone drew revered glances from the individuals he passed in the hallway.

As a Marine Corps Critical Skills Operator, he undertook the most diffi-cult and dangerous missions ordered by the Marine Corps and the United States Special Operations Command. MARSOC was a newer force, founded in 2006, tasked with direct-action, special reconnaissance, foreign internal defense, counterterrorism, and information operations. They were proudly dubbed *Raiders* after the famous Marine strike units of World War II's brutal Pacific Campaign.

Wyatt glanced down at the gold pin in the palm of his other hand. Its bright finish glinted in the florescent lighting. He liked the design. An eagle, with its wings outstretched, gripped the hilt of a stiletto dagger that extended upward through a five-starred shield fastened over the raptor's chest. *Spiritus Invictus* inscribed on the top of the pin stood as a testament to the spirit of the Marine Raiders. Wyatt honestly thought it looked more impressive than the eagle and trident of the SEALs. A smug smile donned his face at the thought.

The Raider knocked on the door, more as an alert than asking permission, and walked in. Reyes sat in his bed with an iPad in his lap.

"Hey babe, I got to go," Reyes quickly said. "I love you."

"I love you too. Call me later, okay?" came Sara's reply.

"I will. I can't wait to meet our little man." Wyatt heard Reyes' wife giggle and watched Reyes' smile. They were good people, and he thought Reyes was going to make a great father. Reyes ended the call and lowered the tablet to glance at Wyatt.

"Got something for you," Wyatt said and motioned for Reyes to hold out his hand. He did as desired and received the pin.

"Well, look at that," he said with a grin.

"You earned it, and with Shaw out, I wanted to make sure you got it," Wyatt responded. Reyes didn't know if being rendered unconscious by a grenade meant he earned his place on the team, but he wasn't about to refuse the gesture. He normally would have received the pin after graduation from the Individual Training Course (ITC), but Shaw ran things a bit differently. Reyes understood now as he rubbed his thumb over the pin. He had earned it in combat, and the feeling was all the sweeter. "Looks good, doesn't it?" Wyatt added.

"Better than the eagle and trident, that's for sure," Reyes answered.

"I think so." Wyatt paused, scratched his neck, and continued, "So, listen, York and I were wondering if we could use your tablet to talk to Shaw."

"Yeah of course," Reyes replied. "You guys want to call him in here?"

"Yeah, if you don't mind." Reyes cracked a smile.

"No problem." Wyatt grinned and briefly exited the room. Within a matter of seconds, the door burst open, and York threw his arms wide as he beheld Reyes. Wyatt reentered behind him. Wyatt was tall, six-foot-two, but

York was even taller. If Wyatt was built like a Mustang stallion, lean and strong, then York, in comparison, resembled a grizzly bear, huge and impressive, with a temper to match.

Of Scandinavian descent, York had thrown himself fully into his Viking ancestry, even to the point of pursuing special permission from the Corps to be recognized religiously as a Norse pagan, which was granted after several meetings with the company chaplain. He kept the sides and back of his head shaved but the top long and braided. He even braided parts of his beard and often donned blue or white war paint before a mission. At first, it had been a bit strange for the rest of the team. Master Sergeant Beasley, Shaw's right hand, still didn't approve, but the rest of the team had grown quite fond of York's theatrics. The Raider even carried a RMJ Tactical Custom Raven Bearded Axe with a Viking-style head into battle, and it had saved his life on two occasions. They all agreed that there was not a more fearsome Marine in the entire Corps.

"You're not dead yet?" York teased as he neared Reyes. Reyes cracked a grin, but true to his nature, he replied without joke or jest.

"Just had a checkup with the Doc this morning, he says I'm fine."

"I imagine so, it's been a few weeks," York replied, a bit unenthused with Reyes' humorless response. Wyatt simply smiled at the exchange.

"Let's get this show on the road," Wyatt said. He took the outstretched iPad and input Shaw's phone number for a FaceTime chat. The Raider looked at his reflection as it rang. The tablet continued to chirp, and Wyatt glanced Reyes' way.

"Maybe General Weber hasn't visited yet," Reyes stated. Wyatt returned his attention to the screen, and Shaw's smiling face materialized.

"Hey, Boss!" Wyatt greeted cheerfully. Relief swept over him like the tingling from a large gulp of liquor. He quickly turned and adjusted the tablet to include everyone.

"Hey guys," Shaw greeted. "Reyes, it's good to see you in one piece."

"Not as good as it is to see you, sir," the corporal replied. "I owe you my life," he said seriously. Shaw forced a smile; it was an uncomfortable thing to hear.

"You look rough," Wyatt said. York's large fist playfully slammed into Wyatt's shoulder.

"You'd look worse if you'd just taken a bunch of rounds of seven-six-two," he joked.

"Yeah, six-feet-under worse," Reyes added. Shaw managed a smile, but Wyatt knew him well enough to see past it. Pain lurked behind his eyes. Not physical, but something deeper.

"What's wrong?" he asked. The others looked at Wyatt and then back at Shaw. Apparently, they had missed something. Shaw scratched his bearded cheek and averted his gaze through the window. He bit his bottom lip as he turned to regard them. Wyatt immediately shook his head in disbelief.

"No," he protested, trying to convince himself that what Shaw was about to say was not what he feared to hear. Shaw nodded slowly and deliberately.

"Weber just told me," he said. "I'm out." York, stunned, ran his hands over his braided hair and scratched the back of his head before tugging on his neck with both hands. Reyes, wide-eyed in disbelief, just stared at him.

"But," Reyes started, but Wyatt interrupted him.

"What will you do?" Wyatt asked.

"I hadn't had much time to think about it. I haven't been a civilian in nearly twenty years, and I was just a kid then," Shaw said. The room was silent. Shaw was the greatest Marine any of them knew and the most brilliant. Their team wouldn't be the same without him.

"When is your time up?" York asked. Shaw shrugged, then instantly regretted it as it irritated his shoulder wound. Wyatt recognized the look on Shaw's face, a hidden sadness. Shaw looked at their faces and felt his heart sink upon the realization that he would never deploy with them again. He longed for nothing more than to be reunited with them.

"Could be six months. If I fight it, then longer," Shaw answered.

"You going to fight it?" Wyatt asked.

"I don't know yet." Silence spread uncomfortably between them. Neither one had known the other prior to military life. The knowledge that Shaw would become a veteran didn't feel right for Wyatt. Never before had they experienced such a disconnection.

"Must have been hard," Wyatt said.

"Harder for Weber, I think," Shaw replied. In 2003, Major General Weber, a colonel at the time, had handpicked Shaw to participate in

MCSOCOM Detachment One, a pilot program to assess the value of United States Marine Corps special operations as a permanent addition to SOCOM. Shaw was barely out of recon training when Weber came calling. After additional training with the Navy, he was deployed to Fallujah, attached to Naval Special Warfare Group One. After Det One was disbanded in March of 2006, Shaw would go on to become one of the first Raiders when the Marine Corps established MARSOC later that same year.

"Hard on all of us," Wyatt remarked. "What did the doctor say?" Shaw sighed.

"That I was lucky; that my recovery should be taking three times as long as it is and that I should have needed a colostomy bag but don't. Should be discharged in a few weeks," Shaw replied. "Have they replaced me yet?"

"They put Captain Neeman in command for now, not sure if it's permanent." Shaw bounced his head as he considered the man taking over his team, no not his, the Corps' team. He knew Captain Gary Neeman. Neeman had come to MARSOC straight out of Officer Candidacy School in Quantico. He was a few years younger than Shaw, but he was a straight shooter and a good leader.

"Not a bad choice," he said.

"He's not you," Wyatt countered. He admired Shaw more than the man could possibly know. From the first time Wyatt met him, he recognized Shaw as a man he could follow. It was the simple things, like making sure his men had enough socks, hygiene supplies, and good reading material. He didn't even need to mention the man's tactical brilliance. He made sure every fight was won before it started, and if things went haywire, it was Shaw that patched it up, risking life and limb to save his men. Reyes had experienced that dedication firsthand.

Thinking back to their most recent conflict, Wyatt had never experienced such anger and terror as when he was attempting to patch up Shaw's gut. Despite the officer-enlisted divide, Shaw and Wyatt had grown to become best friends, and frankly, after serving under Shaw for nearly eight years, he hated the thought of serving under someone else.

Unlike Shaw, Wyatt hadn't joined the Marines out of a great sense of patriotism, and it wasn't in the Marines where Wyatt had killed his first man. When he was seventeen, two men had broken into Wyatt's house. His older brother, having just signed a Ranger contract with the Army, met the intruders head on, but they gunned him down. The shots had awakened Wyatt, and his mother's blood-curdling scream dumped a load of adrenaline into his veins.

After loading his hunting shotgun with slugs, Wyatt rushed down the stairs and witnessed his battered and bleeding mother crawling down the hallway toward him. One of the intruders rounded the corner into the hallway from the living room and froze when he beheld Wyatt and his weapon. Finding a deep resolve within his being he didn't know existed, Wyatt aimed and fired at the intruder before the man could raise his pistol.

The slug tore through the center of the man's chest, killing him instantly. As Wyatt cocked the pump action, he heard the front, screen door slap against the frame. Wyatt rushed through the living room and barreled into the front yard. His blood boiled in rage. The second intruder had made it onto the street, but Wyatt aimed and shot the fleeing man through the back at over one hundred meters. The police had said it was an impossible shot.

The city of Leesburg, Virginia didn't press charges given the circumstances, but Wyatt would never forget the endless hospital nights holding his mother's hand until she finally died from the swelling in her brain; his father hadn't been there. For years, his mother had pleaded with his father to leave the State Department and find something so he could be with them, but he had refused, claiming his work was more important than her desires. He always issued the promise of "one day," but the days came and went. He was absent their funerals, and it was as if the man had fallen off the face of the earth. Wyatt hadn't heard a word from his father in years, and he figured he had died somewhere, wherever that somewhere was. That or he was living a double life and had another family in that same somewhere.

Alone, Wyatt turned to the Corps for the sole reason that they would ship him to basic training the soonest. He forged his father's signature on the parental consent affidavit and shipped out to basic at Parris Island right after high school graduation. He didn't care what he did or where he did it, but his marksmanship skills landed him in Scout Sniper training. The transition to MARSOC years later only made sense. He joined the military to escape his pain and found a brotherhood in the Corps that he never imagined.

"Did we lose anyone?" Shaw asked with difficulty. Wyatt shook his head.

"No, just the four commandos in the lead Humvee and Lieutenant al-Sabir and the other guy in your vehicle."

"Al-Attar," Shaw interjected. Wyatt nodded.

"Yeah, al-Attar," the Marine sniper repeated. He knew how important it was for Shaw to remember the names of those that had died under his command. Although those commandos weren't directly under his authority, they often looked to him for leadership and guidance. Shaw exhaled heavily and thought of al-Sabir's children. He had met them once, and he remembered al-Sabir's words to him before he died. He knew it was meant as a joke, but now, he would do his best to help them somehow.

"What are you guys up to?" Shaw asked after the moment of brief silence.

"We're just hanging around now. Nothing is really going on at the moment. Neeman mentioned something about a short op out of Camp Lemonnier in Djibouti. Something's going down in Yemen," Wyatt answered. "But we shouldn't be out there too long." Shaw's gaze drifted off the screen. "You got to go?" Wyatt asked.

"Yeah," Shaw quickly responded, "my doctor just walked in."

"Alright, we'll hit you up when we get back stateside."

"Sounds great," Shaw replied. "Reyes, I'm glad you're in one piece, and York, look after everybody."

"Sure thing, Boss," York replied.

"Thanks for everything, Captain," Reyes stated. Shaw simply smiled. The device chirped and Shaw's image whisked off the screen. Wyatt returned the device to Reyes, and he pressed his lips tightly together as he contemplated their conversation. Shaw out? It just didn't feel right.

3

Over the passing weeks, Shaw grew stronger. His spirits were higher after receiving approval to open a case with the State Department to get al-Sabir's family to the States. Pushing the process through Weber appeared to have worked. However, his mood was still dampened by his doctor's obstinate refusal to pronounce him as operational, but he felt good physically. He hadn't pushed his body to its limit yet, but he felt it would hold up. The Raider rubbed his stomach, a habit that had formed subconsciously after his gut shot, and hoisted his bag over one shoulder. He turned and caught May standing in the doorway.

"Doctor Bakshi isn't pleased that you've decided to leave AMA," May said, using the acronym for *Against Medical Advice*.

"Well, Doctor Bakshi doesn't understand the importance of today," Shaw countered. He knew his body better than Doctor Bakshi did, and he would have stayed had his team not received orders to conduct an operation in Yemen.

"Well, we'll miss you around here, Captain," she said.

"It's just David now," he replied. The young nurse shook her head and grinned.

"No, you'll always be Captain Shaw." If he was going to say anything, the words left him as the emotion tingled throughout his body. He immediately suppressed them and managed a quick nod.

"Thank you," he said. She leaned in the doorway smiling but almost jumped as the hospital phone in her scrubs pocket rang. May looked at him one last time.

"Got to go. Good luck out there, Captain, and don't forget your physical therapy." She answered the phone and left him. Shaw rubbed his stomach again and sighed. He had entered the room as a Special Operations Officer in the United States Marine Corps and was leaving with the realization that his military career was ending. The gravity of his new standing within his country stuck him deeply.

Shaw inhaled heavily and took his first step out of the room. He continued down the hall, chose the stairs over the elevator, and exited the hospital lobby. Summer was yielding to fall, but the leaves had yet to change. Sea salt drifted on the breeze and filled his nostrils. He loved coastal living and relished any time he got on the water. His forty-three-and-half-foot sailing yacht called his name, but more pressing matters required his attention.

He was on track for a medical discharge at the first of the year, and his apprehension grew every time the thought crossed his mind. While he was still in, he wanted to monitor his team and help in any way he could. Shaw's first dilemma, though, was transportation. He could call Sara Reyes, but with her being eight months pregnant with Reyes' first child, he didn't want to inconvenience her. That left the military bus. It ran as scheduled from the hospital to other parts of the base. He knew of a stop not far from his battalion headquarters.

The bus arrived as scheduled, and Shaw boarded. Marines, both young and seasoned, as well as spouses and children, enjoyed the convenience of base transportation. Most took it from housing to the commissary and back, but Shaw, living off base, rarely used it. He rode for twenty minutes before it arrived at his stop. He had gotten in touch with Lieutenant Neil Bateman, an Intelligence Officer, who served with the Marine Special Operations Support Group (MSOSG).

Because of Marines like Bateman, Shaw and his team had all the equipment, logistics, intelligence, communications, air support, and even canines they needed for their deployments. MSOSG linked his team to Joint Tactical Air Controllers (JTAC) and Explosive Ordnance Disposal (EOD) when needed, and it was because of that relationship that Shaw was successful on the battlefield. To him, they were the unsung heroes of MARSOC.

Shaw entered the building in which Bateman worked and preceded to the operations room. It was there that they would monitor the mission in real time, and Shaw was grateful to be invited. The officer pushed through the door and entered the room filled with monitors and personnel. It really was like the movies, he thought. He was normally on the other side of things, but now he was a guest, and so he respected the boundaries. This was their turf, and he wasn't about to encroach on that. He just wanted to remain informed.

"Captain," Bateman greeted with an outstretched hand. Shaw gripped it firmly and offered a quick pump. The Marine was slender and short with his hair freshly cut within regulation.

"I appreciate you allowing me in, LT," Shaw replied.

"We're just all glad you're alright." Shaw forced a smile. He wished people would stop saying that.

"What have we got?" Shaw asked.

"In short," Bateman started, "we've got a link up with the Air Force to provide MQ-9 Reaper support; the pilot's callsign is Cheerleader. She's quite a firecracker." Shaw cracked a grin.

"And a QRF?" Bateman nodded his head.

"The command isn't expecting any conflict, but the 5th Fleet in the Gulf of Aden currently houses SEAL Team 3 and the 13th MEU. We've got it all set up," Bateman explained. He seemed confident enough, but Shaw felt out of his element. He trusted Bateman knew what he was doing and so did the command above him.

"Alright, when does this thing kick off?" Shaw asked.

"Oh-eight-hundred, local time," Bateman replied. Shaw checked his watch.

Thirty minutes.

Camp Lemonnier, Djibouti

The ball bounced against the ground, ricocheted into the wall, and popped into the operator's hand. Again, as it left the Marine's hand, it thudded in quick succession before it returned to the man's possession. He paused for just a moment before throwing it again. The rhythm, soothing in its own way, passed the time for the bored Marine. The quick *thump thump pop* lulled the man as he waited for his orders.

The Marine's M110A1, a 7.62x51mm sniper rifle fixed with an adjustable Schmidt and Bender rifle scope, lay on the bed next to him. His helmet, equipped with night vision binoculars mounted on the front and an integral communication headset, sat on the nightstand to his right. He was dressed and ready for combat sporting his gray jacket, woodland camo pants, and a pair of Salomon hiking boots. He wore a tan plate carrier strapped around his torso laden with extra magazines, an individual trauma kit, a radio, chem lights, and of course protective plates. A tan, desert scarf hung loosely around his neck and exhibited the designs local to the region.

The Raider's senses picked up the boots pounding on the floorboards as they raced toward his room. He knew what the haste meant. He dropped the ball, snatched his rifle, and scooped up his helmet just as Master Sergeant Beasley entered the room. His hair was buzzed short, and he sported a trimmed, dark beard. An M4 dangled across his chest, and it bounced as he came to a stop inside the room.

"Wyatt," he called, "we're up!"

"Rah," Wyatt replied as he followed the other Raider out. With purpose, he moved down the hallway, passing rooms on the right and the left. Out of the rooms poured the rest of the MSOT under Neeman's command. The excitement brought forth by the operation quickened Wyatt's step as they emerged into the op room. They joined the rest of their team as Captain Neeman took a position in front of them.

"You're all up to date on the situation in Yemen, so I'll be brief," Captain Neeman began, "over seventy-five percent of the Yemeni population, twenty-two million people, are in desperate need of humanitarian aid. In short, we're pulling security for a group of NGO reps and media personnel looking to assess the situation and find a new avenue for their aid. The fighting at the country's main port of Hudayda has made their efforts to insert aid into the country that much more difficult. I needn't remind you that we will be protecting American citizens in the midst of this civil war. HQ doesn't expect any resistance on this op, but I want to keep everything tight. Got it?" He glanced over the standing men and received firm nods of confirmation. "Alright, let's get to it."

The fourteen-man team, led by Neeman, loaded into the waiting SUVs and sped toward the adjacent airport reserved for military operations. They pulled into a large hanger and exited their vehicles. Wyatt watched as Neeman strode up to one of the NGO representatives. The rep was dressed in brown and khaki and wore a badge around his neck. He was tall, thin, and balding. To Wyatt, his eyes appeared kind and wise. A nudge from York stole his attention.

"Check it out, man," he whispered. Wyatt followed York's gaze.

"Whoa," he said as his eyes found her.

The tall, thin blonde nodded and smiled as she conversed with an older woman. She wore a gray button-up and tan pants, and her long, flaxen hair was pulled into a ponytail. Her features were delicate and her skin bronzed from the sun. With an athletic figure, she was sure to attract the attention from every Marine present, those married and those not.

"Let's load up!" Neeman commanded. The Raider team moved to the waiting helicopters, and Wyatt found himself fortunate enough to help the attractive blonde onto the craft. He quickly took the open seat next to her and clipped in. He let one foot hang out the side as the UH-1Y Venom's rotors started to spin.

As the Element Leader, Wyatt assumed responsibility for the Marines on his helicopter. Beasley, the team's Tactical Chief, who sat diagonally across the fuselage from him, assumed responsibility for the civilians. That was the beauty of the MSOT. The Element Leaders could focus on leading their respective squads, while the Team Commander and Team Chief focused on operational objectives.

"So, what's your name?" Wyatt asked the blonde seated next to him as the two helicopters took to the skies. Their communication headsets muffled the roar of the rotors and amplified their speech, but Wyatt still had to shout for her to hear him. She glanced his way and grinned as wisps of her golden hair whipped around her face.

"Kathryn Byrd," she answered. "And you are?"

"Don't waste your time with him, Sweetheart!" York shouted. Wyatt cracked a grin.

"John," he answered, unfazed by York's interruption, "What's your role in all this, Kathryn?" he continued.

"Special Correspondent on assignment for CNN," she replied. She patted the camera bag in her lap.

"So, you're a war photographer?" Wyatt asked.

"Not exactly. It's my first time on assignment outside the country. Maybe one day." When Fred Seymour, the senior journalist who was supposed to be in her seat, contracted MRSA from his mixed-martial arts gym, Kathryn was offered his spot. She felt for Fred and hoped he recovered from the dangerous staph infection, but she couldn't deny her luck in obtaining an assignment that should have taken her at least three more years of entry-level work to be eligible. Perhaps, if she really scored here, she could have her pick of assignments upon her return, and maybe, she could finally sink into a groove and focus a bit more on her social life.

"You excited though?" Wyatt asked. The question seemed absurd to her, but she recognized he simply tried to keep their conversation going. She had seen it time and time again with every other guy that showed interest. How could she not be excited? She was surrounded by elite Marines headed to a country at war with itself to help provide aid for a struggling and starving people. It was a story she had dreamed of throughout her journalism studies at Mercer University.

"Oh yeah," she replied. Her smile was as contagious as it was beautiful. However, despite Wyatt's best efforts, York stole the show. His stories had the entire helicopter laughing. Wyatt could only smile. He was no match for Sergeant Cliff York. The guy could hold a conversation with a mannequin.

The Gulf of Aden soon appeared beneath them, and Wyatt leaned back to allow Kathryn a view.

"First time in a helicopter?" he asked. She shook her head.

"First time with Marines through!" she shouted over the roar of the rotors.

"Having fun so far?" Wyatt didn't take his eyes off her, and she met his gaze. More simple questions, was there any depth to this guy?

"Yeah," she replied.

They flew east for an hour, and Wyatt had effectively run the course of small talk. He sat in silence staring out to sea. She hadn't asked any questions in return, so he took the hint. York wore a knowing smile and stared straight at him. Wyatt met his gaze and puffed an exhale before cracking a grin. He pushed the controls to his radio and kept his gaze fixed on York.

"You're a douche," he said after switching his radio to a private channel. The communication came through clearly to York's headset, and he laughed. Wyatt returned his gaze out to sea wearing the same grin. Kathryn turned to Reyes who sat next to her.

"What's your story?" she asked. York laughed again, his deep bellowing drawing Kathryn's attention. He held up a hand to wave her off, and she returned her attention to Reyes.

"I'm married with a kid on the way. Blessed to be serving my country, ma'am," Reyes replied.

"A man of few words," York added. It was true. Reyes was unnaturally shy for a Marine Raider. When the general Marine population dubbed most MARSOC and Recon Marines as *cowboys* for their wild behavior and contempt toward the chain of command, Reyes remained reserved and polite. He always said *sir* and *ma'am* and was quick to volunteer for even the lowliest of duties. York was confident he would loosen up, but Wyatt wasn't so sure. Although he was fresh out of training and only on his first deployment, Reyes hadn't changed much.

As a devout Catholic, Kyle Reyes had struggled a bit after his first kill, but that hadn't lasted as long as they all thought it would. Shortly after, he proved himself a valuable member of the team. He did take some heat for almost getting the captain killed, but that blew over pretty quickly. However, the jokes were just beginning. The coming years would not only test his warrior spirit but his sense of humor as well. Wyatt had little doubt that he would roll with the punches and dish it out when the opportunity arose.

"Here we are," York stated as they soared over the coastline, drawing all eyes to the beaches below. The turquoise watered lapped gently against the rocky shore as the aircraft roared overhead. Mountains shot up beneath them and soon gave way to a sprawling residential area.

"Alright, boys," came Neeman through their comms, "heads on a swivel." It was in that moment that Wyatt sorely missed Shaw.

Aden sat nestled at the base of a small mountain range. The Arabian Sea formed into a bay to the north, and the entire city rested on a peninsula. It was in Aden that the NGO representatives hoped to secure port access to deliver humanitarian aid to the southern region of Yemen. The Houthi faction controlled the capital but not the majority of the country. The different rebel factions that controlled the south, including al-Qaeda, made operational planning more difficult than in Iraq, Afghanistan, and Syria. The fronts in that part of the Middle East were more clearly defined. In Yemen, the good guys and the bad guys shared territory and fought the same enemy, the Houthis, but that did not mean they were all friendly to Western influence. Additionally, many who left to fight for ISIS had returned to Yemen, which greatly complicated matters. Wyatt thought it all was just a big mess, but the people, the innocents, suffered, and that didn't sit well with him.

Kathryn laughed next to him, bringing him back to the moment. She still conversed with Reyes. He was telling a story, but Wyatt hadn't been paying attention. Kathryn turned to address Wyatt.

"Did that really happen?" she asked. Wyatt had no idea to what she was referring. Before he could inquire, the helicopter jolted violently. An explosion ripped through the rear of the aircraft. Kathryn shrieked, and Wyatt gripped the hull to steady himself. Black smoke billowed from the engine, and the tail violently whipped back and forth. The rotor was missing.

"Captain, we're hit!" Wyatt shouted into his comms. The helicopter descended rapidly, too rapidly. "Brace for impact!" he shouted.

"Brace for impact!" York echoed. Those same words resonated through the cabin as the Raiders shouted and readied themselves. Wyatt quickly tugged on Kathryn's harness. It was tight.

"Keep your head back," he shouted, "Cross your arms! Grab your shoulders!" He didn't know if she heard him, but it was too late. The helicopter slammed into the ground and tumbled. The blades snapped and spun in deadly arcs away from the vehicle. Wyatt shouted, a steady cry of defiance in the midst of the deafening crash. Dirt and dust plumed into the air in the wake of the collision. The cabin, what remained of the aircraft, rolled to a stop, and on it settled an eerie stillness.

4

Natalie Hale sipped her coffee as she pored over the report before her. She wasn't tall; maybe five and half feet, and she maintained an athletic physique. She kept her long, dark hair woven into a single, thick braid; it draped over her left shoulder. A few stray strands had fallen to frame her slender face. She wore a maroon, quarter-sleeve shirt and khaki pants. She glanced up from the documents, and her sea-green eyes trailed out the open window. Part of the security detail grunted as they worked out in the afternoon sun. The two men, Jared Becker and Matthew Quinn, were shirtless and drenched with sweat. Becker pounded his chest having just flipped a large tire, and Quinn panted as he pumped his arms to create the quick waves with heavy, black ropes.

Natalie rolled her eyes before returning to her work. Smarter men would have exercised in the morning or late evening, but not in the heat of the day beneath the scorching Yemeni sun. Then again, perhaps they chose the heat of the day for an entirely different reason altogether. She didn't know much about them, only that they were former 1st SFOD-D, or Delta Force as the unit was more commonly known. She never saw them apart, but then again, she never really paid much attention to them. They were on the team that kept their compound safe, and that was all that mattered.

The compound, which operated under the covering of the CIA Annex in Yemen's capital city of Sana'a, lay situated on the southern outskirts of Aden and served to profile and locate high-level threats returning to Yemen from Iraq, Afghanistan, and Syria. Just a year prior, the port city had over-flowed with culture and vibrancy, despite the civil war raging in the north, but the war had finally reached it and left it scarred and broken.

Natalie funneled through a potential list of fighters returning to the country. On a large white board behind her, a list of names, most with iden-tifying photographs, highlighted the highest priorities. Under orders from Donald Mills, the Chief of Station in Sana'a who oversaw all CIA opera-tions in Yemen, Natalie and her team established their small operation. In collaboration with the Department of Defense and Naval Special Warfare Command, which was the naval component of SOCOM, the CIA requested SEAL Team 3 and Special Boat Team 20 be deployed to the 5th Fleet in anticipation of Natalie's findings. Of all the names, one held her obsession.

Isaam al-Amiri.

That name had sparked the entire intelligence mission in the city, and Natalie, as an operations officer, had proven herself fully capable of managing the compound and leading the search for the terrorist. After word came from agency sources in Afghanistan that al-Amiri had returned to the city of his birth, the CIA had jumped at the opportunity to nail him. As one of bin Laden's right-hand men, al-Amiri was currently the highest priority issued from the Chief of Station in Sana'a. Other orders persisted and those targets would not be neglected, but the opportunity to bag one of the men responsible for 9/11 and countless other acts of terror was to be prioritized.

Perhaps Natalie's Uncle Vic, her mother's brother, would rest easier in his grave if al-Amiri left the land of the living. Having perished during the second tower's collapse, a place he wasn't even supposed to be, Natalie had felt his loss more than her own father's. Uncle Vic was a partner at a contract law firm in San Francisco, and when one of his employees had requested vacation, he had stepped in to fulfill her duties in New York, despite it being below his corporate standing. Natalie smiled at the thought. It was like him to step in for others. She held no doubt he had died trying to save as many people as possible.

Natalie remembered watching the 9/11 attacks in her health class as a sophomore in high school. She still felt the eyes of her classmates as she broke down sobbing. When she watched that second tower fall, she knew her uncle had died. Still, she had hoped he made it. For weeks, she held out for a phone call, but now his name lay engraved on the 9/11 Memorial in New York City.

Raised by her mother after her father, a Naval Aviator, had died in a training accident off the coast of Hawaii, Natalie had always considered her uncle as more of a father than the man that gave her life. Her mother never remarried, and so Uncle Vic had stepped in to fill the role, even after having six children himself. His death was the reason she had joined the Navy and now served as an operations officer in the CIA.

Commotion in the yard stole her attention. She sighed. Why were they so disruptive? She looked through the window, Quinn and Becker sprinted toward their housing unit shouting and pointing. Other security quickly followed.

"What is going on?" she asked herself as she moved closer to the window for a better look. A few moments passed, and Natalie waited. Quinn, Becker, and the other security contractors poured out onto the yard dressed in full battle gear and toting their weapons.

Natalie dropped the report on her desk and pushed through the French doors leading from her office into the main living room, which had been converted into an intelligence floor.

"Someone tell me what's going on!" she shouted as she moved toward the building's exit. A young man fell in line next to her.

"A Marine Corps helicopter was just shot down over the western part of the city," Bryon Tyler explained. Her heart pounded through her chest at the news, but Natalie squared her jaw and nodded. She burst through the door leading to the yard, Bryon in tow. "What else you got, Bryon?" she asked.

"Nothing more, it's going to take time to obtain more intel," he replied.

"How long?"

"I don't know. Ten minutes?" came his reply. Natalie sighed. Ten minutes was too long, and Bryon knew it too.

"Hale!" a man shouted as he sprinted across the yard. She was already facing him. His men piled into the three Land Rovers as he headed her way. "I need eyes in the sky," he stated urgently. He threw a thumb over his shoulder toward his men. "We can get to them," Scott Lincoln added. He was a former Ranger, 2nd Battalion.

"You know as well as I that we don't have any operational authority in this," Hale answered.

"To hell with that!" he retorted.

"If you go, you leave this compound undefended, and if you get stuck out there, no one can come for you," she added. "I've got people getting in touch with SOCOM. I can update you when I know more." He cooled almost immediately.

"I'd appreciate that," Lincoln replied. "Depending on where they are, I can get to them in thirty minutes to an hour." Natalie nodded her understanding, realizing that they could reach the Marines far more quickly than SEAL Team 3 or anyone else. However, their actions could compromise the secrecy of the compound.

"We'll get what we can for you," Natalie said. She turned and headed back inside her building. Lincoln watched her go and didn't protest. He knew going blind into a combat situation was a surefire way to wind up dead.

The door behind Natalie slammed shut, and she cast her gaze over the various desks that littered the main floor. This would make or break her future. She wasn't Chief of Station, so she possessed no authority to send assistance, but it didn't matter. Lincoln was determined to go. She had seen that much in his eyes. Still, the wrong decision could end her career. Marines were in danger, if she could, she would give Lincoln the go, but as a former Naval Intelligence Officer, she was not going to send men into the field without some form of support.

"What happened?" Bateman shouted to the mass of Marines working tirelessly at their stations. Shaw kept his arms folded against his chest as he watched the ordeal. The pit that formed in his stomach prompted him to action, but first he needed information. Unfortunately, information took time. He watched Bateman as he navigated the labyrinth of workstations.

"We lost Saber Two," a Marine responded. Shaw stiffened. Wyatt, Reyes, and York were all on Saber Two. Thousands of miles away, Shaw fought against the wave of helplessness that crashed against him. He looked into his future and shuddered. How could he stand by while the fight continued?

"Where did that come from?" Bateman asked the Marine.

"It appears to be surface-to-air weaponry," she replied. Bateman rose from his hunched position behind her chair.

"In Yemen?" Dumfounded he turned to Shaw. The grave expression he received appeared almost threatening. He turned back around. "It doesn't matter. Let's get our boys out of there."

"Aye, sir," came the multiple replies of his subordinates.

"Lieutenant," a Marine called. Bateman turned his attention her way.

"What is it, Cobb?"

"I've got a line to CIA personnel on the ground in Aden," Sergeant Haley Cobb replied.

"A line from where?" he asked in disbelief.

"SOCOM," she replied.

"Put me through," Bateman ordered. He donned a headset and waited for the connection. As Shaw watched, his muscles coiled and his entire body urged him to spring into action, but again he wrestled back control. "This is Lieutenant Bateman. Who am I speaking to?"

"This is Operations Officer Abby Washington. Lieutenant, we've got a team ready to get to your Marines." Bateman's eyebrows hit the ceiling. What are the odds? "We're requesting any assistance you can render."

"Understood, Washington. Hang tight." Bateman covered the mic with his hand and issued an order to patch the drone feeds and pilot access through their connection. The Marines under his command did just that. "Washington, I'm sending you access to our drone feeds and putting you in touch with the pilot, callsign Cheerleader."

"Thank you, Lieutenant. We'll keep this line open," Abby stated. Bateman kept the headset on and again turned back to look at his guest. The countenance painted across the Raider's face sent shudders coursing through his body.

"I want everyone working on the downed Marine craft. What have we got so far?" Natalie shouted over the rushed buzz of working field officers.

"A MQ-9 Reaper is in the air from Camp Lemonnier," Abby answered. "ETA thirty minutes. We've been put through to a Lieutenant Bateman. He's connected us with the drone feeds and granted us access to the drone pilot."

"Good," Natalie answered. That moved more quickly than she could have ever hoped. "Someone get me linked up with Lincoln's team." Another team member, Rachel Lewis, hastily approached and handed Natalie a radio and earpiece. Natalie quickly donned the equipment. Playing the middleman between a team on the ground and support personnel stateside was not ideal, but it was as good as they could manage with such a short window of opportunity.

"Lincoln, this is Hale, over."

"I read you, Hale. Go ahead," came Lincoln's reply.

"We've got a Reaper in the air. ETA thirty mikes."

"Good copy," came his reply.

"Standby for actionable intel."

"Got the engines running," he replied. Natalie turned to Bryon.

"Get me a line to those Marines," she instructed.

5

Wyatt's eyes opened, and he blinked rapidly to clear his bleary vision. His hands hung toward the ground. He coughed and glanced around. Everything seemed so strange. His head throbbed and ached as his awareness grew.

He was upside down.

The Raider's hands found and unfastened his harness, and he fell the short way to the ceiling. He rolled onto his back before sitting up. He adjusted his helmet, and, as the excess blood left his head, his vision finally cleared. Next to him Kathryn's arms dangled to the ceiling, and across from him York hung as he had. He rushed first to Kathryn's side, and his hands worked to unfasten her harness. She fell into his arms, and he brushed the loose hair from her face and checked for a pulse. It was strong. He checked her over for blood, but she was clean. He set her down and moved toward York. He came to right as Wyatt arrived.

"Hey man, you alright?" Wyatt asked. York glanced around wide-eyed before locking in on Wyatt. His face was covered in dust and dirt, and blood dripped from a small cut high on his cheek. "You with me?"

"Yeah, yeah, I'm good," York replied.

"Good, I'm going to check on the rest of us." York nodded and went to work on his harness.

Wyatt crouched and continued through the fuselage. His eyes snapped to one of the NGO reps, the woman Kathryn had conversed with when Wyatt had first laid eyes on her. The middle-aged woman hung limp in her seat, her head dangling in a way it shouldn't. Her eyes stared blankly past him. Wyatt didn't need to check for a pulse. The impact had broken her neck.

The Marine looked away and checked on Reyes. He was okay, and Wyatt helped him out of his harness. Of the seven Marine Raiders in the helicopter, only three had survived. Master Sergeant Beasley's countenance appeared peaceful, as if he slept, but Wyatt knew otherwise. He pushed the assaulting emotions aside and checked on the pilots. A quick glance at one pilot told Wyatt all he needed to know, but the other cried out in pain. A metal shard protruded from her side, but she had managed to free herself from her seat. Tears streamed down her face, and she gripped Wyatt's arm firmly as he neared.

"Hey, you're alright, Lieutenant," he said warmly. She tried to offer him a smile, but another wave of pain rolled over her. Her mouth was clear of blood, which was a good sign. "Think you can walk?" he asked. She didn't answer, but instead attempted to steady her feet beneath her. Wyatt helped her up and guided her out of the craft.

It was the first time he had exited the helicopter since the crash. The pilots had done well given the circumstances. They stood within a court-yard off a wide road, and Wyatt noted where the initial collision had occurred. They had rolled a long way. The helicopter had come to a stop just before crashing into what was perhaps an apartment building. The entrance to the building lay accessible only through the fuselage. Surrounded by blocky buildings with flat roofs, Wyatt sought a defensible position.

"Saber One, do you read me?" Wyatt said, accessing his radio by squeezing the push-to-talk device fixed on his plate carrier.

"Affirmative, Saber Two. What's your status?" came Neeman's reply.

"Numerous casualties including two of the three civilians," Wyatt answered.

"Good copy, we're still overhead. Coming around for a visual." Wyatt set the pilot down and leaned her against the craft. He glanced back at York who looked after Kathryn. She had awakened, and she seemed surprisingly calm given their situation. Wyatt was relieved he didn't have a hysterical civilian on his hands. Reyes knelt next to him, carbine at the ready. He glanced up as the other helicopter soared overhead.

"We've got eyes on you," Neeman began. "Hang tight and we'll..." The line died as the helicopter exploded. Fiery debris flung outward in all directions, the smoke trail from the missile visible against the blue sky. As the burning fuselage plummeted toward them, Wyatt threw himself on the wounded pilot. The helicopter crashed not fifty meters away.

"Reyes, stay here. York, on me!" Wyatt shouted. The two Marines sprinted toward the wreckage. The chances were slim, but there just might be survivors in need of medical attention. As they neared, the fuel tank ruptured, and another explosion shot upward. The concussive force launched Wyatt and York off their feet. Black smoke billowed from the wreckage.

Wyatt groaned as he sat up. He stared at the wreckage in disbelief before shifting his gaze to meet York's dazed countenance. As anger and pain welled within him, Wyatt did his best to suppress the volatile emotions. He needed a clear head.

He was now in charge.

———

"Just confirmed, a second helicopter just went down," Bryon told Natalie as he moved to her side. Her expression hardened.

"Where's that UAV?" she asked.

"Five minutes out," came his reply. She nodded and hailed Lincoln on the radio.

"We've got another helo down. UAV is five mikes out," she said.

"Good copy, we can see the smoke to the west of us. We're Oscar Mike," came Lincoln's reply. Natalie glanced out the window to see the three Range Rovers pull away. She knew each vehicle currently carried two people, and she hoped there would be enough room for the survivors.

"Alright, Bryon, let's get that UAV feed up on the big screen," Natalie instructed. Bryon nodded. "And let's inform Chief Mills."

"You sure?" Bryon asked. Sometimes it was better to ask for forgiveness rather than permission, but he saw in her eyes that she intended to do neither. She nodded and watched as he returned to his workstation. Natalie pinched the bridge of her nose and exhaled; the next five minutes would span an eternity.

Shaw's eyes rimmed with tears as Bateman slowly removed his headset. Shaw had heard the radio communication between Wyatt and Neeman, and Bateman's reaction confirmed Shaw's suspicions. He attempted to suppress the anger welling up within him but failed. He flipped the table next to him, sending the coffee maker, its contents, and stacks of paper flying. The commotion drew all eyes.

"Captain!" Bateman shouted, mustering courage to confront the dangerous man. Shaw, face flushed, met his gaze. His chest heaved, and he ignored the pain of his healing wounds. He hissed through a forceful exhale and watched as Bateman donned the headset and turned back around.

Wyatt had survived the crash, he and two others. Radio communication would confirm who had made it and who had not. Every fiber within Shaw compelled him to Yemen, but the conflicting force of helplessness warred against it.

"Is the Navy sending in the SEALs?" Shaw asked Bateman. The man didn't respond. Shaw repeated himself louder, "Are they sending in the SEALs?" Bateman turned, and the look of defeat splattered across his face confirmed Shaw's fears.

"No, Command says they can't risk losing the entire team," Bateman replied. "The 13th MEU is being mustered, but they won't move until that drone is overhead." Anger burned within Shaw.

"We have to save them!" Shaw shouted. Bateman didn't back down.

"I invited you here out of respect, but now I think it is best if you leave," Bateman firmly stated. Unlike the general population within the Marine Corps, MARSOC Marines, although they yielded to rank, submitted also to expertise. Deep down, Shaw knew there was nothing he could do standing in that room. He swallowed his pride.

"Do what you can," Shaw pleaded.

"I will," Bateman promised. Shaw believed the conviction behind his eyes and offered him a brief nod before leaving the room. The Raider held his stomach as he marched down the hall and back outside. He didn't know if it was his wound or his emotions that stirred the pain within him. Shaw burst through the door leading outside and gasped for breath. Sweat clung to his face and neck, and he bent over to fight off the pain. He rose to his full height and inhaled the coastal air. His anger simmered, and his mind raced.

There were people responsible, and Shaw intended to root them out and leave their bodies for the crows.

The dark-eyed man watched with amusement as the second helicopter erupted in the sky above them. His fingers rested against his lips, and a smile spread across them as the vehicle plummeted downward. The man clapped his hands together and approached his buyer.

"You see, al-Amiri, my weapons prove far more effective than your RPGs," he said. The al-Qaeda commander simply stared at him.

"I am grateful for your demonstration, Mr. Silva, and I am more than satisfied with our arrangement," Isaam al-Amiri responded.

"These VM-99 Stingers will propel your war fighting capabilities into the modern era," Silva said.

"So it seems," al-Amiri replied. "I must say I am much more enthused about the missile systems you have delivered and the intelligence you have provided."

"I am sure you will put it all to good use," Silva replied. Al-Amiri watched as Silva donned a pair of gold-framed aviators. He wore his dark hair short and neat, and his tanned complexion hinted at his Moorish ancestry. Al-Amiri knew Francisco Silva wasn't obligated to perform a demonstration. The older man could only assume that the pompous,

Western arms dealer was attempting to secure future business through the elaborate display.

It worked. The timing could not have been more perfect.

"I look forward to a prosperous business relationship, my friend," Silva said as he buttoned the top button of his khaki suit jacket.

"As do I," the Yemeni answered. Al-Amiri raised his hand, signaling to the man standing behind him. The man approached the metal briefcase situated on the table between them. Silva and al-Amiri watched as the man entered the appropriate account information. "The money has been wired to the account you provided," al-Amiri stated when his man finished. Silva glanced over to his bodyguard for confirmation. The tall man rotated the briefcase, checked the account, and nodded before closing the case. Silva's smile widened as he presented his hand. Al-Amiri gripped it firmly and offered him a dull grin from behind his graying beard.

"Until next time," Silva said. Al-Amiri watched him leave the rooftop and noticed the length of the man's trousers. They were a tad too short, the hem just above his exposed ankles as was the popular European style.

Silva emerged from the building on the ground floor and nodded his greeting to the al-Qaeda guard as he passed by. His bodyguard, a South African named Rian Mather-Pike, wore a pastel blue suit and followed closely. The two men looked more as if they belonged in the nightclubs of Dubai than in war-torn Aden.

Mather-Pike donned a pair of sunglasses and tossed his long golden hair away from his face. The suit looked too small for him, and his muscles pulled the fabric in the wrong places. In truth, he wouldn't dress the way he did if his employer didn't require it, but Silva possessed a dedication to fashion and style that was unavoidable for the South African.

The SUV's rear passenger door opened as Silva approached. The man, a Frenchman, nodded his head in respect as his employer entered the vehicle. Mather-Pike scanned the area one last time before following Silva inside. The door closed and the Frenchman took the driver's seat.

"How do you feel about your first time in the field, Rian?" Silva asked.

"That was quite bold," Mather-Pike said as the luxury SUV sped down the dusty road. Mather-Pike's demeaning tone not lost on him, Silva stared out the window before checking his Omega Seamaster wristwatch. He was due in Dubai before evening.

"Perhaps," he replied nonchalantly. Mather-Pike knew better than to mistake Silva's response for apathy. The Spaniard's mind constantly whirled with brilliance as he planned several steps ahead in any given situation. The South African had not yet seen him overestimate anyone, but he had only been in his employ for a month. Still, he figured it was the key to Silva's success, and he admired him for it. However, the day's events nagged at his conscience.

"I don't see how bringing down two United States helicopters benefits you," Mather-Pike stated. Silva rested his head back against the seat and turned to regard his friend. Was he his friend? Silva found he didn't care much either way.

"It was part of the deal. Check the account again if you need more validation," he replied. As Mather-Pike expected, one of the Spaniard's famous smirks found its way across his sharp, attractive face.

Mather-Pike didn't respond, and instead, he shifted his gaze out the window. He didn't pretend to know Silva's mind, but he did consider his own role. He knew security services sat at the very bottom of his own ambition, even more so after Silva's display. He was okay with selling to revolutionaries and the oppressed, and al-Amiri had first fit that bill, but Mather-Pike had no way of knowing the Yemeni client had possessed such plans against the United States. Why would he know though? He was simply Silva's personal bodyguard, but Mather-Pike's worry was two-fold: Silva had crossed a dangerous threshold in his business, and the United States would not take kindly to the events that transpired today. It was a risk Mather-Pike hadn't thought Silva would take, and yet he had.

He couldn't deny the lucrative nature of the merchandise, but why did Silva draw the attention of one of the world's most powerful governments? It just didn't sit well with the South African. Perhaps he had arranged certain protections with the supplier, but did the supplier have that much influence or power?

The entire event had him questioning everything. At thirty-one, he hoped to have achieved more, and the reality he hadn't only depressed him. When he had accepted the position, he had resolved to glean everything he could from his employer, but his aspirations still swirled as a thin mist, unknowable, untouchable, unsearchable. What did he desire to achieve? What drive did Silva possess that he lacked? The questions frustrated him, but he refused to show it.

Then there was her. Those vibrant blue eyes, sweet smile, and alluring accent haunted him. He quickly pressed the woman from his mind. Why dwell on the impossible?

He turned to regard Silva, and, as he looked upon the man, a question formed in his mind. Would he take a bullet for Silva? He figured that depended on a multitude of factors, but then again, perhaps just one: would the bullet be fatal?

Silva activated his cell phone, tapped the screen, and directed his eyes toward the Frenchman, Romuald Affré, and said, "How long until we're airborne?"

"Thirty minutes," came the swift response. It was as if the man had anticipated the question. Then again, Affré knew every detail of their itinerary. The man was more organized and calculated than any other Silva had ever met. Despite a few past career concerns, Affré, a former French intelligence operative and Legionnaire, had proven himself time and time again.

"Good," came Silva's response.

Affré was slender with a trimmed beard. His bronze complexion and jet-black hair came from his Moroccan mother, and he received his French father's golden-green eyes and slender features. He was strikingly handsome in an exotic way, the best of France and North Africa. He wore a suit tailored in the same fashion as Silva and Mather-Pike, and, though Silva would never admit it, the Frenchman wore the style best.

6

"Contact!" came Reyes' shout through the comms. Wyatt and York raced back toward their downed helicopter as Reyes engaged an insurgent who had opened fire from the road.

"Get inside!" Wyatt shouted as he ran. His legs pumped furiously, moving faster than they ever had before. He heard the gunfire bellowing behind him, but he didn't look back.

Kathryn helped the wounded pilot back inside the wreckage and out of sight. Wyatt slid to a stop and climbed into the fuselage. He turned, and falling prone, picked up his first target. He fired, and the heavy thirty-caliber round tumbled through the insurgent's back. He acquired his next target and fired. The Raiders' quick aggression stopped the enemy's advance, and the insurgents clung to the corners of the buildings by the road.

"We need to get off the X," Reyes said once the brief fighting ceased.

"Fall back to the apartment building," Wyatt ordered.

"What about the pilot?" York asked. Wyatt slid back from the opening and moved to the pilot's side.

"Kathryn and I will take care of her. Let's move," he commanded.

Reyes led the way as Wyatt and Kathryn carried the aviator between them. The lieutenant hobbled as they moved; her left side burned with each use of her left leg.

"Stay off it," Wyatt urged as he bore the majority of her weight. He was careful not to touch the shard in her side. The slightest bump could move the object causing irreparable bleeding. Just as they crossed the building threshold, Reyes opened fire down the apartment hallway at an approaching group of hostiles.

"Back! Back!" he shouted. Wyatt scuffled backwards, and Kathryn lost her footing. Wyatt gripped the aviator tightly as he spun and guided her back the way they had come. Wyatt's eyes immediately widened as he caught a glimpse of the projectile spinning toward them.

"RPG!" York shouted, but it was too late.

Shaw ignored the pain pulsing in his legs and continued into the room. He paused as he flipped the light switch. The florescent lights snapped on one by one, illuminating the open space. Numerous cages housed various gear, weapons, and equipment. Unlike Afghanistan, where the loadout rooms were constructed of raw-wood shelving, everything before Shaw was state of the art. He had seen it empty before but knowing that most of his team wouldn't return bore heavily on him. He pushed the thought aside. He wasn't there to reminisce. He had Top Secret clearance, and he intended to use it.

Shaw dragged a table into the center of the room and prepped his workspace. He nabbed two laptops and a mobile printer and set them up on the table. He propped up a white board and ensured he had the basic office supplies: markers, tape, pens, and a notebook. Lastly, he put on a pot of coffee.

He took his first sip and dove in. Accessing SOCOM's databases, the Raider pulled up logs of satellite imagery and drone footage from the past twenty-four hours. He navigated through dossiers for which he had clearance and printed off everything he felt held significance.

As time droned onward, more paper lay crumpled at his feet than on the table. The white board had been erased countless times, and each time,

Shaw fought the frustration. Each wrong turn, each dead end ate into valuable time, time Wyatt and the others didn't have. He was on his second pot
of coffee when it clicked. His searching generated a file on a joint operation
between the CIA, DOD, and NSWC. He quickly set down his coffee cup,
spilling a bit over the lip, which he ignored, and dove into the intelligence.
His clearance barely got him access.

"Isaam al-Amiri," he muttered to himself as he read the dossier. That's
why SEAL Team 3 wasn't deployed to aid the Marines. They were on
standby for this guy and rightly so. He was believed to be one of Osama bin
Laden's right-hand men and connected to countless terror attacks across
Europe and 9/11. Why was he in Yemen? Shaw read on, muttering the
words quickly as his blue eyes darted back and forth. When finished, he
turned to the white board. He scribbled the name and then circled it; his
gut nagged him that al-Amiri was his man. Regardless of the feeling, Shaw
would press further. Hard intelligence provided the answers, not gut
feelings.

The Raider printed off an old photograph of bin Laden surrounded by
his commanders and taped it to the white board. He knew men and women
more gifted in intelligence gathering had likely pored over the photograph
in an attempt to identify al-Amiri, but one man in the photo tugged at his
memory. He stared hard into the man's eyes and attempted to recall from
where he knew him.

His memory swept him back to Afghanistan 2012. He sat across from a
sheik in the country's Helmand Province. After the Taliban cut ties with al-
Qaeda two years prior, SOCOM seized a new opportunity to hunt down
high-value al-Qaeda and Taliban targets. Amid the chaos caused by the
severed ties, they sought to disrupt any network present in the country. As a
freshly promoted captain, Shaw deployed to the region with the 2nd Marine
Special Operations Battalion, later named the 2nd Marine Raider Battalion.
He remembered having tea with the village sheik while attempting to
obtain intelligence about Taliban activity in the area. That man's name was
Taaha bin Hashim.

Bin Hashim's intelligence on Taliban forces in the area was accurate and
resulted in the success of multiple direct-action and counter-insurgency
missions. Shaw had always felt the information was too accurate, as if bin

Hashim had mingled with those forces, but at the time, he had pushed those thoughts to the back of his mind.

The face he focused on in the photograph belonged to Taaha bin Hashim. Still the name al-Amiri taunted his memory. It was connected somehow to bin Hashim. He remembered something about a rifle. Shaw's eyes widened as the memory cleared. He remembered bin Hashim's weapon. The bearded sheik had explained the rifle's origin, his warrior heritage, and about his father's involvement in fighting off the Russians in the 1970's. His father's name was Hashim Al Amiri.

Everything clicked as Shaw fought through his knowledge of the Arabic language.

In this instance, Isaam al-Amiri was incorrect. The *al-*, known as the *Nasab* in Arabic, referred to the definite article *the*. The name Amiri meant *Prince*, which translated the entire name to mean Isaam the Prince. However, the correction rested in the proper use of *al*. In Isaam al-Amiri's case, the correct article would be *Al*, meaning *the family of* or *from the clan of*. It wasn't Isaam the Prince, but Isaam of the family of Amiri.

Shaw quickly looked up the meaning of Isaam. After a few clicks on the keyboard, he found it. Isaam meant *Safeguard*.

"Safeguard the family of Amiri," Shaw muttered. "Isaam Al Amiri is Hashim Al Amiri's son." He stepped back from his workplace and stared at the image again. It was the only rational conclusion. What was the likelihood that a village sheik, who was sympathetic to the United States' mission in 2011, would be present in a photograph with Osama bin Laden circa 2003? It was possible that bin Hashim had reformed and left al-Qaeda, but Shaw doubted it. The name connection alone suggested otherwise.

That was why the CIA didn't possess a photograph of Al Amiri. Shaw only stumbled on the truth by sheer luck. Had he not sat and conversed with that sheik, he would never have made the connection. Shaw turned back to the computer and pulled up Taaha bin Hashim's file.

There wasn't much, and it didn't even include a photograph. Perhaps that was why the connection was never made. Despite its expertise, the intelligence network was simply too big and bureaucratic to catch everything.

The file showcased his efforts to aid the US, and Shaw found his own report in the dossier. Something stuck him as odd. Bin Hashim never provided any intelligence on al-Qaeda, just the Taliban. Yet more evidence that he was Isaam Al Amiri. It was the perfect ruse. By helping the United States, Bin Hashim protected himself while his alternate identity spread havoc on US and Coalition troops. No one would think to connect the two.

Disgust radiated through Shaw, Isaam Al Amiri had grown rich from United States taxpayers and turned that money toward terrorism. With each strand of intelligence Al Amiri offered as bin Hashim, the Department of Defense had paid him handsomely. Shaw had personally handed bags of cash to the man. Despite his revulsion, Shaw couldn't deny the brilliance of Al Amiri's operation. Now, only one question remained, how could he find Taaha bin Hashim?

Shaw knew he was in Aden, and the closest he could get to the city was either the 5th Fleet or Camp Lemonnier. To get to either, he needed orders, and getting orders meant going up the chain of command.

Major General Linus C. Weber commanded MARSOC, and he and his staff oversaw the operations of the Marine Raider Regiment, which was commanded by Colonel James G. Boatwright. Underneath Colonel Boatwright, the regiment was split into three battalions, each commanded by a lieutenant colonel. 1st and 3rd Marine Raider Battalions were currently headquartered at Camp Pendleton with plans to transition to the east coast, while the 2nd Raider Battalion, Shaw's battalion, remained headquartered in the home of its conception, Camp Lejeune. Four Marine Special Operations Companies made up one battalion, and four Marine Special Operations Teams made up each company. Shaw would first report to his company commander, Major Christopher M. King, and Shaw, if necessary, would work his way to the top to get what he wanted.

7

Wyatt opened his eyes as he lay on his stomach. He coughed and shook his head in a vain attempt to regain his equilibrium. Dust hung in the air and dried out his mouth with each breath. A strong hand suddenly jerked him up.

"Get upstairs!" York shouted. Wyatt stumbled as York shoved him up the stairs.

"The pilot!" Wyatt shouted back.

"She's gone! Move!" Wyatt, pain radiating from his muscles, tore up the stairs. As he reached the second floor, he cleared the corner and aimed down the hallway.

Clear.

He continued upward toward the third floor. Gunshots echoed below him. If help came for them, they would come by air, and if by air, they could extract them from the roof.

The building wasn't tall, just four stories, and Wyatt soon found himself on the roof. He scurried toward the edge and braced his rifle against the small wall. He took aim and fired, dropping an insurgent. Those around the unfortunate man scrambled for cover, but Wyatt killed two more before they vanished inside the adjacent buildings. Wyatt glanced back as Kathryn and Reyes emerged onto the roof.

"Where's York?" Wyatt asked urgently.

"He was right behind us," Reyes responded.

"Contact TOC," Wyatt ordered, referring to Bateman's team serving as their Tactical Operations Center, "let them know what's going on. I'll find York." Just as Wyatt moved toward the stairwell entrance, York emerged. He shook his head and blinked his eyes as he tried to shake off the pain. Wyatt quickly noticed the blood soaking York's uniform just below his ribcage.

Wyatt ripped into one of York's IFAKs and tore open a chest seal. He yanked York's shirt from his waistline and carefully applied the seal to prevent pneumothorax, a condition that if left untreated would result in hypoxemia and death.

"There an exit wound?" Wyatt asked, as he looked him over. York fought the pain with a strong exhale as he pressed his right hand against the sealed wound.

"Never was a fan of side plates," he joked, "I guess I should've been." Wyatt ignored him and searched for an exit wound. He didn't find one. York winced again, and Wyatt could tell his strength faded quickly. He glanced back at Reyes and Kathryn. Kathryn sat alone with her arms wrapped around her knees. Tears streamed down her dusty face, leaving wet streaks of grime.

"You alright?" he shouted across the rooftop. She didn't answer. Her tears had given way into horrible sobs.

"She's losing it," York managed.

"You okay?" Wyatt asked him. It was in that moment he missed Petty Officer Third Class Jessie Adams, who hung upside-down, broken and bloodied, in the helicopter below. Adams served as the team's Special Amphibious Reconnaissance Corpsman (SARC). He was a highly-trained, Naval, combat corpsman attached to their team, capable of rendering the most advanced medical techniques to save lives. Wyatt knew Adams could have assessed and treated York far better than he could, and without him, their immediate future looked bleak.

"Yeah, I'll be fine," he responded. Wyatt didn't believe him, but he hurried toward Kathryn. She threw herself on him. Any hint of calm she exhibited in the courtyard had given way to shock. The RPG explosion must have taken its toll on her psyche.

"Hey, listen to me." Wyatt's tone was firm. "I'm going to get you out this, but I need you to keep it together, okay?" She looked at him, her blue eyes glistening and rimming with tears. There was longing there, hope that he could deliver on what he promised. For Wyatt, it didn't matter if he could or not, he just needed her calm and in her right mind. The last thing he needed was for her to bolt away and catch a bullet. "Stay right here," he instructed. He didn't take his eyes off her when he called out to Reyes, "Reyes, any luck getting through to TOC?"

"Yeah, we've been connected with a CIA officer here in Aden. She wants to speak with you," he answered.

"York," Wyatt called to him, ready to issue orders.

"I've got the door," he interrupted. He knew the words on the tip of Wyatt's tongue. His sweat-drenched face twisted in pain as he moved into position. He let his carbine hang against his side as he unslung an M1014, a semi-automatic, twelve-gauge shotgun.

"We keep them focused on this entrance. Funnel them through the stairwell and keep the advantage. Reyes, clear the roof, make sure there aren't any other ways to get up here," Wyatt ordered.

"On it," he answered and moved past him. Wyatt checked his radio and pressed his PTT.

"This is Staff Sergeant John Wyatt, who am I speaking with?" he asked.

"Sergeant, this is Natalie Hale, head of Aden operations. We've got eyes on you from a drone overhead. What's your status?" Wyatt grinned in relief.

"There are four of us on an apartment rooftop," he started as he took in his surroundings. The bay glimmered like a jewel to the north, and jagged brown mountains rose to the south. "Three Marines and one civilian."

"Understood," came her response. "I've got a team inbound. Six men highly trained." Wyatt scoffed, only six? "Can you hold for forty-five minutes?"

"We can if that drone bites," he replied. "They coming by air?"

"Negative, a vehicle convoy."

"Good copy," Wyatt responded, less than enthused. York needed medical assistance within four hours if he was going to make it, and that was pushing it. Wyatt didn't know what else that bullet had torn through, but there was nothing more he could do.

"There's another way down," Reyes said as he returned to Wyatt's side. "Looks to be clear."

"Alright, exfil is by ground vehicle; we'll head that way," Wyatt started, but York cursed as thirty-caliber rounds tore through the wooden door. He fell backwards, unscathed, and as the door opened, he met the intruder with a blast from his shotgun. York blasted a second intruder before tossing a grenade down the stairs. Shouts of alarm echoed beneath them before the deafening explosion roared up the steps.

"Hale! Where's that Reaper?" Wyatt shouted into the comms.

"Negative on fire support, Sergeant, the pilot won't engage without a clear and identifiable target. We don't know if the building contains any noncombatants," came Natalie's reply. Wyatt knew she was right. York remained vigilant by the door, and he gripped his shotgun with what strength he had left. New shouts rose from the stairwell, and York fought off another wave of pain and readied himself. Reyes took a position on York's right.

A familiar sound, like the swift ring of metal on metal, reached their ears. Wyatt's eyes widened as the grenade soared through the doorway. Time slowed as he watched the explosive travel through the air. It rebounded off Reyes' shoulder and hit the floor to his right.

Reyes didn't hesitate.

He dove atop it and took the full force of the explosion. His body jolted violently under the blast, and the explosive dropped the remaining Marines to the ground. Wyatt, ears ringing, slowly rose to his feet. York rolled over onto his side and glanced Reyes' way. He adverted his gaze down the stairs as a group of men rushed upward.

"Wyatt!" York called, alerting his Element Leader to the threat. Wyatt snapped his rifle up and rapidly pulled the trigger. The rounds thundered through the advancing fighters who were obviously surprised the Marines remained alive. Their shrill shouts of terror echoed around them, but they returned fire.

As he rose from his back, York released the last devastating blast from his weapon their way. York didn't reload but simply dropped the weapon and swung his M4 back around to a ready position. He flicked the safety lever all the way around and emptied his magazine into the stairwell. Wyatt's rifle clicked, but he smoothly transitioned to his Glock 19. He guided the rifle down to his left side, rotating it slightly so it would remain motionless as it dangled, and drew the pistol by disengaging the holster's active retention with his thumb. The pistol barked as he sent rounds through the doorway. He dropped the empty mag and, with blinding speed, loaded another.

"Get her out of here!" York shouted. Wyatt shot his gaze toward Kathryn. She lay on the ground curled up in the fetal position. She was sobbing again. He knew what York was telling him. "I'm done," he said. "I feel it. Besides, I got to see Reyes through the other side. He won't be able to do it by himself," York managed a bloody chuckle. Wyatt hesitated too long for York's liking. "Go!" he shouted as he shoved Wyatt toward the journalist. The Marine Raider didn't look back. He rushed to Kathryn's side and coaxed her to her feet.

"We got to go," he said tenderly. He started guiding her to the far end of the rooftop before pausing. He hurried to Reyes' side and drew his Glock 19 from its holster. "Thank you, bro. I'll see you on the other side." he managed before hurrying back to Kathryn. "Do you know how to use this?" he asked her. She whimpered as he handed it to her. "Just like in the movies." She nodded fearfully as her shaking hand wrapped around the grip. "Keep it pointed down until you need it," he added. The last thing he wanted was to get shot in the back, but, in the event they were overrun, he wanted her to have a way out. If they were captured, the likely outcome for her was a never-ending, gang rape.

York watched Wyatt disappear down the other stairwell and grunted to strengthen his resolve. He moved as quickly as he could to Reyes' side. He knelt, removed his helmet, placed a hand on Reyes' back, and closed his eyes.

"Odin, father, help me," he prayed, "welcome my brothers and me into your halls." Upon opening his eyes, he dipped his fingers into Reyes' pooling blood and traced a red streak overtop his ears and down the sides of his neck. "Wait for me a little longer, brother," York said as he rose and returned his attention to the doorframe. The weight of his brother's demise bore heavily on his spirit, but he readied himself as he heard shouts spiral up the staircase in growing crescendo.

The insurgents emerged around the corner and came face to face with York. The Raider's rounds pounded through the first man, and York marched down the steps dropping each insurgent as they bounded up the stairs. He paused at the corner and caught his breath. Another wave of pain crashed over him, and fire ate at his insides. He suppressed every alert his brain screamed, but he still took a moment to steady himself before continuing his descent. He gritted his teeth and rounded the corner with authority. He picked up his first target and opened fire.

In the chaos, insurgents ended up shooting those in front of them in the backs. A red mist hung in the air as York descended, chasing those fleeing his presence. Maybe they should have tried to retake the building when Reyes was still with them. York pushed the thought from his head and continued down. He slumped against the wall as pain again radiated from his stomach.

He almost missed it.

The barrel rounded the corner from the third-floor entry, and York nearly deflected it in time. He slapped it downward as the insurgent pulled the trigger. The round shredded through York's stomach, and the Marine advanced on him drawing his bearded axe. The heat in his belly surged and seemed to devour his organs, but York, in his battle lust, roared in fury as he repetitively buried the axe into the insurgent's head and neck. With each rage-fueled hack, a streak of dark blood trailed after the weapon. Only flayed meat and split bone remained of the attacker's upper torso, and his head hit the floor with a strange thud, like a broken watermelon hitting pavement.

Tasting blood, both his and that of his kill, York charged onto the third floor amidst a hail of bullets, wielding his axe in mighty arcs. Bullets sliced through him, and, with painful breaths, York sunk to his knees in defeat. His chest heaved, but little air came. His body armor had failed under the onslaught. An insurgent approached. His dark eyes, filled with awe and hatred, looked over the kneeling Marine. Covered in blood, York glanced downward at his gleaming, red weapon. He smiled in euphoria. His end was fitting; it was more than he could have asked for, and surely, the gods smiled on him now.

He looked up at his adversary and presented a wild and savage grin. The man recoiled, but in one last burst of strength, York hammered his axe into the man's chest and hacked and hacked. Gunfire erupted around him, a beautiful chorus of war drums beckoning him to the halls of Odin.

8

The concussive bellowing of AKMs from the far side of the building confirmed York's fate. Kathryn followed closely behind Wyatt carrying the pistol as instructed. She breathed heavily and still shook as adrenaline and fear stoked her body. It was a fear she had never known; it ate its way from her extremities to her core like an invading force seeking to cripple her body. The mental energy required to ward off such an onslaught drained her considerably, and she wobbled more than walked as her legs barely listened to her commands. Still, she trudged onward, following her only hope.

The pang in Wyatt's heart was hard to ignore, but he had to try. Sergeant Cliff York had bought them considerable time, and Wyatt intended to honor his and Reyes' sacrifice by surviving. In the process of clearing his mind to focus on the task before him, Wyatt fought off wave after wave of grief brought on by the rolling memories of the two men. Only anger staved off the looming fear. Wyatt felt that fear hovering just beyond his senses, ready to assault his body as surely as it had assaulted Kathryn. However, a wall of impenetrable anger and thirst for revenge kept the fear at bay, but it did little to stop it from taunting him.

He was a lone combatant with a civilian in tow, surrounded and outnumbered. Never before had he faced such a dire situation. His heart raced, dumping another load of adrenaline into his veins.

The isolation set like concrete.

"Keep it together, Marine," he muttered quietly to himself, "I am the master of my fate. I am the captain of my soul." The mantra worked. It was a technique Shaw had taught him.

Wyatt's mantra came from the poem *Invictus* by William Ernest Henley. He had first heard it in a movie by the same title, and it stuck. Shaw was always going on and on about how important poetry and classic literature was, and, after hearing that poem, Wyatt finally understood. It calmed him and reminded him how in control he actually was in any given situation. His breathing normalized, and his heart descended back into his chest. His mind cleared, and the images of Reyes and York temporarily faded away. He focused on the stairs before him and what threats he might encounter ahead.

Survival first. Then vengeance.

The pair descended from the second floor, and Wyatt checked his corners before emerging onto the ground level. As much as he wanted to smoke the two insurgents guarding the exit, he restrained himself. They faced away from them, and Wyatt seized the opportunity their lack of vigilance bought him.

He motioned Kathryn toward a nearby apartment, and she tried the handle. It was locked. Wyatt crept toward the next unit, keeping his rifle trained on the first of two enemy combatants. He flicked out his arm with two fingers pointing toward the door. Kathryn slowly turned the knob; it quietly opened, and she rushed inside. Wyatt checked the hallway behind him and the two guards again before backing into the room and closing the door.

"What are we doing in here?" Kathryn whispered, but Wyatt silenced her with a finger over his lips. He carefully picked his way around the abandoned apartment. Dust and dirt covered the worn furniture. Distressed belongings showed evidence of a quick departure, but it looked to have been abandoned for quite some time.

Wyatt moved to the window on the exterior wall. He tightened his two-point sling and slung the rifle down at his side. His fingers worked the window lock, and he, as carefully as possible, raised the window. It resisted, and he dare not strike it to dislodge the pane. The Marine Raider moved to the next window. Again, he worked the lock and tenderly pulled upward. The window glided open, and drawing his pistol, he checked the alleyway.

Clear.

He ducked his head through and again checked both directions before swinging his legs over the sill. He guided his rifle through before setting his feet on the dirt. After holstering his pistol, he took Kathryn's pistol and helped her through. He returned it to her and directed her toward a dumpster just to their right.

Kathryn leaned against the metal side and inhaled deeply. She looked at Wyatt and found courage in his eyes. They held a deep resolve, a firmness she had never seen before. Perhaps it was common on the battlefield, but she had never set foot anywhere near a combat zone, much less in the middle of one, to know one way or the other.

Still, she cared little whether it was a common occurrence or specific to her guardian angel, she was grateful for him and his determination, knowledge, and skill. However, her gratitude did little to stifle the fear that roamed freely throughout her body and ravaged her mind. She felt like she hung by a thread above dark, foreboding water. She shuddered. Drowning was her deepest fear. Staff Sergeant John Wyatt, her thread, kept her alive, but just as he served as a constant reminder of her salvation, he also served as a reminder of impending doom. If he fell like York, Reyes, and the others, what hope did she have?

"You okay?" Wyatt asked.

"No," she answered hastily. He realized how foolish his question must have sounded. He flattened his lips and checked the Garmin strapped to his wrist, but he realized he possessed no bearing for a safe direction. He squeezed his PTT.

"Hale, do you copy?"

"Yes, Wyatt, go ahead," came Natalie's reply.

"We've made it outside the building. We are on the west side in a back alley. What's the update on that exfil?"

"We see you. Standby."

Al Amiri ran his hand affectionately over the wooden foregrip of his AKM. His fingers traced over the familiar nicks and scratches from past generations. The stain had darkened considerably and much of the original finish applied to the metal had worn away. He had made a few changes to it over the years. He had replaced its fixed, wooden stock with an under-folding stock, and he had the barrel shortened. Despite its rough and patchwork appearance, Al Amiri kept it clean and well oiled.

The weapon had belonged to his father, and he had used it valiantly against the Russians during their occupation of Afghanistan. Like his father before him, Al Amiri had answered the call when his al-Qaeda brothers in Afghanistan fought against the Americans. Bin Laden was a personal friend, and Al Amiri sorely missed him. Although the work in Afghanistan was far from over, bin Laden's legacy would endure, but Al Amiri could not ignore the pain and suffering in his home country. He had returned to save his people. Western and Saudi influence must be rooted out and expelled, only then could he freely rebuild Yemen and save his people. With millions and millions of dollars at his disposal, he was in the position to do it. However, certain unavoidable roadblocks required his attention.

He had heard of a hidden CIA operation present in the city, and he had lived in Aden for almost two years before he heard the news. They were hunting him, and he couldn't tolerate that. His Libyan brothers, although not part of al-Qaeda, had won a great victory in Benghazi by expelling the CIA there, and he would accomplish no less in Aden first, then his entire country. Afterwards, he felt confident that he could unite a large population of the country by providing food and other necessities. Once he won that trust, he could continue his rise as a leading political figure and put a stop to Saudi and Western involvement in his country. He would not let what happened in Afghanistan happen to his people. It was time for the Imams of Yemen to return.

The door opened behind him, but he remained seated, cross-legged, unmoved. He inhaled slowly through his large nose and exhaled lightly as he awaited the news.

"You have won a great victory over the West today," the young man greeted.

"The day is not over, Faatin," Al Amiri replied. He rose to his feet and straightened out his garb. The cream *thobe* extended to the floor. The older man reached for his brown *bisht*, a cloak-like overgarment common among the more traditionally dressed Arabic men, and donned it over his shoulders. His beard grayed around his chin and was neatly kept. Deep wrinkles formed on his dark forehead and around his coffee eyes. Faatin Radi always felt he saw a dull fatigue hanging behind those pupils, but Al Amiri had proven countless times over to be a vigorous and wise leader.

Radi, a young man not yet thirty with sharp, attractive features, sported a neatly trimmed goatee, and his eyes held the shade of honey. If anyone possessed the countenance of a successful leader, it was Radi, and Al Amiri knew that too well. However, curbing the young man's temper had proven quite the chore, but he had succeeded. His hatred for the West was well founded by Al Amiri's standards, and Al Amiri, with his sons dead by the hands of the Coalition, hoped that Radi would be his heir.

Al Amiri approached the young man and smiled warmly. He placed a hand on his shoulder and met his gaze, "Do you bring more news?" he asked. Radi grinned, and his teeth gleamed bright ivory, a trademark of a Western upbringing.

"We located a convoy of three SUVs in the city. They are making their way to the crash site now," Radi answered.

"Good. Pull back our soldiers. We will follow them back to their base of operations. Once we know the location of the CIA, our many months of planning will have not been in vain. Remember, the victory today is not in the number of deceased; it is in the acquirement of knowledge," Al Amiri explained. Al Amiri guided Radi back through the door from which he entered. The room, covered with maps and monitors, served as Al Amiri's command center. It was a bit crude but functioned perfectly for his needs. More importantly, he could move it using just the one van he kept ready in the back alley.

All rose from their seats as he entered. The four men in the room, all educated in Europe and the United States in information technology, cyber security, computer engineering, and national security were the keys to his success. He had more than enough soldiers; what he truly valued were intellectual minds, and those he could not afford to lose on the battlefield. These minds gave him their undivided attention and, more importantly, their unfailing loyalty.

"We will allow the Americans to collect their dead. This will put them at ease and provide a false sense of security. It will make them think they are in control. Make no mistake, they will try to hunt us from Langley, but you all will have made that impossible," Al Amiri said. Smiles spread throughout the room. "By the end of the day, we will know the location of our target, and I will rely on you all here for victory." Al Amiri turned to Radi, "Contact our men in the mountains, have them prepare, and update me when we know the location. We will not fail." Radi inclined his head as his leader returned to his room.

Natalie Hale watched the large video monitor with great anticipation. She barely noticed her increased perspiration as her anticipation grew. Years had passed since she witnessed the live deaths of United States personnel, and she wouldn't easily forget the image of the one Marine jumping on a grenade. Several of her staff, having never before witnessed such an act, responded in different ways. Two had vomited, three had stepped outside, and one still lay passed out in her chair, but all had wiped tears from their cheeks.

Her right hand tightly gripped the radio that connected her to Staff Sergeant Wyatt and Scott Lincoln. She listened to their communication as she watched the drone footage. Bryon was in communication with the Air Force Remotely Piloted Aircraft Pilot. The communication set up wasn't ideal, but it was the best they could do with such short preparation, but the RPA Pilot was professional and seasoned. Cheerleader could read the battlefield as well as, if not better, than Bryon or Natalie could, and the CIA officer trusted Cheerleader to do her job and operate within the confines of her orders. Natalie was simply grateful they were able to obtain such support so quickly. MARSOC didn't play around. The radio clipped in her earpiece.

"Good copy, Lincoln, we're headed that way," Staff Sergeant Wyatt said. Natalie watched as the two silhouettes, identified through the drone's infrared display, moved north. Wyatt had activated the IR strobe on his helmet for easy identification. His silhouette blinked consistently, visible only to the drone.

Natalie followed their movements but kept a sharp eye out for any hostiles. The room was silent; no one dared to breathe as they watched the events unfold before them. As Wyatt and Kathryn neared the alley opening, Natalie engaged the radio.

"You've got two tangos at your three o'clock," she said.

"Yeah, I see them," came Wyatt's reply. Natalie held her breath as Wyatt and Kathryn crossed the two intersecting alleys; Wyatt paused at the opening of the next alley to engage any threat in the event they were seen.

They weren't.

The duo continued north down the next alley. Natalie had patched the drone feed through to Lincoln's team. On the ground, they would better be able to devise their approach and exfiltration.

"Bryon, you seeing this?" Natalie asked as she moved closer to the wall monitor.

"I am," he responded. The room watched as four trucks pulled into the courtyard with the downed helicopters. The remaining insurgents swarmed the vehicles.

"They're leaving?" Bryon questioned. Natalie felt in her gut that his assumption was correct, but they had just killed Americans. They weren't going anywhere.

"It looks like they are planning on pursuing," she countered. Bryon smirked as he caught the direction of her reasoning. He opened up his line to the drone pilot.

"Cheerleader, we're seeing a convoy mounting to pursue our survivors, can you confirm?"

"I confirm," came Cheerleader's response. Her tone was light and a bit peppy, living up to her call sign. "We are clear to engage."

A satisfied smile spread across Natalie's face when the missile thudded into the vehicles arranged in the courtyard. The gray screen flashed as a billow of white flame plumed on the monitor, and when it cleared, ivory flames licked the mangled vehicles, and strewn body parts painted the ground a crisp white.

"That's a good hit, Cheerleader," Bryon said. He glanced up at Natalie, and she gave him a quick nod of approval.

"Hale, this is Lincoln."

"Go ahead, Lincoln," Natalie replied through the radio.

"We've picked up the survivors and are headed back," he said.

"Good copy, we'll see you soon." She issued a sigh of relief and turned to face her team. "We got them," she said. Somber smiles donned the faces in the room. Natalie turned back to the screen and hardened her face. Bryon noticed it immediately. "Now, who did this?" she whispered to herself.

9

The three SUVs roared down the tattered and war-torn streets of Aden, Yemen. The first Range Rover turned left and accelerated down the street lined with low, flat-roofed buildings, and the trailing vehicles followed. Each man kept a sharp eye for anything out of the ordinary. Jared Becker drove the lead vehicle while Matthew Quinn, next to him in the front passenger seat, navigated. Within Becker, relief and anger surged and crashed together. Quinn, always reserved, wore his usual calm expression.

"How could this have happened?" Becker exclaimed. His hands wrenched hard the steering wheel. Quinn didn't look up from his tablet displaying their navigation.

"Easy, bro. We'll sort this out when we get back," he assured. "Just get us there in one piece." The vehicles were armored against small arms fire, but that wouldn't protect them from an IED. A wrong turn or a simple mistake could spell disaster.

"How we looking, gents?" came Lincoln's voice over the radio. Quinn pressed his PTT.

"So far so good," Quinn replied.

"Let's pick up the pace. This civ is getting pretty hysterical."

"Good copy," Quinn responded. He looked at Becker.

"Yeah, I heard him," he said as he pressed on the throttle. The Range

Rover surged forward, and Quinn checked the navigation. "Hey, I got a military-aged male on a cell phone just ahead on that balcony; he's staring right at us," Becker said.

"Yeah, I see him," Quinn replied, looking up. "Hey, Lincoln," he called into his radio.

"Go ahead."

"We've got a military-aged male on a cell phone up ahead." Quinn waited for his reply. They had all lost friends to such men. At worst, the man would initiate a call at the proper moment, shredding apart their convoy in a detonation of smoke and flame. At best, he was simply making a phone call.

"Your call," came Lincoln's reply.

"We'll push through," Quinn replied. Becker shot him a look.

"You sure?" he asked. The contractor nodded.

"I figure there wasn't enough time to set up an IED since we've been out in the city, and we're not returning the same way we came. I think we're being tracked," he replied. Quinn watched him as they passed, the man's eyes, dark with anger, met Quinn's. Becker flipped him the bird as they roared past.

"Oh yeah, they're tracking us," Becker said.

"You got that right." Quinn felt it in his bones. "Take the next left. We'll try to throw them off. They can't have eyes everywhere." Quinn spoke into the radio, "be advised, we are being tracked. We are altering our course back."

"Affirmative, your lead," Lincoln replied. The two men in the front vehicle had nearly three times as many years of combat experience than he had. Lincoln commanded Rangers as a captain, which is no small feat, but these men had rumbled in the Middle East for nearly a combined forty years. If anyone knew how to get them back in one piece, it was Becker and Quinn.

The second car followed Becker's lead and made the left turn as quickly and sharply. Wyatt noticed the sudden shift in the vehicle's urgency but continued to comfort Kathryn. Any emotion that she had suppressed in the field now streamed openly. She sobbed on Wyatt's shoulder, and he held her tight. Her tears again left dark streaks on her dust and dirt covered face, and her entire body trembled against Wyatt's stone frame.

She wouldn't be able to explain it, but at the sight of American faces, she broke down. Her fear never left, but relief had rammed into it with such force that it destabilized her entire body and mind. Rational thought had long left, and Kathryn tumbled through the assaulting emotions like a child caught in a violent riptide. She could only ride it out until it released her.

"It's alright. You're safe now," he whispered tenderly as he rubbed her arm. She sat curled up on the seat next to him. Wyatt doubted she could move any closer to him if she tried. "You're safe now," he said again. Just acting on instinct, he kissed the top of her head. "Everything's alright," he assured. She quickly tossed her head up and smashed her lips into his. The action completely caught him off guard. Her tears and mucus wet his face, and he was so shocked, he didn't return the kiss. She pulled back, immediately aware of what she had done. Miraculously, the action broke the cycle of unyielding emotion. How? She couldn't say, but her mind seemed clearer and back under her own control.

She wiped her eyes and ran her sleeve across her nose. Her embarrassment skyrocketed, but, in some way, the kiss had helped.

"I'm sorry," she hastily said. She grew red under the pale dust on her face. Deep down she knew the events of the day would take years to flesh out and decipher, but, in that moment, she felt better.

"No, it's okay," Wyatt said as he wiped his face. He offered her a smile.

"You're not married or anything?" she asked. Wyatt briefly chuckled; it felt good.

"No, I'm not married or anything," he responded. She smiled, and, as the fear left, the relief swept through more of her body like a wave of warmth. She curled her loose hair behind her ears.

"So, I could kiss you again, if I wanted to?" she asked, wearing a shy smile.

"You could," Wyatt replied. She leaned in and offered him a quick peck on the cheek.

"Thank you," she said. Wyatt felt the weight of her sincerity behind the simple words.

"No problem," he replied. In truth, he didn't know how else to respond, but even covered in dirt and grime she was beautiful. The comfort of their interaction stole his mind away from York, Reyes, and the rest of his team, whose bodies still lay where they fell.

"We're coming up on the compound," Lincoln said, turning back to face them. "We'll get you two cleaned up and stateside in no time."

"Thank you," Kathryn answered quickly. Wyatt remained silent. He did not intend to return home, not yet anyway.

———

Natalie Hale and her team waited in the courtyard of the former estate. It had belonged to a family who graciously permitted them use after receiving a new life in the United States. Surrounded by ten-foot walls, the compound held two buildings. The main structure, which was once the primary residence, now housed Natalie's operation, and the upper level served as residence for her team. The opposite structure, a single-story building, housed Lincoln, his team, and their gear. The solid steel gate whined open as the convoy approached.

The heavy doors groaned shut once the three vehicles pulled within the safety of the compound. The men all poured out at once, and Lincoln opened the door for Kathryn.

"Abby," Natalie called to her right. The young woman appeared at her side knowing exactly her intended order.

"Sure thing," she replied. As soon as Kathryn set foot on the ground, Abby was at her side. "Hey, I'm Abby," she said with a wide smile. The short brunette took hold of Kathryn's hand, and as soon as Kathryn saw the array of clean faces, she burst into tears again. Abby rubbed her back and guided her toward the group. Her knees buckled as she neared them, but Natalie caught her.

"We've got you," she said sweetly. Kathryn continued to cry. Her embarrassment rose again, but she knew she shouldn't feel that way. Her reaction was completely justifiable, and anyone else would have reacted the exact same way. Natalie turned to another woman, "Rach, will you help out?" She nodded, quickly took Natalie's place underneath Kathryn's arm, and guided her into the main building.

Wyatt appeared around the front of the second Range Rover and watched Kathryn disappear into the building. He longed to follow her, to still protect her, but he curbed the emotion.

"Hey there," Natalie greeted as she moved toward him. He instantly recognized the voice.

"Hale, I can't thank you enough," he said as he gripped her outstretched hand.

"I'm just sorry we couldn't do more," she replied. For the first time, Wyatt allowed in the unchecked pain of his loss. He blinked quickly and coughed to suppress his tears. He looked over her head and avoided eye contact, fearful it might cause him to lose the grip on his emotions.

"Hale, there's something we need to discuss," Lincoln interjected. She nodded without taking her eyes off Staff Sergeant John Wyatt. How could a man endure what he had and come through on the other side? She thought of the SEALs of Operation Red Wings. Wyatt was not the first, and it was possible for a man to recover from such a traumatic event. "Becker, Quinn, see to our Marine here," Lincoln said.

"On it," Becker stated. He moved to Wyatt's side. "Come on, man. Let's get you a shower and some chow."

"Yeah," Wyatt responded quickly. He blinked away more tears and followed them into the other building.

The air conditioning refreshed him more than he could have ever imagined. He took a minute to breathe in the cool air and collect himself. He closed his eyes while inhaling and opened them after his long exhale. He glanced around the main living room. A large, high-definition television adorned the far wall. It must have been at least sixty-five inches from corner to corner. Beneath it sat a PlayStation 4, a myriad of games, and several controllers. The ceiling fan spun too quickly to follow, and a row of cubbies jutted out from the wall to his left. A large sectional and a recliner took up the majority of the floor space, and a table was built into the kitchen island.

"Pretty nice, huh?" Becker said as he strode in past the MARSOC Raider.

"Yeah," Wyatt responded. Becker moved to his cubby and removed his gear. The rest of their team followed suit.

"Feel free to take the last cubby on the left. It's not being used right now," Becker offered.

"Thanks," Wyatt replied as he moved that way. He cleared his weapons and stowed them in the open space. He removed his plate carrier and hung it on the heavy-duty hanger designed for such loadbearing equipment. Again, he inhaled deeply, and his chest expanded to its full capacity. He was thrilled to be out of his kit.

"Feels good to be out of that monkey suit, doesn't it?" the man next to him said. He was thick with a bright red beard and fair skin. The guy looked like he could compete in the World's Strongest Man competition. Wyatt unzipped his gray jacked, pulled it off, and tossed it on the base of the cubby.

"Yeah, it does," he replied.

"Rick Reeves," he said, introducing himself. He extended a massive hand which Wyatt gave a firm pump.

"John Wyatt."

"Yeah, I know. That's a name I won't forget. You did good out there, brother," Reeves said in deep vocal tones. Wyatt wasn't so sure, perhaps he did, but he knew as time progressed, he would see what he could have done differently. He hoped it wouldn't drive him toward insanity. "Showers are around the corner, down the hall, second door on the left."

"I appreciate it," Wyatt replied.

"Towels and stuff are already in there." Reeves left him and settled into the recliner. He donned a pair of readers and cracked open his book. Wyatt couldn't tell what it was. He could ask but didn't feel like it. The Raider removed his boots and headed for the showers.

Becker and Quinn slumped on the couch while their other two teammates prepped some food. It wasn't long before they jumped to their feet, startled.

The wailing echoed down the hall accompanied by several hard thuds. The two men exchanged concerned looks before heading toward the hallway.

"Let him be," Reeves stated. The two men glanced toward Reeves. "The kid needs to get it out of his system," the older man said without looking up from his book. He flipped a page, and Wyatt's grief continued to echo from the shower.

10

Major King glanced over Shaw's report laid out on his desk. Shaw sat in the chair across from him watching King's every move. The seasoned man's bald dome gleamed like a well-polished shoe as it reflected the florescent light. King's large eyes always appeared to pop from their sockets, and his ears flared outward. His large nose sat smashed on his wide face.

King was a good man and better Marine. He maintained perfect fitness scores and was often sympathetic to the concerns held by those under his command. It was in this trait that Shaw placed his hope.

"You know you're not in the intelligence analyzing business," King critiqued. Although Raiders gathered intelligence, they passed the information on through the channels set forth by whatever agency liaised on the operation, whether it be the CIA, NSA, DIA, their own Marine Corps intelligence teams, or the countless others that constituted the United States intelligence community.

"I understand, sir," Shaw replied. King glanced up at him and then back down to the file.

"And all this," King started, waving his open hand over the documents, "you're sure about it?"

"Yes, sir," Shaw replied.

"And you want to lead this thing?" he asked. Shaw nodded. King cracked a smile.

"You know that is not how this works." Shaw knew he possessed a fifty-fifty shot at winning King over.

"I'm the only one who can identify Al Amiri," he countered. It was a long shot but the only one Shaw had in securing involvement in future operations concerning Al Amiri. King traced over the documents.

"This photograph says otherwise," King replied. Shaw sighed. He had thought about excluding the photograph from the file, but it was the only article that linked Taaha bin Hashim to Osama bin Laden and al-Qaeda. "Also, your report is uncorroborated," the major added. "Everything here is based off your word alone. Now don't get me wrong, your word carries great weight here." He paused. Shaw saw the inner workings of King's mind through the man's light-brown eyes.

King was a rational man, and he was up to date on the events in Yemen. His heart hurt for his lost Marines as much as Shaw's, but his duty persisted with a deployment to Afghanistan around the corner to coordinate head-quarters operations for the remaining teams in his company. That deploy-ment, however, would have to wait until after the funeral arrangements and next of kin notifications for those deceased. He shifted focus. "So, you think this man, bin Hashim, this Al Amiri, is responsible for our downed heli-copters?" King asked. Shaw's hope grew as King shifted the conversation's direction.

"I do," Shaw answered.

"And how did you come to that?"

"Sir, Isaam Al Amiri is the CIA's highest priority target in Yemen. I'm certain that this Al Amiri is Sheik Taaha bin Hashim from Helmand Prov-ince. It all adds up. Bin Hashim is pictured with bin Laden here," Shaw answered rising from his seat. He pointed out bin Hashim from the photograph.

"Yes, I see that," King replied. His tone was kind and understanding, and he allowed Shaw to lead him through the intelligence.

"I met this man in two-thousand-twelve," Shaw finished. King glanced down at the photograph again.

"How do you know that this is Al Amiri?" he asked.

"The name," Shaw began, "bin Hashim shared with me about his father Hashim Al Amiri. If…"

"You know as well as I that we don't operate on *if*," King replied.

"Yes, sir."

"Can anyone support your findings?"

"Yes," Shaw answered. King perked up at his answer.

"Who?"

"Staff Sergeant John Wyatt," Shaw replied. "He was there with me when I met with bin Hashim." Major King mulled over the captain's words and nodded his head several times in quick succession.

"It appears we need to rescue Staff Sergeant Wyatt," King stated.

"Yes, sir." King collected the documents into the folder and rose from his seat. Shaw straightened, unsure of King's intentions.

"Who is overseeing this operation in Support Group?"

"Lieutenant Bateman," Shaw answered.

"Let's pay him a visit," King stated. Shaw cracked a grin.

It was a short walk from King's office, across the lawn, and into Support Headquarters. Shaw followed as King's long strides carried him with deliberate purpose. He pushed through the door, drawing everyone's gaze, but no one snapped to attention, nor were they expected to do so. The operation was still under full swing, and although Wyatt and the civilian had been rescued, their work was far from over. The coordination of departments and assets required their undivided attention if they were going to return their people home safely and secure the remains of the fallen.

"Major," Bateman greeted.

"Lieutenant," he replied. Bateman nodded his greeting to Shaw, which Shaw returned. The presence of Major King with Shaw at his side stirred anger within Bateman. Had Shaw gone over his head? For what purpose? It was hardly Bateman's fault that the operation went awry.

"What can I do for you, sir?" Bateman asked. He braced himself for disciplinary action.

"Captain Shaw has brought it to my attention that Staff Sergeant John Wyatt's recovery is of vital importance to national security," Major King explained. Bateman glanced at Shaw. Had he fabricated some false intelligence to rescue his men? If there was any who would, it was Shaw. There was no doubt in anyone's mind how much that man loved his men.

"What intelligence?" Bateman asked.

"That isn't what you should be concerned with," King replied. "Give me an update on the status of your operation." Bateman again shifted his glance from King to Shaw. "Don't focus on him," King scolded, "focus on what I'm telling you to do."

"Yes, sir," the lieutenant replied quickly. He briefed the major on the most recent events. Units with the 13th Marine Expeditionary Unit were inbound to recover the dead, but for fear of exposing the CIA outpost, Wyatt and the civilian would remain until such a time that covert extraction could be arranged. What remained of the Yemeni government had kept silent on the recent events, despite the US embassy's numerous attempts to secure their assistance in Aden. King took it all in and simply nodded along as Bateman continued.

"Do we know where this CIA outpost is?"

"Yes, sir," Bateman replied.

"Is Staff Sergeant Wyatt fit for duty?" King asked. Bateman sighed. It really wasn't his place to say.

"We've received no indication that he has been wounded or otherwise rendered unable to fulfill his duties."

"That's all I needed to know," King replied. "Lieutenant, I want you to run everything by me prior to taking any action to extract, and I want those SEALs to stay right where they are. This is a MARSOC op, and the Marines will see it through."

"Yes, sir."

"Good," King said, "alert me when our boys have been recovered."

"Yes, sir," Bateman replied. King turned to Shaw.

"You got a uniform?"

"Yes, sir."

"Pack a bag. We're headed to Tampa. We've got important people to see."

The room quieted as Wyatt emerged from the hallway. Bacon sizzled on the stovetop, the grease cracking and popping in the heat. The fragrant smell churned Wyatt's stomach, and it growled fiercely.

"I appreciate the clothes," Wyatt said.

"Yeah, bro, no problem," Becker responded.

"Have a seat, man," Quinn encouraged as he pulled out a chair next to him. Three men sat around the table, one cooked over the stovetop, and Reeves sat in the recliner still reading. "Alright, introductions!" Becker exclaimed. "You met Quinn," he began. Quinn offered him a nod, which Wyatt returned. "Me and Quinn go way back, been together since Basic and then Rangers, then onto SF, then Delta."

"Whoa, seriously?" Wyatt exclaimed. Only a handful of people had served in all three famed, Army units.

"Yeah, kid," Quinn replied. Wyatt was hardly a kid. He was nearing his thirtieth birthday; Quinn and Becker had to be pushing mid-forties to have such a resume.

"You met Reeves. He's a Teams guy, been around for a long time now. And that's Isaac Adara," Becker continued, referring to the man at the skillet. "He's the oddball. Serves currently in HRT, but never spent any time in the service. We give him a hard time." Becker referred to the FBI's Hostage Rescue Team, which was arguably the most highly trained SWAT unit in the United States, perhaps even the world. Wyatt grinned and nodded his greeting.

"How do you like your eggs?" Adara asked, his Boston accent coming out strong.

"It's a little late for breakfast, isn't it?" Wyatt said.

"It's never too late for breakfast," the Bostonian replied. "Your eggs?"

"Fry them hard," Wyatt responded.

"You got it." Adara drizzled some oil in another pan and cracked two eggs.

"Then we got Luis Sotelo, our very own puddle pirate," Becker started again, "but he was MSRT, so he's okay." Sotelo was a former member of the Coast Guard's Maritime Security Response Team. The unit specialized in counterterrorism, anti-piracy, and hostage rescue.

"What's going on, bro?" Sotelo greeted. Wyatt clapped hands with Sotelo in a more modern, less traditional handshake.

"I don't think anyone here has rolled with a Raider before; maybe Reeves," Becker said.

"I knew some Det One guys while in Fallujah back in oh-four," Reeves said, still not looking up from his book.

"He's a real book worm," Becker muttered.

"My old team commander was Det One," Wyatt replied. Reeves finally looked up from his book.

"There weren't many of those guys. What was his name?" Reeves asked.

"David Shaw," Wyatt said. Reeves smiled wide.

"No kidding," Reeves replied. "Small world." Wyatt smiled, and Adara drew his attention as he dropped a plate of eggs and bacon in front of him. "What's he been up to?" Reeves asked.

"He was just wounded in Afghanistan, barely made it, and is on a forced medical retirement," Wyatt explained. Reeves nodded his understanding and noted Wyatt's sadness.

"Sounds familiar," he stated. "Glad he made it." Wyatt felt the sympathy radiating from the SEAL and wondered if Reeves' exit from the Teams had fallen under similar circumstances. Reeves returned to his book, and not knowing how to respond, Wyatt turned around and picked up a piece of bacon. He bit into the savory morsel and relished the rendered fat and crispy meat. "Oh man, this is good," he said, turning to Adara.

"Glad you like it," Adara replied. "You don't have to be polite, I'm sure you're starving." Wyatt smiled, folded one of the fried eggs like a taco, and shoveled it into his mouth. The guys laughed when some of the egg fell from his lips as he chewed.

Becker patted Wyatt on the shoulder before rising from his seat. Wyatt watched him reach into a cabinet and produce a bottle of bourbon. He stretched out the bottle to Wyatt, who took it from him. His eyes fell on the intersected arrow and tomahawk emblem molded into the glass before they moved down the bottle. The image of a Special Forces soldier, sitting astride a stallion, lay stamped on a heavy expanse of silver metal.

"Horse Soldier Reserve," Wyatt noted. Becker set six glasses on the kitchen island, took the bottle back from Wyatt, and poured up a round before distributing to each man.

"Reeves, get over here," he called. Reeves nodded, closed his book, and rose from his chair. Becker turned back to Wyatt and said, "we were saving this to celebrate our homegoing, but," he paused as he thought of the recent tragedy, "this seems more fitting." Wyatt watched as all nodded their solemn agreement. "It's our buddy's label. His team was first in after the towers fell." Wyatt knew well the story of the legendary actions of ODA595, known as the Horse Soldiers. In ninety days, the small team of Green Berets had all but eradicated the Taliban presence in Northern Afghanistan.

Becker raised his glass, and each warrior followed. "You've been through hell, bro, and we're glad you made it," Becker said. "To those who didn't, may their names live forever." A chorus of agreement echoed around the room as the men clinked their glasses together. Wyatt paused, remembering his team, before taking a hefty swig.

A knock at the door stole their attention. It opened and Abby stood in the doorway.

"She wants to see you," she said. All eyes fell on Wyatt. His eyebrows perked up in surprise, and Becker gave him a gentle nudge. The Raider set down his glass, shoved another piece of bacon into his mouth, and followed Abby out the door.

11

Kathryn fought through her wet, tangled mane with a comb. She draped her golden hair over one shoulder and attacked it from another angle. Satisfied, she set the comb down on the bathroom counter and looked at herself in the mirror. Fatigue sat behind her blue eyes, and her face appeared drained of its usual vitality. Would it come back? She didn't know, but she knew she would never again be the same.

As much as she tried to cast the scene from her mind, she kept seeing Reyes leap on that grenade, his mangled body bouncing as it fell back to the roof, and the blood pooling too quickly beneath his broken frame. It replayed in her mind over and over again, sometimes in slow motion, and, despite her best efforts, the image was there to stay. She doubted she would ever forget the events of the day, regardless of how much she wished she would. Perhaps the vividness would fade, and she hoped for at least that.

Then there was John Wyatt, his strong countenance giving her comfort and building trust within her. She would never forget his eyes that moment in the alley. She would much rather dwell on that dusty and bloodstained complexion with those vibrant irises of hope than the scene of Reyes' fate on the rooftop. Could she even begin to decipher the emotions surrounding her savior? The tickling in her heart, was it true affection or was she riding the final wave of highly unpredictable emotions caused by the day's tragedy? She wanted to know, and she hoped that seeing him again would help.

She looked at herself in the mirror again. The navy robe that covered her provided warm comfort, like a blanket, she didn't wish to cast it off for clothes just yet. A swift knock at the door beckoned her that way. She paused before she gripped the handle and breathed deeply.

"Yes?"

"It's Abby, I'm here with John." Kathryn opened the door and again offered Wyatt that shy smile, one that said thank you but was uncertain of the future.

"Thank you, Abby," she said.

"No problem, girl. Let me know if you need anything else." As the officer backed away, she held Kathryn's gaze and teased her by puckering her lips in response to Wyatt's appearance. Kathryn rolled her eyes, but she didn't let her smile vanish. Wyatt, failing to see the jest cocked his head for an explanation.

"Nothing," Kathryn replied as she reached for his hand. Abby was a good and fun woman, and Kathryn was grateful for her kindness and quick friendship.

As Kathryn pulled Wyatt in and the door closed behind him, the Raider felt his heart leap into his throat. He glanced at her bare feet and glistening legs as they disappeared beneath the hem of the robe. He couldn't deny his immediate desire for her. She was even more beautiful than when he first laid eyes on her. A few stray droplets of water rested on her neck and collar. He looked away quickly.

"What?" she asked. She realized she was still holding his hand. It was warm and comforting.

"Nothing, you're just... uh... you know," he replied, returning his eyes to her and glancing down at her robe. She grinned. It was different smile, different from her laughter on the helicopter, different from her smile in the Range Rover. It was sweet and tender, affectionate even.

"Will you sit with me for a moment?" she asked. Wyatt allowed her to lead him to the bed, and they sat on the edge. Kathryn still held his hand tightly in her lap. Wyatt felt heat radiate from his core, was he really that nervous? "John, thank you. I will never be able to repay you for what you did for me, and I'm so sorry about your friends." She started to tear up, and she snapped her eyes to the ceiling as her voice broke. "I don't know if I can live up to their sacrifice," she continued. She brought a hand to her mouth. "I'm sorry," she said, apologizing for her tears.

"No, it's okay," he replied. She collected herself and sniffed. She replaced her hand on top of Wyatt's, which made his heart almost burst.

"You know, I'm feeling a lot right now," she said, a short laugh accompanied. Wyatt smiled.

"Me too."

"I don't feel safe without you." She paused and looked at him. Tears rimmed her sapphire eyes again. "And I have all of these feelings for you, but I don't know if they are just because of what happened or because I really," she paused, "care for you." It took great effort to say, but she had said it. She looked into his eyes, those eyes she found so comforting, and the resolve had not left. It still swirled behind those gems like a mix of smoke and water. The more she thought about it, staring into his eyes, the clearer it became. She wore nothing under that robe, and yet felt no embarrassment, no insecurity, and no timidity. Did she care for him? Yes, she decided. Did she know anyone else like Staff Sergeant John Wyatt? No, she did not.

"Kathryn," Wyatt began. It was the way he said her name that sent a streak of fear through her heart. She had always thought of herself as a strong woman, fearless even, but that persona had shattered on the plummeting helicopter. The realization of her new vulnerability didn't sit well with her, and the fear of potential PTSD haunted her thoughts.

"This is not an easy situation," Wyatt continued. "What we've been through will take years to decipher. I'm going to be honest with you though. I was attracted to you the moment I laid eyes on you," he finished. At his words, delight radiated through her.

"I suspected as much," she replied. Wyatt grinned, and she returned it with the most captivating smile.

"But once we're stateside, all this might go away, and I don't want to take advantage of any emotional state you may be in. Also, I don't want to enter into anything that is going to add pain on top of what's already there."

"I understand," she said. Her voice held a hint of sadness. "But if you are willing, and if there isn't anyone waiting back home for you, I'd like to spend some time getting to know you." Wyatt stood, inhaled deeply, and considered what she was asking. It wasn't a matter of whether or not he wanted to try at a relationship with her; he most certainly would be overjoyed, but the circumstances surrounding the entire matter complicated everything. Surely, she had already considered those circumstances hovering behind her request. Shaw entered his mind, and Wyatt could hear him saying his usual line, *Fear is the mind-killer.* It was from some book Shaw loved and had resonated deeply with him. Wyatt couldn't remember the name of the book. *Was it Dune?* Regardless, Shaw said it all the time, but did it apply now? Shaw would say so, but Wyatt was his own man. After a moment of dedicated thought, he came to his own conclusion, and Kathryn, still sitting on the bed, stared at him waiting for his reply.

"I'd like that," Wyatt finally said.

"So, what now?" she asked, standing and moving close to him. Wyatt kept his gaze on her, and she reached for his hands. Her touch sent waves of affection through him. The urge swelled up within, and he couldn't fight it despite his nerves screaming against it. He looked down into her shimmering eyes and leaned forward. Pausing just before their lips met, he invited her to kiss him. A smile spread across her lips before she gently pressed hers against his. They separated and laughed for a second as they rested their foreheads together. Wyatt had never experienced anything like that moment and hoped she hadn't either. He had no way of knowing, though, he had just stolen her heart.

The Marine Raider wrapped a strong hand around her waist, pulling her close. She pressed herself against him and reached up around his neck. He felt the curves of her body through the robe as they kissed again, passionately, fearlessly. Wyatt's knees almost buckled when they separated, and Kathryn kept her eyes closed as she caught her breath.

"I need to check in with my command," Wyatt said, concerned that things might progress too quickly.

"Okay, don't be too long," she replied. Wyatt grinned and headed for the door. He stole one last glance at her before disappearing into the hallway. Kathryn brushed her lips with her fingers and smiled.

Dubai, UAE

Rian Mather-Pike sat on the edge of the couch with his gaze focused on the television. Romuald Affré also watched intently as the French team, nicknamed *Les Bleus*, attempted a try against the South African Springboks. Rugby was one of the few interests the two men shared. Mather-Pike, a dedicated and sometimes violent Springbok fan, cursed at the television as the Blues neared the Springboks' in-goal area. Affré watched silently and showed little emotion when France scored a try. Mather-Pike swelled with anger but channeled it through a deep inhale.

"The game is not over, my friend," Affré stated as the large man rose from his seat. He noted a heightened sense of agitation than what normally exuded from Mather-Pike, and it sparked his curiosity and concern.

"I'm just getting another drink," he grumbled. He moved across the suite in the high-rise Dubai hotel. He passed the floor to ceiling windows and stopped for a moment to take in the evening scene. Fountains, hundreds of feet below, twirled and danced in an array of colors. Surrounding buildings sparkled in the setting desert sun. He couldn't deny the beauty of the scene, but he also couldn't deny his craving for another drink. He continued to the bar, poured another glass of Japanese whiskey, and before heading back to his seat, glanced at Silva's bedroom door. The South African inhaled deeply to suppress his anger and sipped his drink before turning back toward the television. A woman's shriek spun him around.

The door to the bedroom burst open, and Silva emerged dragging a blonde woman by her hair. The woman kicked and screamed while holding onto his wrist. Silva pulled hard and thrust her forward. She immediately balled up and whimpered softly at his feet.

"Ag man! What the hell is going on?" Mather-Pike demanded. Enraged, Silva shot him a threatening glare.

"Get this woman out of my sight and take her to her room!" Silva ordered. Mather-Pike, with both palms displayed outward to defuse the situation, approached the woman slowly. She wore nothing but the sheets from the bed, and blood flowed from her left ear. Naked, Silva stormed past Mather-Pike and headed for the bar. He quickly poured himself a glass of the same Japanese whiskey and exhaled forcefully before he drained it.

Mather-Pike, kneeling before the woman, feared he would not be able to contain his anger.

"It's alright, I've got you," he whispered. The woman, upon hearing the tender words, nearly leapt into his arms. He gazed upon her face, and the anger flared hotter. He forced an exhale through gritted teeth in an attempt to control himself.

"Mather-Pike, what did I say?" Silva's impatient and aggravated tone was not lost on the bodyguard, and it further enraged the man. Affré, concerned, watched the ordeal unravel before him. He did not know Mather-Pike too well, but he knew him well enough to predict the breaking point of his temper. Even then, he wondered which side he would pick if the two decided to clash. He had good reasons to pick Silva and good reasons to side with Mather-Pike. He hoped he wouldn't have to choose, but he palmed the grip of his concealed handgun just in case.

Mather-Pike cradled the woman in his arms and rose to his full height. She whimpered against his broad chest. The scene angered Silva even more to see Mather-Pike display such tenderness as he headed toward the door.

"Wait," Silva hissed. Mather-Pike had half a mind to continue onward, but he obeyed the command. "Ella, don't ever refuse me or talk about quitting again." She cried harder as the fear drew the emotions out of her. Silva wore a smug smirk and met Mather-Pike's gaze. The man easily saw the warning and turned to leave. "Affré, go with him." Without a word, the Frenchman followed and quickly caught up with his South African counterpart who waited for the elevator.

"He sent you to check on me, hey?" Mather-Pike asked without looking at Affré. The Frenchman remained silent and made no attempt to make eye contact either. Mather-Pike finally looked at him and could visibly see the uncertainty in his expression. They proceeded into the elevator in silence and maintained that vocal distance until they both arrived at Ella's room. Affré produced the hotel key and opened the door, and Mather-Pike pushed past him headed directly for the king bed in the center of the room. The room was a far cry from Silva's suite, but it was still nicer than any other hotel room Mather-Pike had ever seen. It didn't matter though; he directed all of his attention toward the woman in his arms; the woman who always managed to steal his breath.

"Ella, are you okay?" he asked as he set her down on the bed. She had regained much of her composure once out of Silva's reach, but Mather-Pike could see she was still quite shaken. His heart ached and yearned for her, and hatred for Silva simmered as his anger grew stronger.

"My ear," she managed as she reached up to touch it. The pain pulsed with each heartbeat.

"Let me see," Affré interjected. Mather-Pike's eyes shot him a warning, but Affré's confident expression relaxed the South African. Affré approached and gently cradled Ella's head in his hands as he examined her ear. He snapped his fingers twice.

"Can you hear that?" he asked. Ella nodded. "Well, it's impossible to tell without the right equipment, but you likely have a ruptured eardrum. Did he hit you?" Ella nodded again. Mather-Pike's anger flared once more. "Any vertigo or nausea?"

"A little," she answered.

"I think you will be okay, but the hotel has a doctor on call. I shall contact him to examine you."

"Thank you, Romuald," she said.

"Of course, Ella. I'm sorry this happened." Tears rimmed her eyes once more as she recalled the event. She shuddered, drove her face into Mather-Pike's chest, and sobbed once more. Mather-Pike stroked her hair and glanced at Affré, and the Frenchman shook his head.

"Ella, will you be okay if Rian and I step outside for a second?" She pulled away, wiped her eyes, and nodded. "Thank you." He stood and motioned for Mather-Pike to follow. As soon as the door closed, Affré lit into him. "You've got to get yourself under control," he snapped. Mather-Pike fumed before him. "You don't yet know Silva fully."

"And you do?" Mather-Pike countered. The comment stirred up a painful memory.

"Yes," the Frenchman replied sternly.

"Let me ask you something," Mather-Pike said quietly but forcefully. "How do you justify what happened today?"

"I don't," Affré answered.

"But you were a Legionnaire, hey?" Mather-Pike countered.

"Is that supposed to make me a saint?" Affré retorted.

"You were also DGSE." The Frenchman sighed and uttered something in his native language that Mather-Pike didn't understand.

"What?"

"That was a long time ago," Affré translated.

"But Silva just killed a bunch of US Marines and now this," Mather-Pike argued. Affré grew annoyed with the train of conversation.

"No, Al Amiri and his men killed a bunch of Marines, Silva just supplied the weapons. This is how it's done, Rian. What did you think the weapons were being used for?"

"To free the oppressed and provide arms for those under tyranny."

"You are a South African mercenary. Don't tell me you have a conscience?"

"Maybe I do," he countered. Silence grew between them, and Ella entered Mather-Pike thoughts again. He saw her just about every day, but seldom spoke to her. To do so would incur the physical wrath of his employer. He couldn't deny how much he desired her. Her blue eyes held such warmth and innocence, and he could only hope she felt similarly toward him. The more he thought about her and her mistreatment at the hands of Silva, the more a new course of action arose in his mind. A question formed on his lips, "How much is Silva worth?" Affré stiffened.

"What?"

"He's got to be worth a couple hundred million, hey?"

"Where are you going with this?" Affré asked.

"Look, I'm sure we can..."

"Rian, stop," Affré interrupted sharply. The Frenchman's tone unnerved the South African, not an easy feat. "I don't want to hear any more of this. Silva drowned your predecessor in the Nile for far less than what I'm sure you are thinking, and he was far more capable than you."

Mather-Pike held Affré's gaze, and Affré witnessed the conviction in Mather-Pike's blue eyes, beckoning him to seek justice for his fallen friend. Mather-Pike certainly couldn't have known any of that, but perhaps Affré psyche was filling in the gaps.

"I'm smarter than I look, Romuald," he said. It was the first time the South African had used Affré's first name, and it intrigued the Frenchman.

Maybe the South African was on to something. The action against the United States helicopters had surprised Affré as well. It was a risk Silva would not normally have taken, and Affré felt Mather-Pike's predecessor's punishment was too severe. It didn't make sense to the Frenchmen to kill a man for taking a little off the top, but then again, he wasn't paid to make sense of Silva's life or business decisions. Still, he missed his friend, and Silva was to blame for that loss. Even more concerning, Affré couldn't help but feel that Silva's new direction might lead to an early grave, and that was something he could not tolerate. The Frenchmen glanced up at Mather-Pike.

"What are you thinking?" he asked in a hushed tone.

12

"I know we've gone over it already, but you're sure you were being tracked?" Natalie asked Lincoln within the security of her office. She sat in her chair as she listened to the Ranger pacing before her.

"We all saw this guy, Hale. He looked at us like we had murdered his first-born son," Lincoln said. His frustration grew. "He knew who we were. Too much connects for it to have been a coincidence," he argued.

"And you want me to evacuate this outpost," she said.

"I want you to be ready to evacuate at a moment's notice. You are here hunting terrorists, and our nearest allies are hours away." Natalie sighed. "And if it so happens to be this guy," Lincoln said pointing at al-Amiri's name on the white board, "who knows what resources are at his disposal." He made a strong point, and his vocal volume grew with his emotions. "I've got five contractors and a Raider to defend this place. This isn't a fortress, it's an Alamo."

"I get it!" Natalie exclaimed. "And I don't care for your tone, Scott." She rarely used his first name. He removed his hands from her desk and again paced around the room. He ran his hand down his face. His skin was fair and his eyes hazel. His dark hair, cut short, plumed in the front from dried sweat. He was tall, maybe six-three, and his muscles bulged under his gray t-shirt. He still wore his gear, and his rifle lay in the corner of the office.

Natalie knew well his gift of persuasion and charisma, but also his demeaning attitude toward her command. Though not yet forty, he was an old-fashioned man, one who didn't quite appreciate a woman's leadership. It didn't help that she was younger than him by a few years.

"I appreciate what you've brought to me, and I will send it up the chain of command. You know better than anyone that I'll make the right call when the time comes," she said.

"I just feel this in my gut," he said.

"But your gut hardly passes for actionable intel," she countered.

"I know!" he shouted.

"Do you need a minute to calm down, Ranger?" That blow hurt. Lincoln backed away and threw up his hands.

"Fine, I've said my piece," he started.

"Yes, you have," Natalie interrupted. Lincoln scooped up his rifle and stormed out of the office. The French doors slammed against the walls and rebounded back to hang partly closed. Natalie sighed and ran both hands over her hair and down her braid before resting her eyes on her secure line to the CIA Annex in Sana'a. Lincoln spoke truthfully, and as much as she wanted al-Amiri, her team must come first. She scooped up the phone and initiated the call.

***

Washington, D.C.

The light from the streetlamps dimly passed through the sheer curtains and greatly annoyed James Caldwell. Sleep evaded him. He sighed and glanced at his twenty-six-year-old wife. She lay on her stomach, and her bare back intrigued him but not enough for him to wake her. He stared at the ceiling. The fan spun slowly casting distorted shadows across the room and onto the far wall. Without consideration for his wife's comfort, he threw off the covers and sat upright on the edge of the bed. The young blonde exhaled loudly and snuggled deeper into the expensive sheets.

Caldwell rubbed his eyes and rose to his feet. The sharp edges of his defined, yet aged, muscles caught the faint light as he moved across the ornate master suite. The naked man snatched his robe from its usual place on the antique coatrack before exiting the room. He donned the red, velvet garment and tied it in place as he moved down the hallway; the old hardwood floors cooled his bare feet.

He moved down the hallway that opened into the foyer. Large oil paintings and a massive crystal chandelier would have left any visitor awestruck upon first entry, but the man didn't give them a second glance. He pushed through two heavy, wooden doors and entered his study.

The room, painted rich olive, was decorated with original paintings depicting famous battles throughout history, and Caldwell's life-sized portrait rose impressively behind his heavy, ironwood desk. He moved to the small bar and held up the crystal decanter filled with Macallan 25. He poured himself a glass and took a quick sip. Supposedly, it hosted flavors of peach, blood orange, and wood spice with intense tastes of coconut and vanilla and added tones of sultana, lemon, and peat, but he consistently failed to taste them. He drank it for the prestige and that alone.

The man, having just turned sixty, moved behind his desk and picked up the small sleek remote. He clicked play before sitting in the baroque, leather chair, and Tchaikovsky slowly crescendoed throughout the room. He took another sip and closed his eyes, resting in the beauty of the music. His eyes snapped open as one of the doors swung open.

"Hey, Baby?" the young woman called. Caldwell sighed and rose from his desk.

"Yes, Love?" he responded. Vanessa Caldwell strode into the office dressed in a black, silk robe, hemmed mid-thigh, and holding his ringing cell phone.

"Your phone's ringing. I think it may be work," she answered. Her blue eyes blinked to ward off sleep, and her curly, strawberry-wheat hair dangled loosely around her shoulders. Caldwell rose from his seat and met her halfway across the room. He gave her a quick peck and traded her his glass of Scotch for the phone. She took a big gulp and turned to leave. He watched her go, and, before leaving, she leaned sensually against the door. "Don't be too long," she said after the burning liquid awakened her. She took another large swig and twirled out of the room. Caldwell smirked and answered the phone.

"Caldwell," he greeted.

"Director, there's a situation with the annex in Yemen. Station Chief Mills is requesting an evacuation of the Aden compound," the man on the line said. Caldwell, the Director of the Directorate of Operations within the CIA, creased his brow.

"What kind of situation?" he asked.

"He says like the one in Benghazi," the man answered. Caldwell pressed his lips tightly together. The Agency had invested greatly in that compound. An evacuation would set them back years, but, then again, another compromised operation was an embarrassment the CIA could not again afford.

"Permit the evac. I want Reapers on standby and a team ready to get them out. Contact the Fifth Fleet and get them involved," he ordered. "The first priority should be returning the team back to Sana'a where they can resume their work."

"Yes sir, I'll alert SecNav and SecDef." Caldwell ended the call and tossed the phone on his desk. He didn't need to hear what the man planned to do; he knew already. He knew the American public had no idea the CIA had planted a compound in Aden, Yemen; most had no idea where Yemen was, but another incident like that in 2012 would not bode well for his career and, more importantly, his ambitions. He poured himself another glass and drained it quickly; his wife was waiting.

MacDill Air Force Base
Tampa, Florida

Shaw, dressed in his green service uniform with his hair slicked back by a quick rinse, stood in stark contrast to the other individuals. His was the only beard in the room full of high-ranking officers within SOCOM. He hardly cared. Major King had seated him to his right in the row of chairs by the wall. Around the long conference table sat the officers. Major General

Weber, commander of MARSOC, rose from his seat to address the committee and various officers representing Army Special Forces, Navy SEALs, and other special operations components of SOCOM. Four-star General Vince S. Wood, the commander of SOCOM, sat at the head of the table and offered Major General Weber the floor. This was no small meeting.

"Gentlemen," Weber began, "you all have been briefed on the recent tragedy involving Marines in Yemen. The 13th MEU has recovered the bodies of the fallen without incident or conflict, and the sole survivor has been rescued by the gracious assistance provided by our friends at the CIA." Those last words were hard for him to say. He hated the thought of owing the Agency on account of their assistance. He knew that's not how it was perceived in the field, but it would be considered a favor from the upper levels of the intelligence community. It sickened him really, that officials, who hadn't been in the field in decades, if ever, were capitalizing on the hard work of selfless officers not directly under their command.

"One of our own," Weber continued, "Captain David Shaw, recently recovered from injuries sustained in the line of duty, has brought some crucial intelligence to our attention." The large screen at the end of the room illuminated with a picture of Osama bin Laden and his associates. "This man," Weber said, pointing to a man on bin Laden's right, "is Taaha bin Hashim. The CIA knows him as Isaam Al Amiri."

"Impossible," a man interrupted. All eyes fell on him. His dark hair was neatly combed, and his face held a youthful complexion despite his age. Frank Hutchins, an assistant director in the Directorate of Operations and a liaison to SOCOM, shook his head in protest. "We have a full file on Isaam al-Amiri. There is no known photograph."

"Well, you're looking at one," Shaw inserted. His anger plumed at the man's denial. King leaned into Shaw's ear.

"Cool it," he whispered. Shaw composed himself but kept a hard stare on Hutchins. Weber shifted his gaze off Shaw. He loved the man, but there was a reason Shaw wasn't frequently invited to such meetings. Shaw was a man of action and held little patience for such deliberation. That was the main reason he had never received a promotion past captain, not that Shaw would have wanted it. Past the rank of captain, Shaw's options for combat diminished greatly. A career without combat didn't interest the Marine Raider.

"Our intelligence suggests that Isaam Al Amiri is an alias for Taaha bin Hashim. Bin Hashim's family name is Al Amiri, which was kept secret from our dealings with him over the recent years. It is also confirmed that bin Hashim has not been seen in Afghanistan since Al Amiri emerged in Yemen," Weber said.

"We only know that al-Amiri is in Yemen because of financial transaction records recovered in the bin Laden raid. There is no link to bin Hashim," Hutchins stated. Everyone in the room was familiar with Taaha bin Hashim's cooperation with SOCOM forces in Afghanistan. The thought that he was one of bin Laden's right-hand men didn't sit well with anyone present.

"First, it must be clear that Captain Shaw has identified the man as the same individual. There is another that can vouch for the identity of Al Amiri," Weber stated.

"And who is that?" Hutchins asked.

"Staff Sergeant John Wyatt."

"And where is he?" Hutchins asked.

"In Yemen. He was part of the Raider team shot down by Al Amiri's men," Weber answered.

"We don't know that Al Amiri shot down those helicopters," General Wood stated. All eyes fell on him. His salt and pepper hair was cut short and his face weathered from years of service in Army Special Forces. Having commanded the 82nd Airborne Division and the 75th Ranger Regiment prior, Wood held the respect of all in the room. His service as a Green Beret only added to his distinguished resume.

"Who else, sir?" Weber inquired. Wood remained silent. "And does it matter? We have a new lead on Al Amiri. We should take it."

"He is the most likely culprit," Wood stated.

"You mean to tell me that this whole time, since 2001, Sheik Taaha bin Hashim has been the world's third most wanted terrorist?" asked Major General Jerry J. Adler, commander of the United States Army Special Operations Command (USASOC). Weber nodded seriously. "And I'm correct in assuming that he's been using our reward money to fund his terrorism and, at the same time, eradicate his rivals within the Taliban."

"That would appear to be the case," Weber answered. The room silenced, and the gravity of the situation weighed on them.

"So, for all we know, those helicopters were shot down with weapons purchased with our own tax dollars," Adler said. Wood turned to Hutchins, and the man stiffened under his gaze. Of all the people in the room, he alone had not proven himself on the field of battle, and he tried to prevent that insecurity from controlling him.

"Can you find Al Amiri with this new information?"

"We have a team in Yemen right now who would benefit from this intel," he replied.

"As soon as we find out where he is located, I'll acquire an authorized airstrike from the President," Wood stated.

"Absolutely not, sir," Shaw stated, jumping to his feet. King reached forward and gripped Shaw's forearm, but the Raider tore his hand away. Weber glowered at him, but Shaw persisted. "He killed Marines, and Marines will finish it." Wood sighed and traced an eyebrow.

"Captain, don't make the mistake of thinking you're the only one in this room that has lost men. We are not going to send more men into harm's way to satisfy your vengeance," Wood replied. He said his words so calmly, but they still stung Shaw's pride. Major King placed a hand on Shaw's shoulder, prompting him back down into his chair. Shaw obliged begrudgingly. "Hutchins, let's find bin Hashim and take care of this matter."

"Yes, sir," Hutchins replied.

"Gentlemen, we are adjourned," Wood stated as he rose from his chair. The men around the table rose in unison, but Shaw remained seated next to King. He felt Weber's eyes on him.

"Stand up, Son," he stated. Shaw did as commanded and straightened his uniform. Weber waited until the room vacated. "You were wrong to speak out in the way you did."

"Sir, I..."

"This isn't how either of us wanted this to go," Weber interrupted. "But you will submit to your command. Don't blemish your distinguished career by pursuing this. You've done great work. Retire with that knowledge. We'll get Staff Sergeant Wyatt home as soon as we can." Shaw exhaled slowly and offered Weber a reluctant nod. Although disappointed and frustrated, Shaw yielded to the command of his mentor. He disagreed entirely with the course of action, but that was nothing new.

The general patted Shaw on the arm before leaving him there with Major King. After receiving a disapproving glance from King, Shaw followed Weber out, and King led Shaw back toward the tarmac where the aircraft scheduled to return them to Camp Lejeune waited.

"There's a finesse to these types of situations, David," King said as they walked. "I keep assuming that someone with your education level would realize that."

"This is wrong, sir," Shaw stated. King stopped him, and Shaw readied himself for reprimand, but King glanced down both directions of the hallway and lowered his voice.

"This is not how I thought this would turn out either, but you're right," King replied. His unexpected tone stirred excitement within Shaw. "Marines will finish this." A smile spread across Shaw's face. "How are you feeling?"

"Ready to kill, sir." King's smile mirrored Shaw's.

"I want you on the ground ready to take down Al Amiri. I'll see to it that we get you over there," King said.

"What about the airstrike," Shaw asked.

"If the airstrike coordinates are never sent then it can't be launched," King replied, the corner of his mouth curling upward in a satisfied smirk. "We'll have Wyatt convince the lead officer on the ground to withhold the coordinates. You think he's up to it?"

"John can do anything," Shaw replied.

As Shaw boarded the military transport bound to Camp Lejeune from SOCOM Headquarters in MacDill Air Force Base, Major King took the seat next to him, and the rear of the KC-130 aircraft groaned shut. Shaw could not contain his exuberance, and his body tingled in anticipation.

"Once in the air, we'll contact Bateman and have him connect us to

Wyatt on the ground and fill him in. We'll get what intel he has and formu-
late a plan. Can your body handle a HALO insertion?" King asked.

"Not going to be problem," Shaw lied. Truthfully, he didn't know how
the high-altitude low-opening jump would affect his wounds, but he wasn't
going to let that keep him from the mission.

He had fought too hard to let his body fail him now.

13

Thirty minutes into their two-hour flight, Shaw once again looked upon Lieutenant Bateman via a tablet as King relayed orders and the necessary details for his team to prepare for Shaw's insertion. A small team would be put together, and Shaw already had the two other men in mind: Corporals Jimmy Hogan and Salvatore Barone. Major King raised his eyebrows at Shaw's recommendation.

"You sure about them?" King asked.

"Yes, sir," Shaw replied confidently. They were both young and eager Marines who had maintained high marks throughout ITC and subsequent special operations training, required by all those who wish to become Marine Raiders. More importantly, they were available. Shaw always made it a point to keep an eye out for skilled Critical Skills Operators as they came through training. He often had his pick on who would be assigned to his team. Reyes had been one of those men, as had Wyatt and York.

King explained to Bateman that Shaw, Hogan, and Barone would meet up with Wyatt in Aden at the CIA compound, and the four-man fireteam would move on Al Amiri once the CIA officers on the ground located his position.

"We'll have them briefed and ready to go by the time we land," King said to Lieutenant Bateman.

"Yes, sir," came his reply.

"Can we get Staff Sergeant Wyatt connected to this device?" King asked.

"Of course, sir," Bateman answered, "he's already contacted us, and we have him on standby until you're ready."

"You can patch him through," the major ordered. Bateman nodded toward one of his Marines, and the screen darkened for a second before brightening again to show an empty desk chair. "Staff Sergeant Wyatt?" King called.

"Yes, sir?" came Wyatt's voice from out of frame. King waited until the Raider appeared and took the seat. Shaw grinned wide at seeing his friend in one piece.

"How are you doing, Marine?"

"I'm as good as can be, sir, given the circumstances," Wyatt replied. King nodded his understanding and sympathy. Externally, Wyatt looked worn and beaten down, but his eyes still held their vigorous glow. The image drew a smile across Shaw's face. Wyatt was as tough as they come.

"I'm glad to hear that," Major King replied. "I'm here with Captain Shaw. There has been an important development regarding your situation." Wyatt perked up and grinned as Major King rotated the tablet to include Shaw in the camera's view.

"Hey, Boss," Wyatt greeted.

"Good to see you in one piece," Shaw replied. Neither mentioned their teammates, but their gazes consoled and supported one another.

"John, tell me about Taaha bin Hashim," King asked. Wyatt's face showed his confusion, but he easily recalled memory of the man.

"The sheik from Helmand? What about him?"

"Does the name Al Amiri mean anything to you regarding this man?" King asked. Both Shaw and King watched as Wyatt scoured through his memory.

"Wasn't his dad named Al Amiri or something like that?" Shaw nodded and held the picture of bin Hashim with bin Laden. Wyatt's eyes widened.

"Son of a..."

"Sergeant," King quickly interrupted. King abhorred cursing and considered the act a direct violation of George Washington's code of conduct from two centuries earlier.

"Sorry, sir," Wyatt quickly said. "You mean to tell me that bin Hashim has been in league with bin Laden this whole time?" King nodded. "But all that money," Wyatt added.

"Yeah," Shaw said, echoing Wyatt's disgust. Wyatt rubbed his forehead and exhaled before reengaging in their conversation.

"So, what does he and the name Al Amiri have to do with all this?" Wyatt asked.

"We believe it was Taaha bin Hashim, acting under the alias of Isaam Al Amiri, who orchestrated the attack this morning," King explained. "Captain Shaw has listed you as being able to identify Al Amiri alongside him."

"And since Shaw has been benched, you need me to locate this guy?"

"Who said anything about Shaw being benched?" King countered. Wyatt's expression lit up in hopeful anticipation. "Captain Shaw and two other Raiders will rendezvous with you at your location in Aden. From there, with the assistance of the CIA officers present, you are to hunt down the designated target, Isaam Al Amiri. A full mission plan is being forwarded to the outpost. For the sake of time, the mission is direct-action and intelligence gathering."

"I understand, sir," Wyatt replied. Fire burned behind his eyes. Taaha bin Hashim had betrayed them, and Wyatt was eager to put him down.

"You think you can convince the CIA team leader to withhold Al Amiri's coordinates from SOCOM?"

"I can do my best," Wyatt replied.

"Good, I'll make sure Shaw brings you a full combat resupply. Anything else you need?" King asked.

"If we're planning on close quarters stuff, I could use *my* M4A1," he added. Shaw caught the emphasis. Wyatt was extremely particular about his weapons, especially his rifles. He had outfitted them precisely to his strict standards. Everything from optics to triggers had undergone careful scrutiny before gaining Wyatt's approval. "And I could use a new set of SAPI's, swimmers cut if available. I don't know how damaged mine are. They took quite a beating," he said, referring to the cut and shape of his body armor plates. "Oh, and extra mags and some nine mil for my Glock. I prefer Glock 17 mags with the plus two extensions."

"I know," Shaw replied, wearing a smirk. "I'll make sure everything is there. I'll bring all the extras too: batteries, chem lights, TQs, trauma gear, and the like."

"I appreciate it."

"Any questions, Staff Sergeant?" King asked.

"What about the civilian?" Wyatt asked.

"She'll exfil with you after the mission is completed. We're coordinating with the 5th Fleet for a maritime exfil. We don't want to risk any more helicopters. We're lucky enough that the 13th MEU made it in and out without any issues," King explained. Wyatt nodded his head. Relief swept over him as King mentioned the recovery of the fallen. The fact that he had left them behind had torn a hole in his heart bigger than he could have imagined. One day, he'll lie beside them under the hallowed ground of Arlington National Cemetery.

He would have it no other way.

"Anything else?" King asked.

"No, sir," Wyatt replied.

"Good."

"I'll see you on the ground, John," Shaw said.

"I'll make sure to have dinner ready," Wyatt replied. King cracked a smile. The bond he witnessed between the two men was what kindled his love for the Corps, and he relished it.

Camp Lejeune
Jacksonville, North Carolina

Jimmy Hogan reclined in the chair, raising the two front legs off the ground. He studied his new teammate with intense curiosity. He noted the faded, Yankees hat sitting backwards on his head. A curl of thick black hair swept upward from the cap's rear adjustment band. The man had recently shaved, as far as Hogan could tell, but the remnants of back hair follicles gave the appearance of a well-kept five o'clock shadow. His nose was large and round and seemed out of place on his chiseled face. He had thick eyebrows over dark eyes of a color Hogan had yet to determine. He looked every bit as an Italian from The Bronx that Hogan would have expected. His family was probably Mafia or sandwich shop owners, maybe both. Hell, he was even a Yankees fan.

Salvatore Barone, or Sal as his family called him, finished loading the last magazine on his combat loadout before stuffing it into the rucksack that made up his third-line gear. Excitement coursed through every fiber of his body. To be hand selected right out of training for a secret CIA-SOCOM joint mission was far beyond anything he could have ever hoped for, and yet here he stood.

He had checked over his gear twice before deciding to pack a few more magazines and felt confident that he had everything he needed for the mission. It was a gut feeling he just couldn't explain, but after adding the extra ammunition, the feeling dissipated. He turned to glance at his new teammate. They were similar in age, and Barone was surprised they had never met.

When he first heard Hogan's name and place of birth, his face had contorted like he had just eaten a lemon. Surely, Jimmy Hogan came from a stereotypical Irish family having been born in Brooklyn. His mom, not unlike his, probably stayed home, took care of the house, and prepared all the food, but his father, no doubt, was likely a cop and a Dodgers fan. After all, they all were.

Hogan's pointed, slender nose lay centered and straight between two blue eyes on his pale face. His hair wasn't quite blonde, but still held a hint of sand. His face reminded Barone of a horse, long and thin.

"What are you looking at?" Hogan asked.

"Just wondering if you're a Dodgers fan," Barone answered. Hogan smirked.

"What, because you think I'm Irish?"

"You could say that," Barone replied with a grin. Hogan laughed.

"I bleed blue and white," Hogan responded.

"Figures." Barone could not understand how someone could root for a team that didn't represent their city. The Dodgers had left Brooklyn ages ago to play in Los Angeles; he could at least be a Mets fan. Barone then shuddered at the thought. No, he was better off rooting for the Dodgers.

"Did you remember to pack your ice pick?" Hogan asked. Barone chuckled as he finished zipping up his bag.

"Yeah, right next to my baseball bat and Tommy gun."

"Alright, Capone," Hogan jested, "just wanted to make sure you didn't forget anything."

"Well if I forget anything, I'll just borrow your billy club."

"Not a chance, pal, that thing has been in the family since the late 1800s," Hogan replied.

"Really?"

"No, bro, my family sells wedding cakes. Been in the baking business since the twenties," Hogan answered, wearing a witty smile.

"No kidding."

"You think we were all a bunch of cops?" Barone shrugged.

"It crossed my mind." They both laughed. "I see why you joined the Marines then."

"Yeah," Hogan answered, scratching the side of his head. "Baking doesn't do it for me. What about you? Your old man in the Mafia or something?"

"I wish, bro. No, he actually owns a small wedding dress boutique. He does all the dresses for my neighborhood and their families." Hogan laughed so hard and so loud that Barone had to keep himself from being offended.

"I tell you what," Hogan said once he had collected himself. He had laughed due to the sheer coincidence that they had both fled the wedding business and turned to the Marines instead. "If we ever get married, I'll make sure you get a discount on the cake if you make sure my future wife gets a discount on her dress."

"I think that leans a bit more in your favor," Barone stated.

"I don't know, bro; my old man bakes a solid cake. Besides, your wife's dress will probably be free anyway." Barone smirked.

"Alright, deal," he said. Both their eyes snapped to the door as it opened. Hogan jumped to his feet and mirrored Barone by snapping to attention.

Captain David Shaw entered wearing his issued M81 woodland, camou-flaged uniform that matched those of the two younger men. The camou-flage pattern, although officially retired from broad Marine Corps service in 2002, had been resurrected by MARSOC in 2011 as their combat uniform camouflage. Their uniforms though, unlike previous generations, were made of state-of-the-art, flame-retardant material and moisture-wicking, stretchable fabric. They were far more comfortable and practical than the Combat Utility Uniform that the rest of the Corps wore.

Each man wore an American flag and Raider patch on their sleeves. Although the skull and Southern Cross weren't officially adopted by MARSOC as their logo, many Raiders wore it as a tribute to the brave Raiders of WWII. The giving of the patch had turned into an unofficial initiation for new Raiders who had completed training.

"At ease," Shaw ordered as he crossed the room. He extended his hand in greeting, "Hogan; Barone," he said in the order of handshakes.

"Sir," they both responded respectively. Both young Raiders swallowed down the lump in their throats. In such a small, tight-knit community, Shaw was a legend, and both had read up on his exploits; at least those that weren't redacted.

"I want to thank you both for accepting your orders. You both know we are hunting one of the world's highest priority terrorists, so let's do our best not to mess this up and embarrass the Corps, rah?"

"Aye, sir," they both said. Shaw smirked.

"You guys can lighten up. Grab your gear and let's go. Welcome to MARSOC." Shaw grinned at them both before turning to leave. The two young Marines swiftly hoisted their gear, grabbed their weapons, and followed him.

They found themselves aboard a C-17 transport aircraft hurtling down the runway and lifting into the air. Barone and Hogan exchanged smiles as their excitement skyrocketed. Neither could fully express in words the exhilarating feeling of heading into combat. They had seen movies of actors portraying soldiers who rejoiced after receiving combat orders, but neither expected such a powerful feeling to wash over them. They felt invincible.

"You boys feeling invincible yet?" Shaw asked without looking up from his mobile device and map. Hogan and Barone glanced at each other in wonder.

"Yes, sir," Barone answered. Shaw cracked a smile and looked up at them both. Try as they might, their eyes still held the soft glow of innocence, and Shaw valued it more than he could express; even more so knowing that it would be ripped away from them after their first pull of the trigger.

14

"Yes, sir," Natalie Hale replied, "I understand, sir." When she hung up the phone, a mix of dread and exhilaration funneled through her. Her evacuation request had been delayed. Director Caldwell, upon hearing this new intelligence, had altered his evacuation approval. She was assured that the new information would follow the phone call and provide new insight into finding al-Amiri. Upon discovering his location, the Pentagon would authorize an airstrike. She could hardly wait to get her hands on the new intelligence. She must have really impressed some people with her work in Tehran for them to trust her this much.

Natalie opened her laptop and logged in with her Agency credentials. She found the new intelligence waiting for her, and her eyes bulged as she read over the material.

"How did they get this?" she uttered in disbelief. She read everything twice, and, with her mouth agape, she simply shook her head. "How could we have missed all this?" Even though she uttered those words, she knew that she had missed this information only because it was unavailable to her. There was no way her team could have unearthed it. It was the kind of intelligence only gathered on a battlefield, and this David Shaw had done excellently. If he wasn't careful, the CIA would scoop him up and put him to work.

The intelligence she gazed upon was utterly amazing. Shaw had been in the right place at the right time, and, more importantly, he had remembered and put everything together. It was just the break her team needed. The CIA officer stood and left her office. All eyes fell on her as she strode onto the main floor.

"Alright team, new intel from HQ," she started. Everyone stopped their duties and offered her their undivided attention. "We have the name wrong," she stated. "It's Al Amiri, not al-Amiri." The team exchanged confused glances, but Natalie wore a satisfied simile.

"What's the difference?" Bryon sincerely asked. He studied her movements as she wheeled a glass pane, similar to a white board, to the center of the room. She spelled out the two names in white script, and her team immediately caught the subtle difference.

"One is a title. The other is a family name," Natalie said. "Isaam Al Amiri's real name is Taaha bin Hashim Al Amiri. I want everyone searching for this man." Natalie circled Al Amiri's name on the pane with the dry-erase marker. "Reach out to your city contacts and see what we can dig up." Everyone returned to their computers with renewed vigor. Natalie lingered for a moment, observing her team hard at work. If she got Al Amiri, it would be because of them. Gratitude welled up within her, and she offered a nod to no one in particular before returning to her office.

The outside door opened, and the action stopped Natalie before she reached for her office door. Wyatt moved around the perimeter of the room and headed her way. She offered him a smile as he stopped before her.

"Hello, Wyatt," Natalie greeted.

"Ma'am, I was hoping to connect with you about the updated intelligence," Wyatt said.

"I'm sorry, the what?" she asked. She had no authority to share Agency intelligence without permission regardless of the level of clearance the personnel possessed.

"The new intelligence on Taaha bin Hashim Al Amiri," Wyatt clarified. Confusion assaulted her.

"How do you know about that?"

"I'm part of the Raider team that's going to be hunting him," he answered. Natalie's brow furrowed. She possessed no knowledge of any ground element. She turned the handle to one of the French doors and ushered Wyatt inside. Once she followed him through, she closed the door quickly.

"What Raider team?" she asked. She planted her hands on her hips and waited impatiently for the Marine to respond.

"My command has deployed a small team to rendezvous here for direct-action against Al Amiri," Wyatt answered. Natalie shook her head.

"No, an airstrike has been authorized against Al Amiri," she countered. There was a hint of sadness in her tone. An airstrike would reduce the risk to American lives, but it could never confirm the kill like men on the ground, not to mention it destroyed any intelligence that might be obtained. The fact that the Pentagon and SOCOM pursued an airstrike told Natalie that they were more concerned with retaliating for the lost Marines than securing intelligence that might prevent future acts of terror.

It was often a choice the upper administration faced. She knew they hoped that neutralizing any threat allowed for more time to uncover any terror plot or perhaps disrupt that plot entirely. It was always a gamble, and an airstrike wasn't the option Natalie preferred, which made Wyatt's information all the more intriguing. If Al Amiri was planning something, she wanted men on the ground to provide her with as much information as possible.

"I know about the airstrike, ma'am," Wyatt replied. "But my team leader, Captain David Shaw, is currently in the air for a HALO insertion to this compound."

"So let me make sure I'm understanding you correctly," Natalie started, "SOCOM and the CIA have provided my team with new information to locate Al Amiri so they can call in an airstrike on his position, but you're saying that MARSOC is deploying a team for what I'm assuming is a capture or kill mission?"

"That is correct, ma'am," Wyatt replied.

"And if you're in the vicinity when they decide to call in this airstrike?"

"The way I see it, ma'am, if they never learn the location of Al Amiri, they'll have no coordinates to launch an airstrike," Wyatt countered. Natalie smirked and pondered his words. What he proposed would provide her the option to gain the intelligence she so desperately desired and potentially capture Al Amiri.

"Alright, Wyatt, we'll play it your way," Natalie said with a grin.

———

After finishing their timed pre-breathing period to flush nitrogen from their bloodstream and avoid hypoxia, the trio of Marines stood at the rear of the C-17 as the crisp air swirled around them. Normally, they would have witnessed the curvature of the earth, but the night stole their sight; their night vision binoculars (NODs) only cast their vision so far. Each man wore a special helmet equipped with an oxygen mask and goggles. They cruised around 30,000 feet to avoid any surface-to-air missiles, and the trio would freely fall until they opened their chutes at 2,500 feet.

Shaw glanced back at the two excited Marines and activated his comms. "Ready?" he asked. They both nodded, and Shaw waited for the cue from the pilot.

"Philo Actual, you're clear to jump."

"Good copy, Leonidas," Shaw replied, referring to the aircraft by its call sign. He didn't hesitate but threw himself headfirst into the darkness.

Shaw plummeted toward the earth at increasing speeds, his breath echoing through his ears. His uniform flapped about him, but his gear remained unmoved. He had cinched, tightened, and strapped everything down so as not to lose anything.

Reaching speeds in excess of one-hundred-twenty miles per hour, the three Marines kept a close eye on their gauges as they neared their chute deployment window. With darkness encircling them, their night vision goggles did little to help them judge the distance to the ground. For anyone else, it would have proven a frightening endeavor, but for these men it was another day at the office. The infrared chem lights fixed to Shaw's helmet and wrists made it easy for the other two Marines to follow him down. They each possessed similar lights attached to their bodies. The lights blazed neon under the pale glow of their white-phosphor night vision but remained invisible to anyone else.

Shaw's internal clock nagged at him. He had fallen long enough. Just to be sure, he checked his gauge. He just passed the 2,500-foot mark. The Raider yanked his chute and jerked violently upward when the dark canopy fully opened and immediately slowed his descent. His inner thighs tingled from his harness slowly cutting off circulation to his legs. He glanced downward as the mountainside cleared through his NODs and, pulling on his chute adjustment lines, plotted his course safely down.

The Marine captain, his injuries swirling in the back of his mind and generating a small batch of anxiety, prepared for his landing. He lifted his legs as the ground neared, and on contact, he hit the ground running. His wounded muscles shrieked in protest, but they obeyed his orders. Shaw fought through the pain by keeping his mind on the mission. Once on the ground, he wrenched hard on the lines and wrestled his chute under control. It went better than he could have hoped. He exhaled a long sigh of relief before hurriedly doffing his harness. He switched out his helmet and oxygen mask for his ballistic helmet and transferred his night vision goggles to it. Once he had it settled on his head, he searched the immediate proximity for Hogan and Barone.

Both men trotted up to him with grins wide on their faces. They looked like creatures from another world with their silhouettes enlarged by their gear, their heads oversized and rounded from their helmets, and their eyes, shielded by the circular and protruding, night-vision binoculars, glowed a faded, eerie green. Shaw looked no different.

Shaw knew what they felt, because for the first time in several weeks, the urge to touch his stomach was nonexistent. Excitement coursed through his body, revitalizing him thoroughly. The exhilaration could not be explained without several moments of contemplative thought, but simply put, the men felt truly alive and on the cusp of dangerous adventure. The feeling welled upward from their guts, tickled their hearts, and quickened their minds. It was almost like injecting a drug, but the three men would say it was indeed far better than any substance available.

Shaw carried Wyatt's M4A1 strapped to the side of his rucksack, and the rest of Wyatt's gear was dispersed through his, Barone's, and Hogan's packs. Shaw checked their coordinates on his GPS and then again by map and compass just to be sure. He located their bearing and set off toward the CIA outpost.

The brutal climb tore at Shaw's legs as he ascended. His muscles still ached from his wounds, but he pushed onward. He picked his way up a narrow ridge and sweat beaded down his face as he exerted himself. The Raider moved slowly, careful to judge distance accurately. His night vision binoculars severely handicapped his depth perception, and one wrong step could send him tumbling down the mountainside.

The Marines reached the crest of the mountain, and, from their perch in a small clearing surrounded by boulders, they took a moment to catch their breath and gaze down upon the city. Various lights dotted the entire valley, but it was a far cry from luminous San Francisco or New York City. Shaw checked his map and confirmed the location of the compound.

"There," he said, pointing to a cluster of buildings beneath them. Barone and Hogan noted the location and followed Shaw as he began his descent.

The descent, almost as difficult as the ascent, proved challenging. The three men carefully placed each foot as they moved through the rocky crags laden with loose dirt and small rocks. They fought to balance the weight of their gear, but each had carefully packed their kit to aid their center of gravity.

As they neared, Shaw observed the quiet compound. Darkness shrouded every inch of the outpost and nothing moved. He surveyed the mountainside and narrowed his eyes. The breeze picked up, and a piece of fabric fluttered in the wind. The silhouette of a man materialized as he focused in on the waving cloth. The man lay prone behind a scoped rifle pointed toward the compound. Shaw guessed he was about seventy meters away. He pressed his PTT, "I've got eyes on a sniper." A prickling sensation rolled over both Hogan and Barone at the news. They were really in it. After all their training, they had arrived.

"I see him," Hogan stated.

"Me too," Barone said. Shaw brought up his carbine, and the IR laser fluttered for a moment then steadied on the sniper's torso.

"Move in on him from behind. I've got you covered," Shaw ordered. Barone and Hogan carefully picked their way toward the sniper but stopped. Shaw noted their pause. "What is it?"

"I've got movement in the compound," Barone answered. Shaw turned his head slightly and noted the figure stride across the courtyard. It was a woman with light hair; that was all he could decipher through the pale green illumination. His eyes snapped back toward the sniper and watched as the man settled in behind his rifle. The man slowly inhaled as his rifle traced the woman's steps. Shaw aimed for center mass, exhaled to find his natural respiratory pause, and squeezed the trigger.

15

Kathryn shot upright, gasping for air. Sweat glistened on her chest and face, and she felt her ribcage tighten around her lungs. She glanced around the room, Abby lay asleep in the bed next to her, but everything else remained quiet. The journalist touched her cheeks then her forehead before regaining her composure. She crawled out of the bed and, sliding on her shoes, left the room.

The bathroom on the top floor lay between her room and the next but was only accessible from the hallway. She entered, wet a towel, and pressed it repeatedly against her face and neck. Her breath did little to calm her as she inhaled and exhaled deeply. The dream, the first of many she knew, still lingered in her mind. Already a notoriously bad sleeper, the nightmare didn't help. In it, she stood, surrounded by the mangled bodies of dead Marines, covered in blood from head to toe, screaming as the blood from the bodies rose from the floor. It rose to her ankles, then her calves, then her thighs, waist, chest, and neck. Stricken with the horrifying realization that she would drown in their blood, fear had forced her awake.

Kathryn glanced in the mirror and immediately noticed the dark circles under her eyes. She sighed and draped the rag on the edge of the sink. She wasn't going back to sleep, that much she knew. What dreams would she have? She didn't want to subject herself to her uncontrollable subconscious. She could try, but she knew she would just lay there fearful of closing her eyes. No, she would attempt sleep tomorrow night, and maybe it would come easier once she was back home.

The bathroom door creaked open, and Kathryn, dressed in borrowed athletic shorts and a tank top, descended to the main floor. Her thoughts fell on Wyatt, and she smiled. Was he awake too? She thought it couldn't hurt to find out.

Kathryn quietly opened the door leading to the courtyard. The night was surprisingly cold, and her skin prickled in response. She wrapped her arms around her torso and walked across the courtyard. Halfway to the other building, Kathryn shrieked as the suppressed gunshot rang out on the mountainside. It wasn't deafening, but the sound was unmistakable. The same fear from earlier that day surged throughout her body and paralyzed her. The door to the security building burst open, and Wyatt, fully dressed in his combat gear, rushed forward, grabbed her, and hastily guided her into the security building. The contractors were already donning their gear and scooping up their rifles when the pair entered.

"Confirmed suppressed gunshot from the northeast, up the mountain," Wyatt told them. He guided Kathryn to the couch and calmed her.

"Good copy," Lincoln replied. "Guys, keep your heads down until you reach your designated defensive positions. I want to know what's going on out there." He hoped it wasn't what he feared. He was the first kitted up and out the door. The rest quickly followed.

"You alright?" Wyatt asked her. She looked around, panic smeared across her face. "Look at me," he urged. Her eyes snapped to his, and she took a deep breath. "You're okay," he told her. She believed the words and felt the calm wash over her. "It's always easier the second time around." The journalist found truth in the statement. The crippling fear was easier to fight off, and her mind stayed relatively clear. "Stay here, okay?" She nodded quickly.

"Be careful, John," Kathryn called. He paused and looked back at her.

"Always," he said before he disappeared into the night.

Wyatt snapped down his NODs and moved to the edge of the building, careful not to expose himself to a northwestern trajectory. He turned on his radio, which was still connected to Lincoln's team.

"You guys seeing this?" came Becker's voice.

"Yeah," answered Adara.

"Me too," came Sotelo's response.

"We going to check this out?" Becker asked. Lincoln remained silent. Wyatt peeked around the corner of the building and smirked. An IR laser painted a halo in the sky as the green beam, visible only under night vision, spun in quick circles.

"Those your Marines?" Lincoln asked Wyatt. Natalie had filled him in on the planned insertion.

"Appears to be," Wyatt replied. "I'm headed up there; anyone coming?" Wyatt moved toward the steel doors.

Lincoln thought quickly and assessed the situation with what information he had available. From his position, he gazed through his NODs. He made out the clear silhouette of the man tracing the halo. Two others stood next to him. They certainly looked like American military. Lincoln's eyes snapped to the man's left hand. His thumb and pinky flared out in the familiar *shaka*. Lincoln returned it and nodded his head.

"Quinn, Becker, on me," he said into his radio. "The rest of you, hang here until we get back."

Quinn and Becker fell in line behind him as he neared the gate. Receiving a quick nod from Lincoln, Becker activated the controls to open the gate. It screeched open, and the four-man unit, including Wyatt, made their way up the mountain.

Shaw watched them approach and picked his way down to them. Wyatt pushed past the others and embraced Shaw when they met. He squeezed him tight.

"Captain David Shaw, MARSOC," Shaw greeted the others once Wyatt released him.

"Scott Lincoln, SOG. What's going on up here?"

"Follow me," Shaw answered. The group traversed east about fifty meters and steadily ascended the slope.

"Well, this is a mess," Becker said. The deceased insurgent lay slumped over his rifle. There was no question as to where the rifle was pointed. Blood splattered the ground to the left of the corpse, showcasing the exit trajectory of Shaw's bullet.

"Lincoln, Wyatt, this is Barone and Hogan," Shaw introduced. The two Marines stood nearby keeping an eye out for more threats. "What do you make of this?" Shaw asked.

"Just as we thought," Quinn answered.

"Looks that way," Lincoln added. He squeezed his PTT, "Guys, they know we're here."

"How long do you think we have?" Becker asked.

"At most? A couple of days maybe," came Lincoln's reply. Shaw watched and listened intently.

"Out of the frying pan and into the fire," Becker said. The weight of the situation bore down on all of them.

"You could be putting that lightly," Lincoln retorted. He turned to Shaw, "He alone?"

"Yeah, we already swept the mountainside. It's clear," Shaw answered.

"Let's get back to the outpost. We have a long night ahead of us. Shaw, I'm glad you and your men are here. We could use the extra muscle," Lincoln replied.

"We'll help where we can, but we're here for Al Amiri," Shaw stated.

"We fear an attack on the compound, and because of your new intelligence, our evacuation orders have been delayed. I hope it's worth it," Lincoln said. Shaw noted the contempt heavy in his tone.

"We'll work as quickly as possible," Shaw replied. He hadn't known the situation was so dire, and he certainly didn't want to jeopardize the safety of the personnel in the compound. "Excuse me," he said. Lincoln nodded, and Shaw turned away. "Warhorse, this is Philo Actual."

"Go ahead, Philo Actual," came the communications specialist under Lt. Bateman's command.

"We've got a new development on the ground. The outpost is compromised. Please advise," Shaw informed.

"Understood, Philo Actual. Stand by."

"Roger that," came Shaw's reply.

"So, what's the situation?" Wyatt asked, moving next to him. Shaw turned toward him and then glanced back at the dead sniper.

"I'm not one for leaving Americans high and dry. Until we hear from command, we stay our course," Shaw replied. "Let's get down to the compound."

Kathryn perked up as the door opened. Wyatt strode in wearing a wide smile. She returned the grin and rose from the couch. Three men she didn't recognize entered next.

"Kathryn, this is Captain David Shaw. He's my team commander," Wyatt said.

"Nice to meet you," she said.

"It's a pleasure, Kathryn," Shaw said. The rest of the team entered, and Lincoln stepped last over the threshold.

"Alright, we're on watch shifts. You guys know the drill. Let's get a couple pots of coffee going," he said. The team disbursed through the area, prepping for the rotating watches. Shaw turned to Wyatt.

"I want to meet with Officer Hale."

"Sure thing," Wyatt replied.

16

Natalie pressed the top of her fist against her mouth as Lincoln addressed those present. She had dragged them out of their beds as soon as Lincoln had come knocking on her own door. Natalie didn't possess a large team, but they were talented. Despite the haze of sleep, they all listened intently as he spoke.

"I won't sugar coat it. A trio of Marines engaged a sniper who was fixed on our position. The reality of this information suggests that someone knows we are here and has hostile intentions toward us," he said gravely. He glanced around the room as he uttered the words, and he witnessed the fear spread across their youthful faces. "I've got only five contractors and four Marines to defend this place, and I can't promise that we will be successful." He made eye contact with Natalie, "I've got actionable intel that there is a serious threat against this facility." She didn't miss the reference to their previous conversation, but she held his gaze and received the firm warning. All eyes fell on her, and she lowered her hand from her lips to address her team.

"Alright, team," she began, her voice strong and unwavering, "I want everyone prepared to evacuate. Prep all the hard drives for destruction. I don't want to leave anything here that can be used against us." She met Lincoln's gaze again. His eyes showed his approval. "But we are not to forsake our orders to find Al Amiri. We will evacuate only after we have found him." Lincoln's approval slid off his face, leaving behind a scowl.

The door opened, drawing everyone's attention, and Shaw strode confidently inside followed by Wyatt, Kathryn, and two additional Marines.

"Natalie Hale," Shaw greeted, extending his hand, "Captain David Shaw. I want to thank you for your actions yesterday."

"Nice to meet you, Captain," she responded, gripping his hand. "I'm just glad we were in a position to help. I'm sorry we couldn't do more." He nodded before casting his gaze around the room.

"Prepping for an evac?" he asked, observing the commotion.

"I want to be ready just in case. Did you have something you wished to speak about?" she asked. Shaw produced an old cellphone from his pocket and presented it to her.

"Took it off the sniper on the mountainside," he answered. "I want to know if that sniper had any connection to those who launched the attack, and I'm hoping you have someone here that can trace the next call that comes in."

"Bryon," she called, suppressing her excitement. The young man approached swiftly. "I want you to trace the next call this phone receives."

"Will do," he said. He took the phone from her hand and moved to his desk. He plugged the phone into a device on his desk before turning to his computer.

"Now we wait," Shaw stated. "I want to find out who's on the other line."

"Hopefully Isaam Al Amiri," Natalie stated. She couldn't deny the glee she experienced at the sight of the device.

"That's shooting in the dark," Lincoln retorted.

"Who else? He's the highest profile target we know of in the city. If anyone has the gall to shoot down two United States helicopters and plan an attack against our compound, it's him," Natalie countered. Lincoln retreated; she did have a point.

"Al Amiri," Shaw started, "could he get access to a MANPADS?"

"MANPADS?" Kathryn whispered to Wyatt. He leaned toward her.

"Short Range Man-Portable Air-Defense System," he replied quietly. "Like a bazooka for helicopters."

"Thanks," she said. He smiled.

"No problem."

"We don't know much about Al Amiri other than he was within bin Laden's inner circle and now that is confirmed by your recent findings. I assume he has the resources to acquire such weaponry," Natalie answered. She turned toward Bryon. "Bryon, I want to know the minute that phone rings." Bryon simply nodded. Lincoln seized the opportunity the brief silence presented.

"I could use you guys if you're up for it," he interjected. Shaw turned to face him. Lincoln's expression forecasted his annoyance with the entire situation.

"My men need time to rest and get some chow, but we will be ready if you need us," Shaw answered for them. A grateful Lincoln turned to leave. Shaw nodded again at Natalie, confirming his faith in her ability, before following Lincoln out.

The four Marines and Kathryn made their way across the compound toward the security building.

"Shaw, hold up," Wyatt requested. Shaw gave Barone and Hogan a nod and waited for them to enter the security building. Kathryn paused. "Go ahead, I'll just be a second," he explained. She nodded and hurried after Barone and Hogan; she didn't want to remain in the courtyard any longer than she needed. "What are you thinking?" Wyatt asked Shaw after she disappeared inside.

"I want what I came here for," Shaw replied.

"Then what?"

"I'm going to hunt down everyone who's involved in this," he stated. His grave tone struck Wyatt. He had never beheld such a manner within Shaw.

"You mean after Al Amiri? How far are we taking this?" Wyatt asked. Shaw noticed his use of *we*.

"As far as we need to," he replied.

"Then I'm with you all the way," Wyatt said. Shaw gripped Wyatt's shoulder and gave him a thankful nod. In truth, he didn't expect any less from the man before him. Shaw continued toward the security building.

Once inside, Kathryn, Wyatt, Shaw, Hogan, and Barone sat at the kitchen table and feasted on a quick meal. Sotelo had offered them some leftover ground meat, cheese, tortillas, and a spicy sauce he had whisked together. There was enough left for each person to down two tacos, but Kathryn refrained and simply accepted a cup of coffee. Barone and Hogan were more than happy to eat hers.

They stuck to pleasant topics while they ate, and they laughed together as Shaw and Wyatt recounted some comedic stories from their deployments together. Hogan and Barone enjoyed watching the experienced Marines interact, and Kathryn thought Shaw was delightful. He was well spoken and polite, and it was obvious how much the two men cared for one another.

"Well, that was amazing," Shaw said as he finished his last bite. He placed both hands on the table and released a satisfied exhale. He cast his gaze toward Wyatt, and his eyes softened. After a long pause, he said, "Tell me what happened." Wyatt's eyes drifted to Kathryn before returning to Shaw. He began slowly, recounting everything about the previous day's tragic events. When he finished, Barone stared at the floor, and Hogan clinched his fists.

"We'll get them," Shaw calmly promised. Kathryn reached for Wyatt's forearm and gave him an affectionate squeeze. He looked at her and offered her a half-hearted smile. He knew healing would come, but it would be a long road, a long road for all of them.

"I'm the last one, David," Wyatt said. He fought back the grief as it rose within him. Shaw nodded slowly, somberly.

"You're not alone," Shaw said. Wyatt looked at him. He knew that, but the words didn't help him feel any better.

Natalie pushed through the French doors as her team finished their last preparations for the evacuation. Everyone stopped and looked at her. "Where are we on Al Amiri?" Abby rose from her station and addressed the room.

"My sources say that bin Hashim arrived in country in May of 2017. He's been a vocal opponent of Saudi and Western influence. He made numerous trips to the capitol advocating for a return of the Imams of Yemen, no doubt building support for his own claim," she explained. For hundreds of years, imams and later kings, whom the people revered as religious and political leaders within the Shia faction of Islam, ruled Yemen.

"But from what we know of Al Amiri's involvement with al-Qaeda, he's not Shiite but Sunni. Does he have any support?" Natalie asked. It was only to satisfy her own curiosity. It didn't matter one way or another.

"I don't know," Abby replied.

"What else do we have?"

"Bin Hashim seems to care little about Sunni and Shia relations. From the dossiers we pulled on him, his intel has helped the US destroy numerous Taliban networks. Both the Taliban and al-Qaeda are Sunni," Rachel added.

"He's attempting to place himself above that then," Natalie noted.

"I believe Al Amiri is more of a nationalist and may be more politically motivated. He's not a true believer," said Stephen Carson. Natalie looked at him.

"Go on," she said.

"His return to Yemen after rising so high in the ranks of al-Qaeda suggests to me that he wants to see his nation and his people prosper. He only returned to Yemen after things got really bad here. You should see how the people praise Taaha bin Hashim. His name is everywhere, and he is providing for his people: food, water, medicine, you name it," Stephen said. "He's living this double life out to perfection."

"If he's able to provide for the people, then he's certainly able to procure weapons," Natalie noted. She sighed. It was never easy and most certainly always complicated. Removing Al Amiri meant depriving people of hope and provisions necessary for life. "Do we know where he is?" Natalie asked.

"Not yet," Bryon stated.

"Come get me once we find out," Natalie stated.

"Will do," Bryon responded.

The team returned to their work, and Natalie was grateful for how much they had dug up in so little time. However, she was not going to thrust the burden entirely on them. She too had been working to uncover

Al Amiri's location, and, so far, her search hadn't turned up anything promising. She turned around and reached for one of the French doors.

The phone on Bryon's desk vibrated before she could turn the knob. It drew everyone's attention. Bryon nearly knocked over his chair as he jumped up from his workstation. He worked fiercely at the keyboard as his eyes traced back and forth over the computer screen.

"What happens when he doesn't answer?" Rachel inquired, vocalizing what everyone was thinking.

"Do you have it?" Natalie asked. Bryon didn't answer. The tension in the room fell like a thick fog as the phone continued to vibrate on the wooden desk. "Do you have it?" Natalie asked again, more forcefully.

The signal bounced off satellites leaving a trail encircling nearly half the globe. Whoever was encrypting the call was well trained, and Bryon knew immediately that they weren't native, or at least if they were, they were educated overseas. He knew he could intercept the signal with the Agency algorithms at his disposal, but he had to determine the next waypoint the signal would rebound from in order to successfully capture the trace. With little time remaining, he worked to encode the Agency algorithm on all available network satellites. He inhaled heavily and continued after the signal. The room, frozen with deep anxiety, simply watched him work.

"Got it!" he exclaimed. A great relief spread across the floor. Natalie grinned happily and brushed a stray hair from her face.

"Well done," Natalie said. "Abby, get Captain Shaw for me," she ordered.

"Absolutely," the young woman replied.

"Hey Natalie," Bryon started as Abby moved toward the door.

"Yes?"

"That was far more sophisticated than anything I've seen to date over here. It was unusually hard to trace that call," he explained. Natalie pondered the severity of his words as she watched Abby exit.

Abby rushed across the courtyard and into the security building. Shaw and Wyatt's gaze snapped to the door as the young woman burst in. She favored Natalie, with her dark hair and short, slender build, but younger, perhaps five years or so.

"Natalie's asking for you," she told Shaw, "Bryon traced the call." Shaw and Wyatt, still dressed in their full battle gear, quickly followed Abby out the door and raced across the compound.

17

"Hey, something's up," Becker said into his radio as he watched Abby dash toward his building from the other. He stood atop the security building's roof with his rifle resting on the steel-reinforced wall.

"What are you talking about?" came Quinn's voice through the radio. He was positioned on the opposite side of the roof keeping an eye on the mountainside. Becker waited a moment and watched as Abby appeared below him, followed by Shaw and Wyatt. The three hurried across the courtyard.

"Yeah, I just saw Wyatt and that Raider captain follow Abby into the main building. They looked to be in a rush," Becker said.

"That's Shaw for you," Reeves stated, accompanied by a slight chuckle. He and Adara stood atop the main building's roof. Reeves kept his light machine gun trained down the road.

"What's that mean?" Becker asked. Reeves chuckled again and recalled his memory.

"Back in oh-four, Det One was folded into our team as part of a trial to assess their direct-action capability," he began. "But Fallujah sucked, man," Reeves continued, his deep voice taking on a tone none of them had heard before. "Marines were going door to door, and, every time, one or two would come out wounded or dead. It was brutal, and they didn't have the right training for it.

"We got word of a group of Force Recon Marines pinned down by enemy fire, and from the sound of it, they were getting cut up pretty bad. I don't know what happened, but when the unit designation came over the radio, Shaw bolted. He just left us and tore down the next alley, and Petty Officer Ben Tussac was the first to follow. Since Ben went, we all went, angry as hell at the both of them." He laughed at the memory, "and we showed up, got in the middle of this firefight, and Ben catches one. I was right next to him, but if I came off my Bravo, I don't know if we would have made it. Next thing I know, Shaw is there. It's like he just materialized solely for Ben in his most dire moment of need, and he saved that kid's life. He saved more than just Ben's life that day. It's the kind of story that gets lost in the annals of war, you know?

"They gave him a medal for it when it all got sorted out, but Shaw left the podium and pinned the thing on Ben's chest right then and there. Not only did he save a bunch of good Marines, he saved Ben, then had the humility to pass off recognition. I wish the military had more men like him," Reeves finished.

"Dang, dude," Becker stated. He knew Reeves' well enough to under-stand the weight he placed on Shaw's actions that day. "Thanks for sharing, bro. I take it we can count on Shaw when things get tough?" he asked.

"With your life," Reeves answered. With the stress of an impending attack from a hostile force of unknown numbers, the statement reassured them all.

The glow of monitors illuminated the small upstairs room, and the five men had worked tirelessly through the night preparing for the next stage of their plan. Faatin Radi watched from over the shoulders of the four before him as he stood in the center of the room. From this room, he managed Al Amiri's money, orchestrated any deals for additional arms, communicated and planned with other cells, and commanded the militant forces under Al Amiri's control. Additionally, the team kept watch for potential issues that might arise from Western intelligence agencies. His was the warfare side of Al Amiri's operations; someone else handled all the details when Al Amiri paraded as Taaha bin Hashim, and Radi couldn't care less.

Radi wasn't from Yemen, but he had found his path to prominence through Isaam Al Amiri. One day, Al Amiri's influence and, more importantly, his finances would pass to Radi, and that promise alone was enough for him to leave Afghanistan when Al Amiri asked.

"He didn't answer," one man stated holding a cellphone in one hand. Radi folded his arms and thought quickly.

"Try him again," he ordered.

The phone on Bryon's desk buzzed again after sitting idle for a few seconds. It served as a reminder that they needed to move quickly. Shaw held his helmet in one hand and his M4A1 carbine in the other. He looked at Natalie as she discussed the planning details. Natalie highlighted the target building on the large, wall-mounted monitor that broadcasted satellite imagery.

"I can't tell you what you'll find or provide you with an accurate threat evaluation," she said.

"We understand," Shaw replied, "you've given us a target, and that's more than what we could ask for. How long will it take us to reach the building?"

"This time of night, we estimate about twenty minutes," Bryon answered.

"Alright, we need one of your SUV's," Shaw stated.

"It's yours," Natalie replied. "Keys are in the security building in a wall-mounted box to the left of the exit."

"Hogan, Barone, we're on," Shaw said into his radio. "Grab a set of keys on your way out. They're in a box on the wall to the left of the exit."

"On it," came Hogan's reply. Shaw turned and offered Wyatt a firm pat on the chest as he passed. The younger Raider grinned, eagerness burning behind his blue eyes. Having already outfitted his kit with the supplies

Shaw had brought and opting for his M4A1 carbine over his M110A1 sniper rifle, Wyatt followed Shaw out the door.

———

"Still no answer," the man said. Radi's brow furrowed. It could mean a multitude of things, but he had to anticipate the worst. "Pack everything up. We're leaving," he said. He moved to Al Amiri's room. He doubted there was any real threat, but he would rest easy once they were all loaded up and on their way to a secondary location. He knew it would take them no longer than thirty minutes to pack everything up and get out, a time in which he was more than satisfied.

———

The SUV slowed and turned onto an alleyway that ran by the rear of the target building. Advancing through the alley provided the four men additional concealment the main roads didn't provide. Shaw glanced at Wyatt, who gave him a quick nod. The four Raiders exited the vehicle and moved silently into the alley. They moved in single file with Shaw leading. The night wind, coming from the sea, whistled down the lane and tossed light debris, garbage, and various papers around the team as they approached the building. They were seventeen minutes into their mission, which put them three minutes ahead of schedule.

"We're approaching on foot. Target building in sight," Shaw said into his radio. He didn't expect to receive a response but only relayed the information as part of the mission protocol. Natalie and their MARSOC support team, led by Bateman with the designation Warhorse, watched the team's movements through cameras mounted to their helmets.

The two-story building matched the rest in the vicinity with its flat roof and sandy color, but there was no doubt they had the right building. As they neared, they noticed a van with its two rear doors open wide.

"Warhorse, they're preparing to leave," Shaw updated. Again, no response; it wasn't necessary. Shaw and his team crept along the wall of the adjacent house and froze when a man exited through the back door and strode into the alley. He loaded a computer monitor into the van before returning back inside. He hadn't seen them.

Shaw and Wyatt moved fast as soon as the man disappeared into the building. Wyatt took up a position behind the van door closest to the building, and Shaw, grateful that the rear door swung outward, hid behind it. Shaw drew his knife, a Dynamis Alliance Revere Blade, and Wyatt drew his own, a Benchmade Nimravus. They waited, and Barone and Hogan kept their sights trained on the exit.

Anxious voices readied the Marines as the two individuals returned to the exit. As far as Shaw and Wyatt were concerned, everyone present was an enemy combatant. Shaw waited for the first man to pass before seizing the second man from behind, executing a routine both he and Wyatt had performed countless times. Assaulting the second man first ensured that both targets cleared the exit and that neither could flee to alert any who may remain in the building. If there was a third, Barone and Hogan could drop them with a few suppressed shots.

Shaw kicked hard to buckle the man's knees and thrust his knife into the base of his skull. The man instantly fell limp, and Shaw released him allowing the dead man to fall to the ground. Before the first man could react to Shaw's savagery, Wyatt materialized from the darkness, plunged his knife twice between the man's ribs. Wyatt then drove him to the ground before freeing the blade and stabbing it into his neck. Wyatt held the man's mouth shut until he stopped fighting. The man's eyes rolled upward and dimmed, and, when Wyatt removed his hand, the man's mouth contorted open, spilling his loose tongue over his lips. The monitor and computer the men carried crashed to the ground, tumbling and breaking apart.

Hogan and Barone seized the moment and stormed inside while Wyatt and Shaw recovered. Certain the commotion had alerted those remaining in the house, Shaw and Wyatt rushed in behind them.

"What was that?" Radi asked, hearing the crash outside.

"Maybe Jameel and Talha dropped something again," one man said. Radi's anger flared at the thought. It wasn't easy to replace their equipment.

The more he thought about it, the more he hated being in Yemen. He understood, to an extent, Al Amiri's desire to free his people, but their war against the West would not be won in Yemen. It would be won through strongholds in the Middle East that provided access to modern conveniences and were relatively untouched by conflict.

"Go check on them, Abdur," Radi ordered, his anger diminishing slightly. He turned to enter Al Amiri's room.

Abdur froze as two Marines emerged at the top of the stairs. Fear gripped every part of his being, paralyzing him entirely. Their rifles, although suppressed, cracked and echoed through the small room. Radi's ears burst in pain, and his hands instinctively shot up to them. He spun around to see Abdur slump to the floor.

Radi didn't hesitate.

He sprinted for the nearest window. Pain seared through his shoulder and again through his back before he crashed through the glass pane. He tumbled onto the top of the van and cried out in anguish. He attempted a deep inhale but only managed a light shallow breath. Mustering what strength he could, Radi rolled off the van roof and slammed against the ground. He groaned as he rose to his feet. He held his useless arm close to his chest as he rounded the front of the vehicle. The wounded man climbed into the driver seat, cranked the engine, slammed the van in gear, and stomped on the gas pedal.

After firing at the target who threw himself out the window, Barone directed his attention to the last remaining man in the room, who raised his hands swiftly.

"Don't shoot, please don't shoot me!" he cried in English. "I'm an American citizen!" Hogan ignored his convincing accent and rushed him.

"On the ground!" he ordered. The young man complied instantly, not that he had a choice. Hogan's strong hands shoved him downward, and he thrust his knee into the man's back. Hogan pressed his hand against the back of the man's head, smashing it firmly into the floor. He pulled a pair of linked, heavy-duty zip ties from a pouch on his plate carrier and secured the man's hands behind his back. Barone moved to the window and saw the van screech away. He cursed before turning his attention to their captive.

"Look at me," Barone instructed. The man's eyes shot upward though his face remained flattened into the ground. The young man quivered as he stared into the black orbs of Barone's night vision goggles. "Isaam Al Amiri. Is he here?" The captive tossed his eyes toward the door. Barone's eyes followed. He moved toward it, but Shaw's raised hand stopping him mid-stride.

"Get him downstairs, Wyatt and I will handle this," Shaw stated. Barone nodded and helped Hogan yank the man to his feet.

Shaw and Wyatt approached the door, and automatic gunfire erupted from the other side. Shaw sprawled to the ground and slid left. Wyatt dashed to the right and, drawing a flashbang grenade from his kit, neared the door. Shaw rose to his feet once out of the line of fire. He readied himself opposite of Wyatt and nodded his command.

Wyatt pulled the pin, cracked the door, and tossed in the grenade. A flash of light followed by a deafening blast signaled the two to enter. They both checked their corners and then rotated to clear the rest of the room. An older man, holding an AKM and grabbing at his eyes, stood in the center of the room. Both men sent multiple rounds into his chest, toppling him over. Shaw advanced and kicked away the rifle as the man, gasping for breath, reached for it.

Shaw lifted up his night vision goggles and stared into the fading eyes of Taaha bin Hashim, a man he would have once considered an ally if not friend. Any compassion or affection Shaw held for that relationship gave way to penetrating hatred.

"I know you," bin Hashim managed amidst quick, light breaths. Blood trickled from his mouth as he stared at the Marine, his eyes weak and fading. Shaw raised his rifle and loosed two more shots into bin Hashim's chest. The body jerked before settling. Bin Hashim's eyes stared blankly at the ceiling, and Shaw neared so his helmet-mounted camera could focus on the man's face.

"Warhorse," Shaw said, standing and pressing his PTT, "Brimstone is down." He used the designation assigned to Al Amiri by his command.

"Good copy, Philo Actual," came the voice of one of Bateman's Marines.

"Stand by for secondary confirmation," Shaw said. "Hogan, Barone, bring him in," Shaw ordered. A few seconds passed before the two Marines half dragged their captive into the room.

"This Al Amiri?" Shaw gruffly asked him. The young man nodded quickly. "Are you lying to me?"

"No, it's him. I swear to God," he said, trembling.

"I've got a kid here, one of his men, who has also identified him," Shaw radioed to the support team.

"Affirmative, Philo Actual, collect what intel you can."

"We're taking him," Shaw told Hogan. The young man broke down into terrible sobs. "If you don't shut up, I'm going to stab you right in the heart," Shaw threatened. The man's sobs reduced to pathetic whimpers as they exited the room. "Barone, Wyatt, you're on clean up," Shaw ordered.

"Aye, sir," came Barone's reply. Wyatt simply smirked and unzipped Barone's empty pack. He ripped hard drives from computers and stuffed them inside while Barone took a video recording of the monitors and maps arrayed on the walls.

"The van's gone," Wyatt said once they emerged outside. Shaw stomped on the broken computer and yanked on the hard drive.

"Barone," Shaw said as a command. The young Raider hurried forward, turned, and allowed Shaw to stow the drive in his pack. "Let's get out of here."

The four Marines hurried back to their SUV with their captive shoved between Barone and Hogan. Shaw issued a long exhale when he started the vehicle, and Hogan blindfolded the man before taking a seat next to him. He trained his Glock 19 pistol on the man's stomach.

"Warhorse," Shaw said into his radio, "we're Oscar Mike."

18

The young man sat in the chair shaking uncontrollably while tears rolled down his face and dripped off his chin. Abby sat in the chair opposite him. She leaned forward, her elbows resting on her knees, and gazed upon the young man with mock sympathy.

"I can't help you if you don't talk to me," she said. "You said you're an American citizen?" The young man nodded quickly. "What is your name?"

"What's the point?" he managed. "I'm dead anyway. I know the punishment for terrorism." Abby shook her head and offered him a warm smile.

"I can help you if you help me. What's your name?" she asked.

"Armal," he replied.

"Thank you, Armal," Abby said. "My name is Jessica." He bought the lie. "Can you tell me what you were up to?"

Natalie watched on an office monitor as Armal spilled everything to Abby. He shared how his father had gotten him a high-paying job in their home country doing information technology, and he shared that he wasn't able to quit even though he wanted to. Was any of that true? It really didn't matter; Armal, regardless of how he came into the service of Al Amiri, would face the punishment for international terrorism. Abby was a good interrogator and was obtaining satisfactory results. Lincoln watched intently as did Shaw. Lincoln had protested Shaw's presence, but Natalie overruled him. Shaw had done more in a few hours than they had in months, and she owed him for it.

"This isn't a good idea," Lincoln stated. "We need to leave now. We can take him with us."

"Just a little longer," Natalie replied. He sighed and returned his attention to the monitor. He wanted desperately to load everyone into the SUV's and head for the embassy in Sana'a. He didn't care if they possessed orders to evacuate or not. He was responsible for every American life in the compound, but months and months of habitually submitting to Natalie's command caused him pause. A pit formed in his stomach, but he suppressed it. Natalie knew what she was doing.

The camera positioned in the corner of the room recorded and live streamed the footage. Shaw rubbed his bearded chin just as Abby asked her next question. If Al Amiri was behind the downed helicopters, Shaw wanted to know where he acquired the weapons to carry out the attack.

Abby held up a photograph of Al Amiri they pulled from Shaw's video feed. Armal glanced at it and then looked quickly away.

"Can you tell me who this is?"

"Isaam Al Amiri," came his reply. Exhilaration gushed through Natalie, and she almost leaped from her chair. Months and months of grueling intelligence work had finally paid off.

"Was Al Amiri behind the attacks against the United States Marine Corps helicopters?" Abby asked, continuing her interrogation. Armal whimpered and stared at the ground.

"Yes," he managed to say. Shaw's hand fell from his chin, and his lips flattened together. He and Wyatt had done it, and their brothers could rest easy now. It felt good, but Shaw wasn't done. The desire to take his vengeance to the next level could not be sated.

"Ask what weapons were used," Shaw requested. Natalie relayed the question to Abby's earpiece.

"And what weapons were used in the attack?" Abby asked. Armal, his mental resolve completely broken by fear, shrugged.

"I don't know. I just run tech," he answered.

"Think Armal, or I can't help you," Abby pressed. A short sob escaped his lips.

"Man, she's got him wrapped around her finger," Shaw noted. They all couldn't agree more. Armal's eyes shot back and forth as he searched his memory.

"Stingers!" he shouted. Did he mean to shout? The stress bore down on him too hard. "I heard Al Amiri talking about Stingers." Natalie looked at Shaw whose face tightened.

"Those are American made," she said.

"Ask where they came from," Shaw replied. Natalie relayed the question.

"And where did he get them?" Abby asked.

"Yesterday morning," Armal started, "a man... a man arrived with them."

"Just one man?"

"No, there were two more with him," Armal answered, his voice maintained its frightened haste.

"How many weapons were acquired?" Abby asked.

"I don't know, but the cost was more than ten million dollars. And... and the seller promised a demonstration that was planned weeks in advance," Armal explained. Shaw's eyes widened, and he took a step toward the monitor. Natalie watched him.

"Planned weeks in advance?" Shaw repeated quietly to himself. "How?"

"Ten million buys a lot more than Stingers," Lincoln said. He was right. That was a high price tag, and Natalie suppressed a stroke of fear as her imagination filled in the gaps.

"The seller," Abby inquired, "what was his name?"

"Francisco Silva," came the immediate reply.

"And was it Silva or Al Amiri that knew first about the Marine helicopters?" Abby asked.

"Silva," Armal answered. The questions became easier to answer as he told one truth after another.

"Thank you, Armal, you're doing really well," Abby encouraged. "I appreciate what you've shared with me so far. Can I get you anything? Water maybe?"

"Water," he pleaded. His tongue lay parched in his mouth.

"Sure," she responded.

"Wait!" he cried. She turned, keeping her cool, though he had startled her considerably. Despite everything he told her, he was still a terrorist, and if a terrorist, then capable of killing her. She found comfort that Sotelo stood just outside. "Where am I?"

"You don't know?" she asked. He shook his head, sending his long and wavy black hair dancing about his face.

"Tell him," came Natalie's reply in her ear. "I want to see how he reacts."

"You're being held in a clandestine CIA outpost here in the city," she told him. He immediately began to panic.

"No, no, no!" he screamed. He fought against his restraints and struggled to stand.

"Sotelo, get in there," Natalie ordered. Sotelo burst through the door, and at the sight of the contractor dressed in his full battle gear, Armal's panic reduced to a whimper.

"We're all going to die," he groaned.

"What are you talking about?" Abby said. Armal didn't answer but sobbed in his seat. Urine trickled onto the floor as fear took absolute control over his body. Sotelo gripped Armal's jaw and squeezed tightly.

"Speak!" he shouted. Armal inhaled heavily and wailed through his exhale. "I said, speak!"

"There's... there's..."

"There's what!" Sotelo hissed. Armal looked up at him, complete despair clouded his brown eyes.

"A missile."

———————

USS Abraham Lincoln,
5ᵗʰ Fleet,
Gulf of Aden

Captain Griffin C. Yates stood on the bridge of the USS *Abraham Lincoln*, a *Nimitz*-class aircraft carrier. He relished the view of the dark sky and tranquil sea. He often made it a habit to visit the bridge each morning before the rising sun. This was the ship's last deployment as the flagship for

Carrier Strike Group Nine. Next May, the ship would deploy as the flagship for Carrier Strike Group Twelve. It probably wouldn't change much of anything. The strike group would still deploy from Norfolk to the Middle East like it had for the last decade. They would host a new Carrier Air Wing, but Yates, a former Naval Aviator, had not learned of the specific wing the ship was to host; however, he was confident it contained good sailors and aviators.

"Captain!" the sailor next to him cried, "We've picked up a missile launched from the mountains south of Aden."

"Trajectory?" Yates requested, alarmed.

"East, bearing: one zero three," the young seaman responded.

"Sound General Quarters," he ordered. It most certainly appeared to be coming their way. He was a man who refused to gamble with the lives under his command.

"Aye, Captain," the seaman responded. He opened up the fleet wide channel and announced, "General Quarters, General Quarters. All hands man your battle stations. The route of travel is forward and up to starboard, down and aft to port. Set material condition 'Zebra' throughout the ship. Reason for General Quarters: Hostile Surface Contact."

The alarm echoed through the carrier and the rest of the fleet as sailors readied themselves as ordered. Men and women scurried throughout the ship and assumed their positions.

"Update," Yates ordered. The seaman listened into his headset for the requested information.

"We have a confirmed nonnuclear detonation in Aden," he answered. The captain exhaled, relieved.

"Maintain General Quarters," he ordered.

"Aye, sir."

19

Dust hung in the air like a dense fog and silence wove through what remained of the building. The lights in the main room flickered, and the workstations lay in charred heaps. Fire ate at the wooden furniture and feasted on the walls. The French doors, which swung outward to the main floor, had both buckled into the office, their glass panes blown out. The large monitor on the wall swung from side to side before breaking from its mount and crashing to the ground, its screen and plastic components melted and fused together.

Shaw groaned and pushed himself up from the ground. He shook his head and looked at Natalie who lay beneath him. He had done his best to reach her just as the missile thudded into the roof. He checked quickly for a pulse and exhaled in relief when he found it. Blood dripped from a shallow cut along her eyebrow and trickled into her hair. He glanced to his right, and Lincoln blinked rapidly as he came to.

"You alright?" Shaw shouted.

"I think so," he shouted back. The Ranger rubbed his eyes and gave his head a quick shake. Natalie coughed beneath Shaw and opened her eyes blearily.

"What happened?" she asked. She placed a hand on Shaw's arm, still unsure of her surroundings.

"We got hit by something," Shaw answered. Natalie's eyes tried to focus. What was he talking about? Why was he atop her?

Her memory came flooding back, and Shaw slowly rose to his feet. He extended a hand, which she gripped tightly.

"Easy," he said.

"I'm fine," she stated. Pain pulsed over her left eye, but she ignored it. Natalie pushed against one of the French doors, and it fell from its hinges. As she tried to exit, she stumbled against the wall, but Shaw grabbed her before she fell to the ground. "I'm fine," she insisted. She steadied her feet and pushed him away. He honored her wish and strode from the office onto the main floor. His eyes fell on a young woman, her lower half missing and her eyes dull. He tried recalling her name. Was it Rachel? Unable to bear the sight any longer, he looked away.

"Natalie," a man stammered. She rushed to his side, and Shaw quickly followed. Bryon Tyler shook violently and uncontrollably. "I can't see!" he screamed. "I can't see!" Charred, black skin clung to his face, and his plastic glasses had melted into his flesh. He sat against the wall. He couldn't feel his legs. He didn't know it, but they were missing above the knee. His arms rested at his sides as charred, bloody stumps. Shaw knew right away that he wasn't going to make it.

"I'm here, Bryon," she said tenderly. "I'm right here."

"Where? I can't see... I can't see you... I can't..." He couldn't move, and his voice faded as his breathing stopped. Natalie fell back onto her rear and shook her head in anguish. How could this have happened? Her stare grew blank, and her head tilted as she fell inward.

"Hale," Shaw said. She didn't respond. "Hale," he urged more firmly. She still didn't respond. "Natalie," he said tenderly. She looked at him. "You got to get up." She nodded but remained where she sat and glanced around the room. Several members of her team lay motionless on the ground, mangled with the burned furniture. The night, distorted by the rising smoke, flooded in through the gaping hole in the roof, spanning twenty feet or more. Natalie noticed the missile's impact point.

"Abby!" she screamed. The second-floor room, directly above them, in which Abby and Sotelo had interrogated Armal had vanished, like it had been sucked into a void taking the three people with it.

"Shaw!" came a shout from the courtyard. The door was missing, blown outward off its hinges. Wyatt sprinted through the opening and froze when he beheld the carnage.

"I'm here, John," Shaw replied. Speechless, Wyatt didn't respond. Natalie exhaled swiftly and rose to her feet. Something burned in her chest, a boiling sensation that spread throughout her extremities. Her entire team had been in that room, save for Abby, but that hadn't saved her. She looked over the faces of the dead, and immediate remorse seized her heart.

"We should leave," Shaw stated.

"Shaw's right," Lincoln started, "we need to leave." Wyatt's eyes met Shaw's, and Shaw responded with a sigh. Wyatt inclined his head in agreement and turned to leave. Lincoln followed him out, and Natalie, taking one last glance over the massacre, traced his steps outside.

Shaw was the last to leave, and as he stepped over the threshold, he met Reeves' gaze with a firm nod, which the large man returned.

"Headcount," Lincoln ordered.

"We're all here, save Adara," Reeves began. Blood trickled from several scrapes on his exposed arm. "Whatever hit us got him. Where's Sotelo?" Lincoln's expression confirmed Reeves' fears. He glanced down at the dirt before looking back up at Shaw. "Can you get us out?" he asked. Shaw breathed deeply, noting Reeves's desperate tone, and looked at Natalie.

"Can you?" she echoed.

"Let's get those SUV's loaded up," he said.

The three Range Rovers remained intact from the missile attack. Shaw and Wyatt outfitted Kathryn with an armored vest and ushered her into one of the vehicles. Wyatt handed her a set of electronic ear protection just in case, and she quickly set them over her ears. The electronic amplification would provide normal auditory clarity but would deafen the sounds of gunshots and explosions. Wyatt returned to her the pistol he had stored in the seatback on the ride in.

Natalie strapped the same style body armor around her torso, holstered a Glock 19 on her hip, and exited the security building. She cast one last glance toward the main building before climbing into the driver's seat of the first Range Rover. Shaw emerged from the security building with all his gear. He witnessed Natalie take the driver's seat in Wyatt and Kathryn's SUV. He watched Barone and Hogan enter the last SUV and crank the engine. He returned his attention to Natalie.

"Mind if I ride shotgun?" he asked.

"Whatever suits you," she replied bleakly. Shaw took his seat and checked his carbine. Lincoln, Reeves, Quinn, and Becker climbed into the second SUV and started the engine. Natalie pulled forward and turned the wheel toward the gate. She pressed the gate control remote clipped to the sun visor, and, as the steel doors groaned open, Natalie hit the throttle.

A man armed with an AKM, obviously surprised by the gate opening, looked inside the compound. Natalie floored the pedal and ran the man over. Kathryn yelped as the vehicle bounced over the insurgent's broken body, but she quickly regained control.

"It's even easier the third time," Wyatt remarked. She didn't respond, but he was right. It barely fazed her that Natalie had just run over that man. She knew she had cried out in surprise more than fear. Kathryn glanced down at the pistol in her hand, and she found it gave her confidence. How much had changed since yesterday morning, she thought.

The following SUVs bounced over the body and followed closely behind Natalie. Gunfire erupted around them, and the copper-jacketed bullets thudded against the armored vehicles with no effect. Kathryn shrieked and ducked her head instinctively.

Natalie accelerated through the gauntlet and turned onto the main road that led north down the mountain, leaving Al Amiri's forces scrambling and confused. Shaw's hand shot to the handle on the ceiling to steady himself as the SUV bounced over another insurgent.

"We're headed to the beach just south of Flint Island. You know where that is?" he asked.

"Yes," she snapped. "They better be there when we arrive!" Adrenaline coursed through her veins after taking the lives of two men. Honestly, it had felt good to release all her pent-up anger. She tossed her head and brushed a strand of loose hair from her face. She remembered her cut as her fingers brushed across the tender flesh.

The bullet-ridden convoy passed into the residential neighborhood that rested between their outpost and the center of the city. Leaving Al Amiri's force behind, their route would take them directly north before turning west onto Maalla Main Street. She would follow that through the large roundabout then the beach would appear on her right.

The convoy pressed on as the night yielded to the morning's faint glow. The streets were mostly clear, although they usually were, given the state of the war-torn city. The peninsula, however, seemed to have been spared the worst. They passed a hospital and Kathryn noticed a white van that had wrecked just outside the entrance.

"We're nearly there. They should be waiting for us up here on the right," Natalie said. The convoy roared through a wide roundabout and passed a large white mosque with twin spires that rose into the orange sky. Natalie turned right, and the road paralleled the bay.

"Look out!" Kathryn cried, but it was too late.

A truck smashed into the side of their SUV, lifting the vehicle onto its passenger-side wheels and forcing it through the guardrail. The Range Rover tumbled off the road and rolled down the embankment toward the sea. Gunfire bellowed from the heavy machine gun mounted on the truck's bed. The rounds thudded into Becker's SUV, and he swerved to avoid the gunfire. He didn't know how much punishment the armor would take. The former Delta operator veered into the opposite lane.

Hogan watched Becker's maneuver, glanced at Barone, and witnessed the firm resolve splashed across his face. He immediately gripped the handle and braced himself. The SUV surged forward as Barone floored the accelerator. The vehicle smashed into the truck, jostling its passengers. The gunner flew through the air, bounced on the ground several times, and skidded to a stop on the pavement leaving a grotesque blood trail.

Reeves, glancing out the rearview mirror and seeing the ordeal, tossed his machine gun behind the back seat before following it over. The large man struggled, but he finally gripped his weapon and slapped the button controlling the back door. The SEAL steadied himself and trained his weapon out the rear of the vehicle as the automated rear door slowly opened. Becker, viewing Reeves' activity through the rearview mirror, stomped the brakes and jerked hard on the wheel. The tires screeched as the SUV spun out. Reeves, with his feet spread and bracing himself within the vehicle, opened fire as the truck fell into his line of sight.

The light, swift bullets ripped through the back window, cutting down the driver and passenger. Reeves released the trigger. Blood coated the interior glass. Lincoln, Becker, and Quinn burst out of the SUV with their carbines trained on the truck.

"Becker, Quinn, check on those Marines!" Lincoln shouted.

"On it," Becker exclaimed as he and Quinn raced toward the smashed SUV. Quinn reached the driver's door and wrenched it open. Barone swayed as he came to; Quinn helped him out.

"You okay, man?" he asked. Barone blinked rapidly.

"Yeah," he replied. "Hogan?"

"I'm fine, bro," came his reply. Hogan stood relatively unfazed on the other side of the SUV. "That was ballsy."

"Worked didn't it?" Barone replied. He touched his head. "Should've been wearing my helmet." He quickly fetched and donned it.

"Incoming!" Lincoln shouted as he spotted more vehicles headed their way. One separated and bounced onto the beach headed toward the overturned SUV.

20

Within the upside-down SUV, Shaw glanced at Natalie. Unconscious, she hung limp in her seat. The rear driver's side door opened, and instinctively, Kathryn crawled out.

"Wait!" Shaw shouted, but she had already moved onto the rocky beach. A pair of sandy boots stopped her. She glanced up quickly and met the barrel of a rifle, but it moved away, and a young insurgent, maybe twenty years old, smiled devilishly at her. She knew what thoughts floated behind his dark eyes. He gripped a handful of her blonde hair and yanked upward. A gunshot echoed between them, and more followed as Kathryn repeatedly slapped the pistol's trigger rearward. The young man stumbled backward, pressing his hands against sixteen fresh wounds in his torso. He looked at her, and his eyes, wide in utter disbelief, met her gaze before he fell backwards. The others with him shouted in alarm and turned their rifles toward her.

Systematic gunfire erupted behind her, and the three insurgents died before they hit the ground. Two men rushed past her, and, fear guiding her, she snapped her pistol toward the nearest one. It clicked.

Empty.

Grateful for an empty gun, Wyatt gently took the pistol from her grip, but she refused to relinquish it until she recognized Wyatt.

"I shot you," Kathryn stammered, not realizing her pistol was empty.

"No, you didn't," he replied. She released her grip and looked past him to the dead man.

"I killed him," she mumbled, obviously shaken. Wyatt didn't know how to respond. He traced her gaze to the deceased; the four men lay in the sand, and Shaw put an extra round in each one just to be sure.

"Come on," Wyatt instructed. He helped her to her feet and guided her behind the armored SUV.

Shaw hurried back to them and tore open the driver's door. After ensuring she was safe to move, he pulled Natalie from the seat and carried her around and behind the overturned Range Rover. He set her gently on the sand, and, hovering over her, he again examined her for any life-threatening injuries. It appeared that she had hit her head during the crash, but she didn't seem to possess any other concerning wounds.

Her eyes opened, and she blinked rapidly as Shaw's countenance materialized. He smiled.

"Hey there," he greeted.

"You're beginning to enjoy this," she groaned. He chuckled.

"Maybe I am," he replied. "You okay?" Natalie brought her hand to her head and closed her eyes.

"My head is killing me," she replied. Shaw placed a hand over hers. His touch, surprisingly, comforted her, and she fought off tears as they attempted to rim her eyes. Be strong, Nat, she told herself.

"Shaw!" Wyatt called. Shaw jumped to his feet and peered around the SUV. The rest of their companions bolted toward them, sand flinging up behind their boots. At the road, two more trucks screeched to a stop and turned their guns toward the six sprinting men. Shaw and Wyatt immediately engaged. Their rounds soared toward the truck gunners, and those insurgents ducked behind the vehicle cabs. The two Raiders sustained their fire, which bought their approaching teammates precious time. The four CIA contractors and two Raiders slid into prone positions in front of the overturned vehicle and opened fire. Any advance the insurgents intended to make was halted by the Americans' aggression.

The trucks' heavy machine guns barked, but their rounds flew indiscriminately as those shooting hid fearfully behind the cabs. Some bullets arched out to sea and others thudded into the sand and skipped off rocks.

"I got to reload!" Reeves shouted. He worked quickly; they needed his light machine gun back in the fight to keep the insurgents at bay. Seizing the moment, the enemy advanced quickly. They shot their guns wildly from the hip as they moved. They needed to close the distance before Reeves got his gun back up and running. And if the truck gunners found the courage to aim, they would cut the Americans down with ease.

Despair fought for triumph as it assaulted the group's morale. With the sea to their backs, they had no place to retreat. The armored SUV provided the necessary cover, but the insurgents, if they continued their advance, would soon approach close enough to land successful and consistent hits. Even if the Americans could hold them at bay, they would eventually run out of ammunition.

"Where the hell is our exfil?" Becker shouted. He slammed a new magazine into his rifle and picked up another target. He fired four times, three found their mark, and the insurgent fell on the road.

Natalie, her pistol drawn, kneeled in the sand on the passenger side. She dropped her shoulder and leaned beneath the hood of the overturned vehicle. The space provided enough clearance for a direct line of sight. The shots were long, too long for a pistol really, but she knew they needed all the firepower they could muster. She squeezed the trigger and kept it pinned to the rear for upmost accuracy. The pistol cycled, chambering a new cartridge, and she released the trigger. As soon as she felt the familiar reset, she fired again, having already acquired her target. She couldn't be sure she landed hits, but perhaps she kept the enemies' heads down, and that was enough.

Shaw glanced toward Wyatt, who had fished his M110A1 out of the vehicle. His M4A1 dangled at his side. If anyone provided the capability for accurate fire, it was he. With his sniper rifle, he could easily drop the targets at the one-hundred-meter distance. Wyatt exhaled and fired. An insurgent toppled off the heavy machine gun, but another quickly took his place.

"There are too many!" Wyatt shouted. He looked down and to his right. Kathryn covered her head with her hands and had drawn her knees into her chest. Her shoulders shuddered, and Wyatt knew she was crying.

Rightly so, within the span of just over twenty-four hours she had endured, not just one, but two firefights and killed a man. She had already experienced more combat than the average US service member. If she came through mentally unscathed, she would emerge as the strongest person he had ever met.

As she sat there, flanked by two Marines and a CIA officer, Kathryn sobbed. Although grateful for the hearing protection, the blasts from all the gunfire still rolled over her. The sharp sounds didn't stab through her like they had on the rooftop, but each concussive shot brought a new wave of fear. It wasn't just fear of death, that fear, although very real, paled in comparison to her helplessness. Her fear flowed from the reality that if the worst happened, she was incapable of truly defending herself. Had Wyatt and Shaw not come to her aid just moments ago, those other insurgents would have killed her. Yes, she had killed one, but, without proper training and discipline, she was helpless against her other attackers.

The entire notion terrified her, yet she found relief. As she decoded her emotions, she realized that she had truly defended herself and that she did not freeze in that moment of dire necessity. Even now, she actually engaged her mind while the world fell apart around her; her mind wasn't seized by fear to the point of inoperability. She was no longer held captive by her own fear, but in control despite it. The journalist glanced up at Wyatt, she couldn't see his face because of the way he shouldered his rifle, but she imagined his eyes, focused and resolute. The thought comforted her considerably.

"We can't keep this up too much longer," Shaw said to Natalie as she retreated behind cover to reload. She glanced up at him, but she didn't need his grave expression to remind her of the severity of their situation. The heat radiating off her pistol's slide warmed her hands, but she paid it no mind as she slammed home her last magazine. She had fifteen rounds, and she had to make them count.

A guttural whine ripped through the air behind them, and tracer rounds lit up the sky like lasers as they cut through the fading darkness above the small group of Americans. A fifty-caliber, M2 heavy machine gun bellowed amidst the snarling minigun. The heavy rounds ripped through the vehicles and cut down the advancing insurgents with apathy.

Special Boat Team 20, one of the Navy's special operations units manned by Special Warfare Combatant-Craft Crewmen (SWCC), consisted of two eleven-meter NSW RIBs. Since the beginning of the War on Terror, special boat teams have extracted SEALs and other special operations units from the Tigris and the Euphrates Rivers in Iraq. The NSW RIBs, which stood for Naval Special Warfare Rigid Inflatable Boat, contained room for eight personnel in addition to the pilot and two gunners.

One of Special Boat Team 20's boats continued to fire on the enemy force while the other advanced toward the beach. Any resolve the insurgents held to continue fighting broke almost immediately. Many were shot through the back and cut in half as they attempted to flee the onslaught.

As the boat nudged against the shore, an eight-man element from SEAL Team 3 jumped off and, in a wide formation, advanced up the beach. They opened fire on the enemy while moving, and they formed a protective layer around the besieged Americans.

"Let's go!" Shaw shouted. Wyatt reached for Kathryn, but she was already on her feet. He looked back one last time toward the trucks on the road. The minigun and M2 shredded through the vehicles, and one exploded as an incendiary round penetrated the gas tank. As if that were the signal, the rest of the group broke cover and sprinted toward the boat. Wyatt jumped into the craft and hoisted Kathryn onboard. Shaw remained in the surf and provided a step for Natalie. He thrust her upward, and she latched onto Wyatt's strong arms. Shaw helped Quinn, Becker, and Lincoln aboard and remained until Reeves approached.

The second boat now simply put on a massive display of force. No threat lingered by the trucks or along the road, but they continued firing, as was protocol. They would cease only when the other boat was safely out to sea. After Reeves climbed aboard, Shaw waited for Barone and Hogan to board before reaching for Wyatt's hand.

As anticipated, the second boat kept firing until the first craft had retreated safely behind them. Once the first boat was clear, the pilot of the second boat sped toward the beach and picked up the SEALs before turning and gunning the engines to follow the other craft.

The silence was deafening once the guns ceased, and although relief spread among them, no one uttered a word. No one laughed or even cried.

They simply yielded to their fatigue. Kathryn lay against Wyatt's chest. She closed her eyes as he hugged her tight. The wind tossed his sandy hair and cooled his scalp. His neck ached from the weight of his helmet and its attachments, and he was relieved to have taken if off. He looked down at Kathryn. Her beauty stole his breath, and he couldn't ignore the pleasure he felt in keeping his promise to her.

"I told you I'd get you out of there," he said. The engines drowned out his words to anyone but her.

"I know," she replied. He could never know the extent of her gratitude, but she would do her best to show him. Her heart tingled as she considered the future, a real future. The fantasy had faded, and the reality of a life next to John loomed before her. If she was honest, it scared her as much as it excited her. What if, without the fear and stress, the quick highs and lows, they failed? One day at a time, she told herself.

Lincoln watched Quinn pat Becker's helmet and Becker, seated on the floor, reach up and gripped Quinn's hand. His gaze fell next on Reeves who cradled his machine gun and rested his eyes. No doubt, the man thought of his family back home.

Grateful to be alive, Lincoln extended his senses to feel every wave the boat crested and the breeze that refreshed him, but his mind thrust thoughts upon him. Natalie's obsession over Al Amiri had cost them all dearly. He had the power to paint her as the hero or the villain in his report. He had every right to crucify her. This he knew, but he pushed the thought away, and instead tried to focus on the steady rise and fall of the keel.

Barone and Hogan both could not believe the events of the last several hours. Their admiration for Captain Shaw had dramatically increased, admiration neither had thought could grow any higher. The same thought now ran through their minds. If Shaw was appointed a commander of a new MSOT, they both wanted to be in it.

Natalie relished the cool sea wind as it refreshed her face. Her mind, though, thought forward. She knew she would be summoned to Langley to provide account for the last twenty-four hours. Perhaps she would sit before the director; a small amount of anxiety stirred with that thought.

Shaw sat next to Natalie, and satisfaction rolled over his entire being. Not only had his body held up, he had also accomplished his mission. Al

Amiri was dead, and, although Wyatt had effectively saved himself, Shaw had avenged his brothers. Now, a name swirled in his thoughts: Francisco Silva. Who was he, where was he, and, most importantly, how could he find him? He thought of the hard drives stowed in Barone's pack. He hoped the cache would provide information to locate his next target.

PART II
THE ARMS DEALER

21

"He's ready to see you, Ms. Hale," the middle-aged woman stated. Natalie exhaled heavily and rose from the leather chair. She straightened her blazer and built up her resolve. Her fingers traced the fresh scar on her eyebrow, and she fought her nerves as she offered the secretary a smile and followed her into the large, corner office.

The unexpected summons after her return from Dubai didn't sit well with her. While the events surrounding Aden were under review, Natalie had assembled what data she could on Silva, tracked a private plane out of Aden to Dubai, called in some favors, and left to investigate. The director's timing suggested he had discovered her endeavors.

The suite resembled a library instead of an executive office. Bookcases completely concealed the walls, and Natalie figured the director couldn't squeeze in another book. It was arranged neatly though, not disheveled like other offices she had entered, and each case appeared to be categorized by subject. Floor to ceiling windows behind and to the left of the large desk showcased the green, Virginian landscape and cloudy, blue sky.

The secretary closed the twin doors behind her, and Natalie set her jaw and strode confidently forward.

"Have a seat, Ms. Hale," the man said without standing or looking up at her. She did as instructed and found the chair lower to the ground than it ought to have been. It forced her to look slightly up at the man. It annoyed her, but she didn't show it.

Director James Caldwell, wearing a gray suit and matching tie against a starched, white, dress shirt, glanced over the report before him. It contained detailed explanations from each Aden survivor employed by the CIA, including Natalie's own. He struggled to read the blurred words, but he refused to wear reading glasses. Regardless, he got the gist of what had happened. He finally looked at her.

Natalie almost shuddered under his fierce gaze, but she repressed her anxiety. He glanced back down at the reports, and she quietly sucked on her saliva glands to bring relief to her dry mouth.

"I'll start with this," he said, "I am issuing nominations for new stars to be added to the Memorial Wall." He watched her, his eyes prying for some hint of weakness, regret, or apathy. He found none of those things. She remained proud and sat upright. "Those nominations are a direct result of your operations in Yemen. Tell me, are you satisfied with the outcomes?" he asked.

"No, sir," she replied without hesitation.

"But your report indicates that Isaam Al Amiri was targeted and killed, albeit in direct violation of your orders," he countered.

"That is correct."

"So, the mission was a success?"

"From a certain point of view," Natalie answered.

"Hutchins with SOCOM staff reported that you were to relay Al Amiri's location to them so they could authorize an airstrike," Caldwell said.

"Those were my instructions," she replied.

"Indeed they were," he responded harshly. His expression hardened. "Was it worth it to disobey?" Natalie didn't know how to respond. She certainly felt that could be the case, but she would never know. Al Amiri was dead, and perhaps her team's sacrifice might prevent another major terrorist attack upon the Western world. The intelligence gathered by Shaw and his team would answer that.

"The events did not turn out as I would have hoped," she replied.

"That's the understatement of the decade." His gray eyes bored into hers. "To make matters worse, you participated in an unsanctioned operation using unapproved personnel to kill a man. SOCOM wants your head, and there is no way, on paper, to justify your actions."

"I'm sure there are many things the Agency has done that cannot be justified on paper," she countered. Caldwell's eyes narrowed; she teetered on the brink of dangerous territory, but he could see that she would not allow him to ridicule her. "The orders came from Major King in MARSOC. I was given a choice, and I chose the option that provided the greatest opportunity to capture or kill Al Amiri and secure vital enemy intelligence."

"So it seems," Caldwell responded.

A moment of silence passed between them, but Natalie remained unaffected. She kept her poised posture despite his downward gaze. The director stared at her disapprovingly, but only confidence radiated from the woman before him. He flattened his lips before continuing, "Considerable intelligence was recovered, and Al Amiri is confirmed dead. I also recognize that there was no way you could have anticipated such an attack, and I do applaud your flexibility. It is unfortunate that we lost so many talented officers. What I want to know is, how at fault are you, and did you respond to your situation in a way that is consistent with the Agency's policies?" Natalie firmed her resolve and readied herself.

Caldwell knew that had he been in her shoes he would have chosen the same option. He liked to think that any field operative would have. It was only the benefit of hindsight that urged officials within and outside the Agency to crucify her. Caldwell felt differently toward Natalie's situation, and his harsh probing had confirmed his suspicions.

She was worth keeping, but that decision wasn't up to him.

Caldwell felt Natalie held all the traits of a Cold War era officer. She displayed ruthless aggression toward her enemies. Caldwell recalled the drone footage; he and others held the belief that those insurgents were retreating, but Natalie had ordered their execution regardless of their intent. She also appeared to keep her cool in immense danger, returning fire and fighting alongside her security team, Marine Raiders, and SEALs during their extraction. At the same time, Caldwell could see she cared deeply for her fallen teammates, but that even now, she did not allow their deaths to cripple her. He saw immense value in her, and he wondered if the review committee would as well.

Caldwell closed the reports and laced his fingers together. Natalie noted his worn hands.

"This decision isn't up to me, but know that if it was, I would keep you around," he started. Natalie didn't break his gaze, and he admired her for it. "However, your little trip to Dubai wasn't as discrete as you had likely hoped." Natalie's palms moistened, and she resisted the urge to dry them on her pants. In that moment, her sweaty hands frustrated her. How had she endured Aden with such confidence but found herself nervous before her director? Deep down, she knew the committee held the power to end her career, a notion that seemed far worse than dying in service to her country.

Caldwell studied her expressions, mentally interrogating her. He knew what she had sought in Dubai. "What were you doing there?"

"Vacation, sir," she replied.

"Vacation," he murmured. Natalie immediately knew he wasn't buying the ruse. "Whether you are aware of this or not, Ms. Hale, your good reputation did not survive Yemen. Your actions in Tehran heralded you as an Agency hero, but Langley is fickle, staffed by too many who have never borne what we have endured." His eyes glimmered as he recounted his covert past. Natalie knew Caldwell's biography all too well. The vast majority of the redacted reports on his fieldwork listed operations in East Berlin before the wall fell and Afghanistan during the Soviet occupation. "We are a unique breed, Ms. Hale, willing to do and sacrifice everything for the mission." A lump formed in her throat; she did not place herself in that same fraternity.

"What happens now?" she interjected. The left corner of Caldwell's mouth curled upward. Was she nervous or simply apathetic? He couldn't tell, but he hoped for the latter. It showed strength.

"There will be a frustratingly long review process. Our agency will review the case, and SOCOM will review the case, the Senate Intelligence Committee will likely want to get their hands on it as well. We're looking at months, if we're lucky, but in the interim, I have no choice but to place you on administrative leave," he said flatly. Again, her expression didn't reveal anything he sought. It almost frustrated him, but he found himself more impressed than anything. Although collected on the outside, Natalie swirled in turmoil on the inside.

She had left the Navy for the CIA solely for the ability to do more than the military allowed. As she recounted her decade long career with the Agency, she recalled her training at what was mysteriously termed "The Farm," her first assignment in Belarus to her narrow escape in Tehran, and her most recent operations in Yemen. She hadn't lived stateside in nearly eight years. Natalie had heard the stories of the CIA tossing their people aside in such a manner as she now experienced, but she never thought that it would happen to her. However, she would endure the humiliation with grit and determination. Before she could think about future options, Caldwell spoke again.

"I know you went to Dubai seeking Francisco Silva. File an expense report, and I'll see to it that your bill is covered," he said. Natalie studied him and then slowly nodded.

"Thank you, sir," she replied.

"Of course, Ms. Hale," he paused a moment, "I'm not going to sugarcoat it; this looks bad for you. I would encourage you to begin your job search now."

"I understand, sir," Natalie replied. She hid the defeat that attempted to fill her tone.

In a brief moment, she reflected on her career. Like many, she was at first disillusioned with what operations officers were. Hollywood had taken many liberties with the so-called CIA agents in their productions. Natalie later found out that as an officer she would recruit, manage, and support foreign agents in the effort to gain vital intelligence to protect the United States. She herself wasn't an agent but a case manager of sorts at the highest level of risk and reward, life and death.

"Do you have any questions?" Caldwell asked.

"No, sir."

"Then you're free to go," Caldwell stated. Natalie calmly rose from her chair, squared her shoulders, and moved toward the door. "Ms. Hale," he called. Natalie turned. "You'll not want to miss any of your hearings." The message was clear enough. This was her last chance, and she knew that all too well.

"Of course, sir," she replied before she exited through the open door.

Natalie's thoughts whirled as she walked the halls of the Central Intelligence Agency Headquarters in Langley, Virginia. Nothing had changed for her. Silva was out there, and Natalie had already resolved to go after him regardless of the meeting's outcome. She knew a man who would jump at the opportunity to help, and she needed to move fast to secure assets before word of her administrative leave blocked her from doing so.

22

Arlington, Virginia

The green grass softened under his feet as the man strode across the field. Marble headstones rested in meticulous rows, standing at attention within the strict and solemn formation. Fog hung low, and the moisture sparkled as the morning sun cut through the mystical haze. The man stopped in front of an impeccably shaped tombstone. The dark letters honored the man beneath the consecrated soil. He beheld the cross before his eyes traced down the rest of the writing.

KYLE E

REYES

CPL

US MARINE CORPS

AFGHANISTAN

JUNE 26 1994

AUG 8 2020

OPERATION ENDURING

FREEDOM

Shaw immediately snapped his eyes upward as they watered. He placed his hand atop the stone.

"I'm sorry I wasn't there," he lamented. "I should have been." The fall breeze picked up, prickling Shaw's skin. He glanced back at Reyes' name and removed his hand. "I'm working on something though," he continued, "Francisco Silva is the name of the arms dealer who sold Al Amiri the Stingers that shot down your helicopter. I'm going to get him. For you, for York, and the rest of the guys. I promise." He paused, allowing the weight of his promise to permeate the air around him.

"And there's this woman, Natalie," Shaw continued. He grinned as he thought of her. "You'd like her. She's tough, like your Sara, and she's smart; a real fighter. I can't seem to keep my mind off her, you know?" He hesitated for a long moment as he remembered the day in Afghanistan when he risked his own life to save Reyes. How he wished he could trade places with him now. "I don't even know why I'm telling you this. I guess I know that she may be the only hope I have at finding Silva, or maybe I'm just into her, I don't know." Silence radiated from the headstone, and Shaw didn't speak for a long time.

The Raider inhaled sharply. "Your son was born. Sara wanted me there at the hospital; she let me hold him." Tears rolled down his face and into his beard. "He's a healthy little man," Shaw managed. His mind arched back to that day.

"What will you name him?" Shaw had asked Sara as he gazed upon the boy's face. He had slept soundly in Shaw's arms with one small hand pressed against his bronze cheek.

"David," Sara Reyes replied without hesitation. Shaw's face had whitened.

"No," he had answered, not sure of what else to say. Sara had smiled at him as he held her son.

"It's what Kyle wanted," she had said. When Shaw had met her eyes, it was the first time she had seen him cry. As he gazed upon Reyes' child, he had smiled.

"Hey, David," he had greeted affectionately. The Marine had never been so honored as in the moment he held David Kyle Reyes.

As Shaw's mind returned to the present, a wave of emotion rolled over him. He fell into a crouch and put a hand on the grass to steady himself. He wept for a long time. All the emotions he had buried while in Yemen and buried again to remain strong for the families of the fallen exploded from his chest. He cried for them all: York, Reyes, Beasley, Adams, Neeman, and the others he had the honor to serve beside.

Shaw recovered and wiped his face. Mucus ran into his mustache. He exhaled and turned his red eyes back to the headstone. The Marine pressed his palm against the cold marble.

"I love you, bro, and I'll take care of Sara and little David for you." He waited a moment, hoping Reyes had heard his words, before he stood and turned away. His eyes widened in surprise, and he rocked back on his heels as he gazed upon her. A smile broke across Shaw's face as he beheld the woman standing in front of him. He immediately wondered how long she had been standing there.

Her green eyes gleamed against her tanned complexion, and a myriad of freckles dotted her face in mature and dazzling beauty. The woman's dark hair, highlighted with streaks of light brown, tumbled down her shoulders in thick waves, and her slender facial features all dwelled together in perfect proportion. Her neck sloped softly into a foundation of defined collarbones that also appeared decorated with the alluring freckles.

She wore a form-fitting, black pantsuit with flared legs, which almost touched the grass, and an olive blouse with a scalloped neckline, which made her eyes glow even greener.

"Hey, Natalie," Shaw greeted. In truth, he had to catch his breath upon seeing her and hoped she hadn't noticed.

"It's good to see you again, David," she said. "I thought I might find you here." She offered him a consoling smile before shifting her eyes to the tombstone. Shaw half turned and followed her gaze.

"How did you know I was here?" he asked.

"I called Major King."

"I'm glad to know he'll just give my location out on a whim," he joked. Natalie smiled again. She noted his puffy, red eyes, and her heart ached for him. She knew the feeling all too well.

"Well, I did tell him I was on agency business regarding a matter of national security," she replied.

"Of course you did." Natalie felt a bit vulnerable under his gaze. It was the look of a man who beheld something of great worth. "So, is this a social call or business?"

"Both," she replied. Shaw nodded his head.

"How much of that did you hear?" he asked.

"Enough," she answered, wearing an excited and knowing smile.

23

Atlanta, Georgia

The morning sun breathed through the apartment window, and rush hour traffic honked below as commuters navigated their usual routes. The previous evening's clothes lay strewn about the small studio apartment at Post Centennial Park. The sun kissed Wyatt's eyelids, and he awoke, inhaling deeply. Kathryn lay nestled next to him, and his arm, fully numb, lay underneath her head. The limb slowly came back to life as he moved his fingers, and the intense tingling radiated up the extremity with each movement.

Careful not to wake her, he slid his arm out from underneath her and sat on the edge of the bed. He looked affectionately upon her and stroked her cheek tenderly. The Raider then stood and stretched his arms over his head. He moved lazily over to the large windows and gazed upon the Atlanta skyline. He really couldn't believe the location of Kathryn's apartment. From her top floor studio, Wyatt beheld the entirety of Centennial Park, the home of the 1996 Olympics. His eyes fell on the Georgia Aquarium, the World of Coke, and the Center for Civil and Human Rights. Not far in the distance, the CNN headquarters loomed, its bright red letters easily visible. He had only been to Atlanta once before and couldn't deny the energy and excitement that seemed to radiate from the city.

He turned around and smiled as his blue irises again dwelled on her. He could not deny the beauty of the Atlanta skyline, but the beauty before him stirred his heart like nothing else he had ever seen. A strand of her wheat hair lay draped across her face, which now lay directly on the mattress. Her full lips seemed to call to him. He returned to her, cupped her chin in his hand, and gently kissed her. Kathryn smiled as he pulled away.

"Hey, you," she said. Her words, like a warm melody, stirred his heart, and he found himself out of breath.

"Hey," he managed. She kept her eyes closed but offered him a wide smile.

"What are you up to?" Kathryn asked.

"I was thinking of taking a shower," he replied. Her large, blue eyes opened and gazed into his.

"That sounds nice," she said as she stretched and inhaled before yawning.

Later that morning, the two strolled through Centennial Park arm in arm. Kathryn beamed while at his side. The last two months had been surreal, and they were both delighted to find their relationship had not diminished upon returning to normalcy. They both enjoyed much needed leave from their employment. Wyatt, having lost his entire team, was placed on mandatory leave and instructed to check in weekly with an assigned shrink. He supposed the Marine Corps feared he might hurt himself, but no thought had once entered his mind.

CNN had provided Kathryn all the support the company could muster, not only did they offer Kathryn three months of paid leave, they more than compensated her for the trauma she had undergone. In addition to monetary compensation, they paid for her to see a private psychiatrist on a weekly basis. No doubt they felt she sat on the story of the year and would do all they could to keep her happy.

After Wyatt's debrief and evaluation at Camp Lejeune, Kathryn had invited him to stay with her through the duration of his leave. Thrilled, the Raider had accepted without another thought. Together, Kathryn introduced Wyatt to the best Atlanta had to offer, and so far, his favorite attraction was the Beluga exhibit at the Georgia Aquarium.

"What would you like to do today?" he asked her as they strolled. She didn't immediately answer but bit her bottom lip. "What?" he probed, wearing a smile.

"It's dumb," she answered.

"Tell me," he insisted. Kathryn smiled as she fought through the sheepish feeling. She didn't know why she felt that way; it just seemed strange to ask for such a request.

"Will you take me to buy a gun?" The question took Wyatt by surprise, but the Marine nearly jumped for joy when she asked.

"What kind of Marine would I be if I didn't?" She laughed and hugged him tightly. "Let me find a good place, and we'll head that way."

"What's this place called?" Kathryn asked as they pulled into the parking lot.

"Stoddard's," Wyatt replied. The gun store and range, found on Bishop St NW in between the Atlantic Station and Berkley Park neighborhoods and just south of Loring Heights, had met all of Wyatt's criteria. Their professional appearance, great reviews, and a large selection of self-defense firearms proved them to be the best option in the immediate area, and, to top it off, it wasn't a far drive from Kathryn's apartment.

Kathryn parked, and the two entered the brick building. Upon entry, Kathryn's eyes popped.

"I didn't know places like this existed," she said. Wyatt grinned.

"Yeah," he replied, marveling at what the store had to offer, "this place is nice." The industrial interior impressed him, and he especially enjoyed the exposed metal joists and trusses. The spacious layout pleased him as well, and the lighting highlighted the space in all the right places, which made it feel much larger. Kathryn, although a bit intimidated, found the establishment warm and inviting.

"Good morning," a man greeted from behind the gun counter. Wyatt returned a grin and headed his way. "What can I do for you?" he asked.

"My girlfriend would like to purchase her first gun," the Marine answered. Kathryn's face lit up at the mention of the term.

"Awesome," the man said. He turned his attention her way, "you looking for a rifle, a pistol, shotgun?" his voice trailed off as he awaited her response.

"A pistol," she replied. She didn't look at Wyatt for confirmation; she knew what she wanted.

"Right this way," he said.

"So I'm your girlfriend now?" Kathryn whispered in Wyatt's ear.

"If you want to be," he replied. She blushed.

"I do." She slid her hand into his as they followed the salesman to a section of the gun counter.

"I'm George, by the way," the salesmen said.

"Nice to meet you, George. I'm Kathryn. This is John."

"Great, well what kind of pistol are you looking for or should we just run through them?"

"I want a Glock 19 Gen 4," she replied. George's eyebrows snapped upward. She noted his surprised expression. "What?" she asked.

"It's just... that's pretty specific," he said. "Most girls, especially first-time shooters, don't really know what they want."

"I'm not most girls," she said with a sparkling smile.

"I can see that," George replied. He discreetly looked her over while he reached for a new Glock 19 Gen 4. Man, this John guy is lucky, he thought. She was gorgeous.

Kathryn's sapphire eyes beamed against her smoky eye makeup, and her golden hair spilled onto her shoulders in soft curls. Her turquoise top, cinched across her chest, left her shoulders bare, but it flowed loosely down her torso and over her hips. Her dark jeans clung tightly to her legs, and she had rolled the hem to expose her ankles. She wore a pair of light brown leather heels with simple straps that wrapped around her ankle and forefoot. Yes, this John guy was lucky indeed, George thought again.

George ejected the magazine from the pistol, racked the slide to make sure the weapon was empty, and handed Kathryn the firearm. As she gripped it, the memories of that day on the Aden beach poured into her mind. Her hand shook as she held the weapon, but she quickly steadied herself. Wyatt watched, concerned. He placed a comforting hand on the small of her back.

Reassured by his touch, Kathryn exhaled and tossed her hair over one shoulder. Her scalp tingled from where the insurgent had yanked her hair, and his eyes, burning with terrible desire, flashed across her memory. As she strengthened herself, the memory changed, the man's eyes shifted and filled with horror. She had defended herself, and it boosted her confidence. The journalist focused on the pistol again and flexed her fingers around the polymer grip.

"What do you think?" George asked.

"I like it."

"Have you shot one before?" Kathryn cracked a smile.

"I have," she answered, little did he know. She looked over the other Glock pistols in the case below, and her attention fell on a two-tone model. A red sales tag read $499. "What's that one?"

"It's the same thing, a Glock 19, just in a different color," George explained.

"Why's it on sale?"

"We've had that one for a while. For some reason, the two-tone models aren't as popular as the all back versions."

"Can I see it?"

"Sure," he replied. He took the black pistol from her hand and retrieved the other Glock from the bottom of the case. George handed it to her. The polymer grip sported an earthy tone and the metal slide remained black like the others.

"I want this one," she said. She looked at Wyatt, and he smiled at her.

"Great, I'll just need to see your driver's license." Kathryn looked at him, puzzled.

"What for?"

"The federal background check," he replied.

"Oh, you actually do those?" George raised his eyebrows again and glanced at Wyatt. The Marine shrugged.

"Yeah, its federal law. Of course we do them." Kathryn rummaged through her purse, retrieved her wallet, presented her driver's license, and he handed her the necessary paperwork in exchange. "Alright, fill this out, and I'll run your background check."

"How long will that take?" she asked.

"Should be instant as long as they're not backlogged or anything," George replied. He meandered off to the computer at the far end of the counter.

"You going to help me with this?" she asked Wyatt.

"Absolutely not, that's illegal. Let me know when you're done. I'm going to go look at some guns," he replied. He gave her a quick peck on the cheek and followed George down the counter while gazing at their inventory.

"Okay then," she said to herself. She glanced down at the paperwork. "How hard can it be?"

Not long after, George returned and looked over her paperwork. He filled in the necessary information concerning the firearm, logging the model and serial number.

"Alright, your background check is clear. That'll be $533.93," George said.

"How about $525 out the door?" she countered. George, a bit shocked, stared at her.

"I... uh..."

"And I'll buy this too," she said, handing him a Magpul GL Enhanced Magazine Well. At Wyatt's recommendation, the part would help guide new magazines into the pistol a bit easier and provide her a more secure grip. "I suppose we can settle at $550."

"I suppose we can," George replied. He should have said no, but he couldn't. Her confidence was too great to ignore. "Will there be anything else?"

"No, that will be all," she said sweetly.

"Alright, I'll ring you up over here." Kathryn followed him to the computer and presented him with her debit card. She caught Wyatt's eye and responded with an excited shoulder shrug and grin. He made his way over to her.

"I'm going to pick these up for her," he said. He dropped two boxes of

Federal HST jacketed hollow-point 9mm rounds on the counter and a set of Night Fision tritium pistol sights. "Could you put those on for her now?"

"Yeah, I can check with the gunsmith," George replied without looking up from the computer.

"Why do I need those?" Kathryn asked him.

"The sights that come with Glocks are plastic and will break on you. I've had good luck with these. They're a good price, sturdy, and easy to pick up for follow up shots," he explained. She somewhat followed what he said, but if he recommended it, then she wanted it. He was, after all, a MARSOC Critical Skills Operator, and he had saved her life more than once.

"All right, we're all set. Let me drop these off with the gunsmith and he'll install those sights," George said.

"Can he throw this on there too?" Wyatt asked, holding up the magazine well.

"Yeah, no problem," George replied. He took the package from Wyatt and disappeared through a door behind the counter.

After George returned and presented Kathryn with her new pistol, the duo exited Stoddard's, and Kathryn carried the weapon in its case as they headed to the car.

"What do I do with it now?" she asked, once inside her Honda CR-V. Wyatt chuckled as he buckled his seat belt.

"Buy a thousand rounds of ammo and book a training class," he replied. A smile spread across her face. That was exactly what she wanted to do.

"Do you recommend anyone?"

"Yeah, the Warrior Poet Society. John Lovell is a good guy, and he's here in Atlanta."

"Alright, the Warrior Poet Society it is. Can we do that tonight after dinner?" she asked.

"Sure," he replied. She cranked the engine and pulled out of the parking lot.

"Great, any thoughts for dinner?"

"Yeah, I could go for some good Mexican food," he replied.

"Bone Garden Cantina it is."

24

The CIA rented a simple apartment for Natalie in Reston, Virginia near Washington Dulles International. Shaw immediately assumed that she spent very little time there. Although the interior was furnished and decorated in a light, modern style, he, like most would, recognized brand new furniture when he saw it.

"You just move in?" he asked as he traced his fingers across the top of the entertainment system.

"You could say that," Natalie answered as she moved into the galley kitchen. "You want anything to drink?" she asked.

"Water's fine," he replied. He waited a moment, observing the space until she approached with a glass of ice water. "Thanks. So, what are we doing here?" Shaw asked.

"Follow me," she responded with a grin. Shaw, unsure of what to expect, followed Natalie from the living room, down the short hallway, and into the first bedroom. He stopped abruptly when he witnessed the state of the room; it was not at all what he expected. The far wall lay covered in various images, maps, and documents. On the table against the same wall sat a mess of papers and photographs. Discarded materials littered the floor, and a laptop and printer rested on the far end of the table. The entire scene reminded Shaw of his intelligence work in his team's loadout room during his search for Al Amiri.

Order existed within the room only as an individual employed by the intelligence community would see, and Shaw appreciated the sight. However, the nature of the scene nagged at him. Why had Natalie done all this in her personal residence? It didn't bother him, but he realized Natalie perhaps hadn't revealed everything just yet. His eyes fell on the large photograph centered on the wall.

"Is that him?" Shaw asked. His tone hardened at the sight of the man. Natalie nodded, and Shaw approached. "How did you find him?"

"In Dubai. Take a seat, and I'll catch you up to speed."

Dubai, UAE
Two Weeks Ago

Natalie, next in line for her turn at the customs window, gripped her luggage and readied her story should the official probe. The customs agent waved her over, and she complied. She removed her ball cap and presented her passport. The man glanced at her photograph and turned his gaze toward her.

"What brings you to the United Arab Emirates?" he asked in a relatively light accent.

"Vacation," Natalie replied. The customs agent stared blankly at her before turning his attention to the computer next to him. He didn't appear the least bit interested in her story. He clicked away with the computer mouse and then turned back to face her.

"Welcome to Dubai," he said as he stamped her passport. "Next!" Natalie smiled, took her passport, and continued through Dubai International Airport.

Tall silver pillars supported the curved roof, and spotless white floors swept through the entire interior. Light appeared to shimmer throughout the corridor casting an ethereal glow. She strolled past the central gardens and palm trees planted symmetrically throughout the hub. The woman scanned the faces holding signs near the exit and frowned when she didn't spot her name.

"We don't do that anymore," came the voice behind her. She smirked.

"That's probably smart," she replied. The man moved to her side, and she turned to greet him.

"How are you, Natalie?" he asked.

"I've been better, Ari," she replied. The stoic Israeli nodded his understanding.

"We heard what happened and extend our condolences," he said. She offered him a sad smile.

"I appreciate that, but I'm ready to get to work. I'm grateful for your assistance."

"I told you that day in Tehran that all you had to do was ask, and we would be here for you." Again, she smiled, a bit embarrassed. Ari made too much of her assistance in Tehran, Iran two years ago, but she wasn't going to turn down his help in locating Silva. "I have a vehicle waiting where we can talk more privately."

Natalie followed Ari outside the airport and into a waiting sedan. He took her luggage, loaded it into the trunk, and took the driver's seat.

"Hannah is here?" she asked.

"She is. She has talked of nothing but seeing you since you called," Ari said as he put the vehicle in gear and left the airport. Natalie smiled; Hannah was sweet.

As the Israeli drove, the two talked about life developments that had transpired since they all left Iran. His wife had received a promotion at the Knesset, Israel's parliament, and his daughter had just finished her government service and was looking to attend university. Ari's son prepared to enter mandatory government service, and he was hoping to follow in his father's footsteps and serve in the *Hativat HaTzanhanim*, Israel's elite Paratroopers Brigade.

Ari was a third generation Israeli. His grandparents had survived the holocaust and fought in the 1948 Arab-Israeli War, known as Israel's War of Independence. Since that time, his entire family had served in one war or another.

The two intelligence officers shared an interesting relationship. A slight tension loomed over what was acceptable to share and what was not. The Mossad officer, although indebted to Natalie, always maintained professional secrecy, and Natalie responded to their friendship in the same way.

"Did you find him?" Natalie asked after they finished catching up. Ari nodded, and his expression firmed.

"Natalie," he began, "I want you to know that we cannot take any action against this individual. We are here without support and are unable to help you take him."

"I understand," Natalie responded. She had hoped they would, but she had planned for that condition. "I just needed your help in locating him."

"We have done just that, and will support you, and, how do you Americans say, watch your back?" Natalie grinned.

"I appreciate that very much, Ari." He nodded. The Israeli kept his black hair short and maintained a constant five o'clock shadow. He thought it shortened his long face, but Natalie thought otherwise. His brown eyes glanced down to the tablet he pulled out of the bag at Natalie's feet and handed to her.

"This is the man from the private jet," Ari said as Natalie activated the device. A photograph populated the screen. "The plane is registered to a shell company. We've tried to locate more information but have not been successful." Natalie listened and looked intently at the photograph. The man, wearing the gold, wire-framed aviators, held a bronze complexion and maintained a pristine appearance.

"Name?" she asked.

"We don't know."

"Nationality?" she asked. Ari shrugged.

"Middle Eastern, North African, Latino, who knows," he replied. "He's staying at the Giorgio Armani Hotel in the Burj Khalifa. We've booked a suite for us there."

"What about his flight crew?" Ari nodded.

"They are staying there as well, along with two bodyguards." Natalie swiped through the photographs Ari and Hannah had taken. In each new photograph, a different young woman hung on his arm; he appeared most charismatic.

"She is one of the flight crew," Ari stated before Natalie could swipe to the next photo. She studied the scene a bit more intensely. The woman wore a tight-fitting cocktail dress and sat alone at the bar.

"How often is she there?" Natalie asked.

"Every night since we arrived," Ari answered.

"Always alone?"

"Yes, until your man comes and checks on her." Natalie chewed on her cheek as she contemplated her next move. "I know that look," Ari said. "What are you thinking?"

"I think I need to go shopping," she replied with a smirk.

25

The room appeared simpler than she thought as the duo strode inside to rendezvous with Hannah. Considering the ornate nature of the lobby and its intricate design, Natalie thought the rooms would mirror the grand vision of the Burj Khalifa, but she had to remember that the Armani Hotel simply dwelled within the impressive skyscraper, and, that in its entirety, the world's tallest building was more than a hotel.

The mini suite, sporting a modern design of sleek, taupe furniture, existed on the exterior wall of the building and provided captivating views of the oasis city.

"Natalie!" a woman squealed with delight as she rose from a table swamped with surveillance equipment and ran towards the CIA officer. The Israeli threw her hands around Natalie's neck, and with one hand Natalie returned the hug. She held her new dress and shoes in the other. "Oh, it's so great to see you!" Hannah exclaimed.

"It's good to see you too, Hannah. It has been too long."

"It has," she replied with a warm smile. Unlike Ari, she possessed more European traits. With her blue eyes, lighter hair, and olive skin, she stood in stark contrast to her colleague. She did possess a larger nose, a wide, white smile, and round cheeks, resulting in a more adolescent appearance. A Jew, she was born in Paris, and her parents migrated to Israel when she was four. Making *Aliyah*, the Hebrew word meaning *ascent* or *the act of going up*, Hannah's parents had joined almost half of the world's Jewish population in returning to their ancient, ancestral homeland.

"What do you have there?" Hannah asked, noticing the shopping bag.

"Something you'll have to help me into later," Natalie joked. "It's a bit tight." Hannah pursed her lips and tilted her head as she beheld her friend.

"That's uncharacteristic of you," she teased.

"Any surveillance updates?" Ari asked as he set Natalie's luggage by the door to the room she would share with Hannah. The young Israeli woman moved back to her station and accessed the most recent footage.

"I finally managed to tap into the hotel's security feeds, but the rooms aren't monitored," she answered.

"Will you be able to tell me where he is this evening?" Natalie asked.

"As long as he isn't in his room or left the hotel," she replied. Natalie smiled and checked her watch.

"Great, I'm going to get some sleep. I didn't get a chance on the plane, and tonight we'll find out who this guy is," she said. She was risking a lot going after a man she hoped was Silva, but she couldn't deny the trail of evidence. Still, they all could be wrong.

Natalie made her way to the bedroom from the main living area and scooped up her luggage as she entered. She hoped she would be able to sleep, but she couldn't fight the fear that she had called in her biggest favor for the wrong guy. The gamble was worth the risk, she decided.

Natalie awoke and lifted her head from the pillow. Everything blurred until her eyes focused. She checked her watch. It was almost twenty-one-hundred hours. She had slept longer and deeper than she had anticipated. She blamed the bed's luxury, the soft touch of the sheets, and the weight of the comforter for robbing her of valuable preparation time.

She set her feet on the floor and, out of habit, kept the weight on the balls of her feet as she made her way to the bathroom. She showered and focused on her makeup and hair. She parted her hair down the middle in what looked to be the latest Hollywood fashion, and she tossed it regularly to generate volume. Satisfied that it framed her face in the most alluring way possible, Natalie left the bathroom and jumped when she saw Hannah sitting on the edge of the bed. Natalie placed a hand over her heart to slow its thumping.

"Sorry," Hannah said. "You said you needed help earlier, and I heard you were up."

"No, it's okay," Natalie said. She smiled at her friend and retrieved her dress.

"So," Hannah started. The way she spoke churned Natalie's insides. She knew what was coming next. "You seeing anyone?"

"No." Her eyes traced the floor as Natalie dressed.

"Okay," Hannah replied; her long tone drew Natalie's attention as she stepped into the dress.

"I'm telling the truth," Natalie insisted.

"But you have someone in mind," Hannah countered. "Look, I don't get much girl talk on my team, as you can imagine. Come on, tell me." Natalie sighed and smiled.

"Help me into this dress, and I might tell you."

"Deal."

Natalie struggled with more difficulty to don the dress than she had in the store. Perhaps her skin was still damp from her shower and clung to the material in a way it hadn't before, but they eventually succeeded.

"I wish I could pull that off," Hannah said as she tossed Natalie's dark hair over her shoulders.

"It's shorter than I remember," Natalie replied, tugging downward at the hem.

"No, leave it. You look hot, Babe." The CIA officer looked at herself in the mirror. She tilted her head and smiled. The black, sequined dress hugged her curves in the best way possible. She did look beautiful, and she couldn't remember the last time, if ever, she had dressed up like this. "So, what's his name?" Hannah probed. Natalie chucked and exhaled.

"David."

"Does he feel the same?" Hannah asked.

"I don't know. I haven't seen him since we left Yemen." Hannah grinned, biting her bottom lip.

"You were in Yemen together? Is he CIA too?"

"No, he's a Marine." Natalie lifted one foot to slip on her black heels. "But it's nothing. He doesn't even know, and I'm not even sure if anything's there anyway." Hannah simply smiled and met her gaze in the mirror. "What?" Natalie asked. Hannah's expression held some deep sense of knowing.

"Nothing," she said as her smile widened. Natalie rolled her eyes.

"Let's get this thing started. The sooner we're in, the sooner we're out, and the sooner I can get out of this dress."

26

Named *The Lounge*, the hotel's premier bar bristled with people, and live music echoed around the spacious floor. The scene was classier than she imagined, and she most certainly stood out in her dress. It clung tightly to her body, exposed nearly the entire length of her legs, and the neckline broadcasted her cleavage in the most tempting way. She felt vulnerable but refused to show it. The dress matched the style of the flight attendant, and that was all that mattered.

She headed to the bar, which appeared cast in a faint red glow as white light reflected off the polished, wooden ceilings. Natalie saw the flight attendant at her usual place sipping a cocktail. She strode forward mustering her confidence. Some time had passed since she worked over human intelligence face-to-face, but she recalled her training with ease.

"Can I have a house martini?" Natalie asked as the bartender acknowledged her. She took the barstool next to the flight attendant and crossed her legs. The flight attendant glanced over Natalie before returning to her drink. Natalie repositioned herself and turned to face the other woman. "What are you drinking?" she asked. Given recent events, her mock, bubbly personality proved difficult to muster, but she succeeded. The woman perked up at the question.

"Lemon drop," the woman replied, over articulating the last syllable. Natalie smiled.

"I bet that's good."

"It is," she replied. Her eyes brightened as the conversation continued. "I haven't seen you around; did you just check in?"

"Yes, this morning. I'm Miranda," Natalie said extending her hand. The woman smiled and gently gripped Natalie's palm.

"Ella," the flight attendant greeted. The bartender set the martini down in front of Natalie.

"Thanks," she said. She turned back to Ella, "nice to meet you, Ella. Your dress is amazing." Ella blushed and looked at her outfit. The shimmering, ivory garment sparkled in the low light.

"Thanks, I like yours as well." Natalie smiled, noting her accent, and sipped her martini. She'd tasted better.

"I love your accent," Natalie complimented. She placed her hand on Ella's forearm. Rule one: physical touch generates connection. "Where are you from?"

"Norway," she replied. She turned and faced Natalie directly, and Natalie caught a glimpse of her earrings.

"Oh, girl, your earrings," Natalie complimented. Ella grinned and bounced her head a bit to show them off. Rule two: compliments open up conversation.

"They're my favorite," she said.

"They are stunning!" Natalie exclaimed as she reached for one. Ella turned her head so Natalie didn't have to reach as far. The gold earrings, resembling large leaves, caught the light on their polished edges. Natalie ran her thumb over the jewelry as she admired its beauty.

"Thank you. Perks of the job." Ella, her delight growing as they conversed, noticed Natalie's ears. "Oh, you don't have yours pierced?" Natalie laughed.

"I'm afraid of needles," she replied.

"Oh, I like the natural look," Ella quickly said. Natalie surmised she didn't have many friends. She appeared in constant fear of saying something that would drive Natalie away. "So, what do you do?" she asked.

"I'm in private aviation," Natalie replied. Rule three: establish professional or personal connection.

"Me too!" she squealed. "Oh my gosh, are you a stewardess?"

"I am," Natalie replied, wearing a genuine smile.

"Wow, this is crazy! I am too!" Her pitch rose with each word. "To world travel," Ella hastily toasted, lifting her glass.

"To world travel," Natalie agreed as she clinked her glass against Ella's. They each took a large gulp and laughed when they put their glasses down.

"Are you in Dubai often? Where do you normally fly?" Ella asked. The questions came so fast Natalie could only smile, and she had to fight to focus. How long had it been since she had conversed so simply with anyone? Natalie couldn't deny how good it felt to just talk.

"Mainly Europe, but we get to this area occasionally. What about you?" Natalie answered.

"Oh, I'm all over. Asia, South Pacific, Europe, South America, just about everywhere," Ella said. That was good to know. If she was employed by Silva, Natalie now knew he operated globally.

"Wow, that's amazing. Look, it's pretty lonely out there. Do you want to exchange numbers? It's not every day I make a new friend," Natalie said. Rule four: secure future contact as early as possible.

Ella nearly jumped out of her seat as excitement exploded forth. A pang of guilt struck Natalie's heart. Ella seemed like a sweet young woman and didn't deserve to be tangled in this mess, but Natalie reminded herself that she likely already was.

"I would love that!" she exclaimed. This was easier than Natalie had thought.

"We can get drinks and maybe go dancing," Natalie said. She moved her shoulders to the music. Rule five: create hope.

"Where have you been all my life?" Ella asked. She produced her phone, unlocked it, and handed it to Natalie. Natalie quickly keyed her number.

She was in.

"Shoot me a text with your info," Natalie requested.

"I will," she promised. Natalie grinned again and reached for her drink.

"He just entered the lounge," Hannah said. Natalie received the informa-tion through her earpiece but kept her gaze focused on Ella. Her skin prickled as she sensed someone staring. "He's heading your way," Hannah added.

"So, who do you work for?" Natalie asked, attempting to keep the conversation flowing as naturally as possible. Ella's gaze snapped away, and Natalie, feeling his eyes on her, turned her head to behold the man in the cream suit.

———

"Who's your friend, Ella?" the man asked. Ella tensed under his wary tone, and Natalie studied him closely. Perfectly manicured, the man from the photographs stared directly at her.

"This is Miranda," Ella replied fearfully. The man smiled, and Natalie watched the exchange.

"His men are here," came Ari's voice in Natalie's ear. Natalie fought the urge to look for them. "One by the exit and the other at your eleven o'clock, tall with blonde hair. He seems pretty focused on the girl." Natalie picked him up through her peripheral vision.

"That's a pretty name," the man complimented. "Tell me, Ella, are all your friends this beautiful?" His eyes danced down Natalie's figure, and his smile shifted. Natalie knew what thoughts ran through his mind. "It's great to meet you, Miranda. Let me buy you another drink."

"No, thank you. I don't let strangers buy me drinks," Natalie responded. She tossed her hair over her shoulder, which offered him a full view of her cleavage. She brought her drink to her lips and sipped lightly. His eyes brightened at the sight. Her breasts certainly weren't the biggest he'd ever seen, but they were perfectly proportioned with the rest of her body; his desire to touch her intensified.

"We can remedy that," the man said. He had taken the bait. "Francisco Silva, but Silva will do just fine."

At the mention of that name, Natalie's insides flared and burned with hate. She fought the desire to break the bowl off her glass and shove the sharp stem repeatedly through his neck.

"It's a pleasure, Silva," Natalie managed. Had she hid it well enough?

"See, now we aren't strangers anymore. Let me buy you a drink, and we'll see where the night goes," he said. His hand slid across Natalie's lower back as he moved to the bar. She suppressed her shudder and the urge to pull away. She forced a smile, but her mind screamed.

Silva glanced at Ella who produced a strained smile. Maybe tonight, he could have both Miranda and Ella. They were new friends after all. The thought stirred his loins, and his eyes again traced Natalie's cleavage before they rose to meet her gaze.

"Well, you don't hide your intentions very well," Natalie accused. Silva smiled and turned to the bartender. He spoke in Arabic, and the man nodded and quickly moved away.

"I'm a man who knows what he wants," Silva replied unashamedly. "What kind of woman are you?"

"The kind that requires men to try harder than that," she responded as she sipped the last of her martini. If something was going down, then vomit could not rise up.

"Fair enough," Silva replied with a smirk. She readied herself for what was coming. If she left now, it might raise suspicion. It was imperative that Ella feel comfortable enough to text or call her as soon as she was able.

The three talked and drank, and the evening tested Natalie's self-control far beyond its normal thresholds. The more Silva drank, the more he touched her. The invitations to his room grew steadily more forceful.

Before Natalie could execute her planned exit, Silva's hand shot forth with blinding speed and seized her wrist. She tensed, repressed her fear, and stared into his dark eyes.

"You're hurting me," she said softly. His grip tightened.

"Why won't you come up with me?" he countered. His words slurred together, and his other hand slid up her leg. Natalie torqued her arm against Silva's thumb, but his grip didn't break. She fought against the growing fear that welled within her as his hand traced the hem of her dress.

"Please stop," she insisted. Don't make a scene, she told herself.

"I told you I am a man who knows what he wants. Ella, convince your friend to come up with us," he said. Ella froze with fear. Natalie caught Ari moving toward the bar. Her gaze stopped him, and he diverted but kept a close eye. The interaction didn't fall on blind eyes. "Who's your friend?"

Silva asked. His words came through clear and crisp as if he hadn't ordered a single drink. His entire demeanor changed, and he glanced over at Ari who met his gaze; the Israeli's eyes bored hard with warning.

"He works security for my employer," Natalie stammered, putting on a show for him. Silva's hand shot upward and gripped the side of Natalie's neck, and his dark eyes interrogated her for the truth. Behind the sharp pupils, a beast stalked, and Natalie felt Silva's hunger permeate her being.

Ella couldn't take it anymore. Finding courage, she stood and moved to Silva's side.

"Silva, please," she insisted. She hung on his arm. "Please let her go." Natalie remained stiff in his grip.

"Why does he take orders from you?" Silva hissed, ignoring Ella altogether. The commotion drew attention from other patrons.

"Silva, please, people are staring," Ella whimpered as she tugged on his arm. Silva still ignored her and kept his gaze fixed on Natalie's eyes. His breath bathed her face as he held her. His hungry stare traveled from one eye to the other, awaiting her answer.

"Why are you not afraid?" he asked. Alarm rose within Natalie, but she held his gaze.

"What do you want?" Natalie asked. Her tone drew a smile from Silva's lips. He appreciated strength. He let her go but kept his hand on her thigh just to remind her of his authority.

"I want to know why you are so interested in my staff," he answered, turning back to the bar and draining what remained of his cocktail. He set the glass down firmly and returned his gaze to Natalie.

"Just being friendly," she replied. Again, his eyes moved back and forth between hers. "What's your problem?" Natalie asked forcibly. Silva smiled again.

"I just want the truth," he replied.

"Is this how you always treat the women you want to have sex with?" Natalie countered. Ella watched the exchange. She admired Miranda for her courage. How could she stand before Silva in such a way? She could only rationalize that Miranda had no idea to whom she was speaking or what Silva was capable of doing.

Natalie brushed his hand off her thigh and drained her drink before standing. "Ella, your boss is a dick, but it was great to meet you," Natalie said. Her comment spiked fear within the Norwegian. She moved toward Ella and kissed her on each cheek. "Bye," she said. Silva watched her go, and chuckled.

"I like your friend," he said to Ella. Ella kept her eyes focused in the direction Miranda had just taken. She couldn't deny the longing in her heart to follow her, but Silva's strong hand reached around her waist and roughly pulled her into his side, his previous warning still fresh in her mind. "Let's go," he ordered. She reluctantly fell into step with him as they left the bar.

27

Once in the elevator, Natalie leaned against the wall and exhaled heavily. Thinking of her fallen team, tears fought their way to her eyes, but she repressed them and allowed her anger to surge upward. She drove her fist into the elevator wall. Her knuckles immediately burst in pain, but she ignored it. Her skin remained intact and therefore not worth another thought.

In that moment, Natalie had never felt such compassion for an individual and such hatred for another. Her desire to end Silva's life increased with each passing second. The critical question remained.

Did Silva believe her?

If he didn't, would he destroy Ella's phone? The device's destruction would ruin the entire operation. She pushed the thought from her mind; there was nothing to do about that. All that remained was to wait for that text.

As the doors opened, Natalie removed her heels, walked barefoot down the hall, and, after producing her keycard, entered her room. Hannah rose from her chair as her friend entered.

"You okay?" she asked. Natalie answered with a wave and moved to the minibar. She grabbed the first bottle in her path and popped the top. She tossed it back and wrinkled her face as the fiery liquid descended into her belly. Natalie held the bottle out to Hannah who shrugged and accepted. A grin shot across Natalie's face as Hannah coughed after downing her gulp.

"How can you throw this down like that?" Hannah asked. She rotated the bottle in her hand and gazed at the vodka label.

"Well," Natalie said. Her head buzzed. "I was a sailor." She took the bottle back and tilted it skyward again. "I'm going to take a load off," she added. Hannah understood; she had watched the entire ordeal on the security camera. Natalie had shown considerable restraint. She must really want to nail this guy, Hannah thought as she watched her friend head toward their shared room.

With heels dangling from one hand and the bottle of vodka in the other, Natalie closed the door behind her with her foot.

Ella lay beneath the sheets with Silva's arm draped over her. She fought back tears and prayed that he would roll over. He finally did, and she quietly slipped away to the bathroom. She turned on the shower and sat down on the ornate stone floor. Her tears mixed with the hot water, and she held herself tightly. Loneliness cut through her as she sobbed.

Her thoughts then shifted toward Rian, his sweet smile and tender touch from weeks ago constantly filled her mind. Since that horrible night, she found confidence in his affectionate gaze. Whenever their eyes met, she could not refute the desire he had for her. It wasn't like Silva's. Rian's was genuine and caring, and she found that she desired more than anything to be with him.

The thought brought a fresh wave of tears. It was merely a dream. There was no way Silva would allow it. She had tried to quit already and would not do so again. Before dragging her from the bedroom, Silva had said she knew too much. She didn't even know what he did for a living, but she began to guess that his dealings did not align with the rule of law.

At first, Ella served him drinks aboard the plane and maintained the interior as instructed. The job was a dream. She traveled the world and experienced everything it had to offer on Silva's tab, and when he first invited her into his bed, she was excited. It was only afterwards that she realized he was just a dog looking for his next lay. Her inner ear still ached occasionally from the beating weeks ago.

Ella cut off the water, dried, and wrapped herself in one of the hotel robes. She crept across the room and reached for the door. The handle squeaked, and she froze. Silva stirred but quickly fell back into rhythmic snoring.

The flight attendant cracked the door just wide enough to slip through, and as she closed it and turned, she nearly screamed as the large, shirtless man surprised her in the darkness.

"Hey, it's okay," he said. She looked up at Rian Mather-Pike, and tears rimmed her blue eyes. "I retrieved some clothes for you and put them in my room. You're welcome to stay there for the night."

"But where will you..." He cut her off.

"I'll sleep out here on the couch. There's a rugby game on anyway." He smiled warmly and raised a hand to her cheek. She nestled into it, and he wiped away the tear that trickled down. "Go on," he said tenderly. She touched his hand with hers.

"Thank you, Rian," she said. He offered her an affectionate nod, and she moved past him but stopped halfway across the room. The tugging in her heart was too great to ignore.

"Rian?" she called softly. The large man turned to face her. Their eyes met, and a lump formed in the South African's throat. His heart stirred and longed for her more than ever before. He watched her hands undo the robe. She opened it, revealing herself to him. Rian inhaled to gain confidence and returned his eyes to hers.

"Are you sure?" he asked. She nodded and broke into a smile accompanied by a tear. "Ella," Rian started. He would not take advantage of her emotional state. He wanted to be with her, to connect with her on the most intimate level, but not unless she was fully invested in the same endeavor.

The robe dropped to the floor, and Ella moved toward him. His head swirled as her beauty intoxicated him. Her wet, blonde hair clung to her body, and her skin gleamed in the pale light. The sight stole Rian's breath. She placed her hands around his neck and, lifting onto her toes, kissed him. Rian inhaled deeply as their lips parted. She smiled sweetly, grabbed his hand, and led him into his bedroom.

Happier than she had been in a long time, Ella looked up at Rian. He snored loudly, but she found it cute. It was almost sunrise, and Silva wouldn't mind that she had left during the night, but he would mind if he found her in Rian's room. Despite the rational thinking, she wanted to give into the desire to stay at Rian's side. Still, she made herself get up.

She sat up and kissed Rian on the forehead before she got out of the bed. She dressed in the clothes Rian had provided and slowly and quietly closed the door as she exited. She reentered Silva's room. As quietly as possible, she retrieved her phone, dress, and shoes and made her way out of the suite to her own room. Once inside, she powered up her phone, and feeling fresh wind in her sails, sent Miranda a text. She smiled, thought again of her night with Rian, and hoped for many, many more.

That morning, Natalie emerged from her room and walked across the suite to the array of food arranged on the coffee table.

"Hungover?" Hannah asked.

"A little," she lied. The sunlight nearly blinded her and irritated her already throbbing head. She filled a plate with cheese, pastries, and fruit before moving to Hannah's side. She looked at the laptop but made little sense of the Hebrew displayed across the screen.

"Your new friend texted you early this morning. I don't blame her really. I would have."

"You did," Natalie countered. Hannah shrugged, and a smile spread across her face. "Anyway, you in?"

"Of course I'm in," Hannah replied. "We'll be able to track her phone anywhere in the world."

"Good," Natalie said. "I am thankful for all your help."

"No problem, Babe," Hannah replied. Natalie kissed her on the cheek, and Hannah reached up to touch the side of Natalie's face.

"I couldn't have done this without you."

"I know," Hannah replied warmly. The bond they forged in Tehran could never be broken, and Hannah knew she could never repay Natalie for saving her life.

Despite the difficulty and the considerable restraint required, Natalie now possessed a way to Silva. If she could, she would save Ella, but Silva was the prize. She couldn't sacrifice that for an individual. Ari entered the suite and smiled at Natalie.

"Your mission was successful," he said. His tone served as a reminder as to how close they had come to failure. It wasn't condescending but rather concerned.

"It appears so," Natalie replied.

"Don't tell your people, but Mossad has the best tracking software in the world. They will never know that we are watching them."

"Thank you again, Ari. I suppose we're even."

"No," he said, "we can never repay what you did for us in Tehran." Natalie smiled. She doubted that but wouldn't argue the point.

28

Reston, Virginia
Present Day

"The last two months have been quite eventful," Natalie continued, "While in Yemen, we learned that Silva was on site at the time of the attack against the USMC helicopters. I learned later that on the same day a private jet left Aden International with a flight plan logged for Cairo. It never arrived." Shaw followed her train of thought through the provided documents. "Instead, it landed in Dubai at eighteen thirty-two hours. The plane has jumped around since then. Spain, the UK, the Bahamas, Turkey, Kazakhstan, and now, back in Dubai." She provided the photographs, audio recording, and all additional surveillance taken in Dubai.

"What has he been doing?" Shaw asked. Natalie shrugged.

"I don't know. I'm sure he's seeing to his business, but I've been following a shipping vessel named *Vittoria Fortuna*. I believe Silva is using that ship to transport his merchandise."

"Where is that ship headed?"

"Port Tawfiq, Egypt," she replied. Shaw nodded. He fully understood the gravity of conducting an operation in that nation.

"The weapons used in Yemen were of American design," Shaw said, shifting the conversation and glancing from Silva's photograph to Natalie. He already viewed Natalie with great respect and admiration, but after hearing of her exploits in Dubai, he couldn't revere her more. "He also knew ahead of time when our helicopters would arrive in Aden," Shaw added. "That alone, suggests leaked information from a military source. The NGO reps and journalists wouldn't have known the details of the operation, especially not in advance. Do we have any updated information on that?"

"Not yet," Natalie replied. "I believe the only way to glean that information is to bring Silva in." Shaw nodded his agreement.

"When do we leave?"

"Well, I've got all the intel, a plane and flight crew, travel and insertion authorizations, weapons and gear, and all I need is a direct-action and recce element," she replied.

"I suppose that's where I come in." She nodded.

"Do you think you can pull some strings with your command?" she asked. Shaw rubbed his bearded chin as he contemplated.

"Not likely," he replied. "SOCOM isn't thrilled with what happened, nor should they be, and I'm on track for a bogus medical retirement at the beginning of the year." Natalie leaned against the table, her disappointment evident. It was in that moment, Shaw realized that she was alone. Something had happened at the Agency that had driven her to do all this in secret. "You're not alone, Natalie. Silva won't get away with this and neither will the one who leaked him military intelligence. I'm with you through this thing, and I'll see what I can scrounge up. What's our window?"

"We have three days," she replied gravely.

"I need to book a flight."

Tampa, Florida

Shaw slowed the rental as he neared the elaborate gate blocking the winding driveway. The vehicle stopped next to the white gatehouse adorned with red Spanish tile, and Shaw greeted the smiling security guard.

"Well, I'll be. Look who it is! Semper Fi, Marine!" the burly guard exclaimed. He shook his head in disbelief and rested his hands on his hips. "It's good to see you, Davy."

"You too, Lester," Shaw responded. Lester Dean was the only person in the world save for Shaw's mother that called him *Davy*. He had served under General Weber during the Gulf War when Weber was a young lieutenant fresh out of OCS. Lester went bankrupt in 2008 during the Great Recession, and Weber was quick to offer him a job as his gate security guard upon purchasing the Floridian estate. Lester had accepted immediately.

The two men shook hands through the open window, and Lester clasped his other hand over Shaw's. His wide grin showed his genuine care.

"Man, it's been years. Does the general know you're swinging by?" Lester asked. Shaw nodded. "And he didn't tell me? I'm going to have some words with him."

"I have no doubt you will," Shaw replied with a grin.

"Come on through then," Lester instructed as he stepped inside the gatehouse and initiated the gate's controls.

"Good to see you, Lester," Shaw stated in farewell.

"Rah, Captain." Shaw lifted a hand in response to Lester's wave and pulled forward.

Palm trees lined the white driveway that cut through the impeccably kept green grass of the sprawling fifty-acre estate. The white stucco house, topped with the same red, Spanish roof tiles, loomed ahead, set against the azure Floridian sky. The palm branches danced in the light breeze coming off the ocean, and gulls squawked overhead. It had been too long since Shaw's last visit.

Shaw parked the car in the circular drive in front of the house. It had six bedrooms if Shaw remembered correctly, and it was far from being considered a mansion. However, Weber and his wife had spared no expense in building their dream home. Shaw killed the engine, stepped out of the Ford Explorer, and trotted up the few steps leading toward the front door. He rang the doorbell and waited patiently for an answer.

The door swung open almost immediately, and a short woman in her sixties answered. She wore a simple dress that Shaw knew cost much more than it appeared and was probably direct from a designer in Paris or Milan. Her makeup made her look ten years younger, and her hair was meticulously styled. Regardless, Shaw's heart warmed at the sight of her.

"Oh, David," Denise Weber greeted. She quickly stepped over the threshold and hugged him gently. "I am so thrilled to hear of your recovery. You gave us all quite the fright."

"Thank you, Denise. It has been too long," Shaw replied.

"Indeed it has. Well, come inside. We are all out back, and Linus has the skeet shooting all set up."

"We?" Shaw probed.

"Oh yes, Caroline is here. I thought you knew?" Denise answered, wearing a sly smile as she wove her hand through Shaw's arm. Shaw chuckled uncomfortably as Denise patted his forearm with her hand. He led her through the foyer and kitchen before exiting the house through the open French doors, and Shaw had forgotten how fond of Weber's home he had been.

At the edge of the expansive deck, the lawn sloped gently downward toward the calm, private bay. The grass gave way to powdery, white sand in a way that reminded Shaw of a high-end golf course. Out in the crystal water bobbed a Beneteau Oceanis 55.1 yacht sporting a charcoal hull.

"Wow, is that new?" Shaw asked. The sight of the yacht stirred deep wonder within the man.

"Oh that? Yes, Linus purchased it last year. You really should join us for a sail sometime," Denise answered with an air of pride.

"That would be wonderful," Shaw replied.

"Ah, here is Linus now." Shaw watched as his mentor approached with a Browning Citori shotgun draped over his forearm.

"David, I'm glad you decided to come for a visit," Weber greeted happily. The two men embraced.

"Thanks for having me," Shaw replied. Weber smiled and issued him a short, confirming nod.

"Caroline!" Denise called. "There's someone here to see you!"

"I'm not..." Shaw started, but Denise patted his arm to silence him.

"Come now, David, humor an old woman who desires grandchildren," Denise stated without looking up at him. "It's a shame you didn't get her pregnant when you two were sleeping together all those years." Shaw flushed bright red in embarrassment.

"Denise!" Weber scolded.

"Oh stop it, Linus. You've said the same thing yourself," Denise replied wearing a satisfied expression that dared him to protest again. Weber glanced at Shaw, who scratched the back of his neck and smiled sheepishly.

"Who is it?" Caroline called, refusing to look up from her book. She sat among the patio furniture with her blonde hair tied up by a multi-colored scarf. She propped her bare feet up on the adjacent chair and curled a loose strand of hair with her fingers as she read. She wore a pair of high-waisted denim cut-offs that exposed the full length of her bronzed legs, and her white bikini top peeped through her white, sheer tunic.

"Why don't you come see for yourself," Denise countered. Caroline exhaled and shot her gaze toward her mother, and her eyes immediately widened.

"David!" she exclaimed. Her tone exploded with surprise, uncertainty, and confusion. "What... what are you doing here?" she asked as she tried to control her whirling emotions. She closed her book and attempted to better cover herself as the three approached. Caroline recognized immediately that Shaw was just as surprised to see her as she was to see him, and she quickly shot her mother a disapproving look. However, Denise simply smiled and transitioned her gaze from her daughter to the man she desperately prayed would be her son-in-law.

"Hey, Caroline," Shaw greeted. He would be lying to himself if he said he didn't feel anything as he looked upon her, but he also couldn't deny the way he felt for Natalie. It didn't make sense. He and Caroline possessed years of connection while his relationship with Natalie extended back only two months, and, during that time, he had hardly spent a full twenty-four hours with her. How did he know if there was even anything reciprocated? Their relationship had been entirely professional thus far, but he couldn't ignore the pain he felt from looking at Caroline.

"Can I get you something to drink?" Weber asked.

"I made lemonade," Denise chimed.

"That would be great," Shaw replied. Denise smiled warmly.

"Why don't you sit down? Come, Linus, please help me in the kitchen," Denise said. Weber rolled his eyes before they settled on Shaw's, and Shaw witnessed the apology behind the light irises.

As the couple disappeared into the house, Shaw turned to regard Caroline who was now standing before him.

"Hey," he said.

"Hey?" she echoed critically. Shaw chuckled and rubbed his face before casting his gaze out to sea.

"Listen, I didn't know you were going to be here," he said, shifting his sight back toward her. Caroline scoffed and tilted her head.

"After all this time, this is how you start things?" Shaw sighed.

"You look great," he said. Her expression immediately softened.

"I'm really glad to see you," she said. "I would have visited you in the hospital, but I didn't think you wanted to see me."

"It's alright," he replied.

"I'm glad you're okay."

"Yeah, me too," Shaw said. They stood in silence for a time, and the awkwardness was too great for each individual to bear. "They sure are taking their time with that lemonade," Shaw remarked. Caroline laughed and nodded her head.

"That's Mom for you," she replied. Shaw grinned at her.

"So, what are you reading?"

"*Seven Pillars of Wisdom*," she answered.

"One of my favorites," Shaw replied. Caroline glanced down at the hardback resting on the table.

"I know," she said. "Do you want to sit down?" Shaw took the seat to which she directed. "Your hair has gotten long, and your beard too." The Marine captain grinned again and stroked his beard.

"Yeah, I could probably use a trim."

"No, I like it," she replied, drawing a wider smile from Shaw's lips. She grinned back, propped her feet back up on the chair, and kept her eyes fixed on him. Her emotions began to settle, and she remembered fondly their relationship. They were together from 2011 to just last year and had talked many times of marriage and children. She wanted two, but Shaw had wanted four. In the end, Caroline had ended things claiming she was second to the Corps. Shaw couldn't blame her as his deployment schedule only increased as the years went by. He didn't know it, but she had come to regret that decision.

"Are you seeing anyone?" she asked. Shaw chuckled again and rubbed his forehead before looking again toward Weber's yacht.

"No," he replied. "You?" Caroline shook her head.

"I heard you are getting out. Is that true?" she asked. Shaw exhaled noticeably, the question stirring up painful emotions.

"Um, yeah. It is."

"I heard Daddy did all he could for you. I'm sorry."

"It's alright. Got to happen eventually; might as well be now," he replied. Caroline contemplated his words. She was thirty-two, and he was thirty-seven. It wasn't too late. Perhaps, just maybe, they could pick things up where they left off. Before she could ask, Denise and Weber returned from the kitchen.

"Hello, you two," Denise greeted warmly. She presented Shaw a glass of lemonade first before serving her daughter.

"Thank you," Shaw said.

"I got the clays all set up," Weber stated. "You up for a round?"

"Linus, let the two be," Denise interjected. Shaw took a sip of the lemonade as he rose from his chair.

"That would be great, sir," Shaw replied. He set his glass on the table, and Weber clapped him on the shoulder. He bore a wide grin.

"I'll see you soon," Shaw said to Caroline.

"Okay," she replied warmly. Denise and Caroline watched the two men descend the porch and head toward the designated skeet field of which Weber was immensely proud.

"So, how did it go?" Denise asked, wearing a confident and self-satisfied smile. Caroline smiled, donned her sunglasses, and scooped back up her book. However, over the top of the pages, she kept her eyes fixed on the only man who had stolen her heart.

29

Dubai, UAE

Affré paced back and forth as he contemplated his next move. His and Mather-Pike's conversations over the past two months had done nothing to ease the dreadful feelings about proceeding. Mather-Pike was more than ready to take the plunge, and, if Affré was honest with himself, he didn't know why he wasn't. Was it because he considered Silva a friend? Or was it simply the act of betrayal that sat sour on his tongue?

The former Legionnaire rapped his cellphone against his open palm and conversed to himself in Moroccan Arabic. The language comforted him and reminded him of his mother who had passed away when he was a boy. He imagined her voice saying the words, guiding him to the right path forward.

It was late, nearly three in morning, but it was the only time Affré could truly be alone with his thoughts. Mather-Pike was asleep and so was Silva, and Affré enjoyed the warm breeze while on the suite's narrow balcony. He hadn't spoken with her in a long time. How would she react to his call? Was her help worth digging through the garbage it would bring? He forced himself to stop worrying and dialed the number. He hoped she hadn't changed it. It rang several times, and he contemplated hanging up with each ring.

"*Oui?*" came a woman's tired voice.

"*Bonjour,* Gisèle," Affré greeted. The line immediately ended, and Affré simply stared at the phone. He likely deserved that. He redialed the number. It connected almost immediately.

"What do you want?" she asked harshly.

"It's good to hear your voice," Affré said. He meant it.

"Who do you think you are that you can call me at such an hour?" Gisèle snapped.

"I need your help." His tone caught Gisèle off guard. She had only heard him speak that way once before.

"What is it?" she asked. Affré smiled at the concern in her voice. Faithful Gisèle LaRue.

"Can you help me or not?" Affré asked. Gisèle LaRue, Affré's old partner at the DGSE, France's CIA equivalent, bit her bottom lip as she contemplated Affré's request. He sounded on edge, unsure. What had happened? She sighed.

"Yes," she replied.

"Can you set up a shell nonprofit centered on wildlife conservation named the Wild Planet Foundation?" he asked.

"What? Why?"

"I'll make it worth your while, I promise. I just need this done," he said.

"Alright, I'll do it, but you can never ask anything of me again. Do you understand?' Affré smirked, and she heard the associated exhale through the speaker. "Are you going to be okay?" she asked. Affré took comfort in her concern. "I've got a place where you can lay low if you need."

"You are too good to me, Gisèle."

Affré was amazed at how willing she was to help him despite the way he had ended things with her. He was sure the paperwork she had to fill out and the hearings she had to attend in response to his unsanctioned departure from the Agency nearly drove her insane, but he regretted breaking her heart even more. Thinking on the events, he would do it again if it meant saving her life. He always knew he would have regrets in life, and he felt confident that he had chosen the path that resulted in the least amount of pain for those he loved and for himself. He longed to explain everything to her, but it was impossible. He turned his mind back to his immediate needs.

"Thank you, Gisèle. *Adieu, mon amour.*" The finality of his farewell shocked and surprised her, but he terminated the call before she could respond.

"Pull!" Weber shouted. Shaw pressed the button to activate the clay launcher, and Weber's shotgun snapped upward and thundered. The shot disintegrated the bright orange disc, and Shaw, on cue, triggered the second launcher. The following clay disc flew from a different direction, but Weber placed his shot well. The fine orange dust gently floated toward the ground. Weber wore a satisfied smile as he broke open the over-under shotgun, ejected the two spent casings, and turned to face Shaw.

"You were a bit quick on that second clay," he critiqued.

"Didn't seem to faze you, sir," Shaw replied. Weber smirked and looked back over the field.

"No, it didn't." He turned back to face Shaw. "I heard about your hearing in Quantico. That was quite a mess."

"Yeah, it was," Shaw replied.

"I love you like a son, but you give me the biggest headaches sometimes." Weber laughed as he finished his sentence. "Do you realize the amount of paperwork you and Major King landed on my desk?"

"I can imagine." Weber chuckled again at how nonchalant Shaw's words sounded.

"But that intelligence cache was something else," he added. He glanced down at his open shotgun, grasped two new shells from his vest pocket, and loaded them into the gun. He opened his mouth to speak as he snapped the breechloader closed, "Possibly the biggest find since the bin Laden raid. It'll have us busy for the next ten years." Shaw's expression saddened. Weber took note and placed a hand on Shaw's shoulder. "I didn't mean to…"

"I know," Shaw said quickly, "but I didn't come to talk about the hearing." Weber furrowed his brow and lifted his chin as he awaited Shaw's next words.

"Caroline then?" Shaw chuckled and shook his head.

"I need a team," he said.

"A what?" Shaw remained silent and let his words sink in. "What for?" Weber probed.

"I'm going after the man responsible for killing my men," Shaw answered.

"You're what?" Weber's voice dripped with disapproval. "I think you need to let this go, David. We're all mourning, but you're taking this thing too far."

"I can't," Shaw stated firmly. Weber sighed and shook his head.

"Who are you talking about anyway?"

"Francisco Silva, the arms dealer who provided the Stingers and intelligence about the operation to Al Amiri," Shaw answered.

"I was not aware that we had unearthed that information. Who are you working with?"

"The lead CIA operations officer from Yemen, Natalie Hale," Shaw answered. Weber bobbed his head in contemplation.

"And the CIA doesn't have a team to tackle this?"

"I requested to be involved, and I figured we would want a shot at this guy," Shaw said. It wasn't the truth, but it wasn't entirely a lie either. He figured Weber would do the same if their positions were switched.

"You're not wrong. Where is he located?"

"Suez."

"That complicates things," Weber remarked. Hope welled up within Shaw as Weber considered his request. "Your unorthodoxy kills me. I guess that's why you fit so well in MARSOC. Hell, you helped set the culture back in Det One." Weber sighed, obviously torn. "Are they going after him anyway?" Shaw nodded.

"I am too, but I'd like to have Raiders beside me. You can understand that, sir."

"I do," Weber replied. A long silence followed as Weber chewed on the inside of his cheek. He gazed into Shaw's hard eyes and nodded repeatedly as he made up his mind. "Alright, but I want all operational details run by me. No more going behind my back, got it?"

"Yes, sir," Shaw replied, beaming with satisfaction. Weber clasped him on the shoulder again before handing him the shotgun and taking the launcher controls.

"Alright, enough of this. Let's see what you got." Shaw grinned and stepped up to the firing position.

"Pull!"

"You're sure you won't stay the night?" Denise asked. Shaw smiled but shook his head.

"There are some urgent matters that require David's attention," Weber said. Denise did little to hide her disappointment and shifted her gaze toward her daughter.

"I'll walk you out," Caroline said, to her mother's approval. Shaw turned, embraced Weber and Denise, and followed Caroline from the porch and into the house. She led him through the front door and down to the rented Ford Explorer. Shaw pulled the keys from his pocket, and the vehicle's lights flashed as he pressed the unlock button.

"David," she started. He sensed the longing in her tone, and it stirred old emotions within him. He turned to face her, and she closed the gap swiftly and kissed him lightly on the cheek. "It was really good to see you," she said as she sank down from her toes.

"Yeah, you too," he replied. She smiled sweetly and touched the edge of the car door as he opened it. She guided it closed, and Shaw rolled down the window. She rested her arms in the opening and gazed at him.

"Come back when you get out. Maybe we can pick things up where we left off," she offered. Shaw forced a convincing smile and nodded his head, unsure how to respond. She had hurt him far worse than she knew.

Caroline patted the SUV and backed away. She folded her arms low across her torso and watched him throw the vehicle in gear. She waved, shyly, feeling a bit foolish over her words, but Shaw smiled and returned her wave before taking off down the driveway.

As the gate to the estate closed behind him, Shaw scooped up his cell phone from the cup holder in the center console.

"Yes?" Natalie answered. The hope and excitement in her tone drew a swift smile across his face.

"You got your direct-action element," Shaw congratulated.

30

Atlanta, Georgia

"What is it?" Kathryn asked as Wyatt hung up the phone. She leaned on his shoulder as he sat on the edge of the bed. He turned his head to look at her.

"Duty calls," he replied solemnly. Kathryn straightened, and her face creased in confusion.

"But you have another month of leave," she protested.

"Not anymore." Although frustrated and upset, Kathryn secretly delighted in Wyatt's sadness. She recognized that he didn't want to leave, and she cherished that thought. As she looked at him, everything in her stirred, longing for him. It was unlike anything she had ever experienced. Although the emotion ran deep, a strong and willful dedication to Wyatt had emerged as the relationship's cornerstone. From their conversations, she knew he felt the same way.

"When do you leave?" she asked.

"As soon as my ride gets here," he answered. He stood and glanced around the small studio for his bag.

"Your ride?"

"Yeah, my flight leaves out of Dobbins Air Base."

"Dobbins?" Her mind whirled. To leave from Dobbins was quite unusual for a Marine halfway through mandatory leave. "Where are you going?" Wyatt raised his eyebrows as he contemplated how much he could or should tell her. He figured his first destination wasn't off limits. Then again, she was a journalist. He gave in.

"Andrews," he replied.

"In D.C.!" she exclaimed. Her excitement poured out more than her disappointment. Wyatt smirked. It wasn't the location that excited her, but the haste of everything. She was certain the CIA was involved.

"Yeah, that one."

"You have to spill to me," she insisted. Wyatt shook his head.

"You're a journalist," he simply replied. She grinned.

"I guess that's fair." Kathryn wrapped her arms around his neck. She kissed him, and he hugged her tightly. "Do you know when you'll be back?"

"I can't say," he replied. She raised one eyebrow.

"Won't say or don't know?" Wyatt laughed.

"I don't know, but I will come back," he promised. Kathryn didn't respond, but simply rested her head against his shoulder. He squeezed her tightly, and she returned the hug. Wyatt inhaled deeply, committing the sweet smell of her hair to memory.

"I love you," he said. Her heart leaped into her throat as it fled the tickling affection. She felt it and knew he felt it, but to vocalize it seemed so surreal.

"I love you too," she replied. It felt so easy to say, so effortless. She looked up at him and melted as she gazed into his eyes. Their lips met, and they fell into the bed.

Joint Base Andrews, Maryland

Shaw stood on the tarmac at Joint Base Andrews as the cargo plane's rear door groaned open. Wyatt stood dressed in jeans and a quarter-sleeve, baseball shirt with his duffle bag slung over one shoulder. The Raider grinned when he saw Shaw waiting for him. His skin prickled as the cold,

Virginian wind raked across his exposed flesh. It was colder than Atlanta, and he wished he had packed a jacket.

"I should have known you were behind this!" Wyatt exclaimed as he approached and embraced the man.

"Sorry to have ripped you away from your leave," Shaw said, wearing a wide grin.

"Yeah, you don't know the half of it," Wyatt replied. Shaw clapped him on the shoulder and led him into the hanger behind him. "So, what are we doing here?"

"I'll let the boss fill you in," Shaw stated. As they passed into the shade of the hanger, the Gulfstream private jet stole Wyatt's attention.

"You remember Natalie," Shaw said as the two approached her.

"It's good to see you again, Wyatt," Natalie said.

"Hello, ma'am," Wyatt greeted as he grasped her outstretched hand. "If you don't mind me asking, what are we doing here?"

"We're going after Silva," Natalie replied. At the mention of his name, fire erupted behind his eyes. "That's what I like to see," Natalie remarked after witnessing his resolve. "Get acquainted with your gear. David put together a case for you. Briefing is at fifteen-hundred hours, and we're wheels up at sixteen-hundred."

"Yes, ma'am," Wyatt replied. Wyatt waited until she walked away before turning to Shaw.

"So, you two on a first name basis now?" he teased.

"Go check your gear," Shaw responded in like manner. He followed Wyatt to his kit and briefly turned his gaze back toward Natalie. She stood next to a large white board with posted portraits and satellite images. Despite the challenge arrayed against them, he cracked a smile.

Finally, everything was in place. The terrorist was dead, the arms dealer was not far behind, and his body truly felt up for the challenge. For the first time in months, Shaw found himself content in his direction.

Over the Atlantic Ocean

The Gulfstream jet's exterior lights blinked in stark contrast to the dark night. Shaw watched their rhythmic pulsing through the window to his left. He faced the rear of the aircraft, and he relished the comfort of his seat. With its clean lines and leather chairs, Shaw couldn't deny that traveling on the CIA's dime had its benefits.

Wyatt slept, but Shaw's mind kept him awake. The opportunity to discover who leaked the Marine flight plans to Silva proved too stimulating.

"May I join you?" came the soft voice to his right. He glanced up at Natalie's smiling face.

"Of course," he replied. "I thought you were asleep."

"No, I can't sleep." She brought her braided hair over one shoulder as she sank into the seat.

"How are you doing?" he asked.

"I guess I'm doing okay," she replied. "I just keep going over the plan." Shaw chuckled.

"I get that." A moment of silence passed between them.

"Have you been to Africa before?" she asked him.

"Yeah, a few times, but on military transport. I know you must do this type of thing all the time, but I could really get used to this."

"It beats the cargo planes I used to fly on while in the Navy," she said. Shaw's eyebrows perked up.

"You were in the Navy?"

"Yeah, in intelligence," she replied.

"Fitting," he said, wearing a grin. Natalie returned his smile, and she drifted her gaze out the window as silence grew between them.

"Silva," Shaw finally said, "what's he like?" Natalie sighed.

"Probably not like you imagine. I can't seem to shake that hungry look behind his eyes," she answered. Natalie looked down and traced her eyebrow with her fingers. Her scar reminding her of the events in Yemen and the actions of the man seated before her.

"Is he a fighter?"

"Yes," Natalie answered boldly, of that she held no doubt. She looked up at him, and his stern gaze caught her off guard. He was preparing, she real-ized. "I need him alive," she quickly said.

"I know," he replied. His countenance didn't change.

"I will get him alive," she added.

"I know," he said again. However, he didn't know how he would react until he laid eyes on the man. Would he immediately place three rounds in Silva's chest? He liked to think he was more professional than that, but some things ran deeper than professionalism.

Camp Lemonnier, Djibouti

"Welcome to Camp Lemonnier," Natalie stated as the aircraft touched down.

"Déjà vu," Wyatt muttered as the plane rolled to a stop. Shaw main-tained a grim expression. The last team of Marines that deployed out of this base all died in Yemen, save for Wyatt. It was a stark reminder of the dangers of their profession and the unbearable loss they had endured.

As the two Marines stepped onto the tarmac alongside Natalie, a SUV rolled to a stop in front of them. The driver's door opened immediately, and a man dressed in a United States Navy uniform quickly strode towards the three newcomers with a hand outstretched.

"Officer Hale, welcome on behalf of Captain Evan Pierce, Base Commander," the lead sailor greeted. She took his hand and glanced at his nameplate.

"Thank you, Petty Officer Jones," she replied. "My colleagues," Natalie added, turning to regard Shaw and Wyatt. They each shook hands with the sailor and nodded cordially.

"I'm here to transport you to your assigned location," Jones said.

"Lead on," Natalie replied. The three climbed into the SUV. Jones, having left the vehicle running, shifted gears and sped away.

Wyatt suppressed uneasy emotions as they slowly rose within him, and he was grateful for the short car ride. He recognized the staging ground immediately; and smiled when he saw the familiar M81 camouflage of fellow Marine Raiders. Two MSOTs mulled about two MV-22B Ospreys. The vertical take-off and landing (VTOL) aircraft resembled a cross between a helicopter and a turboprop airplane. Two short wings extended outward from the fuselage, and two, massive, rotating props fixed to the end of each wing allowed for the aircraft to take off like a helicopter but fly like a plane once in the air. An Osprey allowed the Marine Corps to carry twenty-four Marines and travel five times farther in half the time than a standard military helicopter.

"This is bigger than I thought," Wyatt whispered to Shaw. Wyatt received a grin in return before Shaw opened the rear door and stepped outside. Petty Officer Jones shook Natalie's hand again, waved farewell to Shaw and Wyatt, and returned to the driver's seat.

Natalie proceeded confidently forward, and Shaw and Wyatt fell in step behind her. One Raider approached as she neared.

"Officer Hale, welcome," Captain Heckman greeted.

"Captain, thank you for getting here so quickly," she replied. They shook hands, and her grip impressed him. Applause erupted behind them, and Natalie turned to behold the praise.

A chorus of hoots celebrated Wyatt who bore a sheepish smile. He didn't want to smile, but he couldn't help it. He always had a hard time controlling his facial expressions anyway, but amidst their praise and the numerous pats on the back, Wyatt could only think of his team, of York, Reyes, and the others.

Natalie turned back to Captain Heckman and said, "I didn't know I was bringing a celebrity." Heckman grinned.

"Yeah, we're a small community. Word got around of his survival in Yemen, and if Shaw wasn't already enough of a legend, having helped found MARSOC and all, he is now. I don't think the boys have recognized him yet."

"Dude, that's Captain Shaw," a Marine exclaimed.

"No way, man, Captain Shaw is retiring, he wouldn't be here," another Marine countered.

"It's him," a familiar voice echoed. Shaw smirked as he beheld the man.

"Hey, Barone," Shaw greeted. The two embraced, and Shaw offered

Barone a solid pat on the shoulder. Barone was new to the team, but that action had elevated him up a few notches. "Hogan here?"

"Right here, Boss," Hogan replied.

"Good to see you too, kid," Shaw said as he moved to embrace him as well. "So, you got stationed at Camp Lejeune?"

"It's where the best are," Hogan replied with a smile. He turned to Wyatt, "what's up, bro?"

"Hey, man. Good to see you again," Wyatt replied. It felt good to reunited with the men with whom he had bonded during such a pivotal mission. The rest of the team, unaware of Barone and Hogan's involvement in Yemen, wondered at the connection. The specific details surrounding the Aden operation was classified at the highest levels, but the rest of the team, knowing the gist of what had happened, began to put together the missing pieces.

"You guys ready for round two?" Shaw asked.

"Rah," they both said in union. Shaw got the feeling they didn't know the whole story behind Silva. It was probably better to keep it that way.

"Captain Shaw, Staff Sergeant Wyatt," Captain Heckman called. Shaw had not met Captain Heckman before, but he knew a bit about him. Unlike Neeman, Heckman embodied the cowboy nature of a Raider, having transitioned to MARSOC after a stint commanding in Recon.

Shaw and Wyatt strode over to meet him. They exchanged greetings, shook hands, and briefly acknowledged roles within the op.

"Captain Lopez and I've got full teams here, Shaw," Heckman began.

"No need, Heckman," Shaw started, cutting him off, "we're here as a CIA attachment, nothing more. I'll explain more during the brief." Heckman nodded, a bit relieved. Captain Lopez strode over from a long row of packs and weapons lined up neatly across the hanger floor. Shaw, Wyatt, and Natalie all shook his hand.

"Let's get this brief started, Captain," Natalie urged the two officers.

"Alright, listen up!" Heckman shouted, gaining the attention of each Marine Raider.

31

Inside the hanger, a large monitor displayed a mirror image of Natalie's laptop, and the group of twenty-eight Marine Raiders sat arrayed around the screen and looked upon the satellite image with stern gazes. Shaw stood to the right of the monitor with Wyatt; Natalie stood to the left.

"We're all familiar with what happened in Yemen two months ago. Today, we have the opportunity for some pay back," Shaw started. The surrounding Marines issued solemn nods in agreement. "Major General Weber will serve as TOC for the op, callsign Sage. Staff Sergeant Wyatt and I will be deploying as a recce team on site for target identification and over-watch. Officer Hale, here, will be serving as our TOC in country, callsign Ozark." The two separate MSOTs, with notepads open and pens ready, listened intently. "Captain Heckman will lead Bravo Team, and Alpha will be led by Captain Lopez. As usual, each team will be split into two squads led by their element leader." Shaw turned toward the monitor.

"At thirteen-thirty we'll arrive in Suez, Egypt at the target location. It's one of the country's largest port cities. Once on the ground, we will secure the target's location, and both teams will commence their infiltration on Ozark's command," Shaw continued. "From there, Alpha One and Bravo One will serve as the primary direct-action force," Shaw stated, "while Alpha Two and Bravo Two will hold the perimeter and secure our E&E

once we nab the target. Natalie?" Shaw turned to regard her and took a step back as she stepped forward.

"The target is Francisco Silva, a known arms dealer, who is confirmed to have supplied the weapons used in the attack against US personnel in Yemen in August," Natalie said. The image on the monitor shifted to display a picture of Silva.

"Silva is the priority mission objective. Secondary objectives are to locate and recover any intelligence on site," she explained. "We believe Silva, in addition to his two bodyguards, will likely possess a security detail. We've got satellites in orbit over Egypt for the next seven hours, and the Egyptian *Mukhabarat* has offered their cooperation. Our recce team will be meeting one of their officers in country. Our intelligence comes from a reliable source, who indicates Silva's next destination is indeed Suez. We believe he will be at Port Tawfiq, but we will relay new intel to you as it becomes available."

"Thanks, Natalie," Shaw said once she finished. "For consolidation purposes, your transports, the MV-22B Ospreys, will be armed with Hydra rockets for aerial fire support. We don't anticipate that level of resistance, but we aren't taking any chances here. There is no room for failure," Shaw finished. He met the gazes of the men seated before him. "To recap, once we identify and confirm the target, Sage will authorize a thirty-minute window of opportunity to grab this guy. Sync your watches now." The Raiders all checked their wristwatches to ensure accuracy and looked up when finished.

After receiving a nod from Shaw, Captain Heckman rose from his seat and turned to address the group. His silhouette covered the monitor, and he gripped the top of his plate carrier with both hands.

"Lopez and I have agreed that Bravo One, which I will be leading alongside Gunnery Sergeant Alday, will serve as the HQ element on the field. As a contingency, should Bravo One be compromised, Captain Lopez with Alpha Two will assume operational authority. Rah?"

"Rah," the Raiders echoed.

"Alright then," Heckman said, capping his hands together, "let's roll." The twenty-eight Raiders rose, moved to their gear, and made their way out of the hanger. Heckman scooped up his helmet, offered Shaw a pat on the shoulder as he passed, and followed his men out of the hanger. Shaw watched him trot away before turning to Natalie.

"I'm glad to hear your contact came through for us," he said.

"Yeah, me too," Natalie replied. She thought of Ella and the text she had sent inquiring after their next destination under the guise of wanting to meet again. Desiring to grow their budding friendship, Ella appeared to be all too eager to reveal Cairo as her next stop. The Israeli tracking software would confirm the jet's trajectory once it was airborne. Cross-referencing *Vittoria Fortuna's* navigational trajectory with Cairo proved effortless and pointed solely to Port Tawfiq in Suez.

"Shall we?" Wyatt said as he approached.

"Lead on," Natalie replied.

Over Africa

Mather-Pike watched Ella serve Silva his drink. She quickly turned and came back his way. They had left Dubai not thirty minutes ago bound for Cairo. Silva wanted to personally inspect the next shipment of merchandise coming in for his new client. The leaders of Hamas' militant wing, the Al-Qassam Brigades, in the Gaza Strip had reached out after hearing about the success in Yemen, and Silva was happy to oblige.

The private jet's roar remained faint inside the luxury interior, but Mather-Pike hoped it would be loud enough to drown out his conversation. Ella knowingly smiled at him as she passed, and the large South African rose from his seat and followed her into the stewardess compartment.

"Rian, what are you doing?" she asked, a bit alarmed.

"I need to speak with you," he said. She looked fearfully behind him at Silva. The Spaniard sipped his cocktail and kept his gaze on his laptop.

"Be quick about it," she whispered.

"I can get us out," he said. The statement completely rocked her back on her heels.

"What are you talking about?" she asked. Mather-Pike glanced behind him at Silva; he remained fixated on his computer. The South African's insides turned over as he found the courage to speak.

"I want to be with you, Ella, and I can get us both out of here." Ella flushed and looked into his blue eyes.

"Okay," she said quickly. Mather-Pike's face erupted into a smile.

"Okay, great," he replied. "Great, okay," he said again. Ella smiled; he was cute. Their interactions had been a bit awkward since their night together two weeks ago. Neither knew how to proceed, but they both still longed for each other. Soon, Ella hoped with more hope than she had ever before mustered. Rian's question had breathed new life into her future, just as their passion in Dubai had.

Mather-Pike turned and matched Affré's gaze. He nodded and Affré rolled his eyes. The man, as hard as he tried, was not discrete.

"Something you care to share, Mather-Pike?" Silva asked.

"Just signaling to Affré that the stewardess will bring him his tea," he said. At least he is quick on his feet, Affré thought. Silva stared at him for a moment. It was new, unexpected, and that unnerved him.

"You're ordering tea for Affré now?" He cut his gaze to Affré who sat across the cabin to his left. The Frenchman didn't regard him. Silva closed his laptop, narrowed his eyes, rose from his seat, and moved toward Mather-Pike. The South African tensed, ready to smash the man into the floor, but Ella pushed past carrying a cup of hot tea.

"Here you are, sir," she said, presenting the saucer to Affré.

"Thank you," he replied without looking up. Ella returned past Mather-Pike, and Silva glanced down at the tea. He looked back up at Mather-Pike and smiled before patting the large man on the cheek. Mather-Pike fought against the rising anger in response to the demeaning gesture.

"I'm glad you two are getting along so well," Silva said before retaking his seat. The scrutiny and the threat behind his words were not lost on both the Frenchman and the South African.

Kibrit Air Base,
Suez, Egypt

"I'm amazed you pulled this together," Natalie said as the plane touched down and Wyatt disappeared into the aft hold. Shaw shrugged.

"General Weber is as invested as we are. He didn't take much convincing. Besides, it's you I am amazed with. It must have been hard orchestrating all this without authorization." The blood drained from her face, and the horror of his discovery descended upon her. Shaw looked at her, wearing a smile. "You'll have to tell me how you did it sometime," he said, offering her a wink. The startling sensation that seized her throat released, but her concern didn't fade.

"Thank you," she managed. He placed a hand on her shoulder, drawing her gaze up from the floor. He stared into her eyes.

"Thank you, Natalie," he said sincerely. She mustered a smile, which he gladly returned.

"Be careful out there."

Shaw gazed into her eyes longer than he intended before turning away. "Wyatt, let's go!" Wyatt emerged from the aft hold carrying a compact duffle bag and a backpack. He nodded his farewell to Natalie as he headed for the plane's exit. Shaw followed, stopped just shy of the exit, and glanced back at her one more time. She raised her hand slightly and offered a wave, and he grinned widely back. Natalie couldn't ignore the flutter in her heart as their eyes met.

As Shaw stepped onto the tarmac of the military base, he approached the man with whom Wyatt conversed. Osman Maloof smiled and shook Shaw's hand as he neared.

"Welcome to my country," he greeted in perfect English.

"We are grateful for your assistance," Shaw replied. Maloof offered Shaw's hand an extra shake.

"We are allies, no? It was no small matter for us to approve your country's request for military action on our soil, but your general assured us of the mutual, beneficial nature of this operation," Maloof explained. Shaw nodded his agreement. Maloof served in Egypt's General Intelligence Service, known in Arabic as the *Mukhabarat*.

He was short with a light complexion and dark eyes. Black stubble covered his narrow jawline, and his hair, wild and curly, danced in the desert wind. He wore a light-brown, cotton jacket over a plaid, flannel button-down. Shaw and Wyatt, attempting to appear as civilians, wore similar clothing.

"How far to Port Tawfiq?" Shaw asked as Maloof directed them toward an SUV parked nearby.

"It is approximately thirty-five kilometers from here, so maybe forty-five minutes," he replied.

The three men loaded into the vehicle, and Maloof pulled away. Shaw felt good about Maloof, and he trusted his gut regarding people. Wyatt, however, felt otherwise. He appeared a bit too welcoming, but the sniper disregarded it. He was probably just nervous being in the field again after all that had transpired in Yemen. Wyatt shifted his gaze out the window as they left the air base and sped south toward Port Tawfiq.

32

Cairo, Egypt

The plane taxied to a stop, and Mather-Pike's eyes cut to the aft of the jet as Silva disappeared into his private room. The South African quickly rose from his seat and moved to Affré's side.

"Did your people with the DGSE come through with setting up the foundation?" he asked quietly. Affré glanced toward Silva's closed door.

"They did, for a cut," he replied. Mather-Pike nodded. He knew they couldn't pull this off by themselves.

"What about your people?" Affré asked.

"They're ready to do their part," he replied, "for a cut."

"You're enjoying this too much," Affré warned. Mather-Pike simply shrugged and glanced at his watch.

"We're cutting this pretty close, hey?"

"You let me worry about the itinerary; just be ready when the time comes." Mather-Pike grunted and turned toward the arms closet. He strapped on his bulletproof vest before throwing on a loose, button-down shirt. He would have preferred a plate carrier with armor rated for rifle rounds, but the stiff Kevlar should be enough to stop any bullet from a typical weapon the Egyptians possessed.

He holstered a FN Five-seven pistol on his hip. The pistol's light and fast 5.7x28mm rounds would punch straight through Kevlar body armor. The South African also took comfort in the twenty-round magazine capacity. He could easily carry over one hundred rounds. The pistol was nearly triple the cost of a Glock, but for Silva, price had never once been an issue when it came to arming his protection detail.

A printer churned out a sheet of paper and drew Mather-Pike's attention. At the same time, Silva reemerged from his room.

"Affré, are we ready?" Silva asked as he worked his cufflinks through their designated holes.

"Yes, but I received a form from Kormann regarding your beneficiary information. He's asked for an update," the Frenchman answered. Silva held out his hand for the paperwork.

"The old man's timing is always terrible," he complained. He glanced down at the document and exhaled in annoyance. "What is the Wild Planet Foundation? The old fool and his environmental convictions; did he gain a seat on their board or something?" Silva really didn't care what happened to his money after he died, but Kormann required all accounts to have a primary beneficiary.

"I can't say," Affré replied.

Since Silva didn't care either way, he allowed Kormann to appoint a foundation of his choice. Perhaps one day, if Silva found something or someone he cared enough about, he would have the information changed, but at the moment, Kormann's choice was as good as any, and it wasn't unusual for Kormann to change the primary beneficiary regularly. It was annoying, but it was the price to pay for the secrecy and unparalleled confidence. That was the reason professional thieves, crime syndicates, arms dealers, and terrorist organizations all came to Kormann. He was discreet, and that type of reputation could not be bought.

"We should address this matter after our meeting with Mr. Morgan. We don't want to keep him waiting," Affré stated after noting Silva's hesitation.

"I decide what we should and shouldn't do," Silva stated sharply. "Give me a pen." Satisfied with his persuasion, Affré handed Silva a pen and watched as the Spaniard signed the document. "Send it now."

Affré didn't respond but took the document and placed it on the scanner. Within seconds, the document would reach Switzerland.

"May we leave now? The shipment will be waiting for us," Silva asked Affré. His tone dripped with sarcasm. Affré withheld an answer and instead lifted his hand toward the door. Silva pushed past Mather-Pike and exited the plane. The large man exhaled. Without realizing it, Mather-Pike had held his breath during the entire exchange. He offered Affré a nod well done before following his employer out of the craft.

Affré glanced at the ceiling before rubbing his face. Why had he not done this earlier?

Fear.

The harsh reality was that Affré was afraid. He was still afraid. Silva carried himself in such a way that showcased his apathy for the rule of law. Affré recalled the woman at the bar in Dubai. He had acted without regard for the ramifications, not because he hadn't considered them, but because he held the influence and power to subvert the consequences.

He wasn't as ruthless as many with whom Affré was acquainted, but he held his own. What made Silva so intriguing was his rise to power. He didn't inherit a global empire but built it from nothing. He had amassed his wealth through smart dealings with both legitimate and illegitimate businesses, and Affré believed Silva had only entered into the black market from sheer boredom. At first, he had dealt in black market jewelry, then art, and finally weapons. The only major criminal enterprises he hadn't entered involved drugs and human trafficking, but Affré could see that weapons stirred Silva's spirit and generated the sense of adventure, risk, and reward that he so desperately sought.

Silva had hired Affré nearly five years ago, and everything had gone smoothly until Silva had drowned Marco Capra, the man Mather-Pike had replaced. Affré had grown close to Capra during their tenure together, and the Italian was the best fighter Affré had ever seen until he went toe to toe with Silva. If Silva was going to die, it had to come from the barrel of a gun. The Frenchman wanted nothing more than to pull the trigger himself, but the events he witnessed that day on the banks of the Nile paralyzed him.

It was absurd. Affré had fought in the Middle East as a Legionnaire and faced immensely dangerous situations while with the DGSE. Perhaps his experiences confirmed within him his own mortality. He hadn't expressed it, but he revered Mather-Pike for his ability to drive forward and cast the risks aside. He would be lying if he said he would have crossed Silva regardless. Without Mather-Pike pushing him, he might have found himself floating face down among the reeds of the Nile.

Affré paused at the top of the stairs leading to the tarmac. The heat stifled him. Already, Affré's sweat glands opened up, saturating his chest and back. The heat proved unbearable, especially while wearing body armor.

A black, Mercedes-Benz G-Class SUV sat idle at the base of the stairs on the private landing strip. Affré watched as Silva took his usual position behind the driver's seat and Mather-Pike the seat next to him. The Frenchman's hands caressed the Five-seven pistol on his hip before he descended the stairs toward the waiting SUV. Now, only one thing remained, and he hoped his trust in Mather-Pike was not ill placed. Everything had to look right. If one detail was off, their fortune and freedom would vanish forever.

Zürich, Switzerland

Henri Wolf rapped his pen against the wooden desk as he waited for the printer. As a junior associate at Ziegler & Rohr Financial, Henri hardly qualified, or was even permitted, to touch accounts like Francisco Silva's without prior authorization, but the temptation proved too great. He glanced around, not nervously, but with an aura of excitement. He had to admit that the risk stimulated his normally drab life, and if he pulled this off, he would wave goodbye to Ziegler & Rohr from the back of a half-million-dollar sailing yacht.

When Henri received the call from Romuald Affré last week about the job, he had been hesitant, but as soon as the Frenchman had revealed his cut, Henri jumped at the opportunity. The Swiss had questioned Affré on how he planned to obtain Silva's signature for the beneficiary update, but he had cut Henri off. The more Henri thought about it, the more he was glad the Frenchman had. It was better he didn't know. To Henri, updating the beneficiary information meant Silva had to die for him to receive his payout. The less he knew, the better. Then again, did he really care about Silva's life when three million dollars lay on the line?

No, no he did not.

The printer spat the paper out, and Henri carefully laid the document in his portfolio and breathed deeply. He mustered all the charisma he possessed. If he failed, at worst, he would be fired, at best, he would remain a junior associate for the next ten years. Honestly, he didn't know which one was worse, but it didn't matter. He was confident he would succeed.

He left his small, shared office and headed for the main elevator. Hugo Kormann personally managed Silva's financial affairs, and, fortunately, was a partner for which Henri closely served as an aide. No doubt that was why Affré had reached out to him. Henri smirked as the elevator doors opened. It paid to be in the right place at the right time, literally.

The Swiss followed the familiar route to Kormann's office and, wearing his widest grin, knocked on the frame of the open door.

"Henri!" the tall, thin man greeted. He wore a white smile, and Henri didn't know which was whiter, his teeth or his hair. Still, Kormann's youthful persona was undeniably genuine. At this point in the senior partner's career, Kormann focused more on pouring into the next generation of financial advisors and, in turn, only handled a few accounts. Those few accounts, however, made up over thirty percent of the company's astronomical revenue. "What can I do for you?"

"I have some paperwork that needs your signature," Henri said. Kormann furrowed his brow. It was an unusual situation for a junior associate to approach a senior partner with that type of information. Normally, Kormann would have sent for Henri to do all the legwork first.

"You do? Very well. Let me see," Kormann instructed, holding out a clawed hand. His youthful demeanor could do little against the arthritis that nearly crippled his body. His hands had remained fixed in the same position for nearly five years. Henri handed him the portfolio. Kormann glanced over the single document. "What is this?" he demanded, removing his spectacles after reading the print.

"I just got off the phone with Mr. Romuald Affré. He told me that he attempted to contact you, but was unable to connect," Henri started.

"I've been in my office all day," Kormann countered.

"He did sound spotty over the phone, perhaps they are in the air."

"Spotty?" Kormann repeated for clarification.

"He didn't appear to have a strong signal."

"Ah." Kormann again glanced over the document. "Still, this is very unusual. I have never heard of this foundation," the old man said as he read the new primary beneficiary.

"Mr. Affré stated that Mr. Silva has requested this change to save the elephants should he pass. He does, if I'm not mistaken, care deeply for the environment," Henri explained.

"That he does," Kormann replied. This was the first time Silva had requested a beneficiary change. The notion puzzled the financier, but there was no reason Silva could not, at any time, propose that change.

"I can look up the organization for you if you would like," Henri said.

"No, his signature is here, and everything seems to be in order. It's just a strange order of things for you to bring this to me. Forgive my skepticism, but normally I would be informing you and directing you or one of my other associates to handle the sending and receiving."

"I understand, sir," Henri responded. Kormann's hand gripped the gold-plated pen and moved toward the paper. It wobbled in his grip as he hesitated. Henri's stomach flipped as Kormann's hesitation endured. "Shall I inform Mr. Affré of your hesitation?" Kormann's gaze shot upward and met Henri's. Was that fear?

"No, not at all," the old man answered. He scribbled his illegible signature on the appropriate line and held out the document for Henri. "We shan't keep Mr. Silva waiting. Have this processed immediately," Kormann instructed.

"Right away, sir," Henri replied as he took the document. He handled it as if it was made of gold, as if a single crease or fold would void its validity.

As he left the office, Henri had never before worn a smile so wide in all his twenty-six years. His work was over, and all he had to do now was wait.

33

The setting sun painted the sky with wide strokes of red and pink. Various high-rise apartment complexes lined the coast, and numerous boats bobbed in the golden sea. The SUV parked at the base of an office complex under construction, and the three men exited. Maloof rounded the front of the vehicle to stand next to Shaw.

"The construction is mostly complete except for the top floor. It should provide you with a three-hundred-sixty-degree view of the port and surrounding area," the Egyptian explained.

"Wyatt, what do you think?" Shaw asked.

"It should work," he replied. Maloof proceeded forward, and the two Marines followed. Wyatt glanced over his shoulder but didn't notice anyone or anything out of the ordinary. Again, he pushed the nagging sensation away.

The three men took the elevator to the highest completed floor then took the stairs the rest of the way. The trio emerged onto a construction site, and the robust breeze from the sea whipped around them.

"You can see to what I was referring," Maloof stated.

"Yeah," Shaw replied. He moved across the exposed area, produced a pair of binoculars from his backpack, and surveyed the port. Their perch offered them a clear view of the twin piers that extended out into the Gulf of Suez. "Ozark, we're in position," Shaw said, his earpiece picking up his voice.

"Good copy, Philo," Natalie replied.

"You're positive this is the place?" he asked.

"Yes," Natalie confirmed. He trusted her answer and watched Wyatt unzip his duffle. The sniper assembled his M110A1 sniper rifle by fixing the upper and lower receivers together and ratcheting on the suppressor. Shaw crouched and unzipped his backpack and produced the upper and lower receivers of his MK18 carbine. In similar manner to Wyatt, he threaded on his sound suppressor and found a quick sight picture through the low-powered, variable optic. Maloof watched with interest as the two Westerners checked over their weapons.

"Alright Ozark, we're settled in," Shaw informed Natalie.

"Good copy," Natalie replied. "Sage will be on comms once we have proper target identification."

"Roger that," Shaw replied. "Now we wait," he said to Wyatt. The sniper had settled in behind his rifle. "Maloof, you going to join us?"

"Yes, of course," the Egyptian replied as he fell prone next to Shaw. The group remained several meters back from the edge of the building. The unfinished level lacked its floor-to-ceiling windows, making the position a perfect perch to canvass the entire pier. Darkness settled on the sea, and the trio waited.

"How long to rendezvous?" Silva asked.

"We're nearing the port now, sir," came Affré's quick reply. Silva leaned to gaze out the windshield. He couldn't deny the scale of the operation. It was larger than any previously undertaken, and it had showed in his stress level. It was that initial stress that gave Affré the confidence that Silva would sign the beneficiary form without contacting his financial advisor, Hugo Kormann.

A smile cracked across Silva's face as they approached the security checkpoint leading onto the twin piers at Port Tawfiq. Affré slowed the SUV to a stop and conversed with the guard through the open window. The arm soon raised, and Affré sped into the port.

"There she is," Silva noted as they neared the vessel that carried his merchandise. Affré parked, and the Spaniard stepped out onto the pier. A man, dressed casually except for his body armor, gun belt, and carbine, approached Silva with an extended hand.

"Mr. Morgan," Silva greeted, "I trust everything went smoothly."

"It did, sir. No trouble with the import. We're ready to proceed on your command."

"That is good news, Mr. Morgan," Silva stated. He checked his watch and glanced at Affré, who gave him a nod. Silva's stress gave way to the cool and calm demeanor that usually rested on his countenance. He returned Affré's nod. Morgan turned and, rotating his fingers in the air, signaled to the rest of his team to begin transferring the product to the waiting trucks. Silva stood with his hands on his hips and watched the massive cranes at work.

The Spaniard found it odd that even now thoughts of Miranda swirled in his mind. He admired her strength and her beauty; something in her eyes simply captivated him, not to mention her body that he desperately desired to see atop him. His encounter with her had appeared too coincidental. He could have sworn that she worked for some government agency, perhaps CIA.

He felt his actions were justified given the recent happenings in Yemen, but surely the United States hadn't connected him to that event. He hadn't heard from Al Amiri about any such developments, but then again why would the Yemeni contact him for anything other than business? Al Amiri was one of the world's most wanted terrorists, certainly he would have heard something if the United States or anyone else found him.

Was he being too paranoid?

The deal in Yemen had breathed greater life into his arms business. Soon, as he figured, his net worth would exceed half a billion. He could only thank his new supplier for his continued rise. He credited the enticing merchandise with drawing Isaam Al Amiri's and now Hamas' interest. The arms dealer grinned as he looked to the future.

Today: small arms and light weaponry.

Tomorrow: heavy weapons systems.

The thought of dealing in tanks and jets quickened Silva's spirit. The entire notion added a new complexity and exhilaration to his booming business, and that, more than anything, drove his ambition. Perhaps soon, governments would come beckoning for a taste of America's military capability.

Strangely, his mind shifted back to Miranda. Confusion assaulted him. Why was she, when such exciting business developments unfolded, constantly on his mind? Was his subconscious trying to tell him something, warning him? Or were his loins speaking? He couldn't deny the desire he had for her, but she was just another woman. Would it pass? He hoped so.

"Ozark, this is Philo. We've got movement. Standby for visual confirmation," Shaw stated into the comms.

"Good copy, Philo, awaiting confirmation," Natalie replied. Shaw gazed through his binoculars and focused on the black Mercedes as it pulled onto the first of the two piers.

"I've got armed combatants," Wyatt noted as he peered through his riflescope enhanced by a night-vision device. "Count, fifteen tangos," he added. The group of armed men descended from the cargo ship onto the pier.

"I see them," Shaw confirmed. He fiddled with the binoculars and activated a live feed to Natalie and his command.

"I've got visual," Natalie confirmed. Viewing her monitor, she focused on the individuals broadcasted through the feed, and her anger rose as she beheld Francisco Silva. "Target confirmed and on site," she said.

"Good copy, we see him," Shaw replied. Wyatt's index finger fondled the trigger as his sights fell on Silva. He wanted nothing more than to drop him where he stood, but his better judgement cooled him. He removed his finger from the trigger and sighed. Shaw knew Wyatt's feelings too well. He fought hard against the urge to command Wyatt to shoot Silva. He was certain his friend would obey without a second thought.

"The operation is a go," Natalie confirmed, "Alpha and Bravo teams are refueling over the Red Sea."

"We've got another vehicle incoming," Shaw quickly added. He turned to Maloof, "your men?" The Egyptian intelligence officer shook his head. The trio watched as a second, larger SUV rolled onto the pier and came to a stop some distance from the first. Five men exited and took up positions in a line between their SUV and Silva's. "Ozark, I think we may have a buyer on site," Shaw said. A sixth man exited the vehicle, and Shaw focused in on his face.

"Good copy, Philo, I'm running his identity now," Natalie replied, "stand by."

Silva turned to greet the newcomers and offered them a friendly wave. The six men approached deliberately with their hands on their weapons. Their leader, wearing dark clothing, with his black hair slicked back, led the pack and extended his hand to Silva as he neared.

"Good evening," Silva greeted as he clasped the man's hand. "It is a pleasure to meet you, Mr. Farrah."

"The pleasure is mine, Mr. Silva. My father sends his regards," Ghassan Farrah stated. "I wish to convey how excited we are to secure this business relationship."

"The feeling is mutual," Silva replied. He presented Farrah with a confident smile.

"May I inspect the merchandise?" Farrah asked. Silva smiled again.

"In one moment. There is a pressing matter that I must see to first," Silva replied. He turned, ignoring Farrah's wary and dissatisfied gaze. "Mr. Morgan!" Silva called. Morgan approached. "Now is the time."

"Certainly, sir," Morgan replied.

34

"His name is Ghassan Farrah. He's the son of Eyad Farrah, the leader of Hamas' Al-Qassam Brigade," Natalie explained upon finding a match for the buyer's identity. "I'm sure Mossad would be very interested in this development," she added. Shaw took in the information as he watched the exchange between the two men.

"Excuse me, I need to piss," Maloof stated. Shaw came off his binoculars and issued a quick, approving nod. Maloof slid backwards before rising and heading down the stairs.

"What do you make of this?" Wyatt asked.

"Nothing's changed. Why?" Wyatt inhaled and adjusted his cheek against the rifle stock.

"I just can't shake this feeling I've got," the sniper answered. Shaw glanced at him.

"What feeling?" he probed.

"Like we shouldn't be here."

A sharp clatter behind them drew both men's attention, and a blinding, disorienting blast followed, stealing their senses. Their ears throbbed and vision pulsed flashes of bright white, and both men were unable to make sense of their surroundings. They both knew immediately that they'd been hit by a flashbang grenade, and there was no way they could respond responsibly or accurately.

"Ozark," Shaw groaned, "we're compromised!" If Natalie replied, Shaw couldn't hear her. He felt hands jerk him to his feet, and fingers probed into his ear to dislodge his communication earpiece. Hands searched around his waistline and removed his Glock 19 and holster from his belt. He stumbled as multiple assailants pushed and pulled him forward.

"Philo Two?" Shaw called out.

"Here," came Wyatt's reply from behind.

"Shut up!" came an accented voice followed by a quick slap to the back of the head. Shaw tried to place the accent, but his ears deceived him amidst their trauma. Shaw's mind quickly raced through his SERE training, an acronym referring to survival, evasion, resistance, and escape, and he knew immediately Maloof had betrayed them.

Shaw fell inward for a moment preparing himself for whatever might come next, and as his vision slowly returned, he took note of everything he could about their attackers. Something, some detail, might provide a clue to his advantage, but they quickly pulled a dark sack over his head.

Kibrit Air Base,
Suez, Egypt

"Philo?" Natalie called into her headset. "Do you read me?" No answer came. His previous words sent dread coursing through her body. "Philo?" she called again. She waited a moment longer than she should. If he were there, he would have replied. She hoped he wasn't dead. She inhaled deeply to steady herself before contacting the upper command. "Sage, this is Ozark."

"Go ahead, Ozark," came General Weber's voice through the comms.

"Philo is compromised," she stated, attempting to strengthen her voice. Silence streamed through her headset as she awaited Weber's reply.

General Weber dragged his hand down his face as all eyes fell on him.

The young Marines waited anxiously for his command. Weber removed his headset and muted the microphone.

"How far out are our Marines?" he asked Lieutenant Reynolds, who led the team arrayed around him. Reynolds could tell by the general's tone that he was trying to keep his emotions in check. Everyone present knew his close connection with Captain Shaw and couldn't imagine the position in which he now found himself.

"They're currently refueling over the Red Sea just off the coast of Yanbu," Reynolds answered. Weber rubbed his eyes.

"They know we are coming," he stated, his tone bore the full gravity of the situation. The silent Marines waited impatiently for his next words. "Shut it down," he ordered solemnly.

"Sir?" came the confused reply of his subordinate officer.

"You heard me, Lieutenant," Weber said calmly. "Shut it down."

"But what about Philo?" he asked.

"If they're not dead now, they will be soon. Alpha and Bravo won't be able to reach them in time, and I'm not endangering any more Marines. If they knew about Philo then they surely know about the following teams and will be prepared for them. Shut it down."

"Yes, sir," the Marine officer replied soberly. Weber replaced the headset around his ears.

"Ozark, we're pulling the plug. I'm ordering you to leave the country as soon as you can. This will be the last communication you have from me. Good luck," Weber said. Before Natalie could reply the connection ended.

"Sage," she stammered. "Sage!" She threw her headset across the cabin and sank her head into her hands. She waited for a moment contemplating all her options. Barry Moses, the flight attendant, approached slowly.

"Ms. Hale," he said softly. She glanced up at him, her eyes red. "We've received orders to take off."

"No," she retorted, but Moses shook his head.

"I'm sorry, Ms. Hale, but we will be leaving as soon as we are cleared for takeoff." He reached out to offer her a comforting touch on the shoulder, but she recoiled. Helpless and fearing for Shaw and Wyatt, she sank into her chair and fought off fresh tears.

Over the Red Sea

Barone shot Hogan a concerned look as he felt their VTOL bank right. Hogan's expression relayed the same troubled thoughts. They both shot Heckman questioning stares.

"Captain!" Hogan called. "What's going on?" Heckman appeared to ignore them until Hogan realized he was communicating through his radio on a private channel.

"Understood, sir," they all heard Heckman say. Seated toward the cockpit, Captain Heckman lifted his eyes to face them. "Brass has called off the op. Philo's been compromised," he stated.

"What?" Barone stated in disbelief, voicing what the entire team was thinking.

"I don't know any more than that, but the pilots are taking us back," Heckman explained.

"Sir, we've got to press on. Captain Shaw and Staff Sergeant Wyatt, they need us," Hogan argued.

"We have our new orders, Corporal. I'm not happy about this either, but all we can do is roll with the punches and hope Philo Team makes it out of there." He wanted to tell them that he was going to force the pilots to continue onward and disregard General Weber's orders, but he knew aviators wouldn't listen. Perhaps he should put on the display just to save face. He decided against it, rested his head against the hull, and sighed.

Hogan cursed loudly and shook himself against his harness, and Barone sat still, struggling with the reality of leaving Shaw and Wyatt to face a likely death. How does one work through those emotions? He didn't know and felt terrible.

Port Tawfiq

Ghassan Farrah spun around quickly as the sharp crack reached his ears. The sound echoed from the top story of the building behind them.

"Relax, my friend," Silva stated. "I'm just taking care of a few uninvited guests. Come; let me show you the product. Your men will need to remain here." Farrah nodded, regaining his confidence and attempting to appear more collected for the sake of his father's reputation.

"Of course," he said. He nodded his approval to his lead security, and the team remained behind as Farrah followed Silva up the gangplank. Once on board, Silva led Farrah toward the ship's accommodations. He held a special arrangement with the captain who had allowed his entire crew a night's leave in the city, thereby leaving the ship empty for Silva's deal.

"Right in here," Silva said as he ushered Farrah inside a large room. It appeared to be the ship's mess hall. A tall blonde man greeted them both.

"If you'll wait here, sir," Mather-Pike stated, stopping Farrah in his tracks. More than understanding, the young Palestinian did as instructed. Silva moved to Farrah's side and watched as Mather-Pike entered the unlock code on the keypad of the unopened crate in the center of the room. Farrah's eyes gleamed as he beheld the weapons arrayed within the large, deep case.

"The contents of this case hold an example of each weapon ordered."

"May I?" Farrah asked. Silva smiled, nodded, and extended his hand. The Palestinian moved forward and hoisted an M249 Squad Automatic Weapon. It was an older model, but Farrah ran his hands over the heavy weapon and grinned. "It is belt fed, yes?" He turned to look at the arms dealer. Silva nodded, and Farrah's smile widened. "And this!" Farrah exclaimed as he scooped up the M32A1 Multi-shot Grenade Launcher. "Six shots of forty millimeter, yes?" Silva again nodded.

"You'll find everything is in order."

"I am very impressed, Mr. Silva," Farrah replied. He glanced down at the remaining weapons in the crate: an FGM-148 Javelin missile launcher, an M16A4 rifle, and an M9 pistol. "I am ready to conclude our business on my father's behalf," Farrah stated.

Silva nodded toward Mather-Pike, and the South African opened the briefcase and linked to a satellite signal. The case contained a computer with which to transfer funds from one account to another.

"If you will, Mr. Farrah, input your account information," Mather-Pike instructed as he positioned the case before the man. Farrah leaned forward and with one finger, punched in his account information. As he leaned back, the South African drew the case back into his lap. Silva's pleasant gaze remained on Farrah while Mather-Pike worked.

Rian Mather-Pike suppressed the desire to exhale heavily as he prepared. As he pressed the keys in the correct order, he felt his perspiration hasten. The exhilaration overwhelmed his insides as he punched in a different account number than Silva's. The account provided would buy his and Ella's freedom.

Only one thing remained.

Get back to her alive.

35

Gulf of Suez,
Aboard Scarlett's Bosom

Johan de Jager stood at the edge of the helipad as he awaited his payment. The dark sea foamed beneath him as he gazed northward. It hadn't been easy to smuggle his strike force in from Sudan unnoticed, but he had done it. Now, all that remained was his payment. The Afrikaner mercenary usually didn't accept jobs without some type of payment upfront, but Rian Mather-Pike was a good kid and, as far as de Jager knew, never backed down from his word. In truth though, the payout was simply too good to ignore. He might not retire, but he would surely have more than enough to put his children through university, perhaps even in Germany or the Netherlands. Yes, that would be nice.

The grizzled man, dressed in tan and brown tiger stripe camo, held his R4 rifle vertically as he gazed westward. Port Tawfiq lay nestled at the mouth of the Suez Canal, and his mission was to destroy the *Vittoria Fortuna*, an Italian shipping vessel docked at the port. When Mather-Pike had first contacted him about the operation, de Jager vehemently opposed. He stated that his career thrived because he kept his operations under the radar, doing jobs for warlords and even at times intelligence organizations from a variety of nations, including the United States and the United Kingdom. Attacking an Italian vessel in an Egyptian port was far from under the radar, but his tune had changed when Mather-Pike revealed the payout. De Jager had done his research. They would be in and out before the Egyptians could respond. His advance team had already planted the charges to sink the ship. All that remained was to receive payment from Mather-Pike.

"Can we trust this Englishman, Colonel?" came the fluent Afrikaans behind him. De Jager hadn't officially held the title of colonel in nearly thirty years, not since the South African Border War, but the title had stuck. After Nelson Mandela came into power, he and his troop were tossed aside as the South African government decreased and disbanded most of its military. As former members of the South African Special Forces Brigade, or Recces as they were casually known, de Jager and his men, with no other skills or trades, had turned soldiers of fortune, taking jobs where and when they could.

He thought about the word his companion had used to describe Rian Mather-Pike: *Englishman*. It was accurate but antiquated. Although both men were South African, Mather-Pike's ancestors came from England, while de Jager's migrated from the Netherlands, but the former colonel never considered that to be a negative factor.

"I know Rian. He'll come through for us," de Jager replied in the same language. Marick Haarhoff, a former lieutenant in the Recces, wasn't so sure.

"You know him?" Haarhoff asked.

"I got him into the business. His father died in Angola; saved my life and only God knows how many more." Haarhoff remained silent but observed de Jager's solemn expression. "Now it seems the Mather-Pikes are coming through for me again."

"Colonel!" came a shout from behind the two men. They turned to regard the soldier waving them in. The two mercenaries trotted over, and the rest of the strike team mustered around them.

"What is it, Flick?" de Jager asked.

"The account transfer has successfully been completed." He laughed halfway through his sentence. "We're rich." He handed de Jager the tablet and the old colonel grinned as he witnessed the twenty million displayed in the account.

"Well done, Rian," he said to himself. De Jager had stood firm on one condition: he had to receive payment before he attacked Egyptian soil. Mather-Pike, although he had protested at first, had apparently found a way. De Jager turned his attention to his men. "Alright, boys," he stated, even though most were well over thirty. Each man wore grim expressions and nodded their heads at the words. The words appeared to flip a switch in each man. Even Flick, who a moment ago was laughing, had hardened his expression. They moved with deliberate purpose to the two small helicopters on the bow and aft helipads.

The rotors on the two MH-6 Little Bird helicopters began their slow rotations before quickly picking up speed and becoming invisible to the human eye. They were older models built in the 1990's, but they were too expensive to replace, and their capabilities still too valuable. With enough room for six, including the pilot and co-pilot, the two helicopters each carried four men, two gunners and two aviators, which left more than enough room to extract Mather-Pike and the three other men whose identities remained unknown.

De Jager, serving as a co-pilot in the first helicopter, unfolded the mission in his mind as he envisioned each step of the operation, and he hoped no surprises lay in store for him and his men. He also hoped his man would find this Ella in Cairo and extract her without any problems. There were many pieces to the operation, and at any point, the mission could spin out of control.

Shaw, blinded by the black sack draped snugly over his head, complied with his captors' orders and proceeded forward. He felt the texture of the ground shift under his shoes and incline upward. He realigned his balance and continued forward. Wyatt again issued a timed grunt to inform Shaw he was still with him, and Shaw responded with a fake cough.

Their captors ushered them onto what Shaw could only surmise was the ship when the texture beneath his shoes shifted again. They prodded him along for several minutes before old door hinges squeaked and Shaw felt cool, interior air on his neck and arms. He forced himself to remain calm, but it was difficult. He had never before found himself in such a circumstance, but the Marines under Heckman and Lopez would be arriving soon. He placed his hope in their capable hands.

"Sit," one of his captors sternly ordered. Shaw hesitated, and hands on each shoulder shoved him downward. He braced himself, anticipating hitting the floor, but a chair stopped his descent. Both his legs and hands were then zip tied to the frame.

"Ah, my distinguished guests," a dignified voice stated. The black sack soared off Shaw's head, and the bright, florescent light irritated his tender eyes. He tossed his head to clear his hair from his face and quickly surveyed the room. The buyer, Ghassan Farrah, watched on with concern, and two other men, who Natalie had identified as Silva's bodyguards, stood a short distance away. Both his and Wyatt's weapons lay arrayed on a table near the entry.

The Egyptian intelligence officer, Osman Maloof, picked his teeth with his pinky as he observed the two Marines. Disgusted, Shaw glanced to his left and met Wyatt's hardened expression. Then, both men turned their attention to the man wearing a blue blazer and white pants.

Francisco Silva looked upon them, and Shaw now understood what Natalie had shared with him on the plane. Behind the man's eyes prowled a primal hunger that desired nothing more than to devour both Marines, but his eyes suddenly changed. A smile donned his face before he turned to address Maloof.

"Well done, Mr. Maloof," Silva congratulated. He strode over to the man and wrapped one arm around Maloof's shoulders.

"I am glad to be of service," Maloof replied. "About my payment?"

"Ah, yes, of course," Silva said offering Maloof a smile the Egyptian gladly returned. The sum alone would set him up for the rest of his life. Silva saw the greed in the Egyptians eyes, and Shaw watched as Silva's hand slowly crept to the small of his back then explode into motion.

The knife slammed into the man's midsection, and, working like a jack-hammer, the blade opened up the man's belly, spilling his entrails onto the floor. Maloof, eyes wide in horror, shrieked and slapped at Silva's hand.

Satisfied, Silva backed away, and Maloof dropped to his knees, scooping up his intestines as his primal instincts directed. The fire that ripped through his stomach was too much to bear. Tears flowed freely from his eyes, and his shrieking only increased in intensity.

Silva watched the display and scratched an itch on his neck with his clean hand. Maloof's blood covered his knife hand and darkened his blazer's sleeve.

"You understand, dear Maloof, the less who know about my dealings the better," Silva explained. He turned toward two of the men who had captured Shaw and Wyatt. "Throw him into the sea." Maloof screamed in protest as the two men seized him by his arms and dragged him from the room. The fall alone might kill him, but if it didn't, the shock of the salt-water on his wounds would paralyze him. Silva figured he'd drown before the sharks got to him.

"Now," Silva said as he returned his attention to the two Marines before him. He approached Shaw, dropped into a crouch, and patted Shaw's thigh with the bloody weapon. Shaw fought to maintain his composure, but his eyes remained a bit wider than usual and his heart quickened. "Let's find out how you knew where to find me." Shaw remained silent, and Silva drifted his gaze toward Wyatt. He smirked before turning back to Shaw. "You hide your hate well," he complimented as he bounced the blade in front of Shaw's face. "But your friend here," Silva continued, "not so much." Silva looked up at his men who stood behind both Wyatt and Shaw. "You can go. Please escort Mr. Farrah to his merchandise and make sure it is loaded up to his specifications. I'm sure Mr. Morgan will appreciate your assistance."

The four remaining men nodded. Two prompted Farrah to follow them while the other two carried the weapons crate from the room. Silva patted the knife against his palm and watched them leave before turning back to his bound captives.

"I know you are both Marines, and I'll ask again, how did you know where to find me?" Silva asked. Both Shaw and Wyatt remained silent. Silva smirked. "I won't ask again." Shaw locked eyes with his captor. "Ah, there it is!" Silva exclaimed. He pulled a chair up and sat in front of Shaw. "I do not even know who you are, and yet you hate me so deeply. What is it that I did to you and your friend to make that the case?"

Shaw's mind raced. What answer could he give to gain the advantage? He began to doubt he even could.

"I'm going to count to three, and then I am going to cut open your chest," Silva threatened. "One." Shaw inhaled sharply and prepared himself for the pain. "Two."

"Wait!" Wyatt shouted.

"Three," Silva finished. He applied steady pressure against Shaw's chest, and blood welled up beneath his shirt as Silva drove the knife deeper into the Marine's flesh. All of Shaw's muscles tightened and shook as the searing pain crashed over him. His face contorted in a mix of agony and hatred, and his breath escaped in short, forceful bursts.

"Stop!" Wyatt hissed, but Silva didn't listen. He dragged the knife in an arc overtop Shaw's left pectoral and flicked his wrist downward, cutting cleanly through the muscle. Shaw screamed, and the metal chair rattled with his physical exertion.

"I'll kill you!" Wyatt snarled.

"Oh really?" Silva replied, taking far too much pleasure in the man's response. He patted Shaw on the cheek a couple times in a display of authority. He grinned at Wyatt, his tongue polishing a canine.

His countenance suddenly shifted, and confusion overtook his confident expression. His eyes cut toward Affré.

"What is that sound?" he asked. Shaw despite his pain had heard it too. A faint thundering slowly filled the room. "Check it out," he commanded. Affré nodded his head and quickly exited the room, but not before he offered Mather-Pike an assuring nod.

Silva turned his attention back to Shaw who offered him a tired smile.

"End of the line," he muttered. Furious, Silva shot out of his chair, seized a handful of Shaw's dark hair, and ratcheted his head backward. He pressed the knife against his throat, and Shaw closed his eyes, inhaled deeply, and relaxed his body. He thought of little David Kyle Reyes and of Natalie before finding the peace he sought in the face of his death.

"David!" Wyatt screamed. He lurched his body toward Silva, but his chair toppled over, and he slammed against the floor. Tears rimmed his eyes and bestial howls broke forth from his lips as he tried to break free from his bonds. "I'll kill you!" he shrieked, spittle soaring wildly from his lips.

Two quick gunshots deafened everyone in the room. Silva, eyes wide in shock, stumbled sideways into a nearby table. He touched his chest and looked at his hand, wet with his own blood, before shifting his gaze toward his assailant. Mather-Pike stood with his pistol drawn. Silva laughed in surprise, but it gave way to gurgled coughing before darkness engulfed him.

Wyatt, stunned by their stroke of good fortune, gawked at the blonde man as he lowered his pistol.

"There isn't much time," he stated as he produced a pocketknife to cut their bonds.

"You alright, David?" Wyatt asked once he was free. Shaw, his chest throbbing, stared at Silva who now lay sprawled on the floor with blood soaking his clothes.

"Yeah," he managed. He glanced down at his wound but only saw the blood that saturated his shirt down to his waist. "Let's get out to our boys," he added. Mather-Pike showcased his confusion.

"We've got Marines inbound," Wyatt explained.

"I afraid you don't," Mather-Pike countered.

"What do you mean?" Shaw asked.

"There is too much to explain. Just follow me. I'm confident I have earned your trust. This ship is set to blow once my colleague and myself are safely away. I've made arrangements for you as well," Mather-Pike said. Both Marines recognized they had little time to decipher the depths of the man's plans, and machinegun fire drew all three's attention. The two Raiders scooped up their weapons and turned toward Mather-Pike.

"Lead on," Shaw urged as he slung his MK18 carbine around his shoulders.

36

Shaw, Wyatt, and Mather-Pike raced toward the aft of the ship. Shaw's chest throbbed sharply in pain, but he pressed on. He had endured worse. Two of Silva's armed protection detail raced the opposite direction down the corridor.

"Get outside!" Mather-Pike shouted, "we've got to protect the merchandise!" The two men didn't even look at Wyatt and Shaw and continued right past them. "This way," Mather-Pike instructed as he took a left turn down another corridor. They neared an external door, and Mather-Pike produced a green flare from his inside jacket pocket.

"What are we waiting for?" Wyatt asked, but Mather-Pike held up a hand to silence him. Footsteps echoed behind them, and both Shaw and Wyatt turned to face the newcomer. The second bodyguard raced toward them.

"Hey, bud," Shaw alerted as he raised his weapon toward the approaching man.

"It's fine. He's with me," the South African replied. Shaw and Wyatt visibly relaxed as Affré slowed. He acknowledged them both with a nod before moving past them to join Mather-Pike at the door.

"Let's go," he urged. Mather-Pike nodded, and the four men proceeded outside. Mather-Pike continued to lead them rearward and up a ladder to the top of the stacked shipping containers. Gunfire continued behind them as the Little Birds buzzed overhead raining fire down on the security detail.

Once on top of the shipping containers, Mather-Pike lit the flare and tossed it a few yards away. The green light burned brightly and cut away the darkness. Shaw turned his attention upward as one of the Little Birds rounded the stern and approached for landing. As soon as it touched down, Mather-Pike turned toward the two Raiders.

"You first!" he shouted over the roar of the turbines. Shaw and Wyatt didn't argue and, keeping their head's low, sprinted toward the aircraft. The two gunners on either side quickly helped them strap into the platforms above the skids. Once settled, both Marines readied their weapons as the craft lifted upward. Their helicopter returned to the fray, keeping any attention off the second Little Bird as it descended to pick up Mather-Pike and Affré.

Anger coursing through them both, Shaw and Wyatt fired upon Silva's security detail. They appeared as frantic ants as they raced back and forth attempting to return fire. However, the gunners, seemingly experts in their craft, cut them down, and Shaw and Wyatt picked their shots with deadly accuracy. It was certainly more difficult to land shots from a moving helicopter, but Shaw and Wyatt had done so many times in the past.

"There's Farrah!' Shaw shouted through the fuselage toward Wyatt and pointing at the lone man running down the gangplank. Wyatt looked backwards and saw the man. "Bring us around!" Shaw shouted to the gunner. Upon relaying the request, the pilot banked and lined up Wyatt with the fleeing man.

The former Marine Corps Scout Sniper lined up his shot and trained the reticle just ahead of the fleeing Farrah, anticipating his quarry's speed and direction.

He fired.

Farrah's foot hit the pier before he jolted sideways. He felt as if a sledgehammer, swinging at full force, had hit him in the ribs. He crumpled to the ground still not fully sure of what had happened. He tried to inhale but couldn't and terror seized him. His bulging eyes realized the blood pooling around him was his own, and his hands searched his side for the wound. He was operating on primordial instinct. His rational mind had already shut down. His hands slowed and his eyesight darkened. There was no saving him. Wyatt's slug had ripped through both lungs and his heart, and Farrah died as a wild animal taken as fresh game.

"Nice shot!" the gunner next to him congratulated, but he had no idea who the target was. The scene settled as no one returned fire from the vessel or the pier. Dead bodies littered both, and Shaw felt the Little Bird bank right and change direction out to sea.

Relief swept over him as did the satisfaction of knowing Silva was dead. Although he hadn't pulled the trigger, he couldn't deny the peace he felt for his fallen brothers. However, a truth still nagged deeply at his spirit. Silva had known about the operation in Yemen and the operation to capture him. How? Troubled, Shaw fixed his eyes on the dark horizon.

Onboard Vittoria Fortuna

The man groaned as he pulled himself forward. Pain seared through his chest, and his breath came in labored gasps. The Spaniard rolled over and cracked a bloody grin.

"Well done, Rian," he managed before a coughing fit overtook him. Silva mustered his strength and forced himself upright. The chest wound bubbled and hissed as it drew in air, and he immediately realized his dire need for medical attention. A man rushed into the room, and Silva gripped his pistol, drew it from its holster, and acquired his target.

"Mr. Morgan," Silva wheezed, lowing his pistol. "It's good to see you." Morgan moved to his employer's side. Silva's breathing grew more difficult, and Morgan helped him remove his jacket and, drawing a knife, cut open his shirt. Morgan assisted with removing the soft armor vest, and despite their care, Silva's wound screamed in protest.

He needed air.

The Spaniard gulped repeatedly but couldn't produce the volume he needed. His vision blurred as he tried to focus on Morgan's hands. Morgan ripped into his trauma kit and tore into the chest seals. He wiped away the blood with gauze before applying the sticky seal over the sucking chest wound. Morgan patched the exit wounds in like manner, and Silva's breathing grew easier. Morgan wasn't done though. Silva looked at the decompression needle Morgan prepped and inhaled as deeply as he could to build his confidence. It only brought him more pain.

Morgan removed the case and stared at the sharp needle. He found the appropriate location on Silva's rib cage and pierced through the flesh. It burned, but the sharp pinch didn't compare to the pain from the gunshot wounds. Morgan removed the needle, leaving behind the small white tube. Seconds passed, and Silva's breathing grew steadily easier. He was still far from fixed, but he would survive.

Morgan helped Silva to his feet, and, with Silva leaning on him for support, the two men exited the room.

"Get me back to Cairo," Silva wheezed. Morgan didn't respond but kept his gaze up and alert. He paused at the exit and peered outside. The helicopters had peeled away, and the two men rushed outside. They descended the gangplank and stepped over Farrah's body. Silva's Mercedes-Benz SUV, although riddled with bullet holes, waited for them.

Morgan opened the rear door and helped Silva inside before climbing into the driver's seat and taking the wheel. He threw the vehicle in gear and slammed on the throttle, propelling them forward, off the pier, and out of the port.

De Jager ginned widely as his strike force cleared the area. The operation had gone better than he had expected. Ever the pessimist, de Jager always expected the worst, but Mather-Pike had planned everything splendidly, and it didn't hurt that de Jager was personally two million dollars richer. As commander, he took a ten percent cut of the total sum before cost, and then the rest would be divvied up after expenses to his ten-man team. Marick Haarhoff, his second in command would receive a higher cut, likely around a million dollars.

"Good to see you again, Colonel," came Mather-Pike's voice through a borrowed headset.

"Just like old times, hey?" de Jager replied, wearing a wide grin.

"You going to blow it?" Mather-Pike asked. De Jager chucked and caressed the detonator before he pressed the switch.

Natalie kept her gaze fixed out the window as the aircraft soared westward. Port Tawfiq remained out there somewhere with Shaw and Wyatt captive. She closed her eyes briefly and offered them both a silent apology. She yearned to save them, to find a way, but it was too late. She knew that deep down.

The operations officer reopened her eyes and ran her hands down the length of her braided hair. She glanced back out the window and shot upright as the orange light cut through the night. A bellow of flame roared into the air to the south. Was that the *Vittoria Fortuna*? What else would it be? What had happened?

Weber had called off the operation, had the Egyptians moved in? Were Shaw and Wyatt aboard when the ship exploded? A pit formed in her stomach, and grief forced itself upward. Tears again rolled down her cheeks.

37

Cairo, Egypt

Ella sighed and glanced down at her phone before tracing her gaze around her private room. It wasn't as private as she would have liked. Silva saw to that. Despite the extravagance, adventure, and massive salary, she felt alone. Her hatred for her employer brewed, and at the same time, her hope in Rian increased. Could he really deliver on his promise? She could only hope, and the thought of being with him drew a smile across her face. No, she wasn't alone.

She fell back onto the bed and puffed her hair from her face. Her brow furrowed as she interpreted the noise that echoed through the cabin.

Shouting?

The flight attendant rose and approached the door. It slid open effortlessly, and she shrieked as she gazed down the barrel of a rifle. It lowered, but she shook uncontrollably as fear assaulted her.

"Come with me," the hard voice ordered. Ella complied without realizing it. She no longer thought; she just did as instructed. He grabbed her by the hand and raced toward the exit. "Rian Mather-Pike sent me," he explained, reciting the words as Colonel de Jager had instructed him. Hope immediately welled up within her. She glanced at the young man. He was likely close to her age, early to mid-twenties. He kept his face shaven and his bright blonde hair mirrored her own. "Let's go," he said as they approached the jet's exit. He was the first through the opening, but several gunshots echoed from the tarmac. The young man fell backwards, and Ella shrieked at the sight of so much blood. She backed away and watched as the young mercenary coughed, spewing blood all over his face.

A man Ella didn't recognize boarded and stared apathetically at the young man dying on the floor. The South African's eyes popped with fear, and he trembled before his killer. The gunman looked up at Ella, his face expressionless, before he looked back at her rescuer. He raised his carbine slightly with one hand. The barrel hovered just slightly above the young man's face. He pulled the trigger, and Ella shrieked again.

The gunman slung his rifle around his back and hoisted the man over his shoulder before turning around and stepping through the exit. Ella watched as he dropped the body over the side of the stairs, and she heard it smack against the tarmac. The sound sickened her, and she couldn't fight the bile rising from her stomach. She vomited on the floor, and the gunman turned to regard her, his face wrinkled in revulsion.

Morgan could handle blood and guts but not vomit. As soon as the smell reached his nostrils, he gagged and covered his mouth with his hand before quickly exiting the plane. He returned a moment later bearing the majority of Silva's weight.

"The couch," Silva wheezed. "Get me a bottle of whiskey," he ordered. "And get us airborne." Silva thought of Mather-Pike as Morgan led him to the couch, his desire for revenge stronger than his own lust for life. However, his wounds needed immediate attention. Without medical intervention, he would likely die. What good was taking revenge if he wasn't around to relish it?

"Yes, sir," Morgan replied. Ella, horrified, looked at Silva and then at Morgan.

"Who is he?" she asked.

"An associate who just received a promotion," Silva replied with difficulty.

"Where's Rian?"

"Rian?" Silva inquired. His eyes narrowed, but a coughing fit overtook him. Ella immediately felt uneasy; then terror spilled over her. She had used his first name. Her eyes shot toward the exit, and she bolted for the door. It was armed, so all she had to do was pull the lever and the focused explosions would launch the door outward and deploy the inflatable slide.

She never got close.

Morgan's strong arms seized her and threw her to the floor. He advanced toward her, his dark eyes devoid of any emotion, like a shark's eyes. He ripped her upward and violently dragged her back to her quarters. She screamed and kicked, but her efforts did little to break Morgan's grip. He threw her onto the bed, and sobbing she scurried to the far corner of the room and drew her knees to her chest. However, Morgan held no other plans for her.

"If you come out, I will strangle you to death," he threatened before he slammed home the sliding door. She quickly located her cellphone, and within minutes, Ella heard the engines groan to life, and she bore the force of takeoff.

Gulf of Suez,
Aboard Scarlett's Bosom

Shaw winced and downed a swig of the presented Witblits. The grape-fermented brandy was the South African counterpart to American moonshine. Shaw was glad he was seated when he took the swig because it would have knocked his feet out from under him. He coughed in response to the potent drink. Everyone around laughed, and Shaw quickly passed the bottle to Wyatt.

"It'll take the edge off," de Jager stated as his team's medic neared Shaw with a sutures kit. Shaw, shirtless, glanced down at the wound. It resembled a question mark without the dot, and the raw muscle grain was easily visible between his slashed skin. They had stemmed the majority of the blood flow, but a few streams still trickled out of the laceration, and dried blood caked down his abdomen. With the wound already cleaned, an act that had nearly sent Shaw into shock, the Raider readied himself for the stitches. Each insertion of the needle felt like a stinging pinch or the popping of a bad zit, but Colonel de Jager was right, the swig of Witblits had taken the edge off.

"Why did you save us?" Wyatt asked. The question silenced everyone in the room. De Jager glanced at him and shrugged.

"Ask him," he replied, pointing at Mather-Pike. Wyatt shifted his gaze toward the reclining South African. Mather-Pike rotated a bottle of Witblits in his hand before he met Wyatt's gaze.

"It was the right thing to do," he replied before taking a swig. Both Wyatt and Shaw felt there was more to the story, but they didn't press it.

"Thank you," Shaw said. Mather-Pike inclined his head.

"You're welcome."

"What do you think of my ship?" de Jager asked, eager to gain the approval of United States military personnel. He patted Shaw on the side of the knee as he moved to the open seat next to him.

"It's nice," he replied. De Jager grinned and turned up his own bottle of alcohol.

"She may not be a cruise ship or like one of your American navy ships, but she is a good home," de Jager said.

Shaw hadn't been surprised when the two Little Birds nested on the vessel waiting to the south of Port Tawfiq. The ship resembled an explorer's vessel that Shaw imagined hosted submarines to comb the seafloor in search of missing ships from ages past, but this ship, although a bit rusty, was a floating armory hidden in plain sight. He had to applaud Colonel de Jager. The ship would fit right in with the rest of the vessels that came and went in the various ports throughout Africa.

Shaw's thoughts drifted toward Natalie; he needed to contact her as soon as possible but wasn't sure how. It was obvious by now that General Weber had called off the mission, and Shaw wasn't entirely sure how he felt about it. He could see both sides; however, Shaw withheld his judgement, but he doubted Wyatt would be so forgiving.

The medic finished his work, and Shaw gazed down and approved. He wet a towel and began cleaning the dried blood off his body. A cellphone rang, drawing his attention.

Mather-Pike wearing a wide smile scooped it up and pressed it to his ear. His face immediately changed, and everyone witnessed the concern splashed across his countenance.

"Ella, what is it?" Mather-Pike asked. If his face wasn't enough of an indicator, his tone confirmed their suspicions. Something was wrong.

"Rian!" she exclaimed. Her sobs disrupted her words, "You're... you're alive!"

"I'm fine," he relayed sternly, "what is going on?"

"A man came for me and said you sent him, but another man shot him," she explained. Her hysteria grew as she recounted the traumatic event. "He brought Silva on board. He's been shot too, and the other man confined me to my room." Mather-Pike's anger soared to new heights as he listened. "Where are you?" she asked.

"Wait, did you say Silva is there?" Dread assaulted him as he considered her words.

"Yes, he's hurt and angry," she started, pausing as she mustered her courage, "he knows," she finished. Mather-Pike nearly dropped the phone. He didn't fear for himself but rather for Ella's safety, and the reality that he could do nothing to save her bore down on him like a collapsing building. "Did you shoot him?" she asked.

"Yes," he replied without hesitation. As quick sob issued forth from Ella's lips. Her despair wasn't in that he had taken that action but in that Silva had survived. "I swear to you I thought he was dead," Mather-Pike said. "Ella, I will save you," he promised.

"I know," she said. Her door slid open, and she raised her gaze to meet Morgan's cold eyes. He stood before her in the doorframe to her room. Tears trailed down her cheeks in wide streaks. The look in his eyes betrayed his intent, and her sobs intensified. "I love you, Rian," she said.

"I love you too, Ella," Mather-Pike said back. Tears moistened his blue eyes as the longing emotion gripped him. His eyes suddenly popped as Ella shrieked.

"Ella!" he shouted. He heard the struggle through the phone. Ella fought for breath as Morgan's hands closed around her throat. "Ella!" Mather-Pike screamed. Horrified, a surge of helpless rage coursed its way through his body. Shaw never removed his eyes from Mather-Pike's face. His expression told him everything she needed to know.

This Ella was dead.

Mather-Pike, tense and heaving, stilled as the chilling voice passed through the phone's speaker.

"This is your fault," Morgan stated. The line ended, and the phone fell from Mather-Pike's grasp and clanged against the floor. The large man, his mind swirling with grief and anger, looked blankly into Affré's eyes. The Frenchman's gaze sowed compassion in return, and he moved to his side.

"He killed her," Mather-Pike mumbled. Affré had never heard the proud man speak in such a way. The words rolled off his tongue lazily as if he had forgotten how to speak. Affré's brow furrowed, and he turned toward Shaw after he had eased Mather-Pike back into his seat. The South African, upon touching down, exploded into powerful sobs. De Jager quickly rushed to Mather-Pike's side and embraced him.

"Oh my boy," he said, sympathizing with his pain. He knew his man was likely dead as well.

"Silva will seek medical attention before rendezvousing with his supplier," Affré shared with Shaw. Affré's mind raced toward damage control. He thought as quickly as he could, but he soon realized that in their failure they had doomed themselves. Perhaps the two Americans could provide the assistance he knew they would soon need.

"Why are you telling me this?" Shaw asked.

"You want him dead just as much as I do," Affré replied. Shaw nodded, beckoning him to continue. "He will wish to continue his business, of that I have no doubt. He will meet with the supplier to discuss what he will acquire as merchandise and negotiate the costs."

"Who is his supplier?" Shaw asked.

"I want your assurance that when this is over you let us walk," Affré countered. Shaw looked at the whimpering South African and nodded.

"You have it," he promised.

"Silva's supplier is a Marine Corps major general by the name of Linus Weber."

PART III

THE OFFICER

38

A round of oo-Buck would not have hit Shaw harder. The name that passed through Affré's lips slowed time for the seasoned Marine captain. His mind immediately clouded as it subconsciously rejected the information presented. He fought through the haze, finding his voice and regaining control of his faculties.

"What name did you say?" Shaw asked, his voice barely above a whisper. He rose from his seat and took a step toward the Frenchman.

"General Linus Weber," Affré repeated, alarmed at Shaw's reaction.

"Major General Linus Charles Weber?" Shaw probed. Affré tilted his head in confusion before he nodded.

"Yes, the same." Shaw grunted and stumbled backwards as if kicked in the chest. He caught himself on an empty chair and guided himself slowly into the seat. All those men, his brothers, dead at the hands of the man they all revered above any other.

"How could he do this to us?" he murmured to himself. How many others had fallen to Weber's deception? His life mentor had betrayed good men to their deaths. He glanced at Wyatt. His friend wore the same bewildered look of one betrayed.

"Do you know where they will meet?" Shaw asked.

"I do," Affré answered. "General Weber owns a property in the Abaco

Islands; specifically, on the south side of Green Turtle Cay." Shaw knew the property all too well. He and Caroline had sailed there many times. The entire thought enraged him.

"I'll help you get Silva, if you help me get Weber, and then and only then, will we go our separate ways," Shaw stated firmly.

"What assurances can you give to insure you will keep your word and not reveal our identities to your people?" Affré asked.

"Done," Mather-Pike stated strongly, rising from his seat. Affré's eyes snapped toward his companion. The South African, a man whom Affré had grown to care for as a friend, bore a determination that Affré had not seen on his countenance. If he was so committed, then Affré would commit himself with the same effort. Besides, his fortune dangled in the middle of this mess, and he did not intend for it to slip through his fingers.

"Agreed," Affré added. Shaw nodded.

"We need to get back to the United States," Shaw said. Affré turned to de Jager, his look beckoning for his assistance.

"I can take you to Cape Town, and you can secure transportation to the States. I got to lay low for a while anyway. Might as well see the family." Affré nodded, satisfied.

"There is a US Consulate General in Cape Town," Shaw said. "We can secure transportation through them." Affré nodded again. "And there's someone I need to call."

Tampa, Florida

The runner's shoes fell lightly in a steady rhythm on the abandoned river walk. Sweat bled through his heather-gray shirt on which *Marines* was printed in large, black capital letters. His shirt was tucked into his nylon PT shorts, and his aged muscles shook as each step sent waves of energy radiating up his legs.

General Linus C. Weber's mind remained restless as he kept up his vigorous pace. Had he done the right thing selling out Shaw and Wyatt to Silva? It was only a matter of time before Shaw discovered his involvement.

At that point, the situation would progress into a kill or be killed scenario, and Weber had simply struck first. However, his preemptive strike meant taking out Wyatt as well; it had to be done. The two men were inseparable, and neither would let up on their crusade, especially if the other perished. That meant they both had to go. Besides, Wyatt should already be dead anyway. He convinced himself he had done it for Denise and Caroline's future.

Caroline.

How would he explain this to her? Shaw was encroaching on his family's way of life. Neither Denise nor Caroline knew that though. Weber touted that his wealth came from smart investments in the markets, but he had made his fortune selling phased-out Marine Corps weaponry over the last ten years.

He thought of his older brother, and his mouth turned bitter as his mind dwelled on him. Donald Weber was the founder and CEO of Brightmark Industries, a multi-billion-dollar, international enterprise. Weber's anger increased. He was twice, no three times, the man his brother was. Had he entered the private sector instead of the military he wondered how his life might be different. Would he own multiple yachts? Perhaps a private jet or two? A penthouse suite in New York City? It was impossible to know, but Weber was determined to make up for lost time.

Shaw had simply gotten in the way. He tried to convince himself again that he had done the right thing, but the pang of guilt wasn't so easily defeated. It was done now. There was no turning back. Weber locked his gaze forward and continued his run.

He neared the end of the boardwalk and slowed as the sun crested the horizon. He laced his hands over his head and panted heavily before stretching out his legs. He was not a spry Marine anymore, but he still managed to run five miles every morning. He placed his hands on the railing and watched the water turn from dark black to rich gold.

"I'm so sorry, Caroline," Weber said.

"She'll get over it," came a calloused voice from behind. Weber recognized the owner and didn't turn to address him.

"Yes, she's strong."

"Like her old man," the voice said. Weber chuckled and finally turned around. The man he beheld was a man for whom he cared little but appreciated greatly. "You tell her the same thing you've told the other families. That her beloved died heroically on the field of battle for this great nation." Weber easily deduced the sarcasm that filled the man's tone. He was not amused.

"Did you find out anything, Mr. Roark?" Weber asked. Connor Roark smirked and approached the railing.

"Yeah, she's in Atlanta. Lives in an apartment complex near Centennial Park."

"And?"

"It's been arranged," Roark replied. Weber sighed.

"She may not know anything," the general countered. Roark laughed.

"Can we take that chance?" Weber knew he was right. If she published a story with CNN detailing her experience in Yemen, then a congressional investigation was bound to follow. He couldn't afford to have that hearing summon anyone to testify. He wouldn't have to act against them if Kathryn Byrd was eliminated.

"Fine," Weber replied. "And what about Natalie Hale?"

"She's a tougher nut to crack, but I'm working on it."

"She was on the op with Shaw and Wyatt. She knows too much. She'll be landing at Andrews this afternoon. Get it done," Weber hissed. The threat was not lost on Roark, but before he could react, Weber jogged off, back the way he had come. Roark let it go and checked his watch. He grinned.

Almost showtime.

39

Atlanta, Georgia

Kathryn lay awake in her bed thinking of Wyatt, as she did every morning before rising for the day. Atlanta's radiant, morning glow filtered through the sheer curtains and dimly lit the dark studio. She thought of Yemen and the insurgent she had killed. His eyes no longer dominated her memory, and she was truly grateful for her weekly therapy sessions. She had taken up Muay Thai in addition to her consistent firearm practice at Stoddard's gun range.

She had taken both Pistol 1 and Pistol 2 training courses with the Warrior Poet Society, and Wyatt had been right. John Lovell was truly a delightful yet disciplined instructor. His welcoming and excited demeanor created a pleasant learning environment, and Kathryn couldn't deny how quickly her skills had improved under his tutelage. She now outshot most that visited Stoddard's.

The journalist felt powerful and capable, yet vividly aware of her own limitations. She still awaited her concealed carry permit, but she had applied for it at the probate court. Having submitted fingerprints and authorized a background check, she was confident she would receive it in the mail soon.

She hoped to see Wyatt sooner.

Kathryn hadn't heard from Wyatt in nearly a week, but she never expected she would. She missed him terribly and longed for his presence daily, and to keep her mind occupied, when she wasn't training, she was writing. She had contacted her editor and informed him she had started her story. He was elated and promised any support he could muster, but she had simply requested time, which he was more than happy to give.

Her thoughts dwelled on the media release yesterday stating two Marine Corps helicopters in Yemen had crashed due to mechanical failures, killing all onboard. The story had angered her beyond her normal limits. It wasn't unusual for details to be released by the Pentagon to the press weeks or months later, and considering the classified information revolving around the CIA outpost, Kathryn tried to understand why the government was lying to the public. In the end, it didn't matter, she knew what happened and would report it in detail. That was the beauty of a free press, and she was grateful CNN was waiting on her story before releasing their coverage of the event.

Kathryn stiffened at the muffled shuffling outside her apartment door. Her adrenaline spiked. She rolled off the bed and grabbed her Glock 19 in the same fluid motion. Before Yemen, she would have reasoned with her fear and attempted to convince herself that nothing was wrong, but after receiving training, she listened to her gut.

Her gut told her to get ready for a fight.

A fear-filled yet exhilarating sensation rolled over her. The disturbance was likely nothing to worry about, but Kathryn wasn't risking it. With her senses heightened, she listened. A thought immediately entered her mind. Was Wyatt attempting to surprise her? The idea caused her to drop her guard. She lowered her pistol, and a smile traced its way across her face. She moved toward the door. Her excitement growing, she glanced through the peephole.

She gasped and attempted to recoil, but the door jolted open, slamming into her forehead and nose. Dazed, she stumbled backwards, and the intruder advanced with indiscretion. Blood ran into her eyes, mixing with the tears and blurring her vision. Realizing the severity of her predicament, Kathryn wiped her eyes and blinked rapidly.

The intruder advanced, and Kathryn's eyes caught the gleam of steel jutting forth from his right hand. She raised her pistol, and the man hesitated too long. She couldn't find the front sight, but it hardly mattered; the man was close enough. Falling into muscle memory, she took up the slack in the trigger, finding the familiar wall, and sent the first round into her assailant.

He grunted but advanced. Kathryn, surprisingly collected, fired again and again. The man retreated backwards a step. Remembering the fatal T box that would "turn out the lights" as her instructor had said, Kathryn finally found the front sight post and trained it on his face. She tightened her grip and isolated her trigger finger. It took more effort than she could have imagined implementing the fundamentals in a state of heightened stress, but she succeeded.

The intruder's head snapped backwards, but she hardly noticed having reacquired her sights in the event she needed to shoot again. He fell backwards, a gaping hole replacing his nose. The round had passed through his skull and severed the spinal cord from the brain.

She rose to her feet and again John Lovell's words echoed through her mind, *Does anyone else want to play?* She checked her surroundings, ensuring her assailant was dead and that he was alone. Relieved and yet shaken, she raced toward her phone and dialed 911 before leaving her residence.

"Nine-one-one, what's your emergency?" asked the dispatcher.

"I've been the victim of an assault and home invasion," Kathryn replied breathlessly.

"Are you in a safe place?"

"Almost," she answered. She pounded on her friend's door at the end of the hall. "Patricia! Let me in!" Patricia, a consistent morning person, answered the door immediately. Kathryn pushed her way inside, and Patricia froze when she saw the gun.

"Wait, those were gunshots?" she asked fearfully. Kathryn ignored her and bolted the door. She provided the dispatcher with her address, detailed the situation, and requested EMS.

"Help is on the way," the dispatcher assured. "I will stay on the line with you until they arrive."

"Thank you," Kathryn said. Her body shook as the adrenaline faded. She exhaled forcefully and was surprised at how quickly she had recovered.

"Kathryn, what is going on?" Patricia asked warily.

"A home invasion," she replied through her heavy breathing.

"What?"

"Yeah," Kathryn confirmed. Something in her gut nagged at her. There was no denying that that man had come to kill her, but why? Had he desired to rape her, he would have retreated at the sight of the gun, wouldn't he? Even after being shot, he continued his assault. It suggested that he was accustomed to such experience. A hitman? She couldn't deny that he wasn't. But why? The only rational conclusion fell on Yemen. She should have died, but alive she could reveal what really happened to her, the NGO reps, and the Marines.

Why now? She had told her editor she was working on the Yemen project. Had someone else found out? Had he told someone? The questions scared her more than she would dare admit.

Aboard Scarlett's Bosom,
Off the Coast of Mozambique

Shaw sipped his coffee as he watched Affré at work. His eyes glanced toward the metal briefcase he also kept close. If the case contained what he thought it contained, a plan was already forming in his mind.

Wyatt entered the mess and headed their way. He took his seat across from Shaw and leaned forward. Shaw inclined his ear.

"I just don't get it," he started, "why would Weber sell us out?"

"Isn't it obvious?" Affré interjected. Their stares did little to unnerve him.

"Fill us in, Professor," Wyatt sarcastically remarked. Affré looked up from his laptop and gazed directly at Wyatt.

"For the money," he answered.

"Obviously," Wyatt stated. He looked at Shaw, "but why?"

"What do you mean?" Shaw asked.

"Why risk exposing yourself to the weight of United States intelligence? Why not just sell to uninvolved parties?" Wyatt explained. Shaw scratched the side of his forehead before looking down at his coffee.

"Maybe he thought he could cover it up," Shaw offered.

"But it can't be that simple?" Wyatt protested.

"Sometimes it is," Affré added. The comment carried a weight neither Marine expected. It focused in on the notion that Weber might really have just killed Marines for the money, and that thought brewed deeper betrayal within Shaw and Wyatt. Neither man wanted to believe that their brothers had died for something so trivial. No one wants to die for money.

"What's in the case?" Shaw asked, changing the subject. Affré's golden eyes glanced at the silver briefcase that rested on the table next to him.

"It's a computer that links to a satellite network for funds transfers," the Frenchman responded.

"How does it work?" Shaw asked. The question surprised him, but he didn't show it.

"Once I boot up the software, Mather-Pike or I have the client enter their account information and then enter Silva's."

"Then it transfers the money to Silva's account?"

"Yes, but if you're looking to access that account, you can't, or rather there's no money in it," Affré said. Shaw mulled over his words. He had little interest in Silva's accounts.

"Hey, can I use that?" Wyatt asked, noticing the satellite phone resting next to Affré's laptop.

"Be my guest," the Frenchman replied. Wyatt scooped up the phone and rose from his seat as he punched in the memorized number. He paced around the mess as it rang.

"Hello?" came the timid voice on the other end of the line.

"Kathryn!" Wyatt exclaimed. She immediately burst into tears.

"John," she whimpered.

"What's wrong?' Wyatt's gaze snapped to Shaw's, and the veteran Raider recognized the expression painted across his friend's face as he listened to her.

"What is it?" Shaw probed urgently.

"I need to get to Atlanta ASAP," he stated sternly.

"Wyatt?" Shaw asked for clarification.

"It's Kathryn. Someone tried to kill her."

40

Hamburg, Germany

Silva groaned and passed in and out of consciousness as he lay on the surgical bed at *Asklepios Klinik Barmbek*, one of Germany's and the world's most premier hospitals. His eyes attempted to focus on the faces swirling above him, but the bright light and the pain mingled to blur his vision and cloud his mind. He remembered the ambulance and the awful sirens, but had he lost consciousness? Where was Mr. Morgan? Was his contracted surgeon present?

"Mr. Silva, I am going to administer anesthesia now," came a distant voice the Spaniard didn't recognize. He tried to source its owner, but blackness encroached from the corners of his eyes.

Over Maryland, USA

The Gulfstream entered United States air space, and Natalie rapped her fingers against the cellphone lying on the table in front of her as she gazed out into the morning sky. She sighed. The cellphone rang, but she didn't recognize the international number.

"This is Hale," she greeted.

"Hey, Natalie, you alright?" the man on the other line asked. The joy that gushed within her radiated throughout her bloodstream and sent tingles up and down her spine. A smile wider than any she had ever worn traced its way across her face.

"Is that becoming our thing?" she asked.

"What?"

"Asking how each other is doing," she clarified. Shaw chuckled, and she relished the sound.

"I guess so," he replied.

"I'm glad to hear from you. How's Wyatt?"

"He's fine," Shaw replied.

"And you?" she asked. Shaw smiled at the tenderness in her tone. He opened his shirt collar and looked at his wound dressing.

"I'll make it," he replied. "Where are you?" Natalie fought against the guilt that tried to surface.

"Just entered US airspace," she answered. "Look, David, I... I didn't have a choice." Shaw nodded his head.

"I understand." The forgiveness present in his tone relieved her greatly and subdued the pang in her heart.

"What happened?" she asked.

"Silva knew we were coming," he replied.

"How?"

"I'll explain everything in person. Wyatt and I are headed for the US Consulate in Cape Town where we will obtain transportation to Atlanta. Can you meet us there?"

"What's in Atlanta?" she asked.

"Kathryn Byrd," he replied. "She's been attacked, and we don't think it's coincidental."

"What are you saying?"

"I know everything, Natalie. I know who Silva's supplier is and who leaked the intel about Yemen and likely this too."

"Who?"

"I can't say over the phone. Can you arrange a safe place for Wyatt to lay low with Kathryn?"

"I'll see what I can do," she replied.

"Thanks, Natalie. Meet me in Atlanta and be careful." Natalie nodded along with his words.

"Alright, you too, David."

"See you soon," he said. The call ended, and Natalie rubbed her eyes. When had she last slept, really slept? That night in Dubai? She couldn't remember, but she wasn't finished. Although relieved that Shaw was alive, the questions she had and Shaw's tone suggested she had a long way still to go before she won justice for her fallen team.

She glanced down at her phone. She had another call to make. She knew a senator with an estate in Shenandoah. It should be safe enough for Wyatt and Kathryn until all this was finished. She dialed the number saved in her phone. It would be good to hear her old commanding officer's voice again.

Silva awoke and blinked rapidly. Fatigue assaulted him, but he pushed through the feeling. He took in his surroundings. His suite was decorated in a glossy, modern fashion, and natural light poured in through the large, one-way windows. Morgan sat on the couch watching Arsenal compete against Leicester City on the large, flat-screen television.

"Mr. Morgan," Silva managed. The man didn't remove his gaze from the game.

"Yes?"

"What happened?"

"You got fixed," he replied, his English accent only added to the perceived apathy, and Silva immediately missed Affré. The Frenchman's attention to detail would have propelled him to provide a comprehensive account of the recent hours. Morgan was far less sophisticated. What had happened to Affré? He didn't know but assumed he was dead in Egypt. It was really a shame, but Silva was confident he could find someone to take his place.

He turned his attention inward. He felt significantly better, and, other than the overwhelming weakness and dull pain, his body responded well to his commands, but his mind seemed fuzzy, likely due to the pain meds. He found the remote to his bed and pressed the blue call button, and within seconds, a nurse entered.

"*Ja?*"

"Get my doctor," he commanded. She left as quickly as she had arrived. Thirty minutes passed before a man in a white coat entered the room. "Kasper," Silva greeted, "how did it go?" Dr. Kasper Doevelaar, a Dutch surgeon whom Silva kept on retainer, pressed his lips firmly together as he prepared to respond to his VIP client.

"You were very lucky, Francisco. The first round missed your left atrium by two centimeters and your spine by three, and the second missed your aorta by only a few millimeters. Your left lung briefly collapsed and was subject to tissue damage from the first round; the chest seals and the decompression needle saved your life," Dr. Doevelaar explained. "The two bullets simply poked two small holes in your thoracic cavity as if someone stabbed you twice with an ice pick. Again, you are very lucky. What were you shot with?"

"Five-point-seven millimeter," Silva responded. Dr. Doevelaar chuckled. Silva's expression contorted in anger.

"The five-seven round is a proven underperformer. Sure, it penetrates Kevlar, but doesn't do much damage after that." Doevelaar's eyebrows arched as he put together the pieces. "Oh, that makes sense. You were wearing armor. Well, had those bullets acted as they were designed, you probably would have died instantly. If I had to wager, I'd say someone shot you at pretty close range, not allowing for the bullets to drop in velocity enough to expand or tumble, and they just passed right through and kept going." Silva's eyes followed Doevelaar's hand as it passed through the air mimicking the bullet trajectory.

"Fascinating," Silva replied sarcastically. For fear of appearing weak, he dared not show his relief or gratitude for Dr. Doevelaar's aid, but he did trust his word wholeheartedly. Dr. Doevelaar had served in the *Korps Commandotroepan*, the special forces unit of the Royal Netherlands Army. It was only after medical school that he was recruited by the hospital for which he now worked. The salary alone was enough to persuade him to leave his beloved homeland. In short, the man knew his craft and knew it well.

"When can I leave?" Silva asked.

"Normally, not for several weeks, but I understand our arrangement. And since the damage isn't too severe, you are free to leave whenever you like," Dr. Doevelaar answered. "But give it a few days." Silva had no intention of doing any such thing.

"My business demands my immediate attention," Silva replied.

"Of course it does," Dr. Doevelaar replied flatly, making his offense known. "I've already written you a prescription for the pain. I'll have it delivered from the pharmacy." He turned to leave but paused, "Oh, I tried my best to keep the scars small." The doctor's condescending tone irritated his patient, and Silva watched him until the door closed. The fact that Morgan kept his gaze on the game the entire time greatly annoyed Silva, but the Englishman's loyalty could not be denied.

Or rather, his loyalty to his generous salary.

How unnerving, thought Silva. That was hardly grounds for true loyalty. Could anyone with enough money sway his new bodyguard's allegiance? He assumed so, which drifted his mind toward Mather-Pike's actions. What had spurred his betrayal?

Silva had laughed when he saw his bodyguard with pistol raised. Did he simply appreciate the execution of Mather-Pike's plan? Perhaps, Silva thought as he contemplated the last several hours. Marco Capra had simply taken a little off the top with each transaction, but Mather-Pike had taken betrayal to a higher level. It baffled the Spaniard. Was it about Ella? Had Mather-Pike possessed some deep infatuation with the girl? Had he been so blind to have not seen it coming?

Apparently.

It didn't matter. Silva had underestimated Mather-Pike, and now the South African had to die. He knew too much about his business, and the real question remained.

Where was he?

A thought spurred in his mind, and he glanced at Morgan. The Englishman still kept his gaze on the television, enticed by the game.

"Mr. Morgan, have the jet ready to depart for the Bahamas in a week. I will keep my appointment," Silva said. His words drew the man's attention.

"Still? You don't want to reschedule? Mather-Pike knows when and where the meeting is," Morgan countered.

"Exactly. I want a team outfitted and ready. Handpick them. Make sure their loyalty is not in question, preferably men you know. Pay them whatever they want. I want them on the ground in the Bahamas before we arrive. When Mather-Pike comes for you and for me, he will die."

Joint Base Andrews, Maryland

The jet rolled to a stop on its designated runway at Joint Base Andrews, which lay to the southeast of Washington, D.C. The Gulfstream taxied off the illuminated runway and came to rest among four C-130s. As the stairs unfolded from the side of the craft, Natalie appeared at the opening and glanced down at the man dressed in casual, fall clothing who waited for her.

"Ms. Hale," he called, "if you'll kindly come with me."

"Why?" she asked.

"Director Caldwell has requested to see you," the man answered. She nodded as she descended the stairs, and her mind raced to figure out how she could make it to Atlanta.

"May I see some identification?" she asked.

"Certainly," the man replied with a smile. Natalie took the bifold he presented and opened it. She gazed at the picture that matched the likeness of the man before her. She recognized the seal of the CIA. His name was foreign to her, but the Agency employed over twenty thousand individuals all around the world.

"Alright, Mr. Roark," she said confidently. "Lead on."

41

Kathryn received the cup of coffee from the detective and took a sip before setting the mug on the man's desk. She pulled the wool blanket tighter around her shoulders. Despite the loaned Atlanta Police Department sweatshirt, she still felt cold, however the blanket draped over her shoulders provided a sense of comfort after the night's trauma. Two butterfly bandages closed the cut just below her hairline. She looked up from the mug to the detective who smiled warmly.

Detective Devon Edwards had treated her with nothing but kindness throughout the entire ordeal. She had learned that he was a 2009 Morehouse graduate with a wife and three young children. He had been on the force for just over a decade.

"So, I've got some good news, Ms. Byrd," he started, "the city is not going to press charges. This is as clear-cut as self-defense gets." Despite knowing the unlikelihood of legal action being taken against her, the words relaxed her significantly. Detective Edwards, seeing the relief across her face, smiled again. "I have to say, you handled yourself really well. Even now, you're quite calm. It's," he paused as he sought the right word, "unusual." Kathryn quickly reached for her coffee in hopes to settle the rising anxiety.

She had killed two men in three months, and although Wyatt had been right that recovering from the trauma gets easier, it still shook her to the bone and left a permanent scar on her psyche. Both men's faces, although different in practically every way, remained seared in her memory. She doubted she would forget even the slightest detail.

Detective Edwards watched her, probing for some type of explanation revealed through her body language, but her gaze, hovering over her coffee, remained fixated on the ground.

"The department should thank you, Ms. Byrd. We've connected your assailant to seven cold cases, all ending in rape and homicide. Who knows what else this guy has gotten away with? Needless to say, you're lucky to be alive." Kathryn nodded in comprehension, but her mind was elsewhere, dwelling still on the timing and the why.

"Did you find a motive?" she asked. The question took Edwards by surprise, and he raised his eyebrows in response.

"Well, your case seems to follow the other cases. Young, single woman," he started.

"I'm not single," she protested.

"Are you married?"

"No."

"Then that's hardly a major deviance from his profile," Edwards stated. Kathryn didn't buy it, but she also didn't trust Edwards enough to spill to him. Wyatt was coming, and he would try to sort this all out. At the very least, he could protect her from future harm. There were too many questions, and not enough answers.

The door to the office opened and a sergeant greeted Edwards and said, "There's a John Wyatt here for Ms. Byrd." Kathryn leaped out of the seat and pushed past the portly officer. She raced down the hallway, her blanket billowing as she ran.

Wyatt burst onto the floor, drawing all eyes. His blue eyes scoured the sea of cubicles, desks, and windows until he caught her gaze. Kathryn froze and whimpered as her eyes watered. Seeing him again broke down the wall she had thrown up in the wake of the violent encounter. Wyatt rushed forward and gently embraced her.

"Are you okay? Are you hurt? What happened?" His frantic questioning drew a slight laugh of relief from Kathryn's lips. She pressed herself into his chest, and he kissed the top of her head. Immediately, sobs issued forth uncontrollably, and her knees buckled. Wyatt caught her and slowly guided her down to the floor. He sat with her as she cried.

"I'm glad you're back," she managed. She pulled away and inhaled sharply to clear her nose. Wyatt curled her hair behind her ear and kissed her. She threw her arms around his neck, and her tears saturated his face. Wyatt found himself breathless as they parted, and relief swept over him in a way he had never before experienced. Anger followed on a riptide of emotion, and everyone heard the searing hate in his voice when he asked, "Who did this?"

"A man named Griffin Carney," Detective Edwards stated. His words drew Wyatt's attention. "If you'll accompany me into my office, I can go over everything with you and Ms. Byrd."

Once in the office, Wyatt listened as Kathryn repeated the story she had shared with Edwards, and Edwards filled in the gaps regarding the cases to which his department had tied the villain.

"It's a pretty cut and dry case. No charges will be pressed against Ms. Byrd, and therefore, there is nothing more to do. It's closed," Edwards explained.

"Thank you, Detective," Wyatt said. "I appreciate your assistance. Is Kathryn free to go?"

"Yes, I can show you both out," he replied. He stood and motioned toward the door. Wyatt helped Kathryn to her feet, and the two followed the detective.

Before he saw them outside, Detective Edwards presented Kathryn with his card should she need his assistance in any way. Wyatt led her down the stairs to an awaiting beige Chevrolet Suburban.

"Who's is this?" Kathryn asked.

"It's a rental," Wyatt replied. "We've already got a plan. We just need to know everything you know," he said. "The stuff you didn't tell Edwards." He opened the rear door for her, she scooted in, and Wyatt followed her.

"Hi, Kathryn," Shaw greeted from his seat behind the wheel.

"Hi," she greeted back.

"Where are we going?" she asked as Shaw started the engine. She briefly flashed back to Yemen.

"Your place," Wyatt replied.

"What for?" she asked, alarmed.

"To pack you a bag and retrieve your vehicle," Shaw answered. "It's too coincidental that they tried to kill you."

"Who?"

"It's better if you don't know," Wyatt said. Kathryn didn't agree, but she didn't press the point.

Shaw followed Kathryn's directions, and they soon found themselves sitting idle in the parking deck of the Post Centennial Park apartment complex.

"Stay here. I'm going to head up with Shaw and be right back," Wyatt said to Kathryn. He presented her with his issued Glock 19 pistol. She gripped it confidently.

"Alright," she replied with an accompanying nod. She handed him her key and offered him a kiss before he exited the vehicle.

Shaw and Wyatt worked fast once they entered the bloodstained apartment. Shaw watched and remained alert as Wyatt rummaged through the studio packing Kathryn a bag. He retrieved ample clothing and toiletries for an extended duration away and made sure to grab one of her wool, winter coats. Lastly, he snatched up the keys to her CR-V before turning to face Shaw.

"You got everything?"

"Yeah, I think so. I can pick up anything else that we might need," Wyatt replied. Shaw nodded, and the two men left and made their way back to the parking deck.

Wyatt found the CR-V in the parking deck and tossed Kathryn's bag in the back seat as Shaw moved to retrieve Kathryn from the SUV. Wyatt returned, unloaded his weapons case from the rear of the SUV, and stowed one section of the CR-V's back seats in order to make room for it. Satisfied, he led Kathryn to the passenger's seat and closed the door before turning toward Shaw, hopefully not for the last time.

"And you're sure about this?" Shaw asked, "I want you there with me."

"I know, but I can't explain it. I've never felt this way before. I can't lose her," the Raider explained.

"You keep your head on a swivel."

"You too."

"Tell Natalie that I owe her big for this," Wyatt stated.

"Just keep her safe."

"I will," Wyatt said. He moved to embrace his dearest friend before moving toward the driver's seat. He paused before he opened the door. "David," he started, pausing to muster his next words, "I'm sorry."

"You don't need to apologize, John. I know you're doing the right thing," Shaw replied. Wyatt rolled his lips inward and nodded. It felt strange choosing Kathryn over Shaw, but the feeling was more natural than any other he had experienced. Was he betraying his fallen brothers by not seeing this through? The thought unnerved him, but he quickly realized that protecting Kathryn was just as much part of the mission as finding Weber. York and Reyes had died to protect her, and he couldn't dishonor their sacrifice for revenge. "Hey, Boss?" Wyatt started again. Shaw having made his way back to the SUV stopped and turned to face him. He recognized the shift in Wyatt's tone. He was addressing his captain now. "Kill that bastard."

Shaw offered him a nod before he disappeared behind the SUV. Wyatt turned toward Kathryn's CR-V, and as soon as he closed the door, Kathryn's first question spilled out, "where are we going?"

"Shenandoah," he replied. "Natalie secured a cabin for us to wait this thing out."

"She owns a place in Shenandoah?"

"No, it belongs to a senator she knew from her time in the Navy, or something like that," Wyatt explained. He pressed the push-start button, threw the car in gear, and left the parking deck and Atlanta behind them.

Shaw sat in the driver's seat of the Suburban, having watched Wyatt and Kathryn leave in the rearview mirror. He checked his cellphone.

Natalie had not checked in.

And that alarmed him.

42

Natalie's head rolled to the side as she fought her way back toward consciousness. What had happened? She remembered riding in the vehicle with Roark on her way to see Director Caldwell, when...

Her eyes widened.

She recalled Roark's quick movement and the needle stabbing into the side of her neck. She had attempted to fight back, but the dizzying darkness came too quickly.

The operations officer glanced around the room. Cream-colored tiles lined the floors and walls, and the ceiling above her matched. She tried to move her hands but found them bound together. Her legs, in like manner, lay fastened tightly together. On what was she laying? She turned her head from side to side. It was a glass and metal gurney of some sort, and she suddenly noticed the intense heat radiating from behind the square metal door to her right. Dread suddenly gripped her throat.

She was in a crematorium.

The door at the far end of the room opened, and Roark strode in pushing another cart upon which rested a rudimentary coffin. He paused when their eyes met, and he smirked.

"You shouldn't be awake," he stated. He contemplated his options then grinned. "But since you are..." He wheeled the cart forward, parked it next to the cremation chamber, and approached her. His loins stirred as he looked at her. Natalie attempted to wiggle away, but his rough hands seized her.

"What are you doing?" she demanded, her alarm evident in her tone. His hand stroked her hair, and his eyes traced down her body.

"You're a beautiful woman, Ms. Hale," Roark said, his breath hot on her face.

"Why are you doing this?"

"I've got my orders," he replied casually. Natalie attempted to remain as calm as possible as Roark's hands fiddled with her shirt's buttons. She knew she would likely get only one chance to resist and had to pick that moment carefully. Roark threw her button-down shirt open and glided his fingers over her cleavage before squeezing her breast. Natalie immediately tensed but fought against her impulse to flinch. His hands snapped to her pants and began to undo the button and zipper.

"Please, Connor, no," Natalie pleaded. Her words brought a smile to his face, but a frown immediately replaced it when he realized he could not spread her legs since he had bound them together. He jerked her around and produced a pocketknife. He flicked it open and flashed it before her face.

"Don't move," he commanded. Natalie, her fear nearly stifling her, nodded sharply. He popped the zip tie around her ankles with the blade before closing the knife and stowing it in his pocket. His hands immediately snapped to his belt, and his fingers worked furiously to undo the buckle.

With her legs free, Natalie seized the moment and exploded into action. Roark couldn't react in time to stop Natalie's booted heel from slamming into his face. He careened backwards and slammed his head against the furnace door. Natalie didn't hesitate, she shot upward from the gurney and sprinted for the door. She threw it open quickly and slammed it shut.

She tore down the hallway, her hands still bound in front of her. Light poured in from the window centered on the door at the end of the corridor, and Natalie burst through, stumbling into a parking lot. She felt groggy, sluggish, and her limbs felt distant. Whatever Roark had given her still negatively affected her body, but she didn't have time to dwell on it.

Roark's SUV sat nearby, but she didn't possess the keys and doubted they would be stowed within the vehicle. She heard passing vehicles nearby, and she took off in that direction around the corner of the brick building.

"Hey!" she shouted as she sprinted toward the group of vehicles that slowed for the traffic light. She focused on the black pickup truck with Marine Corps and Colt stickers on the back window. Whoever drove was bound to be armed. She caught the eye of the elderly man at the wheel and received an urgent nod. She threw open the passenger door, and he slammed his palm into the horn and stomped on the gas as soon as she was safely inside. He steered into the opposite lane and accelerated through the intersection.

Natalie, after glancing back through the rear window, exhaled heavily and slumped into the passenger seat. Trembling, she quickly covered her exposed torso with her shirt and worked the buttons closed.

"You okay?" the old man asked. His heart raced and pounded in his ears. The seventy-four-year-old Marine veteran hadn't experienced that level of adrenaline since his time in Vietnam.

"Thank you," Natalie replied. "I'm alright." He noted again her bound hands.

"There's a knife in the center console," he said. Natalie opened the console and noted the cocked 1911 pistol. She looked up at him, and he nodded her a guarantee. If Roark pursued, her savior was ready to fight. She fished the pocketknife out of the console, opened it, and carefully sawed through the zip tie. The plastic snapped apart, and Natalie folded the knife before rubbing her wrists.

"You were a Marine?" she asked.

"Yes, ma'am, and I'm going to take you right to the police station."

"No," she quickly replied. Her response concerned him.

"Look, I don't want to get mixed up in anything. I'm just doing the right thing here." Natalie inhaled deeply and looked at him. His gaze shifted between hers and the road.

"I work for the government, and am on an important mission," she explained. The words sounded so farfetched coming out of her mouth, like something from a cheesy movie. Her savior chuckled.

"I'm going to need a little more than that," he replied.

"Did you hear the Pentagon's statement about the Marine helicopters crashing in Yemen due to mechanical failures?'

"Yeah, I don't buy that for one minute," he said. Natalie nodded.

"They were shot down with United States weapons, and I work for the CIA and am tracking the provider of those weapons." It felt strange telling a complete stranger the brief details, but she saw no other course other than drawing the man's own weapon on him. "I need a phone to contact my partner. I've already missed my check in window." The Marine veteran kept his gaze forward as he contemplated her words.

"You got any ID?" he asked. Natalie almost laughed at the absurdity of that question.

"I was kidnapped, almost raped and murdered, and then cremated to cover it up. I'm lucky I've got clothes on," she retorted. The old man felt stupid for asking such a question. "Your phone." She was no longer asking, and he could see that well enough. He shifted his weight and produced an iPhone from his left front pocket, which Natalie graciously took from him.

Natalie had committed Shaw's phone number to memory after they had connected while he was in Cape Town to go over Wyatt and Kathryn's safehouse location. She tapped the correct numeral sequence on the screen and lifted the phone to her ear.

"Hello?"

"David, it's me," Natalie greeted.

"What number are you calling from," he asked. She heard the concern in his voice. She looked at her savior.

"It's a long story. I don't think I'll be able to make it in time to see Wyatt and Kathryn off," she said.

"They're already gone. Can you meet me in Jacksonville, North Carolina?" he asked.

"You sure are hopping around all over the place, but yeah, I can."

"Good, here's the address." Shaw provided her the address.

"Got it," she confirmed. Natalie lowered the phone and turned to the man driving, "Where are we?"

"Just outside D.C., in Clinton, Maryland," he replied. Natalie raised the phone to her ear again.

"I can be there in six hours," she said. Shaw nodded his head on the other end of the line. Silence spread between them.

"You okay?" he asked.

"A little banged up, but I'll be alright," she assured.

"Okay, stay safe. I'll see you soon."

"Alright, bye," she said. Natalie ended the call and handed the phone back to the Marine veteran. "What's your name?" she asked. He cracked a grin.

"Bernie Bannin," he replied, "and you?"

"Natalie Hale," she said, extending her hand. He gripped her palm lightly. "Well, Bernie, can you take me to get a rental car?" He shook his head.

"Going to Lejeune?" Bernie asked, having overheard their conversation.

"Yeah," she replied.

"I'll take you there."

"Bernie," Natalie protested, but he glanced over at her. His gaze silenced her. He swallowed before speaking. She could see the conviction spread across his face.

"I lost my boy in oh-four and my daughter in oh-nine. Both were phenomenal Marines and taken before their time." His voice wavered, but he continued, "My sweet wife died last month; complications from pneumonia." He paused and exhaled. "I'll take you to Lejeune. All I've got left is my country." Natalie nodded and placed a hand on his shoulder.

"I appreciate that, Bernie."

"Just tell me you're telling the truth, and you're not in the drug business or anything." Natalie smiled.

"I'm telling the truth." He grinned.

"Alright, let's get going."

Connor Roark threw open the door to his SUV and kept a white rag pressed against his bleeding nose. He crawled into the driver's seat and slammed the door closed. He fumed with anger and hatred toward Natalie Hale. At the same time, he scolded himself for allowing his desires to get the better of him. He vowed to finish what he started. He would have his satisfaction. His cellphone rang, and he cursed as he pulled it out of his pocket. He knew who was calling.

"Yeah," he answered.

"What happened in Atlanta?" Weber asked calmly.

"A minor setback," Roark replied. "The case is closed. No one can trace Carney back to me."

"I surely hope not, Mr. Roark. What's the situation with Natalie Hale?"

"I'm still working on it. I'll get it done," Roark replied.

"For your sake, I hope so." Roark didn't respond. "That, however, still doesn't solve the issue with the journalist."

"I'll find her," Roark promised.

"The Pentagon has already released that the events in Yemen were due to mechanical failures and nothing more. The American public bought it, as I knew they would, and I can't have CNN publishing otherwise."

"I'll take care of it," Roark reiterated. "Anything else?" His annoyance steadily grew. The line ended, and Roark tossed his phone on the passenger seat next to him. He glanced at his bloodied nose in the rearview mirror and cursed again.

43

Jacksonville,
North Carolina

Shaw directed the SUV onto the driveway, killed the engine, and looked upon the two-story house with longing. Just months ago, everything had seemed so much simpler. Had the helicopters not gone down in Aden, Shaw might have spent his days fishing and boating until his retirement came to fruition, but now death loomed over them all. If Kathryn had been targeted for what she may or may not know, then Natalie was surly on that same hit list. If Weber knew Shaw and Wyatt were alive, he might try and have them killed too.

Shaw turned his attention to his house and noted the deep blue siding and white shutters in the waning twilight. He opened the door and stretched his legs. The drive from Atlanta had been long, especially considering the gravity of his thoughts. Again, Wyatt was alone, and Shaw worried for his and Kathryn's safety. Natalie had assured that no one would think to look at the cabin for them, but Shaw knew they were all vulnerable until this thing ended. He turned as he heard a vehicle approaching.

A black Toyota Tacoma pulled up and stopped on the street in front of the house. Shaw didn't recognize the old man as he stepped out onto the asphalt, but he smiled wide as Natalie rounded the front of the vehicle.

"You must be Captain Shaw," Bernie Bannin stated. Shaw looked questionably at Natalie.

"And you are?" he asked.

"Private First-Class Bernie Bannin," he stated proudly, offering Shaw a stiff salute. Shaw grinned.

"As you were, Private," he said. Bernie offered him a crisp, approving nod. He turned toward Natalie.

"Are you sure you're going to be okay?" the old Marine asked, holding reservations about leaving her side. Natalie transitioned her gaze toward Shaw, and her heart swelled.

"Yes, I'll be just fine," she replied. She gave the old man a kiss on the cheek and said, "Thank you, Bernie. I owe you so much." His pale face turned bright red.

"Just get this scumbag," he replied, "and if you ever need anything, anything at all," he started. He turned to face Shaw, "and that includes you. Don't hesitate to call me."

"I will," Natalie promised. Bernie nodded again, confirming his offer. He approached Shaw and shook his hand.

"Semper Fi, Cap't," he said.

"Semper Fi," Shaw returned. "Thank you," he added.

Natalie moved to Shaw's side, and they both returned Bernie's wave before turning to face Shaw's house.

"This your place?" Natalie asked.

"Yeah," Shaw replied.

"A bit beachy," she noted.

"I like beachy."

"Come on, I'll show you the view before we head inside."

"The view?" Natalie repeated, intrigued. He encouraged her to follow him. Shaw led Natalie around the side of the house, down a path, and through a decorative gate. As they emerged on the backyard, a large smile found its way onto her face.

"This is beautiful," she said. Green grass slopped gently down to the bank of New River. The sun, nearly set, cast its fading orange glow over the water, turning it to liquid fire. A boathouse rose to the right, and from it, a dock jutted into the river. A sailing yacht floated blissfully with its mast extending skyward. The entire scene pulled serenity from Natalie, and she couldn't deny how good it felt. Shaw had arranged a tasteful fire pit surrounded by chairs facing the water, and it called her name.

"I'm glad you like it," he replied. He closed his eyes and inhaled the fresh air. He was home. "I'm going to head inside and grab a few things," he said.

"I'll go with you." Shaw led Natalie up onto the expansive, back deck, and she noted the large Green Egg near the railing facing the river. He had really poured a fair amount of effort into this place, she thought.

Shaw inserted his key, and the door glided inward. Natalie found herself impressed with the minimalist interior design and open floorplan. Shaw hurried across the dark hardwood floors to deactivate the silent alarm. He had thirty seconds before it blared its high-pitched shriek. He turned back around to see Natalie wander into the kitchen. She ran her hand atop the polished, concrete countertops and marveled at the wood-work on the vent hood.

"You've got a really nice place," she said. Shaw's closed smile made her tilt her head in questioning. Shaw glanced up at the ceiling and around the living area. He had purchased and renovated the place early last year in preparation for his proposal to Caroline, but she had broken off the rela-tionship before its completion. She never knew about it. Natalie watched his reaction. "What?" she inquired, wearing a smile of her own.

"I've never had a woman over," he said. Natalie laughed. She felt safe, secure, and it felt really, really good. For the first time in a long time, she felt normal.

"I guess I'm special," she teased.

"I suppose so," he replied. They locked eyes, and Natalie couldn't handle the tickling sensation in her heart.

"What did you need to get?" she asked.

"Just a few things," he said.

Shaw rummaged through his home collecting the various bits of gear he needed for the mission. The boat was already stocked with provisions, so he needn't worry there. He was quite the minimalist as far as clothing went. He only possessed two pairs of jeans and a handful of flannels, t-shirts, jackets, and shoes. Everything was practical, and nothing extravagant.

His firearms, on the other hand were the exception. He didn't have many, because he didn't need many, but the ones he did own were the best money could buy. MARSOC issued great gear, but Shaw would have preferred to carry his own weapons into combat any day of the week. There were exceptions though. He didn't own any explosives or machine guns, as was the law, but his AR-15, a custom carbine from Sons of Liberty Gun Works in Texas, was far better than the government issued M4A1 he often carried. He had outfitted the rifle with his favorite sling, a Ranger Green Vickers Blue Force Gear sling, and had mounted a Dead Air Sandman-K suppressor on the end of the thirteen-inch barrel. An AimPoint CompM5 red dot sight was his optic of choice.

The Raider broke down the rifle and stowed it in his Haley Strategic rifle case before setting it down on the floor next to the bed. He crammed all his loaded magazines in a duffle accompanied by his personal war belt and Glock 19 fitted with a Trijicon RMR, Surefire X300U light, and Dead Air Wolfman pistol suppressor. On his belt, he possessed a Safariland 6360RDS holster, that he had personally modified, in the spirit of special operations tradition, to allow him to holster his suppressed pistol.

Finally, he reached for the black pistol case on the bed before him. He popped open the brackets and slowly opened the lip. Inside sat a pristine BCM Gunfighter 1911 made by Wilson Combat and an extra, hand-fitted, threaded barrel. He remembered the first time he had laid eyes on the pistol, and apparently so had Wyatt. He didn't know how they had done it, but his team had all chipped in to purchase it for him as a retirement gift while they were still in Afghanistan and before they deployed to Djibouti and then Yemen.

Shaw ran his fingers over the black frame, and he half-grunted and half-coughed to fight off the wave of emotion that crept up within him.

"What's that?" came Natalie's voice behind him. She leaned against the doorframe to his bedroom with her arms crossed over her chest. Shaw didn't turn to address her but simply kept his gaze on the pistol.

"A gift from the guys," he replied. She heard the sadness in his tone and moved to his side. She placed a warm hand on his shoulder as she leaned to see the weapon.

"It's beautiful," she said.

"And it has a purpose," he replied sternly. She rubbed his shoulder, and he appreciated the touch. He closed the case, snapped down the latches, and placed the case in the duffle alongside a SilencerCo Osprey 45 silencer. Shaw then retrieved two items far more precious to him than anything else he owned.

The first was his grandfather's pocket Bible, which he had carried in World War II's Pacific Theatre against the Japanese. Its pages were littered with notes and accounts of his combat on the various islands he had served. It was not only a link to the past but also a link to his present. He was Marine because his grandfather had been. As Shaw stared at the worn leather binding, he remembered the man's kind blue eyes, thinning white hair, and contagious spirit.

He drank Scotch like it was water and only the good stuff. He had cracked jokes at which he was the first to laugh and contained a thirst for knowledge that even Plato and Aristotle would have admired.

The second item was the only physical copy of his grandfather's play, *In This Sign, Conquer*. The language his grandfather wrote was as captivating as any Shaw had ever read. It was his written legacy, his immortality, and Shaw intended to preserve it.

He glanced around the room. Having packed his passport and other important documents and a flash drive containing all the vital information for his life, Shaw zipped up the duffle, hoisted the heavy bag over his shoulder, picked up the rifle case at his feet, and left the room.

"I'm going to load all this into the boat," he said as he passed through the living room and continued outside.

"David," Natalie called. Her tone stopped him. He turned around to face her.

"Why are you packing like this?" she asked.

"Like what?" he asked. She strode forward and looked at him tenderly.

"Like you're never coming back." Shaw broke eye contact.

"I might not be able to after all this," he replied. She understood. She hadn't considered it before, but now that he mentioned that possibly, she considered her own situation. If Roark truly worked for Caldwell, how could she ever return to the CIA? Was Caldwell complicit? "Come on, let's get going," Shaw said. Natalie, drawn back to the moment, nodded and followed him from the home. The duo loaded up the sailboat and, satisfied, Shaw glanced at Natalie.

"We're all set," he said.

"You're forgetting something," she replied. He looked at her curiously. What could he possibly be forgetting?

"What?" he asked.

"You going to return the rental?"

44

Shenandoah National Park,
Stanley, Virginia

The dark, metallic-grey CR-V turned onto the gravel road that led up the mountain, leaving Stanley, Virginia in the valley below. The crossover SUV bounced as it made its ascent, and both passengers tiredly focused on the edge of the vehicle's headlights. The log cabin materialized before them, and they both could hardly call it a cabin. It appeared more as a mountain estate with large floor to ceiling windows built into its multiple A frames.

"Look at this place," Wyatt commented in awe.

"It's amazing," Kathryn added.

Wyatt killed the engine, and the two sat for a moment mesmerized by the home. The exterior lighting painted the structure in the most charming way while still highlighting its grandeur. Wyatt opened the door and inhaled the frigid mountain air. He moved to the rear and opened the hatch to fetch their luggage and his weapons case. The private travel arrangements he and Shaw secured from Cape Town to Atlanta permitted them to maintain possession of the weapons they had in Suez. Wyatt would have preferred his M4A1 given the circumstances, but he settled for his M110A1. He didn't care that it was illegal; he needed to ensure that he could protect them in the unlikely event they were found before Shaw and Natalie could clear up everything. As he followed behind Kathryn, he contemplated how they would even know the coast was clear. It wasn't like someone would just tell them that they weren't being hunted anymore. He only hoped Shaw could squeeze the answers out of Weber.

The couple quickly settled in, and Wyatt familiarized himself with the security system. Afterwards, he readied his weapons, and Kathryn, having changed into an oversized Mercer University sweatshirt, Nike shorts, and a pair of wool socks, watched him work. Her wavy hair lay sprawled over the arm of the couch on which she lay. The sight of her exposed shoulder and firm legs stirred Wyatt's yearning for the warmth of her touch, but he resolved himself to finish his work.

The Marine Raider ensured that his rifle was loaded and situated in the best possible location. He slammed a nineteen-round magazine into his Glock 19, giving him twenty rounds to work with, and toted the weapon around the estate with him. It was never outside an arm's reach.

"Can we have a fire?" Kathryn asked. Wyatt glanced at the large fireplace in the center of the living room. Two massive windows, each twenty feet tall, rose on either side of the equally tall and impressive stone fireplace. A bull moose head, with the most extraordinary antlers Wyatt had ever seen, sat mounted over the mantle.

"I don't see why not," he replied. Wyatt moved toward the pile of wood stacked in a decorative inlay next to the fireplace and went to work. Within minutes, a crackling fire flooded the room with its warmth. "There we go," Wyatt said as he brushed his hands together and rose to his feet. He turned around and froze.

Kathryn stood naked and smiling. Wyatt returned her smile as she moved toward him. Her skin prickled and chills swept over her body as it adjusted to the fire's heat or maybe in response to nearing the man she loved in such an intimate way. Her hands wrapped around his waist, and she hugged him tightly. Wyatt's legs weakened, and he shook briefly as his hormones spiked.

"Thank you," she said quietly.

"For what?"

"Everything," she answered before she kissed him.

Washington, D.C.

Roark scratched another potential location off the paper in front of him as his frustration mounted. He had been thorough in his research and had more locations to check, but the process was proving more time consuming than he liked. Natalie Hale, thus far, had eluded him.

He sat on a bench in the rotunda of the Capitol. Senator Reggie Ramirez would pass by any minute. Footsteps echoed through the rotunda drawing Roark's sharp eyes. Senator Ramirez and his entourage passed through, and Roark quickly rose to his feet.

"Senator!" he called, "a moment of your time?" Ramirez's brown eyes found Roark, and, turning to a member of his party, spoke quietly. The young woman nodded, split off from the group, and headed Roark's way.

"Senator Ramirez is headed for an important meeting. May I inquire as to your business with him?"

"Well, aren't you a cute thing," Roark said.

"That's kind of you," the woman replied, her expression showing her annoyance and disapproval. "Your business?"

"I represent a party interested in the senator's residence in Stanley, Virginia. My employer is hoping to tour the estate this weekend and make an offer," Roark said.

"And you came in person to discuss this?" she asked.

"You know very well that the senator is a very difficult man to get a hold of," Roark countered. She bobbed her head. He wasn't wrong.

"I'm afraid what you are requesting is quite impossible," she began.

"And why is that, Love?" Roark probed. "Surely, the residence is empty."

"Senator Ramirez is not interested in selling the estate," the aid replied, her mood stiffened with each pet name. Roark, seeing her begin to unravel, pressed harder.

"Come on, Beautiful, my employer won't take 'no' for an answer," he said. "Surely, you can arrange a private tour for just the two of us. I can promise you won't regret it."

"Have a nice day, sir," she barked. She turned to leave, but Roark pursued hastily. She stopped and turned to face him again. "You have yet to identify who your employer is or present any credentials whatsoever," she stated, flustered.

"Hey, I'm just doing my job," Roark stated.

"Even if the senator agreed to your proposal, it would have to wait." She grew more agitated as she continued, "an old military friend of the senator is currently staying at the estate, and, therefore, no requests such as yours will be granted." The young woman exhaled sharply and met Roark's gaze with the most unmovable expression she could muster. As she stared at him, something about his eyes frightened her. He looked at her with lecherous desire that overloaded her comfort threshold.

"I'm sorry to have upset you, Miss..." he searched her nametag, but she quickly covered it with her hand. She wasn't quick enough. "Miss Echols," he replied. A shudder coursed down her spine. "I will inform my employer that Senator Ramirez's mountain estate is off the table." He turned to leave, and Johanna Echols, shaken from her encounter, scurried back to Senator Ramirez's side.

Roark trotted down the steps of the Capitol wearing the smug expression of victory. Ramirez likely had hundreds of connections from his military service that he would have considered close, but Natalie Hale was the exception. She clung to him like a father, and he to her like a daughter. If anyone was staying at his estate, it had to be her.

He found his SUV where he had parked it and started the engine. The drive ahead of him would span a few hours and a lengthy hike would surely follow, not to mention all the planning needed prior to his departure. He felt the fire of the hunt heat his belly, a sensation he relished and sought at all times. It was his drug, his heroin, and he now had his next fix.

45

Atlantic Ocean

American Rhetor, a 2007 Beneteau Cyclades yacht, rose gently in the mild surf as she cut southeast through the Atlantic. Her white hull and matching sails contrasted sharply with the dark blue sea. Cruising at a steady six knots, Shaw was pleased with their progress.

The Marine Raider stood at the helm, gripping the steering wheel, with his eyes focused in the direction of the distant Abaco Islands. He dedicated his thoughts toward Weber. He had often wondered how the general could afford such a property in the Bahamas. Shaw had been there many times and was consistently amazed by the three-story, Bahamian residence; it was the main inspiration for the renovations to his house. Now, everything was clear: Weber's vacation home was built off deals selling United States weaponry to the highest bidder. Had it come to light in any other way, Shaw would have been greatly disappointed, but the killing of Marines could not be tolerated.

Shaw inhaled heavily, fighting off the rage attempting to gain a foothold in his body, and focused on the salty breeze. They had sailed through the night, taking shifts and relying on the autopilot.

Theirs was a three-day sail from Jacksonville, North Carolina to Green

Turtle Cay, and, fortunately, they would arrive in time for Silva and Weber's scheduled meeting, according to Affré's timeline. Shaw could hardly believe their fortune, but he wasn't naive. If Shaw were in Weber's shoes, or Silva's for that matter, he would beef up any normal security. He hoped Weber still believed him dead.

Natalie, who Shaw had brought up to speed the night before, emerged from the galley, carrying two mugs of coffee. She had wrapped her hair into a messy and wild bun, and free strands floated about her face. She shivered and dropped her head into her shoulders as the sharp, winter wind chilled her exposed neck.

"Here," Shaw immediately said, removing his jacket and offering it to her.

"No, I'm fine," she replied.

"Take it, I insist," Shaw pressed. She relented with a smile, set the two mugs on the table between the two exterior benches, and put on his coat. Having captured his body heat, the jacket immediately warmed her, and the high collar protected her from the wind.

"What about you?" she asked. Shaw grinned and waved his hand.

"I'm fine. Merino wool," he replied. He pinched a portion of his long-sleeved, crew-neck shirt and raised it up before letting it go.

"Oh, that's *very* nice," Natalie said, her voice laced with sarcasm. Shaw laughed, which drew a smile from the woman. "I brought you a coffee." Shaw raised his own mug he had seated on the dash before taking a sip.

"Thanks for the thought," he said. He didn't want to read too much into the gesture, but he hoped a deeper motive had spurred her actions. "Actually, mine's getting cold," he said, realizing it was far more important for him to accept the gift. Her face brightened. He exchanged his mug for the new one and took a sip, "Ah, that's better." Natalie, having taken Shaw's cup, realized that the ceramic mug was still quite hot.

He was sweet.

"How are we doing?" she asked, moving beside him.

"We're doing great. We'll arrive not tomorrow evening, but the next," he answered.

"Just in time," she said. For a moment, standing next to him, she found serenity being out on the open water in such a way. Despite her six years in the Navy, she had never once experienced the sea in this manner. It was far better than serving on one of the Navy's large warships, more intimate, a deeper connection between humanity and the sea. She loved it more than she could have imagined.

"It'll get significantly warmer by tomorrow evening," Shaw said.

"How much warmer?" she asked.

"Like bathing suit warmer."

"Oh, are you wanting to see a little skin?" Natalie teased. Shaw laughed, embarrassed.

"That's... uh... that's not what I meant," he quickly said. Natalie smiled and winked at him.

"I know." She patted Shaw's corded forearm, which turned into an affectionate rub. "I know," she said again before returning both hands to her mug. She shifted her gaze to the steady rise of the bow. "So how did you manage to afford this thing?" she asked. Shaw smiled.

"They're a bit more affordable than people think. I picked her up in Grenada in 2013. She had been dry docked since 2008. Her previous owner couldn't afford her anymore after the recession began, and I was able to scoop her up for a pretty good deal," he explained.

"And you sailed her back to North Carolina from Grenada all by yourself?"

"Yeah," he replied, "and fell in love instantly."

"I can see why," she said, admiring the freedom and sense of adventure one could only experience at the helm of a sailing yacht.

"What kind of coffee is this? It's quite strong," Natalie asked.

"Black Rifle Coffee: Beyond Black," Shaw answered. She nodded as she took another sip.

"It's good," she said.

"The best," Shaw replied.

"So where are we picking up Affré and Mather-Pike?" she asked, recalling the names of Silva's bodyguards from Shaw's briefing last night.

"Little Abaco Island." She nodded and took another sip of her coffee. Natalie wondered if she should ask her next question. She knew it was a personal one.

"What will you do when you see General Weber?" she asked. Shaw inhaled sharply. He had kept those thoughts at bay. They were too laced with emotion to process, but what he did know he would share.

"I want to bring him in, but I don't know how possible that is," he answered. "It will likely take years for the investigation to unravel what he has done, and who knows how much he'll be able to cover up. Will the threat against your life stop? Or Kathryn's? Or Wyatt's?"

"Or yours?" Natalie added. Shaw nodded.

"I never thought he was capable of such evil, and if he is capable of it now, he will be capable of it in the future." The Raider paused. "There is only one way forward, and I hope I have the strength to do it."

They finished their coffee in silence, and Natalie hadn't moved from Shaw's side, a fact that delighted the Marine. He had never met a woman like her, so resilient and formidable, and to be honest, he found himself concerned with his mission focus due to her presence. What if she didn't make it?

The thought didn't sit well in his stomach.

46

Shenandoah National Park,
East of Stanley, Virginia

The forest-green Range Rover rolled to a stop at the reserved campsite within Shenandoah National Park. The forest was hollow, having shed its leaves for the coming winter, but Roark hardly cared. He trained his mind on setting up camp. He wouldn't be staying, but he had to keep up the facade.

After setting up his tent and filling it with the usual amenities, he returned to the rear of the SUV. The man unfolded the map stowed in his jacket pocket and pressed it flat against the trunk space. He noted his location and the location of Senator Ramirez's estate before producing a Lensatic compass to confirm his bearings. Satisfied, the man slung his hiking pack over his shoulders and checked the ten-millimeter Glock to ensure a round sat in the chamber. He wasn't about to gamble his life in bear country. Roark found his eastward bearing and set off into the bush.

It was late afternoon before he crested the ridge that brought the Ramirez estate into view. His eyebrows arched at the grandeur of the cabin. He chuckled as he thought of how rich senators become only after assuming their office. Maybe he should run one day.

Roark, warm in his Beyond Clothing winter apparel, settled in for his stakeout. If his target was there, he would assault at nightfall. The forecast indicated a full moon and clear skies, which wasn't ideal, but Roark couldn't change the climate or the rotation of planets.

He unzipped his hiking pack and produced a Cliff bar, a Nalgene bottle filled with water, and a pair of high-powered binoculars. He gazed on the structure as he munched on the bar. An hour passed before he saw any activity, and he was immediately grateful for the large windows. A woman in an oversized sweatshirt descended a spiral staircase and moved onto the living room floor.

"Well, how about that," Roark uttered to himself. He recognized the blonde woman as Kathryn Byrd. He licked his lips as he observed her exposed legs and bare feet until she disappeared out of view. She remained hidden for another two hours until she reemerged headed toward the kitchen. She crossed the floor carrying two beers.

The sight excited Roark, who was she with? All intelligence indicated that it was Natalie Hale. It made sense, they did know each other from Yemen, and it wasn't too farfetched to consider that Hale would reach out to hide Kathryn. She certainly had the means.

Despite being unable to confirm the identity of the second occupant, he was confident it was Officer Hale. Who else could it be? Staff Sergeant John Wyatt was likely dead at the bottom of the Gulf of Suez, so even though Kathryn and he were intimate, his likelihood of being there was impossible.

He owed John Wyatt a bit of gratitude. Had he not resided with her for those two months and had the Air Force not picked him up from her apartment, Roark would have had a significantly harder time tracking her down. CNN had of course refused to provide any information about her whereabouts; it didn't matter that Roark had posed as a government official from the State Department tasked with checking on her. CNN, rightfully so, Roark knew, had kept her safe from probing.

He thought of Kathryn's legs again and her feet; he had a thing for feet. He also recalled Natalie's beauty and fought the anger that rose within him. Perhaps, he could finish what he started with Natalie and have a little fun before putting them both down.

The sun fell beneath the horizon of the distant mountains, and the cold saturated Roark's fingers as he readied his equipment. He glanced at the cabin again before checking his watch.

Four more hours.

The lights dimmed inside the cabin, making it all but impossible to see through the windows, but Roark, confident in his intel, settled deeper into the cleft of the rock formation.

———

Kathryn laid her head on Wyatt's shoulder as she watched the movie. Wyatt had come across the original *Star Wars* trilogy and had asked if she had seen them. When he heard she hadn't, he was insistent that they watch all three movies. Seeing his enthusiasm, she agreed, and so far, she had enjoyed the first one for what it was. Halfway through *The Empire Strikes Back*, she found it much more compelling than *A New Hope*. The characters were more complex, and the tension between the protagonist and the villain had increased significantly. Overall, she quite enjoyed herself, but then again, perhaps she only enjoyed the films because of the company. It really didn't matter though.

She glanced up at Wyatt, who kept his gaze fixed on the screen. His mouth hung slightly open, and she grinned at the sight before reaching up to tap the bottom of his chin.

"What?" he asked. He glanced down at her.

"Your mouth was hanging open," she answered with a laugh. He smirked.

"Yeah, that happens." She hugged his arm tighter and snuggled deeper into his shoulder. Wyatt rested a hand on her thigh and turned his attention back to the film. Kathryn reached into Wyatt's lap, picked a piece of popcorn from the bowl balanced on his legs, and popped it into her mouth.

"Who's your favorite?" she asked.

"Boba Fett," Wyatt quickly replied.

"Who?"

"The bounty hunter."

"Why? He's only in it for a couple minutes," she said. Wyatt laughed and rubbed her thigh.

"Yeah, but's he's cool, and his dad is really cool."

"His dad?"

"You'll see. I'm sure we'll get to the prequels while we're here too," Wyatt explained.

"How many are there?"

"There were six when I was growing up, and Disney has made," he paused as he tallied up the number in his head, "five and a TV show, which is beyond awesome."

"What did I get myself into?" she joked.

2300.

Roark sighed as he looked up from his watch. His face stung from the winter cold, and he had balled his fists inside his gloves. The cabin had been dark and quiet for three hours.

"To hell with this," he mumbled. He grabbed his gear and began his trek toward the estate.

After a short fifteen-minute hike, Roark located the power meter and quickly shut off power to the building. Electric companies had made it far too easy to kill the power to modern homes. With the power out at Senator Ramirez's cabin, the security system would not activate; however, that meant he only had a short window before the company called the senator to inform him of the outage. Roark held no doubts that Ramirez would then immediately contact Natalie Hale. He had to move quickly.

Roark produced a lockpick set, went to work on the door, and within moments, he was inside. He stepped over the threshold as the front door swung open, and he was surprised that Senator Ramirez's estate wasn't more thoroughly protected. Despite the instant warmth, his gut did nag at him as he surveyed the room, which caused his eyebrows to furrow.

He felt the strong pull to leave in that moment; however, there were only two women that shouldn't put up too much of a fight. He gained confidence at the thought but then remembered Natalie's foot smashing into his face. He was grateful she didn't break his nose.

With each step further into the cabin, he thought about his situation more. One had bested a notorious, criminal hitman from the Atlanta underground, and the other had held her own against insurgents in Yemen and again against him in the funeral home. Perhaps he was proceeding too hastily. Had he entered too soon? Were they ready for him? He resolved to shoot first and forego any pleasure.

The man's eyes scoured the room, and he kept his pistol ready. He glanced upward at the railing that capped the second floor, and he proceeded toward the spiral staircase. Roark ascended slowly, keeping his pistol trained on the balcony. Once on the second floor, he moved down the hallway. He peeked into the numerous rooms that lined the wide corridor and slowed as he neared the door at the end of the hallway. They had to be inside. He took a step forward.

The wooden floor creaked.

47

Wyatt's eyes shot open, and he rocketed out of bed. A full load of adrenaline dumped into his bloodstream. Someone was inside. Kathryn stirred and groaned at the commotion.

"What's going on?" Wyatt ignored her, and before he could reach for his pistol, the door burst open. Wyatt didn't hesitate. He shot forward, closing the ten-foot distance more quickly than Roark could have anticipated. The sight of a man confused him for a second before he responded as his training dictated, but he was too late. Wyatt barreled into Roark's torso and seized the weapon with both hands. The Raider drove his weight forward, driving with his legs, and pushed Roark back down the hallway and as far away from Kathryn as he could manage. Roark maintained trigger discipline and tried to gain his footing against the powerful force assaulting him. He whipped the side of his head into Wyatt's face, but the Marine, despite the bruising pain of repeated blows, pressed onward and dropped his head, drilling it forward into the man's chest.

Gripping the receiver of the pistol, Wyatt torqued the weapon against Roark's grasp, wrenching it free. It clanked against the ground, and Wyatt seized the opportunity. He snapped his head upward, catching Roark in the chin. Roark's front teeth chipped as they collided with his bottom teeth, but he ignored the shocking discomfort. Wrapping both hands around the back of Wyatt's neck, he drove his knees upward into Wyatt's face.

The first connected, and a flash of white stole Wyatt's vision. Roark delivered another blow, but Wyatt had managed to cross his arms to deflect the incoming attack. Both men growled in primordial rage, each seeking survival.

Wyatt struck out with his fist and connected solidly with Roark's groin. The man squealed and backpedaled, stumbling as he tried to maintain his footing. Wyatt rose to his full height and wiped the blood that ran freely from his nose and upper lip. He had a choice; he could retreat to his weapon or continue the offensive. Not wanting to give his opponent a moment to regroup, he chose the latter.

Wyatt, fists raised, continued toward the intruder, and Roark, not fully recovered from the sickening pain pulsing upward from his groin, reached toward his waist. Wyatt's eyes widened as he recognized the movement, and he lunged forward, tackling Roark. The two stumbled backwards, and they connected with a brittle banister; the railing gave way. Wyatt's foot sought sturdy flooring, but surprise flashed through his mind as he realized what was happening. Both men found themselves tumbling twenty feet to the ground.

Roark hit the floor first, landing square on his back. He had not known pain like that before. It completely debilitated him as he labored in vain for precious breath. He wheezed and wheezed and could barely find the strength to move. It felt like large hands closed around his lungs and squeezed with all their might. He stared at the ceiling, waiting to regain control of his body. His mind screamed, and, in horror of his temporary paralysis, Roark mustered what control he had to keep him in the fight.

Wyatt hit the floor hard. It wasn't audible, but Wyatt felt the series of cracks echo through his body. Wave after wave of debilitating, piercing pain radiated from his left side. He knew instantly that his ribs were broken.

Still able to draw breath, Wyatt gripped a broken railing post and arched it down on Roark's body. The hard, wooden club connected on Roark's chest, and Wyatt reared back for another blow. He aimed for the head.

His eyes wide, every cell in Roark's body shrieked upon recognizing the impending doom. Roark mustered all his strength and raised an arm to block the incoming blow. He felt the bone crack near his wrist, and the pain nearly made him nauseous, but he pressed through it. Wyatt raised the club again, but Roark rolled onto his side and caught the club with his good hand.

Wyatt let go immediately and rose onto all fours. He scrambled toward Roark and took an ill-timed, glancing blow on the shoulder from the makeshift club before he mounted his assailant in the dominant top position. He put his Brazilian Jujitsu to work, but it was far less effective than when training on the mat. It was crude, mixed with primitive striking that originates only in the midst of hectic combat, but Wyatt continued.

With the man straddling atop him and raining blows down on his face, Roark's body fell into habitual motion. He shielded his face with his forearms and grunted each time Wyatt connected with the broken bone. Wyatt reared back, and Roark seized the opportunity. Having regained his movement and lung capacity, he rocketed upward and seized Wyatt by the back of the neck. He discretely hooked his foot around Wyatt's left ankle and thrust upward and over with his hips.

Wyatt found himself tumbling sideways, and Roark gained the upper hand. Wyatt noticed Roark's hand again shoot to the center of his beltline, and, as he reached for Roark's hand, Roark produced a blade and raked it across the exposed flesh of Wyatt's palm. The Marine Raider howled in pain.

Roark rose to one knee and drew back his hand to thrust into Wyatt's side. Wyatt recognized the maneuver; it was one in which he too was well trained. The Marine snapped his heel forward and connected again with Roark's groan. Roark's face tightened, and a slight groan passed through his firmly pressed lips. Wyatt seized Roark's wrist with both hands, controlling the blade, and again shot his heel forward to connect in the same region. Roark screamed and retreated, the pain unbearable. Rising to his feet, Roark hobbled backwards into the living room, but immediately ducked as three gunshots echoed from the second-floor balcony.

Her ears should have rung from the deafening volley, but Kathryn's adrenaline canceled out the thunderous sounds. It was dark, and she couldn't see down into the living room. For fear of hitting Wyatt, she had shot at the ceiling in hopes to startle the combatants. As she focused on the living room, the faint moonlight, filtering in through the large bay windows, highlighted two men. She didn't know which was which.

"John!" she shouted.

"Here!" he cried. That was all she needed. She turned her attention to the standing man and fired quickly. They were long shots, nearly twenty-five feet. None connected, but Roark had had enough. With a broken wrist and permanently damaged testicles, he raced toward the back door, hobbling in a strange way. Kathryn fired again but missed, and the round cut through the glass pane of the sliding door. Roark threw his weight into the compromised pane and burst through the shattering glass as he stumbled onto the deck. "Throw me the gun!" Wyatt shouted. "Just drop it!"

Kathryn did as instructed. It thudded against the floor, and Wyatt quickly found it. Rising to one knee, he sent the remaining rounds through the opening. Roark rolled over the deck railing and tumbled to the forest floor just as the nine-millimeter rounds splintered the railing and continued overhead. He took off up the mountain. The cold assaulted his throat and warred against his warm breath for dominance. It quickly won victory, and Roark's throat burned from the exertion.

"Are you okay?" Kathryn asked Wyatt as he rose to his feet. He placed his hand on his side and exhaled out the wave of pain.

"Get my one-ten!" he shouted, referring to his sniper rifle. The night's cold swirled into the living room, and Kathryn scurried back into the bedroom to retrieve the rifle. In the meantime, Wyatt had thrown on his boots. Kathryn emerged with the heavy rifle and dropped it down to him. He caught it, ignoring the pain in his side.

"Get back to the bedroom," he ordered before he rushed outside. Kathryn watched him go, but she did not intend to return to the bedroom. Because of her involvement, Wyatt had gained the upper hand, and she was not about to let him continue alone. She hurried down the spiral staircase, found the pistol, and loaded a new magazine before racking the slide. She followed him outside, and the cold nearly paralyzed her.

Wyatt braced his M110A1 sniper rifle against the railing and sought out the intruder. Thankful for the full moon and its friendly light, he quickly found the man scurrying up the mountainside. A wave of pain rolled over him and his vision blurred, but the Raider fought through it.

Kathryn watched as Wyatt exhaled slowly and his finger found the trigger. Finding his natural respiratory pause at the end of his exhale, Wyatt watched the reticle sway across the man's profile. He rapidly blinked his eyes; the pain from his side grew deeper and burned sharper. He couldn't get the reticle to steady, but as it passed over Roark's profile, he squeezed the trigger and hoped for the best.

Roark heard the suppressed rifle's breathy chirp just before the searing pain ripped through his left shoulder. He slumped into the nearest tree and rolled around it for cover. He forced his breath through his gritted teeth to fight off the rolling waves of pulsing and throbbing pain, and he cradled his arm at the elbow. He cursed over and over again as he took off once more up the mountain.

Mist rose from the ground obscuring Wyatt's view, and the forest grew thicker and thicker as his reticle traced up the mountain.

"Did you get him?" Kathryn asked. Her voice trembled with fear.

"I... hit him," Wyatt replied, but he couldn't be sure he had killed the man. "We need... we need..." his breathing grew more difficult, "we need... to leave." Kathryn caught Wyatt as he slumped forward. His rifle clanged against the deck, but she ignored it and dragged him inside.

"I'll call nine-one-one!" she exclaimed. Wyatt's hand shot up and gripped her forearm. She looked down at him, and he shook his head.

"My guns... they're illegal for me to have. Pack up the car...and we'll head for the nearest hospital." Kathryn did as he had instructed. She retrieved his rifle and pistol, and, after stowing them in the car and covering them with a blanket, she helped Wyatt to the vehicle. After starting the Honda, she sped backwards, whipped the steering wheel, spun the car around, and hit the gas to zoom down the driveway.

Wyatt passed in and out of consciousness, and Kathryn repeatedly screamed his name to wake him. After hastily finding a hospital using her iPhone GPS, Kathryn sped to Page Memorial Hospital in Luray. It was the nearest one, and, upon arrival, she threw the car in park and raced inside the emergency center.

"Help!" she cried.

"What is it, ma'am?" the staff behind the counter inquired. Her voice held an edge of not expecting what would come next.

"My boyfriend, he's hurt really bad!" Kathryn answered.

"Alright, Miss," the staff replied kindly, "we'll take care of him. Just bring him in," but Kathryn cut her off.

"He will die if you do not help him," she stated gravely. The severity of her words and tone caught the woman off guard. She turned around and shouted, "I have a priority one!" Two men with a gurney meandered from a set of twin doors. They trotted toward Kathryn, and, although their pace agitated her, she led them outside.

"John!" she cried. The passenger door was open, and Wyatt lay sprawled on the ground. The two men quickened their pace.

"Any spinal or neck injuries?" one of them asked as he knelt to examine his patient.

"No," Kathryn quickly replied.

"Alright," the man said to his colleague, "let's lift him up." Kathryn watched as the two men lifted her beloved onto the lowered gurney and strapped him down. Kathryn followed alongside until one of the men stopped for a moment, touching her shoulder.

"You'll need to move your car. There is parking just over there," he said, pointing to the structure.

"But," she protested.

"Ma'am, please. We'll take good care of him." Kathryn nodded, and her tears wet her cheeks as she watched them roll Wyatt inside. She inhaled and ran both hands over her head as she fought off hysteria.

"I'm stronger than this," she told herself. She resolved her emotions and raced toward her Honda. The sooner she parked, the sooner she could be at Wyatt's side again.

48

Great Abaco Island,
The Abaco Islands
Bahamas

Morgan helped Silva from his seat on the plane, and the two men descended onto the tarmac of Leonard M. Thompson International Airport. His chest still hurt considerably, but his breathing had steadily grown stronger. He glanced around the devastated island and noted the repairs the country had initiated. Hurricane Dorian had decimated the small island and was considered the worst natural disaster in the country's history, but Silva hardly cared. His mind already placed him in Green Turtle Cay where his business would continue.

Kevon Pinder waited patiently by his vehicle. His life was better than most, and the black Range Rover behind him and the nice suit he wore confirmed his standing. The vehicle gleamed in the morning light, and Pinder was satisfied with his wax job. He picked up Mr. Silva from the airport three or four times a year and had done so for the last two. He still had no clue how he landed this opportunity, but Mr. Silva paid him well and had imported the Range Rover to keep in Pinder's care. It was a dream job.

"Mr. Silva," Pinder greeted, "Welcome back to the Abacos." He smiled warmly, and his white teeth gleamed in contrast against his dark skin.

"Thank you, Mr. Pinder," Silva returned. Pinder quickly opened the rear door behind the driver's seat, and Silva climbed in. Pinder noticed Silva's weary complexion but did not press the matter. Fear always surged through his body when he picked up his employer. A fair bit of that fear stemmed from a concern of losing his job, as if one small mistake would ruin his good fortune, but Silva himself kneaded a small fraction of that fear. Pinder knew a dangerous man when he saw one, and Silva was no exception. He couldn't place his finger on it, since Silva had always dealt kindly with him, but deep down he just knew. Mistakes were not to be tolerated.

Pinder started the engine and commenced his drive on the familiar route that led north to Treasure Cay Marina, where an ocean-worthy, luxury, sport yacht waited for his patron.

The fifty-two-foot, Windy SR52 Blackbird sat calmly in its slip at the marina. Its black hull contrasted attractively with the clear, turquoise water. The sport yacht boasted a price tag of over a million and a half, and it fit Silva's taste perfectly; however, he was sad he enjoyed it only briefly the few times he visited the island per year. The bright red, leather seating shouted boldly against the light woodgrain of the decking and black accents. The design almost appeared like a combination of a United States Navy PT boat and a professional racing boat. Radar sensors spun over the cockpit, and Silva drew all eyes as he stepped off the dock and onto the luxury craft.

Morgan handed Pinder an envelope containing a five-thousand-dollar, cash tip, to which he was accustomed, and followed his employer onboard. He had never seen such a boat and secretly marveled at its design while maintaining his usual, grim expression. Silva stood at the controls and fired up the engine. It roared like an old mustang before settling into a pleasant purr. Silva eased the yacht out of the slip and piloted it south down the channel and into the open Caribbean.

The yacht cut through the calm water with silky grace, and Morgan admired every aspect of their journey. His promotion certainly came with perks. No longer would he work the back waterways and ports of the developing world moving Silva's merchandise. He had arrived, and he intended to remain at his current standing.

"Is the team in place?" Silva asked without taking his gaze off the northwest horizon.

"Yeah," Morgan answered. "How do you know this guy will come for you?"

"Because of you," he simply replied. The comment caught Morgan off guard.

"Because of the girl," he corrected.

"No, Mr. Morgan, you are the prize upon which Rian Mather-Pike has set his gaze. Having you here assures he will come," Silva explained. The entire notion didn't sit well with the Englishman, but he hardly had time to contemplate before Silva piloted the craft into the strait where his supplier's residence was located. He spotted the blue house sitting alone and separated from the rest of the properties. Silva did not find the three-story villa impressive, but he could see how the general found the place charming. Silva docked the SR52 Blackbird alongside the small pier, and Morgan secured the vessel.

General Weber watched from the second-floor balcony as the two men exited the yacht and approached his villa. He sipped his dark rum and raised his glass in greeting before turning inside. In a few moments, Silva stood before him.

"What happened, Francisco?" Weber asked as he refilled his glass. His condescending tone brewed anger within the Spaniard.

"I was betrayed," Silva replied.

"We can't have that now, can we?" Weber replied, posing the words more as a statement than a question.

"I'm taking care of it," Silva replied.

"I hope so," Weber snarled. The sudden shift in demeanor startled both Silva and Morgan. Silva had killed a fair number of people in his time, but Weber stood on another level to which Silva could not hope to advance. Despite his dapper island attire, Weber had likely put more people in body bags than both Morgan and Silva combined, perhaps even twice over. He commanded one of the world's most elite fighting forces, and Silva was very aware of that fact. There were very few men Silva feared, but Weber was surely one of them. "Now," the general said, "I need to fill you in on some things."

"You burned Al Amiri?" Silva asked, stunned. "You ensured me that you would be able to cover that up."

"And I did," Weber hissed.

"Then why is Al Amiri dead?"

"I am a man under authority, and I posed the best solution to prevent exposure, and, as far as I can see, it worked." Weber took a sip of rum. "Business can resume as usual after we clear up this twenty-million-dollar debt."

"Debt?" Silva probed.

"Yes, you lost twenty million in product. Now, I don't care if you write a check or you negotiate higher prices on the next batch, but you will cover the cost of what you lost," Weber explained. The way Weber spoke, with such superiority, agitated Silva all the more, and his patience wore thin.

"This is a mutually beneficial arrangement," Silva countered. It wasn't about the money, but the principle.

"Indeed, but I can toss a rock and find ten other arms dealers that would kill for our arrangement. How many suppliers of top-tier, United States weaponry do you know?" Weber didn't wait for an answer. "When I found you, you were dealing in Vietnam-era Russian trash. Look at where you are now. Do you want to throw that away over twenty million?"

"I'll repay your cut, and your cut only," Silva countered. Weber shook his head.

"Consider this a show of good faith," the general replied with a confident grin. Silva maintained his composure despite his desire to lash out at the man. Fearful of him or not, Silva possessed his own threshold, and Weber was hovering quite close to the line. He was rich before Weber, and he'll be rich after Weber. However, that level of wealth depended on how well he played his cards.

"I will repay the twenty, plus an additional five if you can secure heavy weaponry," Silva stated. It was Weber's turn to be caught off guard.

"You want to deal in F35s and M1s?" Weber scoffed, referring to the United States' most advanced combat aircraft and tank.

"Perhaps not right away, but eventually, yes," Silva replied. His confidence growing, he rose from his seat and meandered over to the bar. He perused the stock and settled on a bottle of Black Tot British Royal Navy Imperial Rum. When he turned and locked stares with Weber, the general showcased his annoyance. However, the notion of five million, not accountable to anyone, intrigued him. The twenty million would be dispersed to pay off his black-market employees spread throughout the Marines Corps, SOCOM, various ports, and shipping companies. He would take home around four of that twenty, but the extra five tickled his greed too much for him to bear.

"We are phasing out our heavy armor, so I'll see what I can do," Weber replied with a smile. Yes, he had chosen well in his partnership with Silva. The Spaniard was a visionary, and why disrupt a good thing?

49

Green Turtle Cay,
The Abaco Islands
Bahamas

Shaw gazed through the night to behold the well-lit, Bahamian villa as *American Rhetor* glided smoothly through the sea, passing the residence at a distance. Natalie stood next to Shaw, and Affré and Mather-Pike next to her. They had picked up the two men in Coopers Town on the north shore of Little Abaco, which conveniently lay on their route toward Green Turtle Cay.

"You sure this will work?" Shaw asked Affré. "How do you know you both won't be shot on sight."

"I don't," he replied, "but it is the only way to expose the extra security Silva would have acquired."

"And how do you know?" Natalie asked.

"Because I was there when he did this before," the Frenchman replied. Shaw shifted his eyes back to the villa and nodded.

Shaw returned to the helm and steered the vessel to the designated insertion point. He dropped anchor off the beach to the west, out of sight from the villa, and prepared. He assembled both carbines, allowing Natalie to take her pick. She chose Shaw's personal AR-15. Shaw approved of her choice, wanting her to have the lighter, more reliable weapon.

Anticipating that Silva would have Mather-Pike frisked upon arrival, he was to go unarmed, but Affré would carry Shaw's service Glock in his waistline. And finally, Shaw popped open the black gun case and again beheld the 1911 pistol with awe, appreciation, and grief. Having already swapped out the barrels, he threaded on the forty-five-caliber silencer and fixed a Surefire X300U weapon light to the rail on the underside of the weapon's frame. Shaw then slammed home a loaded magazine, racked the slide, and clicked on the safety. He removed the magazine to top it off with another jacketed hollow-point round. He had eight rounds in the gun, but he wouldn't need them all. He stowed the weapon in the RagnarokSD holster and handed Natalie his personal Glock 19. She seated the weapon in the same holster on her belt, and she indicated her readiness with a nod.

The four piled into *American Rhetor's* inflatable tender and sped toward the island. Under the cover of darkness, they would easily infiltrate the island; penetrating Weber's illuminated villa was a different matter. Shaw helped Natalie out of the craft, not that she needed it, and the two other men remained afloat.

"Remember, the security team will be located close by, wait until we draw them out," Affré whispered to Natalie and Shaw. They nodded.

"Good luck," she said. Affré bound Mather-Pike's hands with a single zip tie. They made sure to leave enough room between his wrists so that he could break the bonds against his chest when needed.

Shaw watched the two men speed away in his tender and hoped their plan would work. Shaw was good, and Natalie had proven herself in combat, but they were no match for the fully outfitted security team that Affré had described. Everything relied on perfectly planned execution, and if the special operations community had taught Shaw anything, it was that perfectly planned execution didn't exist. Adaptability was necessary, as was speed, surprise, and violence of action.

"Are you expecting anyone?" Weber asked as he observed the tender enter the straight. He puffed on his cigar, exhaled, and watched as the small boat docked at his personal pier. Silva sat up and attempted to identify the two men. The smaller of the two shoved the larger man out of the boat. He fell, catching his foot on the edge of the dock, and landed on his chest. His hands were bound, and the other man kicked him in the side.

"My dear Romuald," Silva uttered affectionately. He rose from his seat on the balcony and watched Affré hoist Mather-Pike to his feet. Nearly giddy, Silva couldn't hide his wide grin. "Mr. Morgan," he called. The Englishman stepped through the French doors and beheld the scene.

"Well, how about that," he commented.

"Call in the team," Silva ordered. He nodded, produced his radio, and turned inside. Affré, carrying the metal briefcase, met Silva's gaze from the lawn and nodded. Silva returned it before heading inside to greet his most loyal employee.

"There," whispered Natalie. From their position among the low shrubbery in the undeveloped lot next to Weber's home, the two witnessed a six-man team pour out of the boathouse and head toward the building.

"You ready?" Shaw asked. Natalie nodded and braced her rifle against the trunk of the palm tree, taking aim at the last in the line of men. "Alright, stay here. On my go."

Shaw, staying low, rushed to his right, finding a solid position on the other side of a small boulder approximately thirty meters away from Natalie. He took in a deep breath and likewise braced his MK18 against his cover. He flicked the selector switch to full auto and placed the team in his sights. He would shoot first, drawing the immediate attention of the team and ensuring that Natalie took the least amount of fire possible. He didn't know how well trained these individuals were, but even the highest trained operators could be cut down in an ambush.

The Marine Raider squeezed the trigger, sending a three-round burst into the lead man.

"Mr. Affré!" Silva greeted loudly, as the man shoved Mather-Pike to the floor of the second story. "I thought you were dead."

"Almost," the Frenchman replied. He delivered another kick into Mather-Pike's side before moving casually to the bar. Silva glanced at Mather-Pike who seethed upon seeing Morgan.

"See, Mr. Morgan. What did I tell you?" Morgan chuckled, drawing enraged thrashing from the South African. Affré immediately feared that he would ruin everything.

"How did you escape?" Silva asked. Affré treaded carefully. Silva would smell a lie all too easily.

"Him," he replied. Silva's eyebrows shot toward the ceiling.

"Care to explain?" he probed. Affré returned to the center of the room with a glass of liquor in his hand. He gripped Mather-Pike by the collar and tugged hard. Mather-Pike complied and rose to a kneeling position, his bound hands rested at his waist. Laughter filled the room, and Silva turned to regard Weber. The general, having entered from the balcony, held his cigar in the corner of his mouth, and the smoke twirled upwards in a hypnotic dance.

"Is something funny, General?" Silva asked.

"You got bested by this... oaf?" he asked, knowing Mather-Pike well enough. His condescending tone was not lost on him. Silva gritted his teeth in anger, but then his mind cleared.

"What did you say?" he asked. His words, barely above a whisper, immediately alarmed Affré.

"I'm surprised is all," Weber said, extending his glass toward Mather-Pike. "The man's a gorilla, lacking any basic intelligence. You and I know that." Silva turned his gaze from Weber back to Mather-Pike. His eyes rose slowly to meet Affré's golden-green irises.

"Yes, General, you are quite right." Before he could act, a stream of suppressed, automatic gunfire echoed outside, followed quickly by the screams of dying men.

The rock in front of Shaw chipped and fragmented, as enemy rounds thudded into it. Shaw ducked behind his cover for a brief moment. Of the six, four remained, and they had responded with such aggression and accuracy that it confirmed the level of their training. Still, Shaw and Natalie held the advantage of position.

Natalie watched as the four remaining men engaged Shaw, causing him to retreat behind cover. She fought against the rising adrenaline that warred against her fine motor skills and placed the red dot on the torso of the last man. She would need to be fast. Shaw had dropped two, and now it was her turn.

The operations officer squeezed the trigger and sent her first round hurtling toward her target. She fired again toward the same man after he staggered but didn't fall. Natalie quickly transitioned targets as the mercenary hit the sand, and she squeezed off another shot. She didn't miss. A fourth man fell, and the courage of the remaining two faltered. One turned to face the nearest threat while the other kept his attention on Shaw; however, Shaw rolled around to the other side of the boulder and dropped the man aiming at Natalie. Natalie made short work of the last mercenary, and the island fell silent.

Shaw moved from behind his cover and kept his rifle trained in the direction of the fallen mercenaries, ready to send another round into any that moved. Satisfied that none remained alive, he moved toward the villa and directed Natalie to follow.

"Here," he whispered, positioning himself beneath the balcony and offering Natalie a leg up. "Stay to the left, and they won't see you." She nodded, slung the rifle around her back, and gripped Shaw's shoulders. "Up," he said. She felt her body rise, and she gripped the bottom of the railing and hoisted herself onto the balcony. She stayed to the left as instructed and waited for Shaw.

The Raider captain slung his carbine around his back in like manner, and, finding one of the posts that supported the balcony, scurried up it, using his feet, hands, and body weight to easily reach the top. He gazed to his left, and Natalie stood on the opposite side of the balcony. Large bay windows and a set of French doors separated them, and with a nod from

Shaw, the two moved toward the doors with their rifles high and entered the building on the second floor.

50

Silva spun around to regard Morgan, and the Englishman's expression confirmed his fears. His security team was gone. Silva slowly shook his head and a smile crept onto his face.

"Well played, Romuald," he said. "I should have seen this coming." The betrayal fell twice as hard, but he resolved himself. "You and Mr. Capra were close," Silva added, referring to his former bodyguard whom he had drowned in the Nile. "Morgan, kill them both," he ordered. Before the man could obey, Affré's hands flashed with blinding speed and produced the pistol concealed at his waist. He pointed it at Morgan, who slowly raised his hands.

"Your weapon; kick it over," Affré commanded. Morgan reached slowly for it. "No, no, with your left hand," Affré instructed. The gun clangored across the wooden floor, and Morgan raised his hands to shoulder level, palms outward. "He's all yours, Rian," the Frenchman said.

Mather-Pike rose to his feet. His eyes burned with ravenous hatred for the Englishman before him. He torqued his hands against his chest, passing his elbows forcibly beyond his ribcage, and the zip tie snapped with ease. That sight alone was enough for Morgan. He bolted through the open doors behind him and onto the balcony. Mather-Pike roared in rage and raced after the murderer. Silva moved, but Affré quickly presented the pistol his way and shook his head.

Morgan jumped from the second story balcony, rolled to absorb the impact, sprinted toward the SR52, and reached it before Mather-Pike had exited the building. The South African cleared the balcony and likewise rolled to absorb the impact of his fall. He sprinted toward the dock but slowed as he watched the yacht reverse and speed away toward open sea. Shaking his head in denial, he sank to his knees on the wooden dock and wept.

"Have a seat, General," Affré stated. Silva stood in the center of the room, and Weber stood several paces away near the exit Morgan and Mather-Pike had just taken.

"I'll stand," he stated flatly, his grim expression showing no sign of fear or distress.

"I'm going to kill you, Romuald," Silva hissed. Before Affré could respond, the French doors behind him opened, and two individuals entered with their carbines ready.

"David!" Weber stated, failing to hide his alarm. Shaw ignored him, his eyes focused on Silva, but Silva stared at Natalie.

"Miranda?" he questioned. It all clicked, and he laughed in deep appreciation of her abilities.

Shaw strode up to Silva, and his chest wound tingled as he neared. He drew his suppressed 1911 from its holster and sent a round through Silva's forehead. The Spaniard's head snapped backwards, and a spray of blood and brain matter followed the bullet out the back of his skull. His body slumped the ground, and Shaw stepped right over him as he proceeded toward Weber.

General Weber, unfazed by Shaw's savagery, looked from the dead man to Shaw's burning eyes. He refused to look at the pistol the man held at his side.

"I'm surprised to see you alive," Weber said. Shaw holstered the pistol before seizing Weber by the shoulders and throwing him to the ground. It took more personal resolve than Shaw realized to lay hands on the man. Weber quickly recovered and rose to his feet, shaking off the assault.

"I want answers," Shaw demanded. "You killed my men."

"They're not your men, David. They belong to the Corps." Weber's voice held the tone of a condescending parent. "Marines die. You know that as well as anyone else."

"Did you leak the op?" Shaw probed, as if not hearing him. Natalie and Affré watched the exchange, each unsure of what they should do.

"I saved your life," Weber countered. The comment caught Shaw off guard. "You weren't going to be medically retired. I did that and kept you stateside," the general stated.

"What?" Disbelief coursed through Shaw's mind.

"You're alive because of me," he argued.

"And so you let the others die! York! Reyes! Just so you can make some extra cash?" Shaw growled.

"Don't lecture me, David. You understand. We are men of a different breed. Had we gone into the private sector, we would be living like kings. We gave everything to an ungrateful country. I traded my daughter's childhood for war, and this country has done nothing to repay that debt."

"I can't believe what I'm hearing," Shaw stammered. His heart split and lay asunder at the feet of the man he had revered above all others.

"There are kings and pawns in this world, David. I was given an opportunity for kingship, and kings, from time to time, must sacrifice their pawns. Those Marines were fortunate that their blood anointed the altar of freedom," Weber continued. Shaw shook his head, fighting against the new reality he saw in the man before him. Is this how he had rationalized his actions? How had the humble, farm boy from Iowa, a first-generation college graduate from the Naval Academy, become the vain elitist that now stood before him?

Shaw now saw it.

Weber possessed all the traits of victimhood, which had undoubtedly led him down this path of treachery, greed, moral relativity, and ethical instability.

"Have you forgotten everything? Semper Fidelis?" Shaw's eyes showed more pity than anger. "You are no Marine," he finally said. The comment unexpectedly stung Weber deep in his soul.

"The cost was too high," Weber admitted soberly.

"The cost?" Shaw stammered. "What do you know of the cost of freedom? Reyes paid the cost! York paid the cost! Neeman and Beasley paid the cost!" Weber's shame was too much to bear, but his pride would not allow him to relent. He stoked his anger, and the flame spread, unquenchable.

"It was only a matter of time before you came for me!" Weber countered. "Look at you now!" Shaw stared hard at the man, who stared equally as hard back. The emotions that stirred within Shaw were unlike any he had ever experienced. He had to go through it, for the sake of his brothers, but could he pull the trigger? His control teetered on the edge of a knife; one blow in either direction would catapult him into seas of emotional turmoil he couldn't possibly imagine. "What happens now, David?" Weber asked, extending wide his hands and bearing his chest as if inviting the sword.

"Affré, open the case," Shaw ordered without taking his eyes off Weber. The Frenchman moved to his side and opened the case on the table next to him. "You will make this right," Shaw commanded of Weber. "You are going to transfer all of your black-market wealth into the account provided." Weber looked down at the computer installed in the case and then back to Shaw.

"And if I don't, you'll kill me?" Weber asked. The Marine general repressed all affection for the man that stood before him. All he saw was a faceless, enemy combatant threating his life.

"Yes," Shaw replied coldly. Weber smirked.

"Go ahead." He doubted Shaw could pull the trigger. "You can't kill me. I made you." He glanced around the room, his eyes falling on everyone present. "I am MARSOC!" he shouted as his anger increased. "Me, General Linus Charles Weber, and I will command it as I see fit! I tell Marines to go and they go! I tell them to come and they come! I tell them to die and they di..."

Shaw's pistol cut him short. The slug tore through the man's abdomen, and he fell into the couch clutching the spurting wound. Shaw horrified by his own actions glanced down at the weapon in his hand. He wondered if his own consciousness had pulled the trigger or if his fallen brothers had possessed him in that moment, demanding justice for their deaths. The pain of watching his mentor writhe in agony was almost too much to bear.

Weber, facing death, glanced up at his protégé. The aura of integrity surrounding Shaw permeated Weber's soul. Who had he become? What had he done? For what, money? His father's words echoed in his mind, *all you have in this world is your good name, Linus, and once it's gone, it's gone forever and there's no getting it back.* What had his endeavors gained him? What had they robbed from him? The answers were too great to face. Staring into the eyes of the man he and his wife had always hoped would marry their daughter and provide grandchildren, Weber came face to face with his inequities. Death, the great philosopher, had a way of clearing the mind.

"What of my wife? My daughter?" Weber managed to ask through labored breaths. The question snapped Shaw out of his trance.

"They will be cared for," he promised, "as will the families of the Marines you killed."

"I will have to make multiple transactions," Weber explained.

"That will be fine," Affré said, presenting Weber with the open computer. After several moments, Weber, exhausted with sweat soaking his clothes, nodded his head toward Shaw.

"It's done... but... but..." He found speech difficult as each moment brought a new wave of agony. "I've left my joint accounts with Denise alone. I... I... hope you can appreciate that." Emotion welled up within Shaw as Weber looked up at him. They both knew there was no veering from what came next, and Weber's tired eyes, so vibrant just moments before, begged him.

"Meet me by the tender," Shaw said to all present. Affré first retrieved the case before leaving, but Natalie lingered and touched Shaw's arm before doing as he requested. Shaw watched her leave, then turned his attention back to Weber, and raised his pistol.

Upon seeing the weapon, Weber inhaled solemnly. Shaw shook as his imagination led him through his next course of action; he felt the spirits of his brothers radiate from the weapon.

"Go ahead, Son," the defeated man stated, "I'm sorry." Shaw's eyes reddened and tears flowed freely down his cheeks and into his beard. He raised the pistol and leveled it with Weber's forehead. The general closed his eyes and leaned into the suppressor. "I love you," Weber said. The words tore at his heart, but Shaw averted his gaze. He inhaled, mustered his courage, and pulled the trigger. Shaw felt the weapon recoil and chamber a new round.

Weber fell back into the couch as his lifeless muscles failed to support him. His blood soaked into the white fabric, but Shaw refused to look at the body and left immediately. On the way down the stairs, his devastating grief staggered him into the wall, and he shouted in anguish. He slid down, sobbing hysterically. It all crashed over him. He had lost so much: his career, his life, his brothers-in-arms, and now his mentor. It was too overwhelming, and all the suppressed emotions bubbled upward and spewed forth in agonizing reality. His pistol fell to the ground, and he buried his face in his hands.

Natalie jumped at the suppressed gunshot and instantly feared the worst, but she checked herself. She kept her gaze on the door leading into the bottom floor. Minutes felt like days, and, eventually, Shaw emerged alone, his face red. Compelled by affection, she ran toward him and threw her arms around his neck. Shaw buried his face into her shoulder and cried again. She stroked his long hair and held him tightly. He collected himself, sniffed, and looked away.

"Hey," Natalie said tenderly, drawing his gaze back to hers with a move of her hand against his cheek. He grunted, fighting off the wave of emotional pain. She curled his loose hair behind his ear and kissed him, and before Shaw could process the new emotions swirling inside, she pulled away. "Come on," she said. Natalie wrapped her arm around his waist and led him to the tender.

Mather-Pike stared blankly in the direction Morgan had fled, and Affré sat at the idling engine. Natalie and Shaw climbed in. Affré backed the boat into the channel, gunned the throttle, and sped them back to *American Rhetor*.

51

Luray, Virginia

Wyatt's eyes opened blearily, and dark circles underneath contrasted with his pale complexion. The various monitors blinked and beeped, and he inhaled intentionally and deeply; his left lung screamed, setting a grimace on his face. He looked to his right; Kathryn lay asleep, curled up in a chair she had pulled close to the bed. A light blanket lay draped over her body, exposing only her head. He couldn't see her face but took comfort in the waves of golden hair.

The Raider attempted to recall his last memory and vaguely remembered the drive from the cabin to the hospital. Did he remember arriving? He wasn't sure. He pushed himself a bit higher on the reclined bed and touched his side. He remembered laboring for breath and feeling faint. He must have passed out at some point.

"Kathryn," he called softly. She stirred but resettled into her sleep. What time was it? Wyatt found the digital clock on the bedside table.

4:32.

It was dark outside the window; had he been out for only a few hours, or more than a day? He led himself through self-diagnosis. The pain in his side was assuredly the result of a couple broken ribs. Due to his weak condition and painful breathing, he could only assume that a rib had punctured his left lung, but that didn't explain his passing in and out of consciousness.

Wyatt looked at the palm of his hand. The bandage concealed what was no doubt a stitched wound. He flexed his fingers and was grateful no serious damage had occurred. He touched his nose, finding it uncomfortably surrounded by a brace.

"Kathryn," he called a bit louder but still tender so as not to startle her. She rolled her head toward him.

"Yeah?" she replied tiredly as if she really wasn't aware of her surroundings or Wyatt's situation. Wyatt smirked.

"How long was I out?" he asked. He was surprised by how weak his voice sounded. Kathryn rubbed her eyes.

"What?" she asked. Her eyes opened and focused on him, and, as her brain caught up with her waking body, she realized what was happening. "You're awake!" she exclaimed. Wyatt smiled as she rose from her chair and gently hugged him. He kissed her forehead, and she held him longer than he expected. "You've been out for more than a day. You lost so much blood, and they had to remove your spleen," she explained worriedly.

"Did they?" he replied. Kathryn was relieved to hear the humor in his tone. She chuckled with relief. If his humor was back, then he surely would be fine. "Any word from David?" he asked. Kathryn shook her head, and Wyatt feared the worst.

Nassau, Bahamas

The anchor splashed into the turquoise water just off the coast of Nassau. Satisfied it had found solid bedding, Shaw turned to his companions. The morning sun barely crested the horizon, and the city still slept. He turned to Affré and Mather-Pike.

"I stand by our agreement," Shaw stated, "but I still acknowledge both of your roles in Yemen."

"Trust that we are most sincere in our apology," Affré replied. Shaw wore a dissatisfied expression, but he nodded.

"I ask that you no longer partake in any such actions against the US or our allies." Natalie supported his reasoning.

"You have our word," Mather-Pike said. He extended his hand in good faith. Shaw hesitated. "I never wanted any of this, and I hope our actions have proven our position." Shaw finally gripped his hand and nodded. Their actions had earned his forgiveness. Afterall, bitterness only infected the one who held onto it.

"Thank you for your help," Shaw said. "You both saved my life and without you, we never would have succeeded."

"It is we who should be thanking you and Ms. Hale," Affré replied. Mather-Pike nodded his agreement. "We have some affairs to sort out, but we wish to show you both our gratitude." He produced a card and handed it to Shaw.

"What is this?" Shaw asked, looking at the numerals listed on the card.

"An account with Ziegler & Rohr Financial in Zürich. It is the least we can do. All I ask is that you allow us a few weeks to arrange everything," Affré explained.

"I don't understand," Shaw stated, but Affré merely extended his hand. Shaw smiled and gripped it before transitioning his gaze to Mather-Pike.

"Take care of yourself, hey?" the large man said.

"You too," Shaw replied. They both climbed into the tender at which Natalie sat at the helm, and Shaw watched them speed away.

The Raider set his hands to the boat, keeping his mind preoccupied with simple tasks. He chose to dwell on the kiss from Natalie instead of the recent events that plagued him. The prospect of the unknown excited him and helped fight against the grief. How could he possibly go back to the Corps? He reminded himself that the actions of one man, no matter how influential, did not tarnish the proud and honorable history of the United States Marines. However, someone would find Weber, and they would likely figure out that it was Shaw who pulled the trigger. No, he couldn't go back to his old life, and so he pushed the possibility out of his mind.

An hour passed.

Natalie returned, but Shaw, having checked the engine in the galley, didn't see her board. He wiped his hands with a towel, climbed the steps back outside, and froze.

Natalie stood before him, dressed in a black bikini and matching sarong. She grinned wide and removed her sunglasses.

"This enough skin for you?" she teased. Shaw laughed.

"You look great," he stammered. Natalie set the shopping bag containing her previous outfit on one of the benches as she advanced toward him.

"I was kind of hoping for a vacation after all this; get lost at sea. That sort of thing," she said. Shaw's grin widened.

"I think I can arrange that," he replied. She stood before him and gazed into his deep blue eyes. She removed his ball cap and tousled his long hair with her fingers. He wrapped his arms around her waist, she his neck, and their lips met. The kiss catapulted both individuals into tranquility and vibrant joy. They gleefully laughed as they parted, and Natalie bit her bottom lip as she looked back up at him. Had it ever felt this good? She found the answer didn't matter.

"Where to, Captain?"

EPILOGUES

1

Tucson, Arizona

Sara Reyes rocked gently back and forth in the old rocking chair that had belonged to her grandmother. She nursed three-month-old David, who repeatedly patted his small hand against her downturned cheek. His big brown eyes stared into hers, and the sight brought a smile to her face and tears to her eyes.

The decision to leave North Carolina was an easy one after the death of her husband. Little David had only his grandfather to teach him of manhood, and Sarah really could think of no one better who currently walked the earth. Her father, a full-blooded Apache, umpired little league baseball and worked as a park ranger in the Saguaro National Park. As a retired Marine Master Sergeant, he had approved of Sara's marriage to Kyle as soon as he returned from Basic Training. Not all Marines were good enough for his daughter, but only a Marine would be. Kyle had proven himself worthy, not just through his support and respect for Sara through high school, but in his dedication to the Corps.

Sara's heart still longed for her late husband and always would, but she knew she would see him again. Her greatest goal was to raise David to serve the Lord so that he could meet his father in heaven one day. The thought brought a fresh wave of tears, as did the possibility that he might follow in his father's footsteps. She didn't know if she could let that happen but would cross that bridge when that day came.

Sara considered her situation as she reached for David's little hand and relished the sight of his little fingers curling around hers. Her parents had welcomed the two of them into their home with open arms, and really, they had not touched her old bedroom since she left with Kyle for North Carolina just over two years ago. She glanced around the small room and observed the changes she had made.

David's crib sat opposite of her new twin bed, and she had repainted the walls from faded pink to light blue. She installed small white shelves, which sat decorated with her husband's flag, medals, and portrait. She smiled as she gazed into Kyle's eyes, but a knock at the door stole her attention.

"Sara?" called the soft voice.

"Yes?" The door slowly opened, and her mother, Nan Boyington, entered. She had met Sara's father while she was visiting her extended family in Okinawa and was immediately smitten with the mysterious Marine she had met at a local bar. They dated through the summer and maintained correspondence throughout the year. When Bobaway Boyington returned to the United States, they married a month after Nan graduated from the University of Arizona.

"You've got some mail," the woman said. She stopped as she observed the sight of her daughter nursing her grandchild. Tears welled up in her almond eyes, and Sara simply smiled. "How is he?" she asked.

"He's doing well," Sara replied, looking down at him. "I have some mail?"

"Yes," her mother replied.

"You can open them," Sara said.

"Oh, right," Nan replied, gazing again at her grandson. She ripped open the letter and briefly read the correspondence. She staggered and braced herself against the wall, drawing Sara's alarm.

"What is it, Mom?" Nan stammered incoherently before taking a seat and handing the letter to her daughter.

Mrs. Reyes,

First and foremost, I wish to offer you my deepest and sincerest condolences on the loss of your husband. I know the following in no way can make up for his sacrifice, but we hope that this enables you to live comfortably and provide for your child.

A trust has been set up in your name through the Philo Initiative containing $2,458,321.83. A board of financial advisors will manage the trust and is available to discuss all matters pertaining. Please contact me at your earliest convenience to discuss the details.

Sincerely,
Richard Rasmussen, CEO
The Philo Initiative

Sara could not believe the words she read. Her heart hastened at her new reality, and all her worries vanished in that moment. However, something tugged at her about the letter. One word caught her attention: *Philo.*

It was the call sign of Reyes' team, Shaw's team. Was it coincidence, or was this a gift from Shaw? Her heart led her to believe the latter. She looked down at little David and smiled.

"We're going to be just fine, Love," she said. He looked up at her and giggled.

2

The rows of bright, pastel buildings and passing cars from the mid-twentieth century did little to spark the man's appreciation. He sat at a restaurant table that spilled onto the sidewalk to attract patrons and cater to the Cuban culture.

The man took a deep swig of his mojito and enjoyed the minty flavor. His muscles bulged through his white linen shirt, and the Caribbean breeze that swept down the street, funneled by the row of buildings, tossed his long blonde hair. He waited for his companion, a Frenchman, who had for some reason or another stuck by his side when Silva's death should have separated them.

They both had dissolved the Wild Planet Foundation, into which Silva's wealth had been poured per his beneficiary mandate, and diversified their new, impressive fortune. They had paid their debt to Henri Wolf, who had promised them his services at any time they should need them, but both men had little faith in Wolf's financial ability. He was a pawn in the right place at the right time. They had also kept their promise to David Shaw and Natalie Hale by setting up the account at Ziegler and Rohr with Hugo Kormann.

Even with over one hundred million to his name, Mather-Pike's insides still churned in mayhem. Morgan was out there somewhere, and Affré had promised to find him. As if on cue, a teal 1958 Chevrolet Impala convertible rolled to a stop next to his table.

Affré removed his sunglasses and motioned with his head for Mather-Pike to enter. The South African drained his drink, having already paid double its cost in tip at the bar, and headed toward the car. When the door closed, he looked at his friend.

"Did you find him?" he asked. Affré nodded and threw the car in gear.

They came to a stop twenty minutes later in front of an old hotel of colonial Spanish design.

"Room three fourteen," Affré said. He dropped open the glovebox exposing a snub-nosed revolver. Mather-Pike immediately shook his head. He got out of the car and glanced up at the third floor.

"I'll be right back," he said. Affré watched him enter the hotel. He drummed his fingers against the wooden wheel to pass the time.

Mather-Pike entered the lobby and nodded his greeting to the clerk before approaching the desk.

"Can I help you, *señor*?" the clerk asked.

"I need a key to room three fourteen," Mather-Pike stated. The clerk immediately shook his head.

"I cannot help you. That room is currently occupied," the small man protested. Mather-Pike leaned forward.

"It's government business," he uttered menacingly. The man's face drained of color. It wasn't unusual for the government to requisition the services of foreign nationals. The clerk nodded profusely and produced the spare key.

"*Gracias*," Mather-Pike said before heading toward the stairs that opened into the center of the lobby. He followed the steps as they split to the right from the first landing and continued to the third floor. He quickly found the correct room. He inhaled deeply and exhaled slowly, preparing his mind for the coming task.

He inserted and turned the key. Mather-Pike slowly and quietly opened the door. The room was quite bland and did not mirror the ornate Spanish design of the lobby. A woman moaned loudly with fake pleasure, and Mather-Pike's eyes snapped to the couple making love in the bed.

Morgan's eyes widened and his gut twisted as a strong hand gripped the back of his neck. A moment later, he was airborne. He crashed against the floor and rolled before slamming into the wall. The prostitute screamed, but one savage look from the intruder silenced her to a whimper.

"Get out," Mather-Pike threatened. She didn't need to be told twice. She fled, naked from the room, not caring to cover herself. The South African turned his attention to Morgan who had risen to his feet. His expression reflected his fear as he gazed upon the man nearly double his size and seething with hate.

"Listen, I've got lots of money. I can pay you whatever you want," he pleaded. The words fell on deaf ears.

The South African advanced, and Morgan lunged for the door, but Mather-Pike proved the quicker. His hand snatched Morgan's trailing arm and pulled him backwards. Mather-Pike's other hand gripped Morgan's throat, and he steadily applied pressure. Morgan's feet dangled off the ground as Mather-Pike lifted him. Instinctively, Morgan raked his fingers across Mather-Pike's hand but could not break the hold.

Mather-Pike thrust him downward, connecting his body solidly with the floor. The room shook and a lamp toppled off the bedside table. The agony that radiated from Morgan's lungs and back was unlike anything he had ever experienced. He gulped for air, but his shocked lungs would not expand, and the air never entered his throat.

Like a vice, Mather-Pike's hands locked down on Morgan's throat, and the man barely thrashed, paralyzed from the trauma. Mather-Pike watched the life fleetingly fly from Morgan's eyes, but it wasn't enough.

Affré sat in the driver's seat as he waited. Glass shattered above him, immediately drawing his sight upward. The Frenchman watched as Morgan's naked body, bloodied and cut from the broken glass, crunched against the pavement. Blood pooled beneath the corpse, and Affré simply smirked. Mather-Pike was anything but discrete. He looked left and

Mather-Pike emerged from the hotel, stepped onto the street, rounded the front of the vehicle, and climbed inside. He looked at Affré who simply stared at him despite the growing cries and horrified shouts of pedestrians.

"Do you feel better?" he asked.

"Yes, actually. I do," Mather-Pike replied, his gaze on Morgan's broken body in the street.

"Good," Affré responded as he threw the car into reverse. They sped down the street toward the marina where the stolen SR52 waited. It was through the GPS of the craft that they had known Morgan was in Havana. After that, Affré simply put his old agency skills to use while Mather-Pike had waited. "What will you do now?" Affré asked, shifting his gaze toward his friend. Mather-Pike watched the vibrant passing buildings as he contemplated his answer.

"Go home," he finally said. Affré nodded and returned his attention to the road.

"I've not been to Johannesburg," he said. Mather-Pike smirked and looked at the Frenchman.

"You'll hate it."

"Probably so," he replied.

Mather-Pike laughed, and Affré joined him.

3

Arlington, Virginia

The thick snow crunched underfoot as the couple walked arm in arm through the famed McClellan Gate at Arlington National Cemetery. The white blanket covered the hallowed grounds and stirred tranquility within them both as they continued onward. Various wreaths, adorned with a red ribbon, decorated each headstone, and snow collected in the crevasses of the old, barren trees.

Wyatt inhaled heavily and watched his breath rise into the frigid air. Kathryn glanced at him and smiled solemnly. She knew he missed Shaw. The only evidence of his survival arrived in the form of a text message from an unknown number stating: *It's done. - Philo*. Wyatt had taken comfort in the fact that Shaw had made it through and that the threat to his and Kathryn's lives was over. He then made it a point to visit his brothers' grave to let them know they could rest easy.

Still, Wyatt wanted to know if the man that assaulted him in Shenandoah was connected to Weber. He didn't even know if that man had died in the woods. Although he tried his best to stay up to date with any bodies found in the national park, none had yet been located this winter. He pushed it from his mind and focused on the headstones surrounding him.

Placed on medical leave, Wyatt took every advantage to resume his time with Kathryn, and now, after what seemed like closure, Wyatt set his gaze on the future. There was no reason to stay in the Corps. He had made his mind up about that. He had two more years left on his enlistment, and, since everyone he loved had passed on or disappeared, he saw little value in reupping now that he had Kathryn. She was, after all, what he had been looking for. He joined the Corps to find a family after losing his, and, again having lost his Marine family, he had found a new one. He had no intentions of leaving her side. He knew he wouldn't survive if he lost her too.

"Kathryn," he started. He stopped and looked at the sky and the surrounding headstones. She paused and looked up at him. He turned to face her. Dressed in his Blues with his winter overcoat, white belt and cover, she found him quite dashing.

"Yes?"

"You know this, but I lost my family a little over ten years ago. I found a new one in the Corps. Now, I've lost them," he said. His eyes trailed from hers to the rows of headstones. He gripped both her hands and stared back into her blue eyes. "But I found you through the craziest of circumstances." She smiled. "I have no intention of spending another moment apart from you." He dropped to one knee, and Kathryn's heart leaped into her throat.

"John?" she managed. He produced a small, velvet box from his coat pocket and cracked it open. Her jaw dropped as she beheld the white-gold ring. A halo of smaller diamonds encircled the round brilliant, and the diamond-adorned band bordered the halo, giving the appearance of a double halo intersected on each side of the setting.

"Will you marry me?" he asked as he gazed into her tearful blue eyes.

"Yes!" she jubilantly replied. She tore off her leather glove and presented her ring finger. Wyatt grinned wide and slid the ring onto her finger. She laughed, having never known such joy. She met him as he was rising and kissed him, pressing her lips passionately against his. She wrapped her hands tightly around him, and the couple relished their moment of joy and the bright future that awaited.

The Defection Protocol
David Shaw Book 2

A man on the run. A traitor on the loose. One last chance to set the record straight.

After months on the run for an assassination they call justice, David Shaw and Natalie Hale have built a new life in the shadows. But when a hit squad tracks them down in the Caribbean, it's clear their enemies aren't done with them yet. Someone with deep connections wants them dead—someone with the power to erase them for good.

That someone is Connor Roark. A dirty CIA officer with everything to lose, Roark has spent years operating in the darkest corners of international crime. Now, with his illicit enterprise crumbling, he's tying up loose ends. And Shaw and Natalie are at the top of his list.

From the Caribbean to Washington, D.C., and deep into the criminal networks of the Mediterranean, Shaw and Natalie are chasing one goal: exposing Roark's true allegiance. But with time running out, they may only have one last shot to stop him before he wreaks havoc on an unprecedented scale.

Get your copy today at
severnriverbooks.com

ABOUT THE AUTHOR

Harrison is ardently committed to story and narrative, that a good narrative is driven by believable and compelling characters whose struggles are sincere, difficult, and meaningful. Story has spurred humanity into the greatest of endeavors, and valuable contribution is made to the larger human narrative with the telling of a good story.

Inspired by the great stories of Tolkien, Pressfield, Dumas, and others, Harrison strives to build on the foundation of humanity's story to inspire to action, provoke to thought, and call to integrity all who choose to read his work. His gratitude to you is sincere and deep.

Harrison lives in Alabama with his wife and two daughters.

Learn more about Harrison's books at
harrisonkone.com